ADDITIONAL PRAISE FOR *PEOPLE PERSON*

"Carty-Williams is a careful, astute observer of the human psyche and the complications of unconventional dynamics. . . . I can think of no better description for Carty-Williams's writing and her grasp of her characters. That she can present them to readers so openly and use them so expertly to explore themes like obligation and duty, grief and love, solidifies her role as a voice to be reckoned with—a real people person, if you will."

—*Bookreporter*

"A hilarious romp."

—*O, Quarterly*

"A bighearted story of a young woman coming to terms with her complicated London family from the author of the game-changing *Queenie*."

—*The Guardian*

"The ambition behind Carty-Williams's novel calls to mind what Zadie Smith brought to her first novel, *White Teeth*. And to some extent, Carty-Williams is to south London what Smith is to the north: a sharp, humorous voice that paints greater London's Black communities with the nuance they deserve."

—*The Washington Post*

"A witty and tender portrayal of how our childhoods affect how we relate to our family as adults."

—*Real Simple*

"A bighearted reminder that a messy family is still a family."

—*Time*

"From the author who gave us the unflinching and heartfelt *Queenie*, Candice Carty-Williams brings us her second novel, *People Person*. . . . Sweet and funny."

—*BuzzFeed*

"A vibrant and charming celebration of discovering family as an adult."

—*The Nerd Daily*

"From the author who brought us the deliciously messy *Queenie* comes a lively untraditional story of a family reunion in *People Person*."

—*PopSugar*

"Epic . . . Carty-Williams is a natural—an elite-level storyteller with a sustained interest in the ways we find ourselves in our families."

—*Goodreads*

"A tender portrait of a nontraditional family. *People Person* is a wonderfully huggable book full of humor, heart, and hope."

—*Bust*

"A darkly comedic novel of family . . . as heartfelt as it is hilarious. Carty-Williams probes hard questions about race, microaggressions and abandonment within a larger, somehow softer story about what makes a family, what makes a friend, and what happens when the two are one and the same."

—*Shelf Awareness*

"*People Person* is more than just the title of this phenomenal second novel. It's a statement of intent. It's a declaration that when Candice Carty-Williams writes, she captures the hearts and minds of readers everywhere."

—**Melissa Cummings-Quarry, Black Girls Book Club**

"Wonderful. *People Person* is about five half-siblings (one dad, four mothers) who, in response to a crisis, meet as adults and start shaping themselves into a family. It's a warm novel, funny and full of emotional intelligence. The tone is lighthearted, even comic at times, but underneath there's an undertow, a steady drumbeat reminding us of all the microaggressions black people experience on a daily basis—and that white people are mostly oblivious of. I cannot recommend it highly enough."

—**Marian Keyes**

"*People Person* is a portrait of a family that is as poignant as it is hilarious. It had me belly-laughing, then picking up my jaw from the floor, then nodding in delighted agreement. Candice is a writer who is not only revealing modern Britain with each of her novels; she is defining it. Cyril Pennington is a character for the ages, but this story truly belongs to the children he never managed to parent. I loved it."

—Sara Collins

PRAISE FOR *QUEENIE*

"[A] hilarious, heart-shattering, deeply lovable novel . . . Debut author Candice Carty-Williams has created a truly one-of-a-kind heroine in Queenie, whose story is universally relatable without ever flinching in the face of challenging subjects that are more important now than ever . . . All hail Queenie."

—*Newsday*

"So raw and well-written and painfully relatable. It's also clever and funny and has the most glorious cover."

—**Ruth Ware, #1** *New York Times* **bestselling author of**
The Woman in Cabin 10

"My favorite novel this year. *Queenie* is the sort of novel you just can't stop talking about and want everyone you know to read. Snort-your-tea-out funny one moment and utterly heartbreaking the next, (and with the best cast of characters you'll read all year), I absolutely loved it. I can't wait to read whatever Candice writes next. If there is anything right in the world, Candice Carty-Williams is going to be a literary superstar."

—**AJ Pearce, author of** *Dear Mrs. Bird*

"A black Bridget Jones, perfectly of the moment."

—*Kirkus Reviews*, **starred review**

"The vibrant Queenie is a modern-day *Bridget Jones's Diary*, and so much more . . . [Carty-Williams's] debut reads a lot like its smart, sensitive protagonist: full of flaws and contradictions, and urgently, refreshingly real."

—*Entertainment Weekly*

"Written by a new and exciting young woman, [*Queenie* is] articulate, brave, and, in the new parlance, 'woke.' Funny, wise, and of the moment, this book and this writer are ones to watch."

—Kit de Waal, author of *My Name Is Leon*

"[A] smart, fearless debut . . . Carty-Williams doesn't shy from the messiness of sexual relationships, racial justice issues such as police brutality, or Queenie's promiscuity, and the narrative is all the more effective for its boldness. This is an essential depiction of life as a black woman in the modern world, told in a way that makes Queenie dynamic and memorable."

—*Publishers Weekly*, starred review

"A really special book with much to say about black female identity, sexual politics, group chats, emotional becoming, in a way that feels totally unforced. Filthy, funny, and profound."

—Sharlene Teo, award-winning author of
Ponti

"Carty-Williams creates an utterly knowable character in Queenie, who's as dimensional and relatable as they come as she tries to balance her own desires with what everyone else seems to want for her. . . . This smart, funny, and tender debut embraces a modern woman's messiness."

—*Booklist*, starred review

"Queenie is the best mate we all want—funny, sharp, and more than a little vulnerable. I loved climbing inside her mind and wish I could have stayed longer. I adored this novel."

—Stacey Halls, author of *The Familiars*

"With resonant reflections on race, relationships, sex, and friendships, *Queenie* is a terrific debut that's delivered with a touch of British humor and plenty of feel-good moments."

—*BookPage*, starred review

"*Queenie* has all the things you want in a debut novel—a startlingly fresh voice, characters you fall in love with from the very first page, and a joyous turn of phrase that makes this book almost impossible to put down. In turns hilariously funny and quietly devastating, *Queenie* is an important, timely story."

—Louise O'Neill, bestselling author of
Asking for It

"*Queenie* is the book for anyone who has ever asked: Who am I? And how do I get there?"

—*PopSugar*

"Sometimes achingly sad, at other times laugh-out-loud funny, *Queenie* is a welcome debut from a seriously talented author."

—*The New York Post*

"Candice gives so generously with her joy, pain, and humor that we cannot help but become fully immersed in the life of Queenie—a beautiful, compelling book."

—Afua Hirsch, author of *Brit(ish)*

"A charming read for fans of women's fiction; Carty-Williams sets herself apart with her relatable and poignant writing."

—*Library Journal*

"Adorable, funny, heartbreaking. People are going to love it."

—Nina Stibbe, author of *Love, Nina*

"[A] heartbreaking, hopeful, sometimes funny, and always relatable journey."

—*Refinery29*

"Meet Queenie Jenkins, a twenty-five-year-old Jamaican British woman who works for a London newspaper, is struggling to fit in, is dealing with a breakup, and is making all kinds of questionable decisions. In other words, she's highly relatable."

—*Woman's Day*

"[A] wry, candid novel . . . feels like listening to a good friend's woes and wins—and cheering her on along the way."

—*BuzzFeed*

"The story of how twenty-five-year-old Queenie Jenkins balances her Jamaican and British heritages while navigating professional inequalities and romantic dilemmas is Black and brilliant all on its own."

—*Essence*

"I ate up *Queenie* in one greedy, joyous gulp. What a treat of a book. Lots to enjoy and think about. I loved Queenie and was cheering her on all the way. I thought all the mental health stuff was brilliant and so well done and authentic—it so often isn't, in novels—and also all the unhappy sex rang so true. Is there a sequel planned? All I wanted to do when I finished was to open book two."

—**Cathy Rentzenbrink, bestselling author of**
The Last Act of Love

PEOPLE PERSON

CANDICE CARTY-WILLIAMS

SCOUT PRESS

New York   London   Toronto   Sydney   New Delhi

People Person *is dedicated to all the single mothers.*

*Especially the ones who try their best to raise their children
with the love of two parents.*

Scout Press
An Imprint of Simon & Schuster, Inc.
1230 Avenue of the Americas
New York, NY 10020

First Scout Press trade paperback edition October 2023

SCOUT PRESS and colophon are registered trademarks of Simon & Schuster, Inc.

For information about special discounts for bulk purchases, please contact Simon & Schuster Special Sales at 1-866-506-1949 or business@simonandschuster.com.

The Simon & Schuster Speakers Bureau can bring authors to your live event. For more information or to book an event, contact the Simon & Schuster Speakers Bureau at 1-866-248-3049 or visit our website at www.simonspeakers.com.

Manufactured in the United States of America

10 9 8 7 6 5 4 3 2 1

Library of Congress Cataloging-in-Publication Data is available.

ISBN 978-1-5011-9604-1
ISBN 978-1-5011-9605-8 (pbk)
ISBN 978-1-5011-9606-5 (ebook)

"Hello? Hi, is this Nikisha? Hi, it's Dimple. Number three in the line, last time I checked. Yeah?! It's been a while, hasn't it? You good? Yeah, no, I'm not so good, actually. I'm in a bit of a sticky situ, and I remembered what you said about calling you if— Okay. Uh-huh. Yep. Yes. I'll text you my address now. Okay. Yeah, I'll see you in a bit."

CHAPTER
ONE

THEIR FATHER, CYRIL PENNINGTON, was not a discriminatory man. He had five children. Five children that he claimed, with four different women. Though claiming isn't the same as paying child support, or being physically, mentally, or emotionally present. Claiming, in Cyril Pennington's way, was being generally *aware* that he had five children (and possibly more, but he wasn't going to go looking), remembering their names and sometimes their birthdays, and asking them for money when times were hard. He worked as a bus driver, spending his days doing very little in addition to his job but flirting with passengers, chasing women much too young for him, and playing dominoes with his acquaintances at the barber shop near the bus garage. Although he was unknowingly a master of detachment, Cyril saw himself as more of a people person than a father. Sadly for his children, this sociability didn't extend to the five of them in a way that was mutually beneficial.

Cyril's eldest was Nikisha Pennington. Fiery, driven, and bright, she'd decided long ago that having a man in her life was never *essential*, more like something nice to pick up when she needed to and put back down when she didn't. She had very little time for daddy issues, and actually found the term offensive; the suggestion that she had the issue as a result of being left behind was unbelievable to her.

Nikisha's mother was Bernice. Bernice's mum had worked at the dental practice Cyril's mother, Delores, ran with her husband. Cyril had known Bernice for a while before he'd gotten her into bed and subsequently got her pregnant.

Bernice was a slim and captivating, wildly flirty Jamaican woman with an outwardly sunny disposition but mainly a tongue that would, and could, lyrically destroy you. Nikisha had picked this up from Bernice as she'd grown older, and sometimes deployed it, but only when she needed to.

Then came Danny Smith-Pennington. His mother was Tracy Smith, a friendly and more than accommodating petite white woman with a dark blond bob, who lived on the block near the bus garage where Cyril worked. Cyril would help Tracy carry her shopping up the dull stone steps to the flat until the day she asked him if he'd like to come inside for a cup of tea. When she became pregnant, Cyril, in his own optimistic way, vowed to himself that he'd make strides to be present in the life of this child, and also to Nikisha, the two-year-old daughter he already had. That was the first time Cyril had ever notably lied to himself.

Three years later, Cyril became father to Dimple Pennington and Elizabeth Adesina. Not twins, but born three weeks apart. Dimple arrived, weeping as gently as a baby could, three weeks early, while Elizabeth, who would be known as Lizzie by those close to her, arrived silently, precisely on schedule, and already seemingly unimpressed by the world she'd been born into.

Cyril had met Janet, Dimple's mother, at a nightclub on Old Kent Road he was DJing at. His DJ name was Fireshot. It was also the name of the sound system he'd built back in Jamaica before London called his name. Cyril had liked Janet because she was *big*. His type was usually smaller, more lean women, but when he laid eyes on Janet's heavy chest and big, round bottom from the decks, he was so distracted by what he saw that he dropped a bottle of Red Stripe on the turntables. Her full body piqued his interest in a way he hadn't been able to let go of, physically or mentally. Cyril had promised her the world, and, suitably, had left her with a child. Janet, an Indian Jamaican woman who had aspirations to be a legal secretary, knew nothing of Cyril's previous children, and when she found out, she was equal parts livid and heartbroken, though she hid her disappointment. She wanted a child to love, yes, but she also thought that what she'd found in Cyril was a man who would love and support them both, not a man who could whisk up, on the spot, seventy-five reasons he couldn't pay child support this week, but that he "might be able to help in a couple weeks' time."

Lizzie's mother was Kemi Adesina, a young nurse Cyril had met when visiting his mother, Delores, in the hospital. Kemi, the picture of dignity, was athletically built with a long, slender neck, and was a proud and firm Yoruba woman who was committed to a full and prosperous relationship with this man who was to be the father of her child. When she found out that this wasn't going to be the case, she put the encounter with Cyril down to a lapse in judgment and didn't speak a word to him until the day Lizzie asked where her dad was. This was around nine years after her conception. Kemi called Cyril, exchanged some quick pleasantries with him, and put him on the phone to his daughter.

When Nikisha was ten years old, Cyril had gone to visit his eldest daughter for the first time in six years. He had given up all of his false aspirations of being a father to her, but it had been Nikisha's birthday a couple of weeks before and he thought it might be a good thing to take her a card. Nikisha had looked at her father, and the card, with derision, then went out to play with her friends. Cyril stayed and reacquainted himself with her mother, Bernice, who looked just as good to him as she did when Nikisha had been just a glint in his eye.

Nine or so months later, one frosty December day, came Prynce Pennington. Nikisha, who was probably more suited to being an only child, actually took to being an older sister well. Mainly because she realized there was no point in fighting it; the first time Prynce took food out of her mouth to eat it for himself, she knew this sort of activity wouldn't be a one-off. Everything she had became her little brother's. Even her time. Prynce grew up to be a schemer and a dreamer. Selectively forgetful but sharp, charming, and excited, but largely uncommitted to anything.

———————

One day, when all of his children were of what he believed to be approaching courting age (apart from Prynce, who was nine), Cyril decided that this day, this Saturday, would be the day they all met. He jumped out of the bed that sat in the corner of his little studio flat, padded over to the window, and pulled aside the sheet he'd been using as a curtain for the last three years. The sun was shining and the sky was as blue as the sea he remembered from back home. He loved days like this. His mood was entirely dependent on the weather, though he didn't know why. If he ever let his mind roam to interrogating any possible reasons, he chalked it up to missing the sun he'd known on his skin every day when he'd grown up in Jamaica. Things were very simple to Cyril, so if you'd said the term "seasonal affective disorder" to him, he'd start a fight with you and accuse you of trying to put a spell on him.

He went into the bathroom, splashed cold water on his face, and brushed his teeth. He only had one full front tooth, plated in gold. Of the other front tooth, he only had half. He always told women that he lost the other half in a fight, when actually he'd fallen over when he was drunk and smashed his face on the steps going up to his flat. He swilled water round his mouth, spat it out, and smiled at his reflection in the cracked mirror above the sink. He decided that today was going to be a good day.

Cyril left the bathroom and sauntered over to the sound system that took up most of his living space: a record player he'd won in a game of cards hooked up to three once-broken speakers that he'd found outside a nightclub, convincing a friend to help him carry them home. He flipped through his prized record collection, deciding that this morning he was in the mood for some Johnny Nash.

He took time and care to remove the record from its sleeve, then its plastic sheath, balancing it delicately between his thick, otherwise clumsy fingers. He smiled as he lowered it down onto the platter, feeling the same buzz he felt every time he lifted the needle slowly from its place and dropped it on the spinning disk.

The crackle of the vinyl felt like a balm to his soul, and when the music began, Cyril felt his whole body relax.

The shower in his house was broken, and he hadn't remembered to pay the gas bill on time, so Cyril had a bucket bath with some hot water from the kettle. The electricity bill was always paid on time because Cyril couldn't live without music. And it wasn't like he minded not having hot water. This way, he was reminded of bathing back home. When he'd first come to London, the functionality of a shower was so luxurious to him that he almost didn't trust it.

After his bucket bath, he moved across his little flat, towel round his waist, the once-taut stomach that had been threatening to become a pot belly for a little while peeking over the top of it.

He took his time moisturizing himself before he got dressed, opting for a pair of black trousers with a black leather belt and a salmon-red short-sleeved shirt. He liked this shirt a lot. He couldn't remember which woman had given it to him, but he knew he definitely didn't buy it himself. He finished his look with a small gold chain. From it hung a cross pendant from his mother that dangled down between the space where his pecs had once been.

When he was fully dressed, Cyril danced small steps around his flat until the needle lifted itself off the vinyl and signified that it was time to leave for the day. That was how Cyril did things. He tried not to rely too much on actual time, more on feeling, on instinct, how the world was moving around him. How he had kept a job was a mystery to everybody who knew him, especially his employers.

Cyril left his flat, carefully locking the door behind him lest anyone broke in and stole anything to do with his music. He strutted down the steps to the ground floor, left the building—an old Georgian house that had been converted into way too many flats—and smiled widely at the postman coming up the path.

"Anyting for me, Bill?" Cyril asked the postman. "Unless it's bills you bring me, Bill. You cyan keep dem."

The postman, a white man named William with a curious mustache, laughed politely, shook his head, and shrugged his shoulders at the same time. It wasn't that Cyril's accent, one that he'd refused to drop since he'd arrived in England decades ago, was particularly strong, but William still had no idea what he was saying to him, even though they'd spoken to each other in some way pretty much every day for the last year.

Cyril climbed into his vehicle, a shining gold Jeep. It was his pride and joy. Most, if not all, of the money he should have spent on child support, or even living slightly more comfortably, was spent on the gold Jeep. He truly loved it more than anything else in his life and he didn't see a problem with that. He put the key into the ignition, wound the windows down, and slid a reggae mix CD he'd gotten at the barber shop into the drive. Before he took off, "Inna di Bus" by Professor Nuts blasting through the speaker, he pulled the sun visor down and smiled at his reflection in the mirror, his gold tooth glinting back at him.

"You is a handsome man, Cyril!" he said to himself. He was definitely not a man who needed lessons in self-love.

First, he arrived at Bernice's. He'd timed it so she was out doing Saturday shopping in Brixton market. He didn't want to get into it with her, didn't want to have to answer any questions about what he was doing with *his* kids on *his* own time. When Cyril pulled up, Prynce was already outside, eyeing the gold Jeep suspiciously. The loud reggae blaring from it had already disturbed him from roller skate practice.

"My yout!" Cyril smiled, pulling up and sticking his head out of the window. "How yuh still so small?"

Prynce knew not to talk to strangers, so backed toward the house as quickly as his roller skates would let him.

"Nikisha!" Prynce called into the house behind him. "Stranger danger!"

Nikisha, now nineteen, ran out of the house, frying pan raised above her head.

"Back up!" she shouted. "Oh."

She rolled her eyes at the gold Jeep, and the man inside it, and lowered the frying pan.

"It's your dad." She stroked Prynce's head with her free hand.

"Who?"

"Well, your dad and mine," Nikisha told Prynce. "He's called Cyril."

"Ohhh." Prynce blinked slowly, looking at this man with fresh eyes.

"Y'all right, Nikisha?" Cyril called out. "Since when yuh know how fi cook?"

Nikisha looked back at Cyril blankly.

"Why are you here, Dad?"

"I'm taking you out for the day."

"Are you?" Nikisha laughed. "What's the occasion?"

"How old is this one now?" Cyril asked Nikisha, pointing at Prynce. "Six? Seven? Him small!"

"He's nine," Nikisha said. She thought about hitting him with the frying pan.

"Nine!" Cyril exclaimed, looking at both of his children. Nikisha already looked exactly like her mother did when he'd met her. Prynce looked like Cyril did when he was nine. But much skinnier.

"There doesn't have to be an occasion," he told Nikisha and Prynce. "It's a nice day, so I thought, why not? Lemme see mi kids dem, lemme take them somewhere nice."

Nikisha opened her mouth to ask her dad why he'd turned up today of all days, when it had been years since he'd seen them. She was ready to ask why he thought he could drive up to their house in this oversized and garish vehicle with no notice and disturb their peace for the day, to ask why he wouldn't be nice to Prynce, who hadn't seen him since he was about two. But instead, she told Prynce to swap his roller skates for sneakers and use the toilet before they went out. Maybe it would be good for Prynce to see what their dad was like instead of always asking. Nikisha did not have the answers.

"And wash your hands, Prynce!"

Nikisha put the frying pan on the cabinet by the front door and made her way into the Jeep.

"How are you?" she asked her dad, immediately turning his music down. It wasn't that she didn't like reggae, it's that she liked to be able to hear a conversation without having to guess 80 percent of what was being said.

"As you find me." Cyril smiled, turning the music back up and re-starting the CD so Professor Nuts played again.

"Wha' you know 'bout this tune?" Cyril shouted over the song.

Nikisha blinked back at him.

Once Prynce was in the car, seat belt on, Nikisha shook her head in wonder at the day's change of plans. This was her experience of having Cyril as a parent in a nutshell, though. You think you're about to have a normal day and suddenly you're reminded that (a) you have a dad, and (b) your dad wasn't actually a parent. Cyril started driving, zipping around the streets of south London, not concentrating enough on the road, but slowing down and eyeing pretty much every woman they passed.

"Dad, can you remember that we're here, please?" Nikisha pleaded, checking that her seat belt was secure. "Where are you even taking us?"

"We're going to the park," Cyril told her. "But we've got a couple—no, t'ree stops first."

———————

They pulled up to an estate, a cluster of high-rise buildings whose top floors nestled in the clouds in West Norwood that Nikisha had never been to but recognized because it was close to the bus garage she knew her dad worked at.

Cyril unclipped his seat belt and jumped out of the gold Jeep.

"You two wait here," he told them, disappearing into the estate. When he returned, following him was a mixed-race teenage boy who couldn't have been that much younger than Nikisha. Handsome, taller than Cyril but a lot slimmer, and with loud acne dotted across his forehead and cheeks.

Cyril climbed into the driver's seat, and the boy opened the back door and slid in behind Nikisha.

"Who is this? Who are you?" Nikisha asked, turning to her dad, then to the boy, for an answer.

"It's your brother." Cyril shrugged as if Nikisha had asked a silly question.

"I'm Danny." The boy smiled, holding a hand out for Nikisha to shake.

Nikisha ignored the hand.

"I'm Nikisha, that's Prynce," she told him.

Nikisha turned back to Cyril and stared daggers at him. He didn't notice, though; they were back on the road and the music was back on. Cyril didn't have a care in the world.

"Nikisha, run the CD back for me, track one again," he asked his eldest.

"Where are we going?" Danny asked their dad over the music.

"The park," Cyril told him. "But we've got one or two stops first."

They drove to Norbury, a strange little area that was nestled between Streatham and Croydon, not taking any trait from either surrounding area but not really having any defining traits of its own.

The gold Jeep pulled up outside a compact little house. Cyril parked swiftly and expertly in a space that had before seemed physically impossible for the Jeep to fit into.

"Actually, lemme jus' move down there a piece," Cyril said, driving out of the space and parking a little farther down the road.

Again, Cyril jumped out of the Jeep. When he returned, behind him was a plump teenage girl, hair big and wild, most of it escaping what was once a loose bun on top of her head.

Cyril got back into the Jeep, and the girl opened the door behind the driver's seat, looking frightened when she saw a strange older teenage boy and a strange quite young boy looking back at her.

"Move up, Prynce, let your sister get in," Cyril called to the back. "Dimple, you don't need to look so frighten!'"

Nikisha rolled her eyes as Prynce took his seat belt off and shuffled up next to Danny.

While Dimple took a running jump to get into the gold Jeep, Danny leaned over Prynce and clipped the middle seat belt over him.

"Thanks," Nikisha, who was watching from her visor mirror, said to Danny.

Danny nodded.

"Dimple?" Cyril turned the music down.

"Yep?" Dimple asked quietly, not looking at anybody.

"This is your sister Nikisha. Your eldest sister." Cyril gestured loosely at Nikisha. "That's Danny, the bigger one, and you see the smaller one? Him name Prynce. They're your brothers."

Cyril turned the key in the ignition. "An' we got one more stop."

"You sure it's only one?" Nikisha asked Cyril.

Cyril laughed, even though nobody in that gold Jeep was finding anything funny.

———————

Close to half an hour of the most silent journey ever later, Cyril stopped the gold Jeep again. This time in Clapham, close to the common.

"Won't be long," he said, taking his seat belt off. "Talk amongs' yuhselves."

A few minutes later, he returned to silence. Nobody in that gold Jeep was saying a word. For a second, he wondered if they were even still breathing. Behind him was a slim and pretty girl who, to Nikisha's eye, seemed like she was around the same age as the last girl Cyril had collected.

"Someone will have to sit on laps," Cyril said, opening the back door and peering in at the three sets of eyes, all like his in some way, staring back at him.

"Such a big car and not enough space for all your children?" Nikisha asked Cyril.

"It would seem that way!" Cyril replied cheerfully, the bite of the question lost on him.

"I'll get in the back, Prynce can go on my lap," Nikisha said. "Why don't you come in the front? What's your name again?"

She pointed at Dimple, who looked embarrassed.

"Why her?" Cyril asked. "Let the little boy go on her lap, nuh?"

"Because she's the *biggest* one," Nikisha said, unclipping her seat belt. "She's taking up the most space in the back."

Nikisha's comment hit Dimple in the chest and landed at the bottom of her stomach, where it would stay for a long time. Dimple's face got hot and she tried not to cry as she also unclipped her seat belt, then swapped places with Nikisha as the new addition to Cyril's unwilling gang stood outside and crossed her arms.

Nikisha pulled Prynce onto her lap as this new girl climbed into the Jeep with long, slender legs.

"I'm Elizabeth," she said. "I'm assuming you're my brothers and sisters?" she said, her tone surprisingly dry for someone her age.

"Smart girl. Does anyone ever call you Lizzie?" Nikisha asked.

"Only family," Elizabeth said pointedly.

"Okay, Lizzie," Nikisha said, ignoring this. "I'm Nikisha, eldest. This is Prynce, youngest. I dunno how old these two are. You two can introduce yourselves."

"I'm Danny, hi." Danny smiled from the middle. "Seventeen."

"And I'm Dimple," Dimple said, almost in a whisper, from the front seat. "I'm fourteen in July."

"How old are you?" Nikisha pointed at Elizabeth.

"Fourteen in August," Elizabeth said as she pulled her seat belt on smoothly.

"Eh, Lizzie, I know your mum doesn't play you any reggae when you're at home—listen to this!" Cyril laughed, putting Professor Nuts on again and turning the volume up.

"Dad! I've heard this song a hundred times now," Nikisha said.

Cyril turned up the volume.

When they arrived at Clapham Common, all walking behind their dad and very separately from each other, Cyril bought each of his children ice cream, having to borrow some money from Nikisha to pay for all five.

"Good thing I brought my purse." Nikisha sighed.

Before he went over to the ice cream van, Cyril made them stand in a circle.

"Right," he said to them. "Know each other's names, and know each other's faces." He watched them, nodding as they all took each other in properly.

Cyril smiled as they recognized the similarities they shared and wondered why he hadn't had them all in the same place sooner, before swiftly realizing that the answer was their mothers.

Nikisha, despite looking so much like her mum, had the same nose as Danny, while Dimple had the same eyes as her nontwin,

Lizzie, and to an extent Prynce, who had the longest eyelashes of all
of them. Lizzie and Prynce had the same smile; they'd inherited their
dad's big teeth, when he'd had the front ones intact. Only Dimple
had two dimples, while the rest had one each, on the right side of
their face.

Despite them all clocking how they did and didn't look like each
other, none of them felt any connection to the other. Nikisha and
Prynce only had ties because they lived in the same house, but a
nineteen-year-old and a nine-year-old didn't really have a lot in common otherwise.

Dimple looked up from the floor, anxious. She didn't know what
to say to any of these people. She looked over to Cyril, hoping he'd
be on his way back over, but he was locked in a boisterous conversation with the ice cream man. She noticed how he stood as he waited.
All of his weight rested on his left leg, while the other was stretched
out, the toe of his foot touching the floor lightly. She did that when
she was doing the washing up. Her mum always used to say she must
have been a ballerina in a past life.

None of Cyril's children were going to smile the way their dad
was smiling as he turned and looked at his mixed-gender, five-a-side
team.

"Is this the first time you've all met?" Cyril asked them, saunter-
ing back, the cones of five dripping 99s in his hands.

"Yes, Dad." Nikisha couldn't believe her ears. "Obviously."

"Wow." Cyril exhaled. "Time really flies, don't it?"

Nikisha was over this; she wanted to get back home. Her boyfriend was coming to knock for her later and she needed to shave her
legs. Danny was sort of bemused by the whole thing. He didn't really
ever let anything get him down. He was probably a bit too laid back
in general, which would come back to bite him one day. Dimple was
overcome with emotion regarding the whole meetup, but was determined not to show it, especially after what Nikisha had said about
her. She wanted to get to know them all. They were her siblings!

Half, whatever, but they were her brothers and sisters. And it wasn't like making friends came easy to her. Lizzie couldn't give a fuck about any of them. She wanted to go home and tell her mum that Cyril had basically kidnapped her and forced her to spend time with a group of Jamaicans.

And what was Prynce thinking? He just wanted another ice cream.

"This is so none of you ever buck up with each other on road and fall in love or have sex or any of dem tings," Cyril stated. "Because that, my children, would be illegal."

"Despite the fact that you got four women pregnant within a five-mile radius of each other," Nikisha said. "I doubt that was going to happen. We all look like you enough to know. Even the mixed-race one."

Danny nodded, dutifully accepting the facts.

"No offense," Nikisha said. "You just are."

"Nah, none taken." Danny shrugged. "I just am."

"Listen, Nikisha," Cyril said. "I just want you all to be clear and know who is who so I don't get any surprises down the line."

"You're one to talk about surprises," Lizzie said. "How many other women have you got?"

"I don't want to think about sex," Prynce groaned. "I'm nine. That's weird."

"Weird or not, I am just doing my duty as your father."

"Your duty?" Lizzie, already bored of Cyril and his ways, scoffed. "As our what?"

"Anyway, look." Cyril clapped his hands together. "Now that you all know each other, it's up to you to make friends if you want to make friends or whatever."

"I don't think we're gonna be friends, Dad," Nikisha said, then turned to her half-siblings, half of whom wouldn't have minded being friends. "But if anything ever happens, you call me, okay?"

Danny, Lizzie, and Prynce nodded, then looked at each other, blinking, ice cream dripping down their hands.

"And I mean it. Anything," Nikisha said.

Dimple, not eating her ice cream because she could still feel the earlier comment about her weight expanding in her belly, didn't consciously acknowledge what her half sister had said. Instead she vowed in her head that she would never ask her for anything ever.

"Talk a little bit, nuh?" Cyril asked his kids, his twinkling eyes wandering over to two twentysomething Black girls sunbathing in shorts and bikini tops.

"Dad!" Nikisha clicked her fingers. "Eyes over here!"

Cyril laughed, stood back, and crossed his arms.

"Why don't you tell each other what you like at school?" He was so out of touch with his children that he hadn't recognized that two of them had long left secondary education.

"I left school when I was sixteen, Dad," Nikisha said. "I was gonna study project management at college, but the course schedule didn't work with looking after Prynce, so. I dunno. I'll see when Prynce is in secondary school."

"So what, you wanna tell people what to do for a living?" Danny asked her. "So you're bossy, basically?"

"Very." Nikisha nodded. "What about you?"

"Errr? I like fixing things. I like working with my hands," Danny told his half-siblings. "I dunno what it is, but when I was in school I'd just fall asleep in lessons aaall the tiiime."

Prynce laughed at this. He liked this older boy in front of him; he seemed silly.

"Anyway," Danny said. "I do a mechanical apprenticeship now. Like, cars and stuff. It's good. Messy. But good."

"What about you?" Nikisha looked at Lizzie, who was licking her ice cream neatly, concentrating so she didn't get any of it on her hand.

"I'm going to be a doctor," Lizzie answered, not taking her eyes off her ice cream.

"Okay!" Danny exclaimed. "Confident, I like it!"

"Mmm." Lizzie nodded.

"So you must already be top of the class, yeah?" Danny asked.

"Yep," Lizzie said.

"I want to be a BMX biker." Prynce smiled.

"Oh what?" Danny exaggerated a jump backward. "Swear? That's the best job I've ever *heard*! I might have to copy you, you know!"

Prynce beamed as he bit into his ice cream.

"What about you?" Nikisha looked over at Dimple.

"Huh?" Dimple had gotten so into her head about having to answer that she forgot she was required to be part of the conversation.

"School? Job?" Nikisha asked.

"Er . . ." Dimple looked up at Nikisha, then back down at the floor. "I don't know."

"You don't know what you study?" Lizzie asked, furrowing her thick, neat brows. "Or you don't know what you want to be?"

"I do the usual classes." Dimple nodded. "I just . . . don't have a favorite thing. Maybe drama, actually. But I don't have a thing that I want to do."

"You're so shy and you like drama?" Nikisha laughed. "I think you're gonna have to find a new favorite subject."

"She'll figure it out," Danny told Nikisha, putting a gentle hand on Dimple's shoulder.

Cyril, thinking that he'd done a really good and worthwhile thing today, smiled, took a deep breath, and looked around him as the sun kissed his face. His eyes went back over to the sunbathing girls, who had gotten up to leave and were crossing the park. As he watched them walk over to the pond, he thought he recognized someone he didn't feel like having a conversation with today.

"All right, it's time to tek you all home now." Cyril strutted into the middle of his circle of children. "I've got things to be doing."

Cyril took his children home in the reverse order he collected them in. Lizzie was first because he knew that Kemi liked to know details, and in hiding the details of today from her, trouble was coming. The second Cyril pulled up, Kemi approached the gold Jeep at lightning speed, flinging the back door open and looking at the weary children inside who were all too young to understand the magnitude of the day they'd had.

"Elizabeth," the woman barked, not acknowledging the rest of Cyril's children, nor Cyril, who'd wound his window down to greet her. "Out, now."

Lizzie flung the door open on her side and hopped out. She closed it behind her, not quite a slam but almost, and trotted around the car to stand behind her mum.

"Kemi!" Cyril exclaimed. "What do you?"

Kemi stepped up to Cyril's open window and held her index finger up to his face.

"When I came after Lizzie to give her a sweater, I looked closer, and who do I see driving away? You, and all of these little heads bouncing around in this stupid big masculinity car. Never again. My Lizzie doesn't need to consort with the rest of your litter."

"Who's this woman talking to?" Nikisha shouted from the passenger seat. "Litter? Litter? Let her meet my mum and tell her about litter."

Cyril let out a low laugh.

"Kemi and your mum have already met. That was really something."

"Come on," Kemi said to Lizzie, pulling her away even though, clearly, Lizzie did not want to stay there.

"One down," Cyril said, pulling away from the curb.

Next to be dropped off was Dimple. When Cyril pulled up to the compact little house in Norbury, her mother, Janet, was already outside. Cyril wondered if he'd ever get the chance to dip back into Janet's curves.

"You see you, Cyril?" she said, opening the driver's-side door. "You're going to hell."

"That's a bit strong, Jan." Cyril laughed as Dimple tumbled out of the gold Jeep and managed to land on her feet.

"No, it's not strong *enough*, Cyril," Janet spat. "I really had to find it in myself to let you rock up here and take Dimp for the day, even though you haven't spoken to her for months, *or* given me one penny in years. And when I do, Sharon calls me and tells me she sees you, Dimple, and your four other children on Clapham Common? Cyril, I couldn't believe my ears."

Cyril laughed again.

"And you're laughing!" she shrieked. "As you always do. Well, you're going to laugh in hell."

Janet turned to her daughter and placed her hands on Dimple's chubby cheeks.

"Are you okay, Dimp? Did they say anything to upset you? You can tell me!"

"I'm fine, Mum." Dimple pulled her mum's hands away from her face, embarrassed.

Janet turned back to Cyril.

"Hell," she told him. "I mean it."

Janet pulled Dimple, who was trying to wave goodbye to everyone in the gold Jeep, into the house.

"You see how mad women are?" Cyril asked, turning to Nikisha.

"Well . . ." Nikisha shrugged. "Aren't you the common denominator?"

"Where you learn these big words?" Cyril asked as he closed the door on the driver's side.

If Nikisha had glared any harder at her dad, her eyes would have bored a hole in the side of his head.

"Your mum won't give me any trouble, Danny," Cyril said, setting off to West Norwood. "She's always been a good girl."

Danny, not sure what to do with this information, just nodded, then quickly forgot what his dad had said when he looked out of the window and got distracted by literally anything in his eyesight.

Danny's drop-off, as Cyril had predicted, was smooth. Danny said a cheerful bye to his dad, Nikisha, and a sleeping Prynce, jumped out of the Jeep, and made his way into the estate.

They took off again. Cyril, optimistic as he was, was silently relieved that this day was almost over. This snap decision to bring all his children together was meant to have been fun; instead, Cyril had taken a verbal battering from a number of women *and* his kids didn't even chat to each other.

Nikisha turned to look at Prynce, who was still asleep, then turned back to her dad.

"Why did you turn the music down when Dimple got in the car?" she asked him. "And not for the rest of us? Why's she so special?"

"What?" Cyril kept his eyes on the road. Even though he didn't really know his children, he loved them all the same. Each got 20 percent of the love he had to offer. No more, no less.

"Is it 'cause her mum is one of them Indian-looking women?" Nikisha pressed, annoyed. "I always hear how you lot go on about 'good hair.'"

Cyril pulled over and made sure he put on the handbrake loudly and in a way that might have seemed authoritative. He turned to Nikisha.

"So that's why you made that little dig about her size."

Nikisha didn't say anything.

"You didn't think I heard that?"

"It's the truth, though. She is the biggest."

Cyril tutted.

"You're too old for alla that. Dimple is soft," Cyril said. "She's always been like it. You, you have fire. Lizzie, she's been giving me a run for my money every age I've known her. Prynce is too young to know anyting, and Danny is, how yuh call it? Happy-go-lucky. But Dimple, she's soft. Everyting affects that girl. The breeze blows the wrong way and she bawls. You look at her in a way she nah understan' and she's weeping. So we haffi treat her wid kindness."

"Since when did anyone get special treatment for not being strong enough?" Nikisha huffed. "That's her problem, not mine."

"You're her sister," Cyril said. "It's your problem, too."

"Half," Nikisha said.

Cyril drove Nikisha and Prynce back to Battersea. As the gold Jeep swung onto their road, Nikisha turned in her seat and saw that Prynce was still sleeping in the back.

"Better wake him up," Cyril said, pulling up.

"Why?" Nikisha said. "He can just be carried in."

"You're as strong as that?" Cyril smiled. "You must be a Pennington fi true."

Nikisha looked at her dad and wondered if it even occurred to him that he, the father of this small boy, might be the one to carry him into the house.

"See you soon, yeah?" Cyril said, finding another CD to put on. He'd lost interest entirely.

Nikisha hopped out of the car and opened the door closest to Prynce. She stroked his face softly to wake him up and said his name quietly.

"What you doing?" Cyril jerked round. He put a hand on Prynce's knee and shook it roughly. "Get up!"

Prynce's eyes shot open and he looked terrified as he tried to realize where he was.

"What are you doing?" Nikisha asked, unclipping her little brother's seat belt. "You scared him!"

"My son isn't going to be no sof' bwoy!" Cyril cackled.

"Well, when you raise him you can have a say in how he's going to be." Nikisha held Prynce's hand as he sleepily lowered himself from the gold Jeep.

She led her brother toward the house without saying goodbye. Before they'd gotten inside, Cyril had already driven off.

Later, after a stop at the betting shop where he lost most of the money in his pocket, and another stop at the Caribbean takeaway down the road, Cyril let himself into his flat and got a beer out of the fridge. He put the food on the side. He wasn't ready for it yet. After the day he'd had, he knew he also wasn't ready for that kind of emotional warfare again for a long, long time.

And so the months and then the years went on, with Cyril promising himself and the mothers he'd take the children out again, and separately this time. But whenever he went to do just that, he grew more sensitive to the conflict he'd face when he'd have to see them, not for one second thinking he was to blame for any of it. The promises to see his children again turned into suggestions, then rumors, until finally, an acceptance on all sides that it wasn't going to happen.

Apart from Nikisha and Prynce, whenever the rest of Cyril Pennington's children saw each other in a shop, or on the street, doing the polite thing of exchanging numbers and saying they'd meet up, none of them really felt any need to speak to each other again. Why would they? They barely had anything in common. They didn't even have Cyril Pennington in common, really.

CHAPTER
TWO

DIMPLE. CYRIL'S MIDDLE CHILD. now thirty, sat at her dressing table. She was slimmer. She wasn't skinny, though, not by any measure of European standards. When she was growing up, she'd seen her solid arms and her legs as problem areas, but now, and only because of the compliments she'd been given on her thighs and bum, she accepted the thick limbs that she'd always accused of letting the rest of her body down.

She was good at doing her own makeup, so that went a long way on the road to being considered attractive. Sometimes she got comments on her selfies calling her "hot" and that went *some* way to making her happy. The fire emojis made her happy, too. When she was in her midtwenties and social media had run her life, she had this sliding scale of how much people loved her based not just on how many likes she got on a selfie but on the emojis they dropped. Fire was the best, obviously. Heart eyes followed, but she didn't like them as much. Her least favorite was the crying emoji. It was meant to be cute, yes, but Dimple didn't want to be cute. She wanted to be sexy, and hadn't yet accepted that some people were born sexy and that she wasn't one of them. But she was definitely attractive. She *was* cute! And she had something about her. Which was better than nothing.

The boiler next to her room rumbled and clanked to remind her how cold it was outside. She turned her ring light on, then checked her face in the mirror. She patted under her eyes gently with her index finger, and wondered if a different pair of lashes would hide how puffy they were.

She clipped her phone into the middle of the ring of bright light and opened the camera, taking a deep breath and smiling widely as she did. She rolled her shoulders back and pressed record.

"Hey, guys! It's me, Dimple!" She stopped recording, cleared her throat, then did a couple of vocal and jaw exercises.

She pressed record again.

"Hey, guys! It's me, Dimple. I'm here with a quick but really sad message."

Dimple looked down at her lap, then up again.

"Now, as you know, me and Kyron have been in a challenging relationship for a while. One that's had a lot of ups and downs. And a few of the downs you know all about."

Dimple paused to tilt her head back and give the illusion that tears were about to fall from her eyes.

"Anyway. I'm sorry to have to break it to you that we've decided to call it a day. Even though we love each other so, so much, we realized that we'd come to the end of the road. We made each other so happy, but happiness can't be everything, can it?" She paused for dramatic effect. "And of course we're going to continue to be friends. I can't imagine a life without him. Please leave your girl some words of encouragement in the comments below! Love ya!"

Dimple stopped recording, took the phone from the stand, and watched herself back before giving it a quick edit. She wasn't happy with it, but thought she'd get more sympathy if it didn't look too polished.

She uploaded the video to her channels, then put her phone on airplane mode, even though fewer than a hundred people were going to watch that video. Followers aside, Dimple was an influencer in the sense that she *believed* she was one. Every influencer had to start somewhere, even though she'd effectively been starting on her influencer journey and had the same amount of followers for at least three years.

Dimple bit her bottom lip hard as she thought about all of the red flags Kyron had shown in the early days. The inconsistency, the angry outbursts, the jealousy, and also the not answering his phone but then turning up when he could be bothered and accusing her of being the tricksy one.

For a while, she'd understood all of those things to be passionate, and not to be actually very bad personality traits that would be used as weapons later on down the line. That'll happen when your dad is almost entirely absent. You can start thinking that any male attention is good attention. Kyron *had* been nice, though. Sometimes. He'd always buy her presents when he'd fucked up, which was something, even though he always forgot her birthday. She'd grown up getting spoiled by her mum when it came to presents, to make up for nothing from Cyril every Christmas and birthday. And so she really *valued* presents from men, even if they were shit. She'd liked having a boyfriend, too, but it ended up being a lot more work than she'd initially envisioned. Plus she'd noticed that the videos she'd uploaded with him got fewer views than her usual solo ones. The difference between seventeen and seventy views is huge when your following isn't quite as high as you'd like it to be.

Dimple had tried to break up with Kyron a few times and he'd always managed to persuade her back, but after a couple of anonymous accounts had sent her messages about the stuff he'd been getting up to when they were together or split, Dimple had ended things, and for good this time. Really. For good this time. She even wrote it on her wall (in pencil) to remind herself of that.

What made it slightly harder was that at this point in her life, she was completely unable to be self-sufficient, emotionally or otherwise, and leaned heavily on her mum (and, before the breakup, Kyron, too, even though when she moaned about things he'd just reply with "gets like that") for everything, up to and including: support, money, and especially love and attention. She didn't think she'd ever leave home. And even though Janet could be a bit overbearing and heavy-handed, her mum was her favorite person, so why would she ever go anywhere?

Her mum had gone on holiday with her best friend, Vanessa, for a few days, so Dimple had been rattling around in the house, trying (and succeeding) not to answer her ex-boyfriend's calls or messages. Kyron had been trying every avenue. When she didn't answer his messages, he called her from a private number. When she didn't answer her mobile, he'd call the landline, even though it had only been installed so they could have the Internet and she had no idea how he'd gotten the number. She knew it was him because the calls came exactly after he'd stopped calling her mobile. She called 1471 just to check the number of the last caller, and every single time she'd be right. When he couldn't get her on the phones, he'd moved over to Instagram. He'd unlike and then like the same selection of her selfies he always did, then he'd message her asking her to call him. Then he'd try Facebook, even though she used it even less than she used the landline. This would happen every time they fell out, and eventually she'd reply to him after a day of bombardment, but this time she was determined not to respond once.

Dimple slipped her phone into her pocket and went downstairs. The stress of the breakup had destroyed her appetite (because she knew it was definitely for real this time), but she knew she needed to eat so she didn't fall over.

She stepped into the kitchen and turned the light on, jumping when the landline rang. She stared at it and bit her lip, ignoring the broken skin that was splitting every time she did so. When the phone stopped ringing, she went to the fridge to see what her mum had left her, telling herself that she didn't need to be so worried. It's not like Kyron could jump through the phone, and if he turned up, she just wouldn't answer the door. She shook her head at the soup on the top shelf of the fridge. As she slammed the fridge closed, the bottle of vegetable oil that sat on top of it fell to the floor, just missing her feet. Dimple clenched her jaw when she saw that some of the yellow liquid had spilled onto the floor, and onto her feet.

"Why?" Dimple shouted at the bottle like it had betrayed her. She picked it up and put it on the kitchen counter before doing half a job of wiping up the spilled oil. She knew her mum would do it properly when she got back. Dimple took her phone out, turned off airplane mode, and swiped away all of Kyron's million notifications as they came through, then ordered some food.

She threw her phone onto the sofa and put the TV on, taking a deep breath and forcing her tense shoulders back down to where they belonged, not up by her ears. She started watching some film she didn't bother to check the name of, but began to doze off after a few minutes. The relief of telling the world, even though that world was, as per the latest insights, thirty people, about her breakup, had made it more manageable, somehow. Even though part of her knew that anybody who would watch, comment, or send messages of love and support didn't really care at all. Her self-awareness definitely didn't stop her from doing what she did. She still had goals. She didn't know exactly what they were. But she had goals.

Dimple woke up to the ringing of the doorbell. She took a sharp intake of breath to try to wake herself up, and shuffled over to the front door. She grabbed a few coins for a tip from the table in the hallway, and called out a sleepy "Just coming!" as she pulled the door handle down. Rubbing her eyes with the back of the hand that held the coins, she held the other out to take the pizza box, but opened her eyes when her hand grasped at nothing.

"Why aren't you answering your fucking phone?" Kyron hissed, pushing Dimple into the house by her shoulders. "You're going to post all my business on the fucking Internet and you can't even talk to me?"

Adrenaline spiked through Dimple's veins. She was fully awake now.

"I was asleep, sorry!" she said, putting a hand to where Kyron had pushed her.

"What, for two days you've been asleep?" Kyron sneered, coming close to Dimple as she backed away from him. "And then my boy sends me a video where you're saying all this shit about how you'll always love me and we'll always be friends? I'm not your fucking friend, Dimple, I'm your man."

"But you aren't!" Dimple said. "We've spoken about this!"

Kyron looked Dimple up and down, then stepped close to her, eyeing her suspiciously.

"Why you got a full face of makeup on? Who you got here?"

"Nobody!" Dimple said. "It was for the video. Obviously!"

Dimple turned and walked back into the living room. Kyron had never just turned up this angry, so she decided to play nice and defuse the situation, rather than force him to leave.

Kyron followed Dimple.

"If I hear about you chatting to anyone else, I swear—"

"Kyron!" Dimple exclaimed. "Why is that always the first place you jump to? Why would I chat to anyone else?"

"I dunno, you know," Kyron spat, his nostrils flaring. "But what else am I supposed to think when you don't answer your fucking phone?"

Kyron wasn't calming down.

"Where's your mum?" he asked. "She here?"

"No, but she'll be back in a bit," Dimple said, lying. Her breathing was getting faster. She didn't like conflict. Even when she argued with her mum she cried, even if it was about the washing up or not taking the meat out of the freezer in time for her mum to get home from work. It was no way to live at thirty, this emotional dependence, but Janet had indulged it so much that neither of them realized it was a problem. She really wished her mum were here as she gave her trembling knees some respite by lowering herself down onto the sofa.

"Give me your phone," Kyron demanded, holding his hand out.

"Why?" Dimple asked. "No. You don't need to see my phone. There's nothing on there."

"Well, if there's nothing on there, then what's the problem with me seeing it?" Kyron sneered. "Give me the phone," he said, louder.

"I dunno where it is," Dimple said. She was annoyed that he refused to trust her.

"You?" Kyron laughed. "Who has her phone in her hand all the time? Doesn't know where it is?"

Dimple's eyes jumped to the other end of the sofa, where her phone sat. Kyron's eyes followed hers, and he grabbed the phone.

"Unlock it."

"No." Dimple tried to be firm even though she was scared. "I told you, there's nothing on there. Can you just trust me, please? What does it say about me that you think I have stuff to hide?"

"Unlock it!"

"I'm not unlocking it, Kyron!"

"Fine," Kyron said, throwing the phone across the room.

Dimple winced as it hit the wall, then went to pick it up. She threw her head back in despair when she saw a gigantic crack down the middle of the screen, and tossed the phone onto the sofa.

"Who you going out to meet, then?" Kyron changed his line of attack.

"Stop this! I fucking hate when you get like this, Ky!"

"You hate when I get like— It's you who makes me like this, you know!" Kyron said, charging over to Dimple and pointing a finger in her face.

"Don't point in my face, Kyron," Dimple said, her lower lip trembling.

At that point, probably the worst point, the doorbell rang.

"Ah, so you've got your new guy coming round now, is it?" Kyron said, turning and running to the front door. "You see, I knew it."

Kyron yanked the front door open, poised to punch the pizza delivery man who stood in front of him.

"Er, good evening ... sir," the pizza delivery man said. "Pizza for you?"

"Give me that, man," Kyron growled, grabbing the pizza box out of the man's bag. "And fuck off."

Kyron walked back into the living room and threw the pizza box down onto the kitchen counter. He turned to a still-trembling Dimple, who was leaning against the kitchen counter.

"Things would be easier for you if you just answered your phone."

"You don't make anything easy for me," Dimple said in a small voice.

"What was that?" Kyron asked. "Speak up! If you're gonna say something to me, say it!"

"I said ... you don't make anything easy for me," Dimple repeated, only slightly louder.

Kyron then transformed, the way he always did, from a demon in a Nike tracksuit to some sort of emotionally available sweet boy who probably drummed for his church choir for free every Sunday.

"But love isn't easy, babe," he said, stepping toward her and gently cupping her chin in his big hand. "And you know, if I didn't love you as much as I did, I wouldn't get so upset when things went wrong between us."

Kyron lifted Dimple's face toward his and bent down to kiss her on each cheek.

"Smile for me," he said. "Let me see those dimples."

A deadly move from Kyron (he knew what he was doing), because about ninety seconds later, Dimple was straddling him on the sofa, her knickers were across the room, and his tracksuit bottoms and boxers were around his ankles.

Afterward, on her way back from the bathroom, Dimple retrieved her knickers from the TV stand where they'd landed.

"You see." Kyron smiled as he lay back on the sofa, slightly breathless and flashing the demon smile that told Dimple she shouldn't have done that. "I knew you wouldn't leave me."

Dimple looked over at him as she pulled her knickers up and remembered the reminder she'd written on her bedroom wall.

"But I have left you," she said. She tried to be firm, and there was a telltale wobble in her voice, but still, she said what she needed to. Again. And the decision was made harder because that particular session was Kyron at his best. The sex wasn't usually that good. The sex is always the best at the end of a relationship. Or when you know you shouldn't be doing it.

"That's not for just you to decide," Kyron said, narrowing his eyes. He'd immediately gone back to Bad Personality A (angry, violent, demon, Nike tracksuit), as opposed to Bad Personality B (manipulative, sorry for himself, church boy, drumsticks).

"It is!" Dimple said, shaking her head. "It's every minute arguing, Kyron. I'm so tired of it! I don't think this can be love."

Kyron exhaled loudly through his nostrils.

"We can't keep stopping and starting something that's so painful," Dimple said. "It can't be nice for you either, Kyron. It's done. And I'm sorry." Dimple rubbed her temples with perfectly manicured nails. "And I hope we can always be friends. I meant that when I said it."

Dimple held her breath. Maybe Kyron had finally accepted it. Maybe he was going to hug her, leave, then send her the money to pay for her cracked phone screen. Instead, though, his big, coarse hands, the ones that had held her face so gently not that long ago, were around her throat. Dimple used all the force she could to push at him, to get him away from her, to get his hands away from around her neck, but it was pointless. Kyron was big, and he was strong, too.

Dimple closed her eyes. She could hear and feel her heart beating fast, then slowing down.

Dimple tried to push Kyron away again, but her arms fell limply at her sides as he increased the pressure on her windpipe. In a final bid for survival, Dimple lifted a hand to Kyron's face and clawed at it, digging her nails deep into his left cheek and dragging them down.

Kyron shrieked and pushed Dimple away before putting his hands to his wounded face. When he drew them back and saw blood, he looked like he was going to faint.

Dimple backed away from Kyron as her breath came back to her in jagged, stuttering bursts.

"Look what you've done to me!" he yelped, so horrified that Dimple wondered if he'd forgotten what had just happened.

"You? *You?* Are you joking?" Dimple shouted, her hands protecting her sore neck. "Kyron, you were strangling me!"

"I thought you liked it when I choked you?" Kyron sneered.

"I fucking hate you!" Dimple screamed at him. "Get out!"

"You fucking witch! Who you talking to like that?" Kyron growled, reaching for Dimple, who ducked out of the way, moving past the fridge, toward the sink. Kyron went for her a second time, springing forward, hands going for the neck again. But on the way toward her, when he got to the fridge, he slipped on the oil Dimple couldn't be bothered to clean up. Dimple watched as Kyron fell backward and hit the back of his head on the kitchen counter. It was all really dramatic, even for a Saturday night.

"Kyron!" Dimple gasped, her hands flying up to her mouth. "That sounded painful. You okay?"

She knew he wasn't okay, but it seemed like the only thing to say in that situation.

Dimple stepped closer to him and saw that his eyes were closed. He looked like he was asleep, except a pool of blood emerged from the back of his head and started to surround it like a sort of anti-halo.

She stared at the crimson puddle, transfixed by how bright it was. Usually, blood made her squeamish, but not right now. No, right now she was wondering what would happen if her mum came home and saw so much mess on a wood floor she'd recently paid to get polished.

"Oh God, what do I do, what do I do?"

Dimple bent down for a closer look and tried to recall the first aid training she'd done when she'd been forced to take part in a youth survival skills course in secondary school. It was so long ago. How was she meant to remember what to do on an actual person when she didn't even pay attention to what you should do to save a mannequin that was so lifelike she was scared to go near it? She got to her knees and went to put Kyron into the recovery position, but then it occurred to her to check his pulse. She pressed two fingers to his neck and felt nothing. She pushed her fingers in harder, worried she was hurting him, then realized nothing would hurt as much as a head injury that had warranted this much blood. Still nothing.

"Right," she said, standing. "Right."

Dimple took a few deep breaths, then patted herself down before seeing that she'd left her phone on the sofa. She ran to it, cursing when she realized that she'd stepped in Kyron's blood and had trailed it across the carpet. It was all truly going from bad to worse with every second that passed.

Dimple picked up the phone and hoped that the cracked screen still worked.

"Phew," she said when she was able to unlock it, momentarily forgetting the situation as the relief of not having to immediately get a phone screen replaced by Apple washed over her.

Dimple turned and looked at Kyron. He was still motionless.

"So, he's probably dead, then," she said out loud. When her emotions were running high, a frequent occurrence, she'd talk things through with herself, and being in a state of acute shock was no exception to that. "Right. Okay."

She turned the phone over in shaking hands. Maybe she should call the ambulance? She went to dial 999 but stopped herself. The ambulance would bring the police with them, and she just needed a bit of time to figure out what had gone on without being slammed against the floor and put in handcuffs. It wasn't just that her mum was a barrister, and that a body in the house would be totally disastrous for her, but the list of reasons Dimple didn't trust the police was obscenely long. Each and every interaction she'd had with them had been traumatizing. The police were who she feared above anyone. Dimple went and sat down next to Kyron's body, trying to control her breathing as tears started to fall down her face. She wiped her eyes with one hand and put the other on his chest, which wasn't moving. "Oh, Ky." She cried. "What do I do?"

Dimple went to call the ambulance again but stopped when her gaze landed on the scratches on Kyron's face. She wiped her face dry with the back of her hand and took a few deep breaths while she collected her thoughts. The scratches were deep, and made it look like they were having a fight and that she'd pushed him.

Who was going to believe that someone could slip on vegetable oil and die? This wasn't the *Final Destination* film franchise, it was real life.

She went to her contacts and typed in the name she'd decided, all those years ago, she'd never call for help.

"Hello?" Dimple put the phone on loudspeaker because her hands were trembling too violently to hold it up to her ear. "Hi, is this Nikisha?"

CHAPTER

THREE

"RAH." PRYNCE, THE YOUNGEST of Cyril Pennington's children, said, impressed. "Small girl like you took out a big man like that?"

"I didn't take him out!" Dimple said, shaking her head. "He slipped on some vegetable oil. And you know how it's one of those things where it might not have happened, but instead it did? 'Cause I was going to cook something, so I looked in the fridge, and the vegetable oil was on top of the fridge, and it fell on the floor, and I was meant to clean it up, but I was like, 'Nah, I'll do that later,' and if I'd actually done it later, or actually at the time, Kyron would still be alive because he wouldn't have slipped on it. And I didn't even end up cooking! So this was all for nothing."

"Take a breath," Nikisha said.

"I think she needs to take a few," Prynce said.

"Who have you called?" Lizzie asked her, biting her bottom lip the same way Dimple did when she was worried.

"Nobody, right?" Danny asked, scratching his head. "I really hope you haven't called anybody."

Dimple looked around at her four half-siblings as they stood looking down at Kyron's body. She hadn't even glanced at any of them on the street for at least five years, maybe longer. They all looked pretty much the same as they had when she'd met them in the park all those years ago, but a bit older, and more tired. Nikisha was still as slender as ever, but had dark bags underneath her eyes that said she'd been looking after two children under six full-time. Danny's difference was that he was . . . thicker. He clearly dedicated a lot of himself to the gym, and he wanted to show it off. Even in the nighttime in the middle of winter, he felt it was appropriate to wear a tank top. Everything had doubled in size, from his neck to his calves. Danny was not a man who skipped leg day. Present-day Lizzie had the body of an athlete. Back then, she didn't have any puppy fat on her, but the extra ounces she'd once had had clearly been jogged away. Prynce had obviously changed and grown the most, but he still had that same childlike look she'd seen on his face when he didn't have dreads and wasn't taller than her. Dimple thought about how she'd have reacted if she had spotted them in the street. She would most likely have pretended she hadn't seen them, and ducked away into some corner. It wasn't that she didn't want to speak to them, it was that she wouldn't have known what to say, and, in her mind, she would have assumed they wouldn't like her. Dimple had some pretty extensive issues when it came to loving herself, and of course these issues extended out to anyone around her who wasn't her mum. And it wasn't as though being with Kyron had done anything to help the idea that she was worthy of unconditional love and kindness from someone who wasn't Janet.

Nikisha, her eldest sister, had her arms folded and looked deep in thought. Danny, who had been the second to arrive, leaned on the kitchen counter and let out a deep sigh. Lizzie, Dimple's nontwin, furrowed her brow and carried on biting her bottom lip.

"Does anyone mind if I eat this?" Prynce asked as he made his way over to the pizza box and opened it.

"Be my guest," Dimple said. "Do you want a plate and a knife and fork?"

"Knife and fork?" Prynce laughed, lifting a slice of pizza and sinking half of it into his giant mouth.

"How is it?" Danny asked his brother.

"Yeah, it's all right. Cold, but it's all right." Prynce nodded, as Danny went over to the box and took a slice for himself. Prynce couldn't help but mention the tank top. "Aren't you cold, man?"

"Nah, not at all." Danny shook his head. "I run hot."

"Are you girls not gonna eat any?" Prynce asked, reaching for another slice.

Nikisha shook her head.

Dimple held her hands up. "No appetite."

"Me neither," Lizzie said. "And I don't eat meat. Or cheese."

"You one of them vegans?" Danny asked.

"Mmm," Lizzie said, bending down to take a closer look at Kyron's body.

"Thanks for letting us know," Prynce said in the direction of Lizzie, who ignored his sarcasm.

"He's the one who asked." Lizzie had grown out of sarcasm as a personality trait a few years back so had no time for it. "How can you get so close to him?" Dimple asked tearfully.

"Medical student." Lizzie shrugged. "I'm always around dead bodies."

"Doctor, yeah?" Danny smiled. "You did say you was gonna be a doctor all them years back. And you really did it. That's so good, man."

"Not a doctor yet. I took a few years out," Lizzie said, leaning closer to the body. "But thanks."

"I checked his pulse," Dimple said when she saw Lizzie reaching two fingers toward Kyron's neck.

Lizzie withdrew her hands and stood, leaning on the marble worktop. Dimple caught Lizzie staring at *her* neck.

"What?" Dimple asked. "What are you looking at?"

"Those marks on your neck," Lizzie said. "You all right?"

"Yeah." Dimple nodded, putting a hand to her neck. The skin

Kyron had pressed his fingers into felt sore and hot to the touch. "Fine."

"So nobody is here, and you didn't call the police?" Nikisha asked Dimple.

"No, and no," Dimple said. "My mum's in Spain with her best friend."

"Weird time of year to go," Prynce said. "Is Spain even warm now?"

"But should I call the police?" Dimple asked her eldest half sister, ignoring Prynce's question. "I did think about it. But then my mum's job, and them being terrifying, and—"

"Why would you call the police?" Danny snorted. "They'll still say it was you, somehow."

"But maybe I should. Because even if I did call them, I haven't done anything wrong, right?" Dimple asked, fear coating her voice. "He slipped and hit his head! Genuinely!"

"We know that," Danny said, walking over and putting a hand on Dimple's shoulder. "But yeah, the scratches. They'll create some story and put it on you."

"If he's the kind of man to put hands on you, why was he here?" Lizzie asked Dimple in a tone that sounded a bit suspicious.

"Just to clarify, I definitely didn't push him," Dimple said for the sibling records. "He had his hands round my neck, and it was seeming like that was the end of the road for me, so I scratched him to get him off."

"Stop saying you didn't do it," Prynce said. "And don't feel guilty or any of that. He shouldn't have put his hands on you, he was wrong for that."

"Well, he didn't need to die, Prynce," Dimple squawked.

"I'm not saying that, am I?" Prynce said. "I'm just saying that if he didn't come here on bad energy, he'd still be alive."

There was a lot of unspoken anxiety moving through the room.

It was thick, uncomfortable, contagious. Danny was the only person who didn't seem shaken by what was going on.

If Nikisha were a different person she'd feel guilty about that. Instead, she understood that she needed to figure out what to do—it was her duty as the eldest. She *did* feel responsible for bringing them all here, though. It wasn't that she'd thought of it as a bonding exercise when Dimple called her after at least a decade. But when she'd heard Dimple's voice, Nikisha could tell that something bad had happened. She didn't know what—how could she?—but she knew that if two heads were better than one, five heads would be able to solve anything. Now that the situation was clear to her, she understood that maybe it would have been better to keep it at two heads.

But here they were. Nikisha knew that this shouldn't be their reunion, and that this being their reunion was completely on her, but she was also a woman who lived life forward; no regrets that way.

Prynce stepped out of the room as his phone buzzed.

"Who's that?" Dimple asked Nikisha, panic flashing across her face.

"Don't be paranoid," Nikisha told her. "It'll be one of his little girlfriends."

A few seconds later, Prynce came back in, a big smile across his face as he ended his call.

"Yeah, you too, Naderah. I'll see you tomorrow."

"If you're finished, we need to get rid of the body," Nikisha said, looking at her brother.

"What, so I can't take a personal call?"

Nikisha ignored him.

"And then we need to clean up. Danny, you're still doing plumbing?"

"What?" Lizzie spluttered. "Sorry, when did I walk into an episode of *How to Get Away with Murder*? Who died and made you Annalise Keating?"

"He did." Nikisha pointed at Kyron's lifeless body. She held eye contact with Lizzie and blinked slowly before turning back to Danny.

"Are we seriously doing this?" Lizzie hissed at Nikisha, who was too busy thinking about next steps to answer the question.

"You're right." Dimple sniffed, her eyes filling with tears. "I'm so sorry, I've really fucked up, and I wouldn't have called any of you to help, and when I called Nikisha I didn't know she'd call all of you, and if anything, I didn't even want her to help, I just needed advice, and I feel so bad, *so* bad, and I feel less bad about Kyron, I feel mainly bad that you're all here, and—"

"Dimple, take a *breath*, my God," Nikisha said, interrupting, holding her hands up. "Look. I know all of you might not be on the family first ting because you're all only children so you probably only know how to look after yourselves . . ."

Nikisha looked pointedly at Lizzie.

"But let me tell you something. I learned from a young age that even if your family aren't your friends, they're still your responsibility. And so, yes, this is an inconvenience, *but*, we're all here, and we're all doing it, because we're family."

"An *inconvenience*?" Lizzie snorted.

Danny went over to Dimple, who was crying so hard her shoulders were juddering up and down, and put an arm around them, mainly to stop them from moving.

Prynce slid over to the counter and pulled a piece of kitchen towel from the roll. He handed it to Dimple, who whispered a thank-you and blew her nose loudly.

"Exactly. We're all in it now." Prynce shrugged. "Might as well help."

"There's a lot at stake," Danny said quietly. "But yeah. We're here."

"And if we do this properly, it goes away," Nikisha said firmly.

"Just because I'm an only child doesn't mean I'm selfish," Lizzie informed her half-siblings.

"I'll believe it when I see it." Nikisha looked pointedly at Lizzie before turning her attention to their half brother. "Danny? Plumbing?"

"Yeah." Danny squeezed Dimple before he let her go.

"Have you got any tarpaulins? Or plastic—whatever you use to line the floor to catch water?" Nikisha asked.

"Yeah, I've got some in my van."

"How much?"

"Well . . ." Danny pondered. "Probably enough to wrap a body in. He's a big guy so it might be a stretch, but yeah. Should work."

"Go and get it," Nikisha said. "And don't let anyone see you."

"Cool," Danny said, pulling his van keys from his pocket and walking out of the kitchen.

"Lizzie." Nikisha beckoned her sister over.

"What?" Lizzie responded sharply.

"What's the best way to clean up this blood?"

"I'm a medical student, not a forensics specialist," Lizzie said. "And I still think there's an alternative to doing *this*."

"Do you know or not?" Nikisha asked. "Because unless you can come up with an alternative, and one that isn't us calling the police and being accomplices, you need to stick with the plan."

"Teamwork makes the dream work!" Prynce said.

"Okay, so we need gloves, first of all," Lizzie sighed, rolling her eyes. "Have you got any here, Dimple?"

"I think we do," Dimple said, stepping over Kyron's body and opening the kitchen cupboard under the sink. "How about these?"

Dimple held up three packets of pink washing-up gloves.

"Those will . . . do," Lizzie said.

"Why so many?" Prynce asked, taking a packet from his sister and putting them on.

"My mum is a neat freak," Dimple said, throwing one packet to Lizzie.

"Okay, stay by the cupboard," Lizzie said. "We need a basin, and we need bleach. And some carpet cleaner. You got any of those?"

Dimple rummaged around in the cupboard and put the bottle of bleach on the floor next to her.

"We ran out of carpet cleaner the other day and I forgot to get some. I think we have some Vanish for clothes, though. Is that going to work?" Dimple asked.

"Well, we're going to find out, aren't we?" Lizzie said flatly. All these years later, her delivery of even the most interesting of sentences was amazingly toneless.

"I'm back!" Danny said, bursting into the room, blue tarpaulin crunching under his arm.

"Volume, Danny," Nikisha said.

"Sorry, sorry!" Danny whispered, putting the folded tarpaulin on the floor. "This house is fancy, init? How long you been here for?"

"Er, about ten years, I think."

"Yeah, 'cause you used to live in Norbury, right?" Danny asked. "I remember when we came to get you. In that gold Jeep."

"Oh God, how did I forget about the gold Jeep?" Dimple nodded her head, remembering their "day out."

"Did any of you know that's what Dad was gonna do?" Danny asked. He was a man who liked to know a lot of things. He didn't even retain a lot of it, he was just broadly interested in talking about stuff.

"I think it's wild that you even call him Dad." Lizzie crossed her arms. "That man is no father of mine. Never has been."

"What do you call him when you see him?" Prynce wanted to know.

"If I ever saw him, and I had anything to say to him, I'd call him Cyril," Lizzie told him.

"Rah," Prynce said. "Firm."

"He didn't say anything to me about any of you," Dimple said.

"And neither did my mum. He just turned up and said he was taking me to the park. So when I got in the car and I saw all of you . . ."

"I bet you didn't think this would be the next time we'd all be in the same place," Prynce said.

"No, I didn't think the next time we'd all be in the same place would be because my boyfriend died in my house 'cause of vegetable oil." Dimple looked at Prynce pointedly through swollen eyes as she replied.

"Life, eh?" Danny said cheerfully, putting his hands on his hips. "I like the—what is it?—the open-plan kitchen/front room ting." Danny gestured to the kitchen; he wasn't changing the topic because of the tension, he was genuinely interested in the architecture of Dimple's house. "'Cause you can cook! But you can also entertain whoever's in the front room, or watch TV. Genius."

"He's got a point," Prynce said. "He's really got a point."

"And even the area is nice, you know?" Danny said. "Your mum must be rich!"

"I guess." Dimple shrugged. "She's a barrister."

"That's why you said you was worried about your mum's job! She's a fucking barrister and you've got us getting rid of a dead body in her house? Nah. Nah." Prynce laughed.

"Prynce," Lizzie said. "This isn't funny. Are you high?"

"Well, yeah," Prynce said. "But when Nikisha told me to get in the car I didn't realize I'd be helping get rid of a dead body, did I? Anyway, I'll be fine. I'm almost always waved. I'd be less use to you if I wasn't, I think."

"Danny and Dimple, you lay out the tarpaulin," Nikisha said, clapping her hands together. "And Dimple and Lizzie will lift the body onto it."

"Shouldn't I help lift the body?" Danny said. "I'm the strongest here."

Nikisha and Lizzie looked at him.

"Fine," Nikisha said. "Prynce, you and Dimple lay the tarpaulin out."

"So what you're saying is, I'm not strong?" Prynce asked. "You know I've been trying, Nikisha. But I'm just a naturally tall and slender guy. You know I've been trying to build mass. You know I—"

"Listen, can we just get this moving?" Nikisha asked. "Girls, roll out the tarpaulin, boys, lift the body onto it. At a time like this and we're doing gender wars, imagine!"

"Nah, it's not about gender wars, it's about the fact that—" Danny said.

"No, it is about gender wars," Nikisha said, cutting in. "And you need to—"

Lizzie added her voice to the mix. "Is this the time to be doing arguing on top of arguing?"

"What was that?" Dimple asked, her back straightening like a meerkat's, horror washing over her face. Her half-siblings stopped talking over each other and looked at her.

"What was what?" Nikisha narrowed her eyes in an attempt to hear better.

"I think I heard the door." Dimple was so stressed she thought her soul was going to leave her body. Maybe she was imagining things. But then, a knock at the door did make some of her soul leave her body.

"Who is that?" Nikisha hissed at Dimple.

"I don't know!" Dimple hissed back. "I'm on this side of the door, aren't I?"

"What should we do?" Prynce whispered.

"I should never have come here," Lizzie whimpered.

"It'll all be fine," Danny said softly, looking at Nikisha to solve this problem.

"Can you go to the peephole and see who it is?" Nikisha asked Dimple.

Dimple shook her head.

"There isn't one."

"Okay." Nikisha thought for a second. "Go to the door, put the latch on—I'm assuming you have a latch?"

Dimple nodded.

"Put the latch on," Nikisha said. "If it's the police—"

"Why would you say that?" Lizzie whispered, putting her hands on her head.

"Because we have to be realistic," Nikisha told her. She turned back to Dimple. "If it's the police, they need a warrant to come in."

A louder knock at the door made them all jump.

"You've got this," Danny said, putting a hand on Dimple's shoulder.

"No, I don't!" Dimple looked at her half-siblings, shaking her head. "Not at all! Maybe they'll just go away."

"Go," Nikisha said, pushing Dimple toward the hallway.

With each step Dimple took, it felt more and more like she was wading through treacle. When she finally made it to the front door and put the latch on with shaking fingers, she felt like she was stuck to the spot.

She opened the door slowly, holding her breath.

"Is everything okay, Dimple?"

It was her neighbor Karen. Her blond bob sat just above her shoulders, and her icy-blue eyes always pierced through Dimple the same way her passive aggression did.

"Karen!" Dimple forced a smile. "Yes, thanks! Everything is really fine!"

"Are you sure?" Karen said. "It's just that I heard some noise, some shouting, coming from here earlier, and I thought, you know, maybe Dimple has just got the TV volume on loud as she usually does, and you know, because my ears are sensitive, even the slightest changes in sound really set off my tinnitus . . ."

Dimple nodded as Karen chattered on and on.

". . . and you know, obviously I know your mum is away, and of course she trusts you—why shouldn't she?—but you know, while the cat's away the mice will definitely play, I know what it's like to be young . . ."

"Everything is fine, honestly," Dimple said, trying to convince herself more than anything.

"Are you sure, Dimple? Because when I was putting the bins out not long ago, I did think I saw someone, and I hate to say it, but you know I'm not saying it like *this*, but when I was checking that everything was okay, I saw what I think was definitely a Black man coming up your path. I wondered if it was your boyfriend, Kyron, that's his name, isn't it? But I looked a little closer and this one seemed lighter."

Dimple was surprised that it had taken Karen this long to Karen.

"And I thought to myself, in the interests of the safety of this community, why are all of these different Black men of all shades and sizes coming in and out of your house—and before you say anything, I don't mean it like *that*, Dimple. You know I voted your mum's front garden 'best lawn' last summer."

Karen peered through the crack in the chained door and into the house, looking past Dimple's shoulder.

"That must have been the pizza guy," Dimple said, not wanting to know how Karen *thought* she meant it. "And I'll turn the TV down. Night, Karen, thanks for checking in."

"I don't think so." Karen smiled a strained smile, the crow's-feet around her eyes deepening and stretching into her temples. "Because I did see the pizza man come earlier. His motorbike was so loud, and as you know—" Karen pointed at her ears and mouthed "the tinnitus."

"Well, then I just don't know." Dimple shrugged. "If someone did come in here, I didn't see them."

Karen looked like she had more in her, but instead she narrowed those icy-blue eyes at Dimple and took a step back.

"Okay." Karen smiled. "Well, I'm here if anything happens."

"Oh, I know." Dimple smiled back. "Thank you."

Dimple closed the front door and went back into the kitchen, where she saw all of her half-siblings piled up by the entrance.

"'Well, then I just don't know'?" Nikisha mimicked Dimple's lack of explanation to Karen. "Are you serious?"

"I didn't know what else to say!" Dimple hissed, closing the kitchen door behind her. "Prynce, can you put the TV on to cover up our talking? She might still be listening."

"But what about her tinnitus?" Prynce asked, genuinely concerned.

Dimple, Nikisha, and Lizzie shot Prynce a look that told him it would be in his best interests to turn the TV on ASAP.

"Can I ask something?" Danny said.

"Yeah, anything," Dimple said.

"Is she actually called Karen?"

"If you can believe it, yes," Dimple told him. "Karen by name, Karen by nature. If she was in a video game she'd be the final boss of Karens."

When Prynce had found an action film, the dialogue of which loosely resembled five people trying to figure out how to successfully hide a body, Dimple and Lizzie each took an end of the tarpaulin and spread it out on the carpet carefully, while Danny and Prynce rolled their sleeves up.

Dimple noticed a scar, which she was pretty sure was a burn mark, that ran across Danny's forearm.

"What's that?" Prynce asked. He'd noticed, too.

"Nah, it's nothing." Danny shook his head, brushing the question away. "Let's do this."

"All right. Gloves," Prynce said, chucking a packet to Danny.

"Are you going to complain about them being pink as well? To add to the list of things that are troubling you this evening?" Nikisha asked Danny.

"Nah," Danny said. "Pink is my favorite color. But I've got a complex about being strong, you know what I mean? I think it comes from—"

"Shall we talk about this later?" Lizzie said.

"You're right." Danny nodded, squeezing the gloves over his large hands.

"Do you want to take the top or the bottom?" Prynce asked Danny.

"I think, because he has a lot of mass at the top, and I am very strong as we've just established, I should take that end," Danny said. "What you saying?"

Prynce nodded and took his place at Kyron's feet.

"You ready?"

"Yeah, course!" Danny said, hooking his arms underneath Kyron's armpits and lifting. "This guy is heavy, you know!"

Together, Danny and Prynce struggled over to the tarpaulin and dropped the body down clumsily as their sisters looked on.

"Be careful!" Dimple shouted.

"Be careful?" Danny asked. "Sis, he's dead."

"I know, but this is just very stressful to me," Dimple said dramatically, not a trace of irony in her voice. "And he was still a person."

Danny shrugged.

"Sounds like he was a prick."

"Okay, we need to fold the tarpaulin over him," Nikisha said. "Or maybe it's better that we push him to the end and then roll him up in it. What do you think, Lizzie?"

"I think roll," Lizzie said.

"Go on then, seeing as you two are so strong," Nikisha said to her brothers, struck by how similar their concentration faces were as they kneeled down next to the body.

Danny and Prynce eventually rolled up the body and stood, both huffing at the effort it took.

"Now we need to clean," Nikisha said as they all looked at the pool of blood on the floor. "Prynce, give Lizzie your gloves."

"Thanks," Lizzie said, taking the gloves once Prynce had removed them from his slim hands.

"So we need to do, from memory, one part bleach and nine parts water," said Prynce.

"From memory of what?" Lizzie asked him.

"YouTube," Prynce responded flatly.

"Why were—" Lizzie stopped abruptly. "Do you know what? Let's just get on with it."

"I'll do that," Dimple said, jumping over the blood, filling the kettle, and flicking it to boil. While she waited for the water to heat up, she poured bleach into the plastic basin in the sink.

"Are you really gonna use your mum's good basin like that?" Prynce asked.

"Good point," Dimple said, trying to push down the waves of nausea that were rising and falling in her stomach and up to her throat. "It's the only one we have, though."

Lizzie rolled her eyes.

"Of all the questions to ask."

"I'm just trying to be helpful," Prynce said, walking over to the sofa and sitting down. He picked up the remote and navigated his way to Netflix. "Any requests?"

Danny joined his brother on the sofa and took the remote from him. Nikisha watched them bicker for a few seconds before she turned back to her sisters.

"You need to pour some of the solution onto the blood and leave it for a few minutes before wiping it up," Lizzie said, crossing her arms again.

When she'd filled the basin and found some disposable rags, Dimple bent down slowly to place her cleaning kit by the blood. She swallowed loudly as she stared at the crimson pool glistening back up at her.

"You all right?" Lizzie asked. "Pass me the Vanish and a cloth and I'll get on to the carpet."

"I'll be fine," Dimple answered, assuring and convincing nobody of this. "But why are you all so okay with this?"

Dimple looked around at them all, still not fully understanding why they were all here, but also not fully understanding why they weren't all running away or feeling as sick as she was.

"I've seen worse than this." Nikisha shrugged.

"Like what?" Dimple asked.

"Another time." Nikisha waved Dimple's question away.

"Same." Danny shrugged, too.

"And me," Prynce said.

"So, what, I've just been living a sheltered life?" Dimple asked.

"Yes." Prynce laughed. "Do we need to explain that to you?"

Dimple looked at Lizzie in solidarity.

"Don't look at me," Lizzie told her. "I already said I'm around this shit all the time."

Dimple rolled up her sleeves and poured some of the solution onto the blood, desperate to prove that she was as tough as her half-siblings.

"Careful it doesn't leak onto the carpet!" Lizzie yelped, grabbing a roll of kitchen towel from the counter and pulling some off to make a barrier between kitchen floor and living room carpet.

"Sorry! I wasn't thinking," Dimple said, annoyed with herself. She wasn't as tough as any of them, or as smart. "I'm so sorry, I'm so stupid."

"You aren't stupid. You're tired, and you're not thinking straight," Nikisha said. "But you need to stay calm. This will all be over soon."

Dimple nodded.

"Okay."

"Why don't you go and sit with the boys while we wait for the bleach to do what it's doing?" Lizzie suggested, wanting Dimple and her emotions out of the way.

Dimple nodded as she held back tears and made her way over to her brothers, delicately avoiding the bloodstains on the carpet. She sat next to Danny, who put a big arm around her shoulders absent-mindedly.

"How long's it been since I saw you last?" Nikisha asked Lizzie as she got to work with the Vanish, spraying the blood and watching as the foamy spray settled on it and expanded as it started to oxidize.

"Three years or so," Lizzie answered. "We bumped into each other in Peckham. At the hair shop."

"Yes, that's right!" Nikisha said. "Time really flies, doesn't it?"

"Yep," Lizzie said in agreement. "What have you been up to since then? And how's Nicky?"

"He's good, you know. And I had another one! A girl. Amara. She's a handful, but she's good, too. Nicky's living with his dad now, because having two children is not the same as having one, let me tell you that. But I have him at weekends," Nikisha said.

"Same dad?" Lizzie asked.

"Yup." Nikisha nodded. "Just like my mum did, I let my memories mislead me into thinking men can change."

"And only one of them lives with the dad?"

"Yup," Nikisha said curtly, wanting to change the subject. "He's one of *those* guys. Bit of a hotep. Comes from the school of thought that boys need their dads and girls need their mums. Anyway—"

"Wow," Lizzie remarked. "You had a whole 'nother kid and I didn't even know?"

"I sent you some pictures a while back. I emailed them. You didn't see?"

"Shit, no. I changed email addresses to a more professional one when I left college. Sorry about that."

"No apologies. I should have checked you had the same one," Nikisha said, stepping over the blood on the kitchen floor and making her way over to the sink. She took a glass from the drying rack and turned the tap on. "Water?"

"I don't think we should be leaving DNA all over this house, you know," Prynce said, walking over to his sisters.

"Finally a good suggestion from you," Nikisha said, putting the glass back on the rack.

Lizzie looked at Prynce to see what his reaction was to something so harsh. He didn't even blink.

"I've got some bottles of water in my van. It's parked round the corner—go and grab some if you want!" Danny called out, pulling his van keys out of his pocket while refusing to take his eyes off the TV screen.

"We can't have multiple people leaving the house now that that woman has seen you," Nikisha said. "Dimple, can you go and get them? At least if she jumps out and asks what you're doing you can say you're going to the shop or something."

Danny dragged himself away from the TV.

"It's fine, if I go I can put on my bally."

"You don't think she'll call the police if she sees you in a bally, no?" Nikisha asked Danny, straight-faced.

"Why would a plumber need a balaclava?" Lizzie sighed, scrubbing away at the carpet.

"I've got to be prepared for all situations," Danny replied.

"And how do you think Dimple's neighbor will react to seeing not just you, who shouldn't even be here, but you in a balaclava, carrying a multipack of Evian into the house at eleven p.m.?" Nikisha asked her half brother.

"Shall we leave the water for later?" Lizzie asked, rubbing her temples. "And we need to figure out how to get the body to the van so nobody sees. This situation is getting trickier by the minute, plus we're all getting tired."

"It's all going to be fine," Danny said, offering his half sister some baseless reassurance.

"If you say so," Lizzie snorted.

"Have you got any kids yet?" Nikisha asked Lizzie once Danny had ambled back to the television.

"Nah. I'm too busy with studies and everything. Plus, I'm only thirty. And when me and my girlfriend decide to have kids, if we do, it's going to be a lot of admin."

"You have a girlfriend now?" Nikisha asked. "How long have you been together?"

"Patrice. She was with me the last time I saw you. Remember? The chatty girl who asked you if you wanted to come round for dinner even though she'd never met you before."

"Oh, her! I thought that was your housemate."

"You know," Prynce said. "If you ever need sperm . . ."

Lizzie closed her eyes and shuddered.

"Please, please, I am begging you, do not offer your sperm to me, Prynce."

"Nah, to your girlfriend, I meant!" Prynce said. "That way, you're keeping it in the family."

"Oh, don't worry, I know what you meant," Lizzie said. "Please keep your sperm to yourself."

"What are you lot talking about?" Danny called over from the sofa.

"I was only saying—" Prynce said.

"Please. Stop saying," Lizzie said, raising her hand to cut her half brother off.

"We ready to get things going, Lizzie?"

"Elizabeth," Lizzie said, removing her gloves and throwing them onto the counter next to Prynce. "Prynce, can you see if you can find a hair dryer?"

"Why a hair dryer?" Prynce asked.

"So I can dry the carpet properly and make sure I haven't missed anything. Why the questions?"

"I like your thinking, you know." Prynce smiled, hopping down off the counter and leaving the room. Lizzie and Nikisha listened to him thunder up the stairs.

"What is he like when he hasn't been smoking, though?" Lizzie asked her sister.

"More annoying," Nikisha told her. She turned to Dimple. "I think it's time to wipe the floors, Dimple."

Dimple got up from the sofa and shuffled over to her sisters.

"Thanks," she whispered as she bent down and dipped her gloved hand into the basin of water. She retrieved the cloth and wrung it out, slapping it down in the middle of the blood and bleach.

She got onto her hands and knees and wiped the floor a few times, methodically and slowly.

"Found one!" Prynce said, walking into the room, hair dryer in one hand, plug in the other. He placed it on the counter and then jumped up onto the counter so he was next to it, watching his half sisters at work.

"How you getting on with that?" he asked Dimple.

"Yeah. Okay, thanks," she replied, sitting back on her heels and squeezing the cloth so the bloody water trickled into the basin.

"You sure you're okay?" Prynce asked. He only had one fear, and it wasn't blood. "I can take over."

Dimple didn't answer, her eyes glazing over. She had many fears, and now that the shock was wearing off, seeing all of this blood was finally affecting her.

"She doesn't look so good, Nikisha," Prynce said, tapping his eldest sister on the arm.

"Dimple?" Nikisha went to her half sister's side and gently placed her hands on either side of her face.

"I'm feeling kind of woozy," Dimple said, her eyes rolling back in her head as she flopped onto the floor.

"Maybe it's the bleach fumes," Prynce said.

"Or maybe she's fainted because she killed her boyfriend?"

Lizzie said, rushing over to Dimple. "Danny, chuck me a cushion, please!"

Danny walked over, cushion in hand. He threw it to Lizzie and laughed as it hit Dimple in the face.

"She'll be fine."

Danny chuckled again and went back to the sofa.

"How is he laughing?" Lizzie asked Nikisha and Prynce as she pulled her half sister's legs out from underneath her and laid her down with the cushion under her head. "There's a dead man in the room, and not one who's been brought into the room by the attending doctor I'm observing! I don't think I'll be able to smile for the foreseeable future, let alone laugh."

Lizzie was being outwardly compliant, but was inwardly livid. What the fuck was she doing here? From what she'd gathered, Nikisha was unemployed, Danny worked with pipes, Dimple was an unsuccessful influencer, and Prynce was somehow even more unemployed than his big sister. She, Lizzie, had the most to lose of all of them. She could lose the job she didn't even have yet, her relationship, her flat, but most of all, worst of all, if her mum found out, Lizzie would additionally lose her life when her mother took it away. When Nikisha had called and said Dimple needed her help, she would never have assumed it would be with anything of this magnitude. She just thought she'd been hurt.

"That's just his way," Nikisha said. "I know I said I've seen a lot, but Danny has seen more. I'm sure he'll tell you one day."

"Let me carry on with the cleaning." Prynce hopped down from the counter.

"Gloves!" Lizzie ordered, pointing at the rubber ones next to him.

"Oh yeah, course," Prynce said, putting them on and getting on with wiping up the blood splatters on the kitchen cabinets.

Lizzie stared down at Dimple, who looked like she was sleeping.

"Do you two ever say happy birthday to each other?" Nikisha asked.

Lizzie shook her head.

"I always thought I should, but then I felt weird about us being the same age. And because she's older than me, I always thought she should be the one to do it first. But she never did, so I thought, why should *I* bother?"

"You know, technically you two should have been born in the same week. But Dimple came early."

"That doesn't surprise me." Lizzie shook her head. "Who told you that?"

"My mum," Nikisha said, walking over to join Danny on the sofa. "She knew all the runnings, trust me."

Lizzie carried on staring down at her slightly older sister's face, trying to pick up the features they shared. Their eyebrows were different. Lizzie's were thicker, darker. Dimple had filled hers in to give them some definition. They still had the same-shaped eyes they'd shared as children, though Dimple's were a darker brown than Lizzie's, and both had long, thick lashes framing them.

Lizzie had a narrow nose that sat straight in the middle of her slim face, while the broadness of Dimple's nose suited the roundness of her face. Lizzie had always loved having her mother's defined Cupid's bow and small, delicate but full lips, whereas Dimple seemed to have a mouth that was entirely her own, judging from the pictures of her mum on the walls.

"Mum?" Dimple groaned, opening her eyes. She tried to sit up quickly when she didn't immediately recognize the eyes looking down at her, even though they were so like hers.

"Relax, relax," Lizzie said, patting Dimple's hair awkwardly. She usually wasn't one to give comfort. "It's me, Lizzie."

"What, so she gets to call you Lizzie?" Prynce couldn't believe the injustice of it.

"Okay, well, if you faint you get to call me Lizzie, too, how's that?" Lizzie asked Prynce, apparently changing her stance on sarcasm.

"Lizzie?" Dimple mumbled, closing her eyes again. "But Lizzie hates me."

Prynce stopped wiping and looked at Lizzie.

"She doesn't mean that."

"Why would she say it, then?" Lizzie asked, clearly offended.

"She's not in her right mind," Prynce said. He went back to wiping, then turned to his sister again. "Wait. Are you offended?"

"Of course I'm offended!"

"Why?" Prynce laughed. "It's not like she said she hates *you*."

"I don't hate anyone!" Lizzie yelped, her voice going up an octave. "Why would she think I hate her?"

"I dunno, she's probably an overthinker like I am." Prynce shrugged. "It doesn't feel like you like me very much either."

"What?" Lizzie's voice had gone up another octave.

"You're quite, like . . . ?" Prynce tried to find the word he was looking for. "That's it. Cold."

"What's going on?" Dimple sat up slowly and blinked at whom she eventually recognized as her half brother and half sister.

"Fuck," she said, looking at the floor, which wasn't quite clean yet. "It wasn't a dream."

"Afraid not," Nikisha said, walking over and handing Dimple a glass of water.

CHAPTER
FOUR

"**ONCE WE ACTUALLY GET** it to the van, we need to think about where we're going to put the body." Nikisha looked down at the four faces that stared back up at her, squished next to each other on the sofa. They all appeared exhausted. "All ideas welcome. It's an open forum. No suggestion is too small, or stupid."

"Well when I was giving ideas about how to get the body to the van, *you* were telling me I wasn't as smart as I thought I was," Prynce told Nikisha.

"Yeah, that's because you aren't." Nikisha sighed.

"Are you two always like this?" Danny asked his half-siblings.

"Okay, so when you say 'put,' do you mean place on a temporary basis, or, like, *bury*?" Prynce asked, ignoring Danny's question because, yes, they *were* always like this.

"I mean bury, Prynce," Nikisha said. "Thank you for helping me to clarify that."

"Do you know any construction sites, Danny?" Prynce asked his elder half brother.

"You know I'm a plumber?" Danny asked back. "Not a builder?"

"Yeah, but you're a tradesman. You might know other tradesmen," Prynce said, "who know building sites."

"You know what, that's a good point." Danny considered Prynce's words, nodding. "I don't know any building sites, but yeah, I hear you. Connections."

"Right," Nikisha said. "So that's a no to any construction sites, I'm guessing."

"What about a graveyard?" Danny asked.

"Wait, what?" Lizzie laughed. "You think we should just go and put the body in a graveyard?"

"That is actually quite logical, alie?" Prynce asked as his phone buzzed. "One second, let me get this . . . Tiffany, you good? . . . Yeah, I'm just in the middle of something . . . Nah, I'm not with another girl, come on."

"Wasn't he just on the phone to another . . . ?" Dimple asked Nikisha.

"I don't try and keep track," Nikisha told her. "And it will save you a lot of time not to try either."

"All right, sweetness," Prynce purred into the phone. "Lemme call you tomorrow . . . you too, you too."

"You finished?" Nikisha asked as Prynce ended the call.

"Yes." Prynce smiled. "Got to make sure everyone is happy."

"Are we going to make a headstone for him as well?" Lizzie snorted. "Have you got a slab of . . . whatever a headstone is made of, and a chisel in your van, Danny?"

"No laughing!" Nikisha told them. "All suggestions are welcome."

Dimple looked over at Lizzie. How could she make jokes at a time like this?

"Yeah, good suggestions, though." Lizzie rolled her eyes as she straightened herself up. "Let me think. How about a body of water?"

"Like the Thames?" Danny asked.

"Yeah, or like literally any sort of lake or pond," Nikisha answered him.

"Not a bad idea," Prynce said. "But unless we tie a block of concrete to him, he'll float up. How about . . ."

Nikisha looked at Prynce as he trailed off.

"How about what? Speak up."

"Nah, it's a bit dark, this one." Prynce shook his head.

"Talk." Nikisha's tone made Dimple flinch.

"Well," Prynce began. "We could take him somewhere and burn him?"

"No." Danny stood to object. "No fire."

"All right, it was just a suggestion." Prynce turned into a little boy at this shutdown from his big half brother.

"There's a new build," Dimple finally said, her voice barely a whisper.

"A what?" Prynce asked.

"You know where that big estate used to be, in Loughborough Junction? At the end of Loughborough Park, past the playground, on the other side?" Dimple tried to paint a geographical picture.

Nikisha, Danny, Lizzie, and Prynce nodded.

"They knocked down all those flats and they're making these fancy new builds," Dimple said. "They've dug up a lot of earth."

"Interesting. They still haven't filled the ground with concrete?" Nikisha asked.

"When I passed the site last week they hadn't done it yet. I looked in on the way to Kyron's."

"I thought you said you broke up?" Danny said to Dimple.

"We did. I was dropping some stuff off for his mum," Dimple said. "We're still friends, me and his mum. Always were, every time me and Kyron fell out." Her eyes started welling up. "Oh God, what have I done?"

"Dimple, man. Save the tears for a sec, please. Surely we can't bury the man on his own road," Danny said. "That feels like a violation."

"How can it be a violation?" Prynce asked. "If anything, it's, like, a mark of respect. We lay him where he used to roam. That way, his spirit is close to home. Like a nine night or something."

"What?" Lizzie snorted. "That's like the opposite of a nine night. Why would we trap his spirit on his road instead of letting it go free?"

"Let's focus, people, let's focus." Nikisha held up her hands. "It's three in the morning, we need to get things moving."

The half-siblings all nodded.

"Everything else is done. The floor is clean," Nikisha said.

"Basin is clean, too," Prynce said. "Everything is so clean. Bleach everywhere. Actually, that's a point. When is your mum home, Dimple?"

"In the morning," Dimple said.

"And can I just add," Danny said. "I know I've touched the tarpaulin and that, but I need to be careful with fingerprints and that."

"Why?" Prynce asked.

"I think my prints might be in the system or something. From some dumb stuff when I was a kid."

"What dumb stuff from when you were a kid?" Prynce asked.

"Oi, Dimple, you're gonna need to do something to cover up the bleach smell. Like, cook or something," Danny said, changing the subject.

"He's right," Nikisha said. "You'll have to do that when you get back home. But for now, here's the plan . . ."

"I feel a bit weird about being back here with a body, do you know what I mean?" Prynce, who was perched on a bag of grout and holding on to a ladder for support, asked Lizzie as he searched her face in the back of the dark van for some solidarity. None of the siblings had clocked that there was never any point looking to Lizzie for sympathy or solidarity.

Lizzie, who was sitting on an upturned bucket, rolled her eyes. What did this boy want from her?

"We've just been in a house with it for so many hours, Prynce," she said as the van turned a corner, reaching out and holding on to a broom behind Prynce before she fell on him. "What could the difference be?"

After they'd waited until every light was off in Karen's house, Lizzie and Prynce had drawn the short straw when it had come to deciding who would sit (sit is a loose term) where in Danny's Vauxhall Vivaro, a small and inconspicuous black van that was full to the brim with every tool, miscellaneous item, or piece of junk a plumber might need.

Danny, the driver, would need to drive, obviously. Prynce wanted to be in the front with his big brother, though he was too cool to phrase it like that. But Nikisha had reminded him that two Black boys in the front of a van in the middle of the night would draw more attention than they needed. So Dimple, who actually wasn't a fan of small or dark spaces but didn't feel like she wanted to draw more attention to herself so hadn't said as much, would go in the front instead.

Nikisha, who had reminded everyone that she was the eldest around seventy times over the course of the night, would obviously be in the front, too, and that left Lizzie, who didn't have a legitimate reason why she should be in the front. So obviously she had to go in the back with the tools, with Prynce, and with Kyron's body.

"Well, we were less likely to get stopped by police in the house, init?" Prynce told her.

"Prynce, is it every second you have to fill with talking?" Lizzie had had enough of his constant chatting. "How far away are we?" she shouted to the front of Danny's van.

Dimple sat snugly between Danny and Nikisha. There was an armrest between her and Danny that boxed her and Nikisha in together. Even though there were three seats at the front, Dimple suddenly felt self-conscious about her size. She wondered if Nikisha had enough room but didn't want to ask in case Nikisha brought up her size like she'd done when they were younger.

The fuzzy radio was annoying Danny, so he found a CD down the side of the van door and slipped it into the disk drive.

When the first song started, Nikisha's ears pricked up.

"Why do I know this song?" she asked. "What is it?"

"Professor Nuts," Danny told her.

"I know it, too," Dimple said, the lyrics that had clearly been somewhere in the back of her head jumping to the front of it. "It's called . . . something something bus?"

"Is this 'Inna di Bus'?" Prynce shouted from the back of the van. "Turn it up! You know this song, right?" he asked Lizzie, who nodded. "Yo, Danny—why is your van so old you've got a CD player?"

They all, including Lizzie, who begrudgingly got involved, and Dimple, who had previously thought herself too traumatized to join in, sang along until the song ended. For one chorus and one verse of that song, they'd forgotten why they were there in Danny's van.

Danny was trying to drive as conscientiously as possible given that he had all four of his half-siblings and a body in his van, and Nikisha was going over and over the plan in her head. She needed to make sure that this went smoothly.

"We're nearly there!" Danny shouted back.

If Dimple wasn't in such a daze, she'd have been nervous. But she just kept replaying what had gone on, as if her brain was trying to go over the incident and trying to find a place where she could have stopped it from happening.

She closed her eyes as they drove past Kyron's house, and she concentrated on the words of whichever song was playing on the rest of the CD, only opening her eyes as the van slowed to a halt just outside the construction site.

It was dark, but sections of the site were lit by the moon when it wasn't covered by a passing cloud.

"The lights are off," Danny said, reversing the van so the back doors were facing the entrance. "Let's go."

"Do I need to go over the plan again?" Nikisha asked.

"Nope," Danny answered. "How about for you two in the back?"

"No," Lizzie answered on behalf of her and Prynce. "Let's just get this over and done with. Please open the doors."

"The side door opens from the inside," Danny told her.

"Okay, and I'd be able to reach it if there wasn't a body in my way," Lizzie said.

Danny jumped out of the driver's side and opened the back doors, grabbing what he needed as he did. Lizzie and Prynce tumbled out, each as nauseous and disoriented as the other. Being in the back of a van was no joke.

The five of them moved into action, working together with a synchronicity that made you wonder if siblings actually had the same mannerisms coded into their DNA.

Danny, bolt cutters tucked up the sleeve of the Champion sweater that had been in his van, walked confidently over to the gates of the construction site, looked around, then broke the chains that secured it shut.

While he opened the gates, Lizzie, Dimple, and Prynce got back into the van, somehow configured themselves and Kyron in the tiny space, then laid a metal sheet and some of the bigger pipes down before lifting Kyron's body on top of them. They laid more pipes on top of and around the body while they waited for Danny to get back so they could lift it all up.

"Was there any CCTV?" Nikisha asked Danny.

"Not that I saw." Danny shook his head as he jumped into the back of his van and grabbed some rope.

Lizzie stared at him.

"I think you need to be a bit more clear about it than that."

"No, I mean, I didn't see any," Danny told her earnestly. "Help me tie this."

He lifted as much of the metal sheet as he could. Everyone but Nikisha secured the pipes with some rope, groaning quietly as they did.

"We'll leave him in here until we know where we're putting him," Nikisha said.

"Makes sense," Danny told them, stepping out of the van and heading onto the site as they all followed.

"Right, it's this way," he whispered, nodding his head to the right.

"It's so dark!" Prynce tried not to get his sneakers dirty as he followed his half brother. "And the moon keeps going off and on. What if we fall into something?"

"Your eyes will adjust!" Lizzie whispered coarsely. "Shhh! Else we're going to get caught!"

The half-siblings arrived at the deep hole that would be Kyron's grave, and ultimately the foundations of a set of flats for middle-class families, and saw that the hole was so big that if they chucked anything in, it would be very clearly seen.

"Wait, we didn't cover this in the plan. What do we do now?" Lizzie asked, panic rising in her voice. "We can't just dash this whole thing in, surely?"

"Do you know how expensive my pipes are?" Danny yelped. "We're not dashing my pipes in, no sir, no way."

"What was that?" A loud rustle made Dimple look left to right.

"Everyone stay still," Nikisha said, holding her hands out.

"Who's there?" Prynce called out in a voice he thought was quiet.

"Shhh!" Lizzie glared at him.

The rustling again. This time they all saw and heard that it came from the high bushes behind a front loader.

"It's your friend Karen, Dimple." Prynce laughed.

"You're making jokes *again*?" Lizzie asked in wonder. "Are you taking this seriously at all?"

"Just ignore him!" Nikisha hissed.

"I make jokes when I'm nervous," Prynce explained. "Reflex action."

"Or a trauma response," Dimple said, even though it wasn't the time or the place for psychoanalysis she'd learned on TikTok.

"I'm gonna see who it is." Danny ran full pelt toward the bush before anyone could tell him it was a bad idea.

As Danny got closer, the rustling got louder, and as Nikisha, Dimple, Lizzie, and Prynce watched, afraid of who was going to jump out, a fox sprang out and ran past them all.

Dimple was so relieved she burst into tears.

"Dimple," Nikisha said. "Cry later, *please*. Someone has to jump down, dig a hole, we tip the body in, then we cover it up."

"I'll do it," Prynce said, pulling his sweater off over his head.

"Thank you," Dimple whispered. "So much."

"Nah, it's nothing." Prynce shrugged. "I, like, like physical activities and shit like that."

"Guys, we're doing so much talking when time is ticking," Lizzie said before looking around to scope out the area. "Let me go and see if I can find a shovel."

"All right, thanks. I'll start with my hands," Prynce said, peering down into the hole. "I dunno how deep this hole is, you know."

Danny, who had been unraveling the rope from around the pipes, handed Prynce the end of it.

"You hold on to this and I'll lower you down."

"Shall I go and keep watch?" Dimple said.

"Yep. But stay close," Nikisha told her. "It's all gonna be all right."

Dimple nodded and shuffled off slowly, looking around cautiously as she did.

Lizzie returned with a shovel.

"Where's Prynce?"

Danny pointed down with the hand that wasn't holding the rope.

"I'm in!" Prynce whispered as loud as he could from the deep pit.

"Okay! I'm going to chuck the shovel in," Lizzie told him as quietly as she could.

"Just be careful you don't hit— Ow, fuck!" Prynce swore as the shovel clanged down and off his shoulder.

"Sorry!" Lizzie whispered down.

"Don't worry about it," Prynce hissed back up, getting to work.

"What's everyone doing tomorrow?" Danny asked Nikisha and Lizzie. "Well, today. What time is it?"

"It's four thirty-seven," Lizzie said, checking her phone.

"Why have you got your phone?" Nikisha asked. "I told you, leave the phone at Dimple's house. Remember what I said about the cell towers! If you get a text they're going to know you were somewhere you shouldn't be."

"Relax, it's on airplane mode," Lizzie said. "I'm not stupid."

Nikisha raised her eyebrows, annoyed that Lizzie was right, even though her being right was in their favor.

"I've got to take Marley to his mum's in the morning, then I've got work," Danny said, rubbing his eyes with a rough hand. He looked exhausted. "I'm working all the hours I can get at the moment to make sure he goes to a good nursery."

"How old is Marley?" Lizzie asked Danny.

"He's one and a half, you know?" Danny told her, smiling proudly. "My life and soul, that boy is. I'd do anything for him. Wait, let me show you a picture."

"Can you do that another time?" Nikisha put a hand on Danny's forearm to stop him from getting his phone out as well. "Just send her the picture tomorrow."

"Did you name him after . . . Bob Marley?" Lizzie asked.

"Yeah!"

"Having a white parent really made you want to prove yourself, didn't it?" Lizzie asked.

"Lizzie," Nikisha said through gritted teeth.

Danny laughed. "I know she's joking!"

Lizzie hadn't really been joking. She asked Danny where Marley's mum was.

"Ah, me and her don't really chat, you know?" Danny crossed his arms. "We were kind of friends, messing about and that. And when she got pregnant she didn't want the baby, but I begged her to keep him. I said she didn't have to have anything to do with it . . . I didn't think she'd take that literally."

"That's heavy," Lizzie said. "I'm sorry, Danny."

"Is what it is," Danny said, upbeat. "Anyway. When are you and your girlfriend gonna have kids?"

"*You* knew she had a girlfriend?" Nikisha asked. "I thought I knew about all of your relationships!"

"Yeah, I always see them together in Brixton holding hands and shit, being all cute and that."

"Wait," Lizzie said. "So you've seen me? Recently? And you haven't said hello?"

"Yeah, I recognized you from when we were kids. When we had to go to that dumb park. You know that ice cream made me throw up when I got home?"

"Why didn't you say anything when you saw me?" Lizzie asked, ignoring Danny's potential lactose intolerance.

"Well, I didn't know how you'd respond, init. I thought you'd be embarrassed because you're all posh and, like, well put together. And I'm . . . me."

"What do you mean, 'I'm . . . me'?" Lizzie asked.

"'Cause I'm always in my work clothes and looking scruffy," Danny said. "I didn't think you'd want to be seen with me."

"That's nonsense," Lizzie said, weirdly annoyed even though she knew he was right. "What perception do you *have* of me?"

"Okay!" Prynce whispered up hoarsely before Danny could respond. "I think I'm ready now."

"You sure?" Danny whispered down.

"Yeah, hurry up, I'm claustrophobic!"

"So why did you—" Lizzie said. "Forget it."

"Lizzie, you go and find Dimple," Nikisha said. "Danny, you and I will go and get Kyron from the van."

"Shall I not leave her to get her thoughts together?" Lizzie blinked slowly.

"She'll want to say goodbye," Nikisha said.

"Okay." Lizzie nodded, turning to go and find Dimple and knocking a couple of bricks down into the hole.

"Fuck! Ow! Get me out of here if you're gonna keep dropping things on me!" Prynce hissed. He was almost too laid back at the best of times, but his ability to stay that way had really been tested while he'd been down there.

"No," Nikisha whispered down. "We're almost done! All you need to do is unwrap the body and then cover it up."

"Why can't Danny do it?" Prynce called up.

"Because we won't be able to pull him up," Lizzie whispered down. "No offense."

"None taken," Danny said. "I've worked very hard to build mass."

"Every time you say it you're not even being sarcastic, are you?" Lizzie asked.

"Why would I be?" Danny said with a smile. "When I was in prison, all I used to do was eat noodles and bang gym."

"You were in prison?" Lizzie asked, furrowing her brow.

"Yep."

Lizzie didn't like that. It meant that he was used to this. This was just nothing to him. He probably didn't care if they got caught. Her heart rate increased as she wondered if the rest of them had been in prison, too. Not Dimple. Dimple was too soft to have even had detention at school. But as for Nikisha, she said she'd seen a lot, which was probably code for prison, too. From what *her* mum had told her about Nikisha and Prynce's mum, they probably didn't grow up with any real discipline, which meant that they were surely *primed* to be criminals, *ready* even.

"What are you thinking about?" Nikisha asked, breaking Lizzie's spiral of thought.

"Nothing," Lizzie said defensively. "Why?"

"Because your face is looking judgmental," Nikisha told her, raising an eyebrow. "Fix it."

Lizzie wondered who Nikisha thought she was speaking to. She might have been the eldest by technicality alone, but that didn't mean she could drag Lizzie into her life and talk to her any which way.

"Can you go and get Dimple like I asked?" Nikisha commanded, rather than asked. "Danny, let's go get the body."

When Lizzie found Dimple, she was sitting on a pile of concrete slabs, hidden from the entrance to the building site, working hard to keep her eyes open.

"Nobody came," she said.

"You're shivering," Lizzie said. "You're in shock."

"I'm okay, I'm just cold. Where are the others?"

"Prynce is in a hole, Danny and Nikisha are getting the bo— Getting Kyron from the van. You wanna say goodbye before we put him in? You need to be quick, though."

Dimple nodded, her thoughts hazy and unconstructed as she followed Lizzie, who was marching back over to the site of Kyron's burial at a pace Dimple's legs couldn't easily keep up with.

"What's taking everyone so long?" Prynce whispered up from the hole when he heard his half sisters return. "I feel like I'm the one being buried."

"Shush!" Lizzie commanded from above. "He's right, though, what is taking them so long?"

"What if the police came and got them?" Dimple said, fear in her eyes. "Oh God. The police came and got them and now they're locked up and it's all my fault."

"What?" Lizzie said. "Don't be so dramatic, we'd have heard sirens. Tighten up, Dimple."

"I can't believe I've done this!" Dimple whimpered as she turned and broke into a run toward the entrance.

"Honestly, I was having such a nice evening," Lizzie muttered, running off after her.

"Hello?" Prynce called up.

When Dimple got to the others, she saw her half brother and Nikisha standing, both with their hands on their hips, staring into the open back of the van.

"Oh, thank God, you're okay!" Dimple whispered as tears of relief brimmed in her eyes. "You were taking so long! I thought someone had found you!"

"What's going on?" Lizzie asked as she caught up with Dimple. "You're quite fast for someone with your BMI."

"What do you mean by that?" Dimple hissed. She'd put up with a lot of things this evening, but she wasn't going to put up with that. Not this time.

"What?" Lizzie hissed back. "You can't be offended by that."

"Yes, I can," Dimple told Lizzie. "Of *course* I can!"

"Girls," Nikisha whispered.

"How? You have a high BMI. That's just fact."

"Just *fact*?" Dimple asked, raising her voice slightly.

"Girls," Nikisha whispered, louder this time.

"Oh, here we go." Lizzie rolled her eyes. "Another thing for you to be sensitive about."

"Girls, shut up!" Nikisha turned to her half sisters and clamped a not-so-gentle hand down on each of their shoulders.

"What?" they asked her in unison.

Nikisha frowned for a second, the cogs turning in her head.

"What?" Dimple and Lizzie asked again. "What's wrong?"

"He's . . . gone." Nikisha pointed into the back of the empty van. "The body's gone."

CHAPTER
FIVE

LIZZIE CLIMBED INTO THE back of the van and, with the strength of somebody more determined than technically strong, started moving ladders, brooms, and loose taps around.

"Yeah, I don't think he's hiding under the broom, Lizzie," Danny said.

"Lizzie," Nikisha said very calmly. "You can stop looking. Go and get Prynce. We're all going to get in the van, and we're not going to say or do anything until we leave here. Okay? And make sure Prynce wipes down the shovel."

Lizzie nodded, and off she went.

"Nik—" Dimple said, panic rising from her throat.

"I *said* we are not talking about anything here," Nikisha said, interrupting. "In the van."

A couple of minutes later, Lizzie and Prynce returned and found Dimple sitting in the front of the van next to Danny, while Nikisha leaned against it.

"What happened?" Prynce asked.

"How many times do I have to say it?" Nikisha pointed at the vehicle, which was already vibrating, ready to leave. "Van. Now."

"Yes, boss." Prynce jumped into the back and Lizzie followed, looking like her world had ended.

Nikisha squeezed in next to Dimple in the front.

"Drive," she said to Danny.

"Is your seat belt on?" Danny asked.

"Danny." Nikisha put her hand up. "Please."

When they'd gotten far enough away from the building site, Nikisha broke the silence similar to the one they'd experienced all those years ago in their dad's gold Jeep.

"Right. I am assuming—assuming—that Kyron was not dead. Dimple, didn't you say you checked his pulse?"

"I did, and I didn't feel anything."

"And you didn't think to double-check, Lizzie?" Nikisha asked.

"You were there when Dimple told me she'd done it!" Lizzie said in protest. "Why didn't *you* do it? Instead of barking orders at us and not lifting a finger?"

"Because I was the one coming up with the *plan*," Nikisha replied. "You're the one with the medical degree."

"Well, as a medical *student*, I saw all of that blood and I assumed he was dead," Lizzie shot back. "Alongside Dimple *telling* me that he was dead."

"You know what they say about assuming, don't you?" Prynce said.

"Don't." Lizzie held a finger up to Prynce's face.

Danny stepped in.

"Look, guys, arguing won't solve anything. Either someone went into my van and took him, or, as Nikisha says, Kyron woke up and left. I say we drive around and look for him, right?"

"Yes," Nikisha said.

"I feel like I should remind you that he does live down that road," Dimple said. "He might have just gone home."

"Or, with any luck, that head injury means he might not have made it very far," Nikisha said.

"With any *luck*?" Dimple said.

"You know what I mean." Nikisha sighed. "Eyes peeled."

"Do you know what pisses me off about this?" Lizzie asked her half-siblings.

"Please tell us." Nikisha turned to look at Lizzie, ready for an argument.

"When the police find out about this, they're going to say we're a gang. I managed to not be in a gang all my life and yet here I am, in a gang." Lizzie folded her arms.

"Nothing wrong with being in a gang," Danny said. "To some people, a gang is family."

"Oh my *God*." Lizzie put her head in her hands.

"They'll probably say we're coconspirators, you know," Prynce said. " 'Cause we don't really look like we're in a gang."

"He won't go to the police," Dimple said. "I promise you, if he is fine, Kyron won't go to the police."

"How do you know?" Lizzie asked.

"He hates the police more than I do," Dimple said. "Very worst-case scenario, he'll come back with his boys. And we really, really don't want that."

"I don't want to be part of this, you know." Lizzie shook her head. "I *never* wanted to be part of this."

"I know, Lizzie," Nikisha said. "We all know. But you are. And we need to figure this out as a team."

Danny drove around until it was light, but there was still no sighting of Kyron.

"I've gotta take Marley to his mum's in, like, forty-five." Danny yawned, rubbing his tired, red eyes.

"Okay. I don't think we're going to find him," Nikisha said, conceding. "I think we just hold on tight to see if he gets in touch with Dimple. And we move from there."

"What's he going to say to me?" Dimple started crying again.

"Well, I don't know!" Nikisha said. "But when we find out, we'll *sort it*."

Danny patted Dimple on the shoulder.

"It's all right, mate."

"We all need some sleep." Nikisha could project-manage the hiding of a body, but she couldn't project-manage all of this negativity.

"Okay, *okay*, who am I dropping home first?" Danny asked.

Nikisha turned to the back of the van.

"We'll drop Prynce back at ours first, then Lizzie."

But when Nikisha's eyes focused, she saw Prynce, asleep, and no sign of Lizzie.

"Prynce!" Nikisha shouted, waking her brother up.

"What, what?"

"Where is Lizzie?"

"She's here." Prynce gestured to his right before opening his eyes and seeing that Lizzie definitely was not there. "Oh shit."

"Yeah, *oh shit*," Nikisha repeated, rolling her eyes. "How did nobody hear her get out?"

"In my defense, I was asleep," Prynce said.

"I thought I heard something about an hour ago, but I figured something fell over in the back of the van when Danny braked suddenly at the signals." Dimple whispered, her stomach churning again.

"Broke *hard at the lights*?" Danny looked at Dimple in shock. "I hope you aren't attacking my driving? 'Cause if there's one thing I can do, it's *drive*."

"And fix a toilet," Prynce said, cutting in. "You think she's gone to the police?"

"Oh God." Dimple looked down into her lap, her head spinning. "Oh God, oh God, oh God."

"If she's smart she won't have," Nikisha said, part hopeful, part threatening. "She probably just needed some space."

"Does anyone know her address? Shall we go to hers and wait outside?" Danny said. "I can text my mum and ask her to take Marley to nursery."

"No." Nikisha shook her head. "I didn't collect her. I gave her Dimple's address and told her to meet us there. I'll reach out to her later today, and there's no point in panicking until I do, Dimple. What we're going to do is nothing. We're going to *do* nothing, and *say* nothing."

Dimple nodded. Twenty-four hours ago her biggest worry was whether or not her hair was retaining enough moisture.

"And Dimple," Nikisha said. "I don't want you to get in touch with Kyron at all. If he's fine, which we have to assume he is, he'll come to you. And as soon as he does, you let me know, and I'll send the message round. Okay?"

Everyone nodded.

"But what if he hurts me?" Dimple asked.

Nikisha smiled, and something quite scary flashed in her dark eyes. "His life won't be worth living if he does."

"Ah, guys!" Prynce looked at all of his siblings, minus Lizzie of course, and grinned. "If only Dad could see us now!" He was met with a tut from Danny and a snort from Dimple. Nikisha sucked her teeth for about an hour.

———————

When Danny dropped Nikisha and Dimple back to Herne Hill, the winter sun was sparkling over the morning frost.

Nikisha had made him drop them at the end of the road in case Karen was already up and about. "See you soon," he said as they slid out of the van. "Text me when you need me."

"In a bit," Nikisha said as she closed the van door.

Dimple could only manage a wave. She mouthed a small "thank you" as Danny drove away.

They walked to Dimple's silently. They were too exhausted to talk for talking's sake.

"You're going to go in, check the floors one last time, put what you're wearing into a bag and hide it," Nikisha told Dimple as they got to her car. She unlocked the door and eased her tired bones into the driver's seat. "Okay? And don't forget to cook something to hide the smell of bleach."

Dimple nodded.

"And if anyone asks, you haven't seen Kyron, and your guess is that he got the message that it was over between you and him after you'd ignored him." Nikisha pressed the instructions onto her sister quietly and urgently.

"Last thing," Nikisha said as Dimple started to shiver. "Those marks around your neck are going to turn into bruises. You need to keep them covered. But take pictures of them when they're at their darkest."

Dimple nodded, even though all of this information was almost painful to process. She watched Nikisha drive away before she turned, walked up the path, and put her key in the door with shaking hands.

"Who was that?"

Dimple jumped, dropping her keys, as Karen popped her head out of her front door.

"Sorry?" Dimple asked, stepping back.

"Early for you, isn't it?" Karen asked. "Or late, depending on how you look at it."

"Oh, yeah." Dimple picked up her keys. "I should get in and go to sleep!"

"It's just that I haven't seen you with any friends around here in a long time, that's all." Karen smiled, her thin lips pressed together tightly. "And especially after last night, I just had to ask, you know? This area has always been very safe. It's important that we keep it that way."

"Er, yeah, that was my big sister," Dimple explained, not that she should have. Karen had always taken it upon herself to be the official neighborhood watch even though nobody in the cul-de-sac had called for it, and nobody even replied to her messages in the group chat. "See you later!"

"Dimple?" Karen said as Dimple put her key in the door. "Are you *sure* something wasn't going on last night? Me and Pete did hear some very strange noises coming from the house."

"It was just the TV." Dimple smiled. "Me and my sister, the one who just dropped me home, were watching this weird experimental film, about—"

"So you watched a film *together*, but she dropped you home this *morning*?" Karen asked, her tone suspicious, saving Dimple from making up the plot of an experimental film on the spot. "Very strange."

Dimple blinked at Karen. Karen eyed Dimple. To speed things up, Dimple pretended to shiver.

"Well!" Karen trilled. "You should get some sleep, as you say."

As she made it into the house, Dimple was sure that wasn't the last she'd hear of this.

The smell of bleach hit her and she had to step back out into the front garden to stop herself from retching.

She walked back into the house, sleeve over her nose and mouth, and moved quickly into the kitchen. She turned the lights on and inspected the floors, cupboards, and counter before opening the windows, even though it was freezing outside, then moved over to the carpet to check for any traces of blood.

Satisfied, if that was the word to use, that everything was clean, Dimple went to the fridge and pulled out the container of soup her mum had left her. She emptied it into a pan on the stove, and looked to see if there was anything in the freezer she could put in the oven to double her chances of hiding the bleach smell.

She pulled out a frozen pizza and turned on the oven. Her hands were still shaking and she felt like she could vomit if she let herself.

While the food heated, Dimple went up to her room and peeled her clothes off. She bundled them into a pillowcase, hid it under her bed, and stepped into the shower, washing every single bit of the night off her. She scrubbed and scrubbed until her arms and legs were bright red, using a whole bottle of Faith in Nature dragon fruit body wash, the stuff her mum got from Waitrose and told her to use sparingly. She smelled amazing, but her skin was sore. The marks around her neck were, too.

When she'd dried herself, the act of which was painful, Dimple dragged her weak and weary body downstairs and turned off the stove and the oven. She poured the soup into the bin, then broke the pizza up and chucked that in after it. She put the empty pizza box into the recycling bin, too tired to think about her mum's empty wine bottles that took up most of the space in there. She'd worry about that when she'd had some sleep.

———————

Dimple had managed maybe one hour of sleep, and with great difficulty. She'd mainly stared at the ceiling, and when she did doze off, she'd woken up and her stomach had churned when she realized that the events of last night hadn't been a nightmare.

She wouldn't have left her bed if it hadn't been for her mum getting home and hollering her name up the stairs repeatedly.

"You ordered a pizza but you cooked a pizza?" Janet asked when her daughter walked into the kitchen.

"What?" Dimple mumbled as she rubbed her tired eyes.

"There's an empty takeaway pizza box and an empty oven pizza box in the recycling. Were you starving, or did Kyron come round or something?"

"I was just really hungry," Dimple said, her stomach flipping at the mention of Kyron's name. "Anyway! How was your holiday? Did you have fun?"

"You know what?" Janet said. "I do not want to go on holiday with that woman again."

"But she's your best friend, Mum."

"Which doesn't mean we should go on holiday together," Janet said. She carried on speaking, but Dimple zoned out. She could see her mum's mouth moving but did not take a single word in.

"Dimple!" Dimple jolted back to the kitchen when her mum grabbed her wrist. "What's wrong with you?"

"Sorry, nothing," Dimple said. "My period is just really bad at the moment."

"But you aren't on your period," Janet said. "You're due on in five days."

"I meant my PMS. I think I need to change my pill or something, because this one is really messing my head up."

"Hmmm. Well. Keep an eye on it and let me know if you need to start seeing my gynecologist. She's very good, you know."

"I will, Mum," Dimple said. "I think I'm going to go back to bed."

"Okay," Janet said, watching her daughter move slowly and clumsily out of the room. "And thank you for cleaning the kitchen."

"What?" Dimple asked, stopping and turning in the doorway.

"I said thank you for cleaning the kitchen," Janet said. "I don't think I've ever seen my floor so clean."

"No problem." Dimple smiled weakly, leaving the room and holding on tight to the banister before her legs gave way.

CHAPTER
SIX

THE LAST FEW DAYS had been unbearable. Dimple had barely slept, and when she did, her nightmares were so bad that the anxiety of real life was a much better option. She hadn't been able to stomach anything, and had had to fake a bug to explain the exhaustion and lack of appetite.

Janet popped her head into Dimple's room.

"Dimple, Lynette is downstairs for you."

"What??" Dimple sat upright, which cost her a lot of energy she didn't have.

"Lynette," Janet repeated. "Earth to Dimple? Kyron's mum? I don't know what she's here for, but she wants to speak to you."

"She, she, h-has to go," Dimple stammered. "I'm not well, I don't want to see anyone."

"You're really not yourself, Dimple." Janet shook her head. "Why have you got that turtleneck on? Have you caught a chill?"

"Maybe. I'm just not feeling great."

"*And* you used the whole bottle of Faith in Nature, so I know things aren't okay with you. One bottle is five pounds, sixty-five."

"Mum!" Dimple exclaimed. "Please!"

"Was it something you ate?" her mum quizzed her as she stood in her daughter's doorway. "I bet it was that pizza you ordered. How many times have I told you about eating takeaway food? You don't know what they're putting in it and you can't see how they prepare it. Me and you both know they're not washing their hands."

"Yeah, Mum, you're right," Dimple said, pushing away the dry toast her mum had left on her bedside table earlier.

"You want me to make you some soup when Lynette has left?" Janet asked, sitting on the end of the bed. "That'll wash you out."

Dimple's stomach was going again. Why was Lynette here? What did she know? Surely if she knew what had happened she wouldn't be waiting downstairs politely, she'd be dragging Dimple out of bed by her hair. It made her want to be sick to think about it.

"Maybe tomorrow," Dimple said, turning away from her mum.

"Have you spoken to him?" Janet asked, closing Dimple's bedroom door so Lynette couldn't hear them.

"To who?" Dimple asked weakly, facing the wall.

"Kyron!" Janet folded her arms. "Every other time you've broken up he's managed to weasel his way back. You can't tell me he's given up so easy? Is that why she's here? Has that boy sent his mother round to get you back? That's something your dad did, you know, back in the day. Cyril's mum, your grandma Delores—not that you could call her your grandma—turned up at my house more than once, begging me to take him back. It usually worked, too."

"No, I haven't spoken to him for a few days," Dimple told her mum, not wanting to hear about her dad right now, and relieved that Lynette hadn't said anything to Janet. "I think he's got the message finally. I had a really big conversation with him about it and I think he understands now."

"Good," Janet said before lowering her voice and saying, "I never did like that boy. I always thought you kept him around to keep your numbers up. Or what you call them? Followers."

"Mmm," Dimple replied.

"Even though you barely have any. All right. Well, go to sleep," Janet commanded as she closed the door.

"She's not feeling very well, Lynette," Janet whispered when she got to the bottom of the stairs. "She's gone back to sleep."

"Poor thing. What's wrong with her?" Lynette asked quietly.

"It sounds like a stomach bug."

"Well, when she's feeling better, can you ask her to call me? It's been a couple of days since I saw Kyron and I'm getting worried."

"When did you last speak to him?" Janet asked. "You know they've broken up? So I don't think Dimple would have seen him."

"Did they?" Lynette asked, forgetting she was meant to be whispering. "I can never keep track of those two."

"Well, look, I'll pass on your message, Lynette," Janet said, ushering Kyron's anxious mum toward the front door so she could make Dimple the soup she'd told her she didn't want today. Janet always knew what was best for her daughter, even when her daughter didn't agree. "And I'm sure he's fine, Lynette. Kyron has never struck me as someone who'd succumb to trouble knocking on his door. Big man like that."

"I hope you're right," Lynette exhaled, her voice threatening to crack.

Dimple waited until she heard Lynette leave before she sat up in bed, realizing that she hadn't posted for a few days. Her two hundred followers might think something was up. She dragged herself from underneath her duvet and went over to her dressing table, flicking her ring light on with weak hands.

She started by covering up the dark marks that were deepening across her neck. Then she did her best to apply a full face of makeup, then realized that if she looked too glamorous, people would think she was fine, so she pulled off her fake lashes.

"But maybe I want them to think I'm fine?" she said to herself, going to put them back on.

Making the smallest of decisions required a level of brain power that she didn't currently have.

Dimple placed her phone in the middle of the ring light, opened video and pressed record. Even *she* could see how worry had changed her face.

"Hey, guys! Hope you're all good on this..." she said. "Wait, what day is it today?" She stopped recording, had some water, took a few deep breaths, and pressed record again.

"Hey, guys!" She beamed at her own reflection in the phone, her voice clearer and higher. "Hope you're all so good on this ... I *think* it's Thursday? Sorry, the days are all blurring into one at the moment. I know I've been quiet, so please forgive me, but you know what breakups are like, right? I know you guys love me and Kyron as a couple, and as I said before, I will always, always have so much love for him, but we've definitely decided that we're done. And as you can see, I haven't slept and I've lost weight. And from all the wrong places. This is so hard. So while I mend my broken heart, please bear with me. Comment your favorite breakup songs below to help your girl through! Love ya!"

She took the phone off the stand and watched her performance twice over, then uploaded the video to YouTube, Instagram, and Twitter before climbing back into bed. Almost immediately, she fell asleep.

CHAPTER
SEVEN

"OH, ISN'T HE HANDSOME?"

"Oh, he's gooorgeous. Even with those scratch marks on his face. *And* the two black eyes."

"He looks like a young Denzel Washington, doesn't he?"

"D'you think? I think he looks more like a young . . . what's his name?"

"Who?"

"You know the one! Tall. Dark. Handsome. The one who plays that detective. Always running around in a suit."

"Ohhh. Idris something?"

"That's it. Idris Elba."

"Oh, you're right. God, what I wouldn't do for half an hour with Idris Elba. He could detect me any day of the week."

"Actually! I think he looks like that one who won the Oscar."

"What did he win the Oscar for?"

"Oh, I don't know, but he's from here! My daughter loves him! What's his name? Daniel something."

"Oh, Daniel Kaluuya."

"That's the one!"

Kyron, who looked nothing like a young Denzel Washington,

Idris Elba, or even Daniel Kaluuya, blinked his eyes open slowly and tried to focus on the source of the mistaken identity. The blurring cleared to reveal two older white women standing over him.

"Oh look, he's awake. HELLO, DARLIN'! YOU OKAY?" the first woman bellowed down at him.

Kyron tried to ask where he was, but all that came out when he opened his mouth was a sequence of dry coughs.

"I wouldn't try and speak just yet if I were you, my love. You had a tube down your throat," the second woman said gently, leaning too close to him. "You just relax."

Kyron looked to his right and saw the winter sun trying to make its way through thick gray clouds. He closed his eyes again and let sleep take him.

———————

When Kyron woke again, he blinked up at the square off-white tiles on the ceiling above him before realizing that it was night. The fat, full moon lit the room he was in, and when he looked down, he saw that instead of the gray tracksuit he'd been wearing earlier, he was in a blue-and-white hospital gown, and he was lying in a bed that wasn't his own. He started to panic. Had he died? No. He took a few seconds to breathe and realized that if he'd died, he wouldn't be wearing a hospital gown. He was clearly in a hospital bed, and everything felt a bit fuzzy and soft. He shook his head to make everything feel like real life again, and it hurt, so he agreed with himself to let everything keep feeling fuzzy and soft.

Kyron needed a piss. He went to swing his legs out of the bed and realized that quick movements were not his friend right now. So, slowly, he lowered his legs to the floor and tried to stand up. It took a couple of tries, and when he was finally firmly on his feet, his mission to find a toilet was thwarted by the drip attached to his hand that pulled him back.

"The fuck is this?" he asked, ripping the needle out of a raised vein. He'd seen people do that in films and hadn't realized it would hurt so much, especially when the tape that had secured it there ripped a few hairs out of his skin.

Kyron looked down at the gray lino floor. It felt so cold on his feet. He wished he had a pair of sliders with him. He stepped out of the room he was in, and in front of him was a nurse, a young white man, sitting at a desk. Kyron had approached him so quietly he didn't have time to put down the book he was reading.

"Where's the bathroom?" Kyron asked the nurse.

"Oh God!" The nurse jumped, throwing the book in the air. "You scared me."

Kyron frowned at the man.

"*I* scared you?"

"Sorry, yes, you snuck up on me there!"

"I snuck up on you?" Kyron said. "You're in a hospital full of people, man."

The man forced a chuckle.

"Well, yes. I must be afraid of the dark."

Kyron was too desperate for the toilet to ask what the man meant.

"Where's the bathroom?" Kyron asked him. "And have you got any slippers I can have?"

"There's a shortage, I'm afraid." The nurse shrugged. "But the bathroom is just down there, to the right."

"Can I have my sneakers at least?" Kyron asked. "None of my stuff is by my bed or anything."

"Ah, yes," the nurse said knowingly. "In the morning, if you're feeling better, everything will be explained to you."

His head still fuzzy, Kyron shuffled in the direction of the bathroom, hating the feeling of the cold lino floor on his bare feet more and more with every step he took. When he found the bathroom, he needed to relieve himself so badly that he didn't bother locking the door.

When he'd finished and was washing his hands, he inspected himself in the mirror, wincing as he ran his fingers across three deep wounds that ran down his cheek. The pain medication he was on meant they didn't hurt; he was wincing because they looked bad. He looked tired, too. Bags under his eyes that weren't there the last time he looked at himself. But mainly, there was a big bandage on his head, running from behind his left ear to his right temple.

He dried his hands on a couple of blue paper towels, then reached up to the bandage. He felt along its path, and in the middle, across the back of his head, was a thick pad of gauze. He pressed into the pad and a pain sliced through his head, so sharp that he bent over the sink and opened his mouth to be sick.

When nothing came, he stood up again, gasping for air. When he'd gotten his breath back, and the pain had subsided slightly, he turned to the side, removed the bandage, and peeled the bloody gauze away. He couldn't see what was underneath, but could see that someone had shaved the back of his head, and badly. His barber was never gonna let this one go.

Kyron dropped the pad of gauze into the sink and gently ran his fingers across the area it had covered. He felt the familiar pattern of stitches that he recognized from his youth when he'd sliced his leg open playing football and had landed on a piece of glass that had been hiding in the grass.

"What the fuck happened?" he asked himself.

———

The next morning, Kyron awoke to a blond, plump nurse standing over his bed. She appeared to be checking his vitals.

"Where's my phone?" Kyron asked the nurse gruffly. He didn't mean to sound rude or anything, his voice just hadn't caught up with the rest of him when he'd woken up.

"Good morning!" she said brightly. Kyron recognized her voice. She was either the nurse who had said he looked like Denzel

Washington, or the one who had said he looked like Daniel Kaluuya or Idris Elba.

"Glad you're awake, my love," the nurse said gently. "Can you tell me how you're feeling?"

Kyron felt less fuzzy and soft than he did last night. The back of his head throbbed.

"Yeah, I'm good."

"Well, we're going to get you a CT scan to make sure everything is good."

"A what?" Kyron asked.

"A scan of your head, my love. But don't worry, all your vitals are fine."

Kyron looked at the nurse and tried to figure out what the fuck was going on.

"Can you tell me your name, my darlin'?"

"Er, yeah. It's Ky— Kyle," Kyron said. She didn't need to know his government name.

"Okay, Kyle. I'm going to go and get you some toast, so as soon as you've had a lovely bit of breakfast, the police are gonna come in and talk to you."

"Police?" Kyron asked, sitting up so fast he startled the nurse. "Police, why?"

"Well, darlin', someone found you on the side of the road with your head bashed in," the nurse explained. "We have to alert the police about that."

"I don't want any police here." Kyron shook his head, not caring how much it hurt. "I don't need police here."

"Look." The nurse lowered her volume. "If it's gang stuff—"

"*Gang* stuff?" Kyron shook his head again. "Nah, it's not that. You need to tell them not to come here."

"My love—"

"I'm telling you, it's not that. I must have had a— An accident or something."

The nurse didn't look convinced.

"My phone," Kyron said, urgency in his voice. "Where's my phone?"

"We've got all of your things somewhere safe in case they need to be given over as evidence, but don't worry, you'll get them back soon." The nurse smiled. "But if you know your next of kin's number by heart, maybe your mum, maybe your girlfriend, I can give them a call and let them know where you are."

"Where am I?"

"You're in King's Hospital, my love. Camberwell."

"Can you just get me my phone, please?" Kyron asked, softly placing a hand on the nurse's arm.

The nurse pursed her lips.

"All right, all right." She smiled.

"Can you just bring all my stuff? I've got some medicine in my pocket I need to take"—obviously a lie—"and I need my sneakers 'cause the floor is cold and that male nurse last night said you lot have run out of slippers."

"Yeah, slippers and everything else." The nurse rolled her eyes as she shuffled away.

When she returned, the nurse handed Kyron a clear plastic bag that contained his stuff. He could see that his tracksuit was covered in blood.

"Jill, can I just borrow you for a sec?" Another nurse popped her head into the room. Though there was no panic in her voice, her eyes were wide enough to tell both Kyron and Jill that she needed urgent assistance.

"I'll be back in a minute, Kyle," Kyron's nurse said, already out of the door.

"Thanks, Jill," Kyron said as he stood up. He shook the contents of the clear bag onto the bed and pulled his clothes on. His blood had hardened the fabric.

Kyron pulled his socks and sneakers on, then felt in his pockets for his keys and his Oyster transit card. His phone was in there, but he'd check it later. He needed to get out of this hospital first.

Kyron twisted and turned his way through the hospital corridors, his head and the wound that had split it open still throbbing, thinking he'd never make it out. Every single one of those long passages looked the same. He squinted as he tried to make sense of the signs and the zones and the names of the wards. Where was the sign that said EXIT?

"Excuse me?" A woman's voice froze Kyron to the spot as adrenaline spiked through his system. "Excuse me, young man?"

Kyron had to decide: Would it be fight, or would it be flight?

"You, with the blood on your sweater!"

This time, it was going to be flight. Kyron ran, those beige walls and those beige floors becoming a blur as he moved as fast as his pounding head would let him. Then, suddenly, he could see it. Outside. He kept running until he hit a set of automatic doors that opened so slowly they stopped him from being able to burst through dramatically.

It was freezing cold, and Kyron's legs started to feel like jelly, so instead of trying to break into a run again, he walked as fast as he could until he was certain nobody was following him, up the hill that led him to Ruskin Park. He slipped through the gates and slowed his pace, finally stopping when he got to a bench.

He threw himself down onto it and bent over, lowering his head between his legs so he didn't faint. He stayed like that, the cold air whipping his back, until his head stopped swirling and the throbbing lessened.

Kyron didn't want to go home, not looking like this. He needed to lie low for a bit, but wherever he was going to go, he needed to decide fast. His skin felt like it was absorbing all the cold around him. While he thought about where he'd go, he started toward the bus stop before he realized that public transport with all this blood on his clothes would be a bit technical. He decided to get an Uber. He finally took his phone out of his pocket, saw that his battery was on red, and tried to ignore all the notifications that were on the screen. Hundreds of missed calls. Mainly from his long-suffering mum, Lynette. Hundreds, hundreds of little green icons telling him he had a lot of messages and WhatsApps to reply to.

Kyron swiped them all away and ordered an Uber to meet him at the entrance of the park he'd stumbled into.

Nikisha had told Dimple to carry on with her life as normal. It had been a week since what she referred to as "the incident" in her head, so she got ready in what she felt was a meaningful way, i.e., putting on a full face of makeup. She didn't need to cover the marks on her neck anymore. They'd finally faded, but when they were at their worst she'd taken pictures of them like Nikisha had told her to. When she felt like she looked nicer than she had in days, she went to see Roman, Kyron's best friend.

"So. How have you been?" Dimple asked Roman as she draped her legs over his lap. She smiled at him, then her eyes wandered to the pockmarks on his dark brown skin. She put her hand to his face and stroked one of the marks. It felt soft against the coarseness of the rest of his face.

"Oi, what you doing?" he asked her, jerking his head back.

"What?" Dimple asked, pulling her hand away.

"Don't do them soppy things," Roman said.

"Why not?" Dimple asked.

"You know why."

"I haven't spoken to him in ages." Nerves crunched Dimple's stomach. She waited for Roman to say that Kyron had finally appeared and told him everything.

"Yeah, but this is you two's pattern," he said instead.

Dimple relaxed slightly. Best-case scenario was that Kyron was somewhere lying low until he was ready to strike.

"You're in your whole fake 'Internet's best couple' with him, and then I'm here having to watch it all, and then when you two break up I see it playing out, all this drama. Then you text me and come round. Happens every single time. You're too sometimeish, Dimple," Roman stated gruffly.

"Ah, you watch my videos?" Dimple smiled. "Seriously, though, it's done for real," she said. "Seriously."

"You say that every single time, man." Roman got up from the sofa and left his living room. "And you know Kyron is my boy. It's like you forget that we chat."

"Are you coming back?" Dimple called after him.

"Yeah, I'm just getting a drink," Roman called back. "Needy."

Dimple put her legs up on the sofa and picked up the remote. She tried to find something for them to watch, which was never an easy thing. They both had different interests; she liked most films, and he exclusively liked documentaries about how rap moguls made it big. She scrolled and scrolled, option paralysis seizing her as she flicked the arrow on the remote to the right, to the right, to the right.

Her phone buzzed next to her. She didn't take her eyes off the screen, but she listened to see if it was one singular buzz (WhatsApp, Insta, or Twitter notification), two buzzes (iMessage), or continued buzzing (phone call). It was the latter. She didn't like phone calls. With narrowed eyes she glanced at the phone and sat up straight when she saw who was calling her.

Dimple's heart sped up as she watched Lynette, Kyron's mum, calling her. Her breath caught in her throat as she saw Lynette ring off.

"What's wrong with you?" Roman asked, walking back into the room. "You seen a ghost or something?"

Dimple could only blink as she swallowed roughly, the lack of lubrication in her throat forcing her to feel every muscle from her jaw to her chest.

"I'm guessing he messaged you so you're gonna bounce?" Roman asked, throwing himself down next to her. "I told you this would happen. Every single time, every single *time*!"

"No," Dimple said, putting a hand on Roman's knee as she got up. "No. I just need to go and make a call."

"Don't put your hand on my knee." Roman brushed her hand away. "I'm not doing this anymore. You must think I'm some kind of prick."

"I don't think you're a prick! Just hold on a sec," Dimple muttered, slipping out of the door and into the hallway. She lowered herself down onto the stairs, phone in her free hand, and chewed her bottom lip for a few seconds.

She stared at the missed call notification for ages, wondering why she hadn't accounted for this happening, and why Nikisha hadn't briefed her on what to do when it inevitably did.

Dimple took a screengrab, then swiped the notification away and found her and Nikisha's message thread. She went to text her the screengrab, then remembered Nikisha very sternly saying they shouldn't text about anything to do with Kyron. She called her instead, her temperature rising as the phone rang and rang. Finally, Nikisha answered, which didn't make Dimple feel any better.

"Hello, little sister," Nikisha said calmly. Her voice was always very calm, very still, very measured. It was actually more disarming to Dimple than it was calming.

"Hey, Nikisha," Dimple rasped. "Are you around?"

"I can be," Nikisha answered. "Where are you?"

"I'm at a friend's in Gipsy Hill."

"Text me the address and I'll come and meet you," Nikisha said. "Give me thirty so I can drop Amara to her dad's."

"Sorry, Nikisha."

"It is what it is. See you soon."

———————

The thirty minutes passed very, very slowly. Roman had chosen a documentary while Dimple was out of the room and neither of them were enjoying it. Dimple went through every single emotion possible for a human to feel while Roman fumed quietly on the sofa next to her wondering how he ended up being his boy's girl's side chick. He always vowed to himself from when he was at school and his first girlfriend cheated on him that he'd never be a side chick, but Dimple just did something to him that he could never make sense of, or walk away from.

When Dimple's phone eventually buzzed with Nikisha's call, she shot up from the sofa.

"Where you going now?" Roman asked. "We're in the middle of a documentary, man."

"I just need to take care of something," Dimple told him. "My half sister is outside."

"Half sister?" Roman furrowed his brow. "You don't have a half sister."

"I do!" Dimple told him. "I have *two* half sisters. And two half brothers."

"You're chatting shit."

"Why would I . . . chat shit about that? I literally have four half-siblings. Dad's side."

"You never told me that."

"Yeah, but I haven't really grown up with them so I haven't mentioned them."

"Listen," Roman said. "If you wanna go making things up just so you can run back to him, don't waste your time."

Dimple threw her head back and asked herself what attracted her to these paranoid men.

"Nikisha is the eldest, then Danny. Lizzie is the same age as me, and Prynce is the youngest. He's got the same mum as Nikisha. The *rest* of us have different mums."

Roman let out a long whistle.

"Your dad was active, init."

"Yup." Dimple nodded. "I'll be two minutes. You can look out the window if you don't believe me. I'll make Nikisha wave at you."

Dimple shoved her feet into her sneakers and left the door ajar. She ran down the path and flung open the door to Nikisha's car, shivering when she got in.

"Hey. Thanks for coming so quickly."

"It's fine," Nikisha said, smiling and turning off the ignition. "What's happened?"

"Kyron's mum called me," Dimple said, watching her sister's smile drop. "Well, she came round. The other day. Oh my God, why do you look so angry? I stayed in bed and my mum sent her away, they both thought I was ill. But what if he's turned up and he's told her everything?"

"Dimple, you're meant to tell me these things. *All* things. When she called, did you answer?"

"No! It rang off. But I don't know what to do. Shall I message her? Shall I say I'm sorry I missed it? Or shall I call her back? But if I call her I don't know what I'm going to say. Maybe I should call her back when you're here. What do you think?" Dimple reeled off all the options, then took a big breath.

"All right, slow down," Nikisha said. "Who is . . . that?"

Dimple followed the direction of her sister's gaze and saw Roman staring out of his living room window.

"Oh, that's Roman," Dimple said. "Wave at him, please."

Nikisha waved at Roman slowly.

"But who is Roman?"

"He's Roman." Dimple shrugged, breaking eye contact and facing ahead. She concentrated on the streetlights flickering on as dusk turned to night.

"And is Roman a friend?"

Dimple laughed awkwardly.

"Why the questions?"

"I'm your sister. I'll always ask questions," Nikisha said.

Dimple pulled the sun visor down and looked in the mirror.

"I mean, I guess he's a friend."

"A friend you have sex with?"

"Nikisha!" Dimple felt her face go hot. "Why would you ask that? You're my half sister!"

"Sister. And I'm not asking to have sex with you, Dimple, relax." Nikisha laughed. "Now *you're* doing the only-child thing!"

Dimple considered this for a second.

"Yeah, you're right," she said. "But isn't it weird to talk to you about sex? Given that we're family."

"I'm your big sister," Nikisha said, quite sternly. "We can talk about anything. And we should."

"Okay, but can we talk about the thing at hand?" Dimple requested. "What shall I do about Kyron's mum?"

"Right." It was Nikisha's turn to stare ahead, but with focus. "You call her back. No mention of Roman. In fact, call her back right now while you're in the car, say you were doing something boring, like food shopping. Not out with friends, nothing. You're going through a breakup, remember."

Dimple nodded along.

"Oh yeah, shit. You're right. And also I don't have any friends."

"You sound as sad as you can, and you ask how Kyron is," Nikisha said. "If she asks if you've seen him, you *do not* say when you saw him last. No specifics. No days, times. If she pushes you for a date, you say you don't remember because the breakup has made all the days blur into one, or something. Then you say you've got to go because you're in the car and need to get the shopping into the house."

"Okay." Dimple pulled her phone out of her pocket. "Now? Shall I do it now?"

Nikisha nodded.

Dimple tapped Lynette's name and pressed the speakerphone

icon. She chewed her lip as it rang and looked at Nikisha, who mouthed "it's fine" at her.

"Hello?" Lynette's voice cut through the silent car, filling the space that Dimple suddenly realized was so small it was constricting. She focused on breathing properly.

"Hey, Lynette, it's Dimp. Sorry I missed your call. I was in Sainsbury's getting some food and some bubble bath and some toilet tissue."

"Too specific," Nikisha mouthed. "Relax."

Lynette ignored Dimple's shopping list.

"Dimp, when's the last time you saw Kyron?" She sounded tired. Her voice sounded hollow and hoarse.

"I . . . can't remember, Lynette," Dimple said. "We're having some space after everything. I told him we should be friends and since then he hasn't spoken to me. How is he?"

Nikisha nodded and mouthed, "Good."

"It's been over a week, Dimp," Lynette said, her voice breaking as she said Dimple's name. "This is the longest I haven't heard from him."

"That's weird," Dimple said. "Are you sure he isn't just lying low or something? He does that a lot. He always used to do that with me—I wouldn't hear from him for weeks sometimes. I used to think he was ghosting me."

Nikisha stared at her sister, telepathically warning her not to say so many words.

"I've rung around everyone, Dimp. I know you two broke up before I went away, but I'm only calling 'cause I know he still loves you so much. I know he had a temper, but it's just because he was so full of love. He didn't know how to handle it. It would just burst out of him."

Nikisha rolled her eyes.

"Is there anything I can do to help?" Dimple asked.

Nikisha reached over and pressed the mute button on Dimple's phone.

"What are you doing?" she asked.

"I don't know!" Dimple threw her hands up. "I felt bad!"

"Hello? You there, Dimp?" Lynette was saying.

"Stick to the script," Nikisha said before unmuting the call.

"Dimp? Where have you gone?" Lynette's pleading, in an even sadder voice somehow, filled Dimple's ears and sank her heart.

"Sorry, I'm here," Dimple said. "Bad reception round here, sorry."

"Stop apologizing, Dimp, you haven't done anything wrong. But look, it would be great to have your help."

"Anything!" Dimple said, a knee-jerk reaction to being asked for help.

Nikisha muted the call again.

"For an only child you're very selfless," she said sarcastically, pursing her lips and exhaling loudly from her flared nostrils.

"I didn't know what to say!" Dimple unmuted the call. "Honestly, anything," she repeated to Lynette. "I'll do anything."

"Well, because I know you've got all them people who watch your videos—"

"Well, it's not really that many," Dimple said. She didn't want to sell Lynette a false dream. Again.

"So I wondered if you could do a little video appeal?" Lynette said. "Everyone will know who he is 'cause they've seen you two together for God knows how long, so if you could put his picture up and ask people to get in touch if they've seen him?"

Dimple looked at Nikisha. Nikisha looked back at Dimple.

"No," Nikisha mouthed. She shook her head aggressively, her headscarf almost tumbling off.

"Of course, Lynette," Dimple said, her eyes locking with her sister's.

Nikisha leaned forward so her head pressed on the steering wheel, the action of which beeped the horn continuously.

"Anyway, I should go! I've got to take this shopping inside!" Dimple tried to be as casual as possible.

"You have a good rest of the weekend, darlin'," Lynette said. "When shall I look out for the video? I'll get the rest of the family to share it. Maybe Monday?"

"Monday." Dimple nodded. "Sure. Great. I'll text you the link once I've done it."

"And what time?" Lynette asked.

"Is she serious?" Nikisha asked more loudly than she should have. "Who's that with you?"

"Nobody— Got to go, Lynette! I'll do the video on Monday, bye-bye-bye!"

Dimple put the phone down and let out an exhale.

"And how do *you* think that went?" Nikisha asked her sister.

"Can you help me do the video, please?"

Nikisha stared back at Dimple for what was effectively an eternity.

"Get out of my car," she said eventually.

"What was that about?" Roman asked Dimple when she stepped back into the house. "It looked like you two were arguing but you were both looking at the dashboard."

"Oh no." Dimple shook her head. "We were on the phone to someone."

"Your dad?" Roman asked.

Dimple laughed for what felt like the first time in months. Life hadn't been very good to her in a long time and things definitely weren't picking up.

"No! Never. We were on the phone to Kyron's mum," she said.

"What?" Roman's hands went to his head. "So this new sister you have knows who Kyron is and is having nice chats on the phone to his mum with you? Does your sister even know who I am?"

"It's not like that!"

"What's it like, then?"

"She thinks he's missing."

"Come again?" Roman laughed. "No, he's not, he's just not about."

"No, apparently he's really missing," Dimple said, testing the waters. "I'm assuming none of you lot have heard from him."

"Rah," Roman said. "I thought he was just quiet. Does anyone know where he's gone?"

"He's—" Dimple looked at Roman. "He's missing, Roman. Nobody knows where he's gone. That's the point."

"Shit," Roman said. "So you were telling the truth when you said you and him were done?"

Dimple nodded.

"I'm really tired. Can we go to bed?"

Roman got up from the sofa and pulled Dimple up with him.

"Can you get me some water, please?" she asked him. "I might have a shower."

Roman nodded and shuffled toward the kitchen.

Dimple texted Janet, who was already tearing her hair out at home, to say that she was staying at a friend's. Before Janet could reply reminding Dimple that she didn't *have* any friends, she put her phone on airplane mode then stood in the shower practicing what she'd say in Kyron's appeal video in her head. She always did her best rehearsals in the shower. Maybe he was dead. Maybe after he climbed out of the van he slunk off somewhere to hide out till he figured out what he wanted to do, then somehow wrote an account of what happened that would be found any day now, and then the head injury really killed him. While she didn't necessarily hope this was the case, it definitely would be easier.

She finished showering, wrapped herself in the special towel Roman had bought her when she first started staying over, and placed herself in front of the mirror. She wiped the steam from it and stared at her reflection. She smiled, and began to mouth her speech.

"You done?" Roman knocked on the bathroom door and jolted Dimple out of her private rehearsals.

"Yeah, one sec." She stared at herself in the mirror for a few seconds. She was worried. But she didn't know what about. She didn't know which part of all this was concerning her. And that worried her the most.

Dimple padded into Roman's bedroom.

"Can you turn the heating on?" she asked Roman, who was already in bed, contact lenses out, glasses on, doing something or other on his phone. The soft light from his lamp made him look even more beautiful to her. Not that she'd ever tell him that for fear of being called a moist yute, or accused of trying to make their thing something it wasn't.

The thing they had had never had a name. She'd met Roman the same night she'd met Kyron, but Kyron was more vocal about wanting her. There'd been something between her and Roman straightaway, something that had felt much deeper and more immediate than what she and Kyron had actually ever had, but Dimple had decided it was better to ignore it. Until she hadn't.

She felt drawn to Kyron; he was exciting, there was a rush and a validation she got when she'd finally hear from him after weeks of quiet, or when he'd chase her and demand that she come back to him. It was toxicity at its finest, and she knew that, but the thrill of it all overrode the part of her that probably loved Roman. Loving someone scared her too much. So she did both, at a level she could manage. And in not giving the thing she and Roman had a name, it made it easier for them both to leave Kyron out of it. Until today, when Roman was suddenly in his feelings about being second best or whatever.

"No," he said. "Can you just get in the bed where it's warm?"

"But the air is what's cold," Dimple told him, hanging the towel on the radiator. "And my face is going to be in the cold air and I won't be able to sleep."

She opened his wardrobe and reached for a T-shirt.

"Why you putting a T-shirt on for?" Roman asked, throwing his phone onto the bed. "Just come here."

"Can we just go to sleep?" Dimple said as she pulled on one of his long-sleeved T-shirts. It was so big it went down to her knees.

"What's up with you?" Roman asked, sitting up and crossing his legs. "Why don't you want to have sex? It's not a pressure ting, I just want to know."

"I'm just tired." Dimple smiled at Roman and climbed into the bed next to him.

"Is it me? Have I done something?"

"No!" Dimple said. "I feel all weird and sensitive."

"Is it that thing?" Roman asked. "That PMS thing. And before you say anything, I'm not saying it's 'cause you're a woman. Even though obviously you are a woman. But I'm just wondering if it's that. Not being like, 'You women all have PMS.'"

Dimple laughed as she moved into him and closed her eyes. "Maybe it's that. Night."

Roman kissed her on the forehead and turned his lamp off.

"Night."

———————

"Hi, everyone." Dimple looked directly into the camera and smiled a sad smile. "Just here in my room, taking some time for myself. I know it's been a while, and I've seen all your messages and just want to say thanks, I'm still here, and I love you all. It's just . . . I'm here with a plea."

"Request," Prynce said from behind her.

"What?" Dimple paused the recording and turned around.

"He's right," said Lizzie, who had, instead of going to the police, undertaken an independent risk assessment at home before deciding to stick with her half-siblings and see how this played out. "Plea sounds a bit . . . I dunno. Like, a bit desperate. Like you're too emotionally involved."

"But I *should* be emotionally involved." Dimple threw her head back. "I'm about to ask people to search for my ex. I'm meant to be all sad and begging."

"Yeah, I think I know what Lizzie means," Danny said from the doorway. "But then I think request sounds a bit serious."

"Say, 'I need you to do something for me,'" Nikisha suggested from the bed. "That way you're asking for help and it sounds inclusive."

The others nodded in agreement.

Dimple faced the camera again, pressed record.

"And Dimple, be a bit more nice," Prynce said.

"What do you mean, 'be a bit more nice'?" Dimple said, stopping the recording and turning back around.

"Like, ask how they are? I know they're all watching you, but it shouldn't be a one-way street."

Dimple rolled her eyes at her half brother and faced the camera again.

"Nobody say anything now, please. I just want to get this done."

"You know we've all taken time out of our days to help you with this, right?" Lizzie asked. "Just checking you know that. If you're going to be snapping at us."

"She knows," Danny said. "She's just tense. You got this. One take, let's go."

Dimple went to press record when Prynce's phone started to buzz. She turned round to stare at him as he answered.

"What's going on, Tajaana? . . . I was just about to call you, you know. What you on tonight?"

"Prynce," Lizzie said firmly. "I want to get out of here, I have things to do."

Prynce waved a hand at Lizzie.

". . . that was just my sister, Lizzie. Tajaana, come on. I don't even have time to chat to anyone but you . . . I promise! Why would I lie, babes? Look, we're in the middle of something so I'm gonna shout you later, yeah? Yeah. You too."

Prynce ended the call and put his phone in his pocket.

"At my last count that's three," Dimple said.

"What can I say? I have a lot of love to give," Prynce told her.

Dimple began again.

"Hey, everyone. Hope you're all good. I—"

Prynce jumped in.

"Sorry, last thing. I think you should turn your light down, make it a bit more dull. The way it is now is a bit too, like, bright and exciting. You know what I mean?"

"Prynce, I really don't," Dimple said flatly.

"Mmm, he's not wrong," Lizzie said.

"Sorry, did you two do the same cinematography course?" Dimple asked.

"Just try what he's saying," Nikisha told Dimple.

Dimple dimmed the ring light.

"Are we all happy?" she asked. "And are we all out of shot?"

"Got a bit of a temper when you're ready, haven't you?" Danny laughed.

"Yes! I do!" Dimple snapped.

"Are you hungry?" Danny asked. "I've got some chocolate in the car, I could grab it for you."

"I don't want any chocolate, I just want this to be over!"

"All right." Danny crossed his arms. "Was just trying to help."

Dimple pressed record.

"Hey, everyone, happy Monday. I hope you're all good. I'm so sorry I've been quiet, but I've been thinking about you all. And thank you so, so much to anyone who messaged me. I've just been lying low in my room and getting my head together. But . . . I need you to do something for me."

Nikisha nodded to herself from the bed.

"I spoke to Kyron's mum, Lynette, yesterday and . . ." Dimple paused. "She told me that he hasn't been seen for a while. I don't know how long for, but it sounds pretty serious. Obviously, he and I ended things on good terms, but even if we hadn't, I would give anything, everything to know he's okay. So, if you've seen him, or you know anything, please, please comment below. And, Kyron, if you see this, please come home. We miss you."

Dimple looked down at the floor and exhaled slowly before stopping the recording.

"Did you study acting?" Prynce asked.

"You did say your favorite subject was drama, didn't you!" Danny said.

"I think you overdid it a bit, you know," Lizzie said.

"Which bit?" Dimple asked, spinning round in her chair.

"Don't tell her, she'll just be annoyed," Prynce said.

"No, it's good for me to know this stuff." Dimple crossed her arms defensively. "For the future."

"No, I've seen a couple of your videos. You're good in general, even though not a lot of people are watching. Even so, you're very much an influencer in spirit, you've got that down," Lizzie explained as Prynce stifled a laugh. "But the thing about 'ending things on good terms.' Did you need to say that, do you think?"

"It's fine," Prynce said. "People will just chalk it up to her being emotional and centering herself. She always does that in her videos, so it's not like it's out of character."

Dimple jerked her head back.

"Do I?"

"Yeah." Danny nodded. "But that's just your thing, isn't it?"

"Sorry, are you all just in your houses watching my videos and talking about how and where I could improve?" Dimple cocked her head as she waited for an answer that she hoped was no.

"No!" everyone exclaimed in unison. She didn't believe them.

"One thing I will say—" Prynce said.

"One thing?" Dimple asked. "To add to all the other things, you mean?"

"Don't you think it's a bit mad? The thing you said about commenting below if anyone sees Kyron?"

"How you mean?" Dimple was so annoyed at this point.

"Like, it's a human life, init?" Prynce said. "Isn't it so mad to be, like, 'comment below' when you're talking about a human life? It's like you're reducing a person to Internet matter. Like, comment below if you're feeling my outfit or something. It's just wild."

Dimple blinked at her half brother and wondered if she murdered him right there as he stood, would the rest of their siblings help her hide his dead body also.

"You got any food in the house?" Danny asked Dimple. "I'm starving and chocolate isn't going to do anything for me."

"Yes," Dimple told him. "There's some curry chicken in the fridge—and some vegetable curry for you, Lizzie. I might center myself in everything, but I remembered you're vegan." Dimple waited for someone to challenge this but they didn't. "Could someone make the rice while I upload this video, please?"

"You don't know how to make rice?" Prynce asked.

"Thank you for offering, Prynce." Dimple smiled as she tried to regulate her temper. "You'll be able to find everything in the kitchen."

Danny, Nikisha, Lizzie, and Prynce left the room, in that order, and Dimple got to work while she listened to them clatter around her kitchen. She wondered if this new and sudden insecurity was coming from the fact that she'd tried to hide a body and the guilt of that was playing tricks with the rest of her mind, or that suddenly she had four people in her life who had no issue with picking her apart every time she opened her mouth.

Dimple chopped and cut the video and added a picture of Kyron to the end of it. Then she thought it might be better to use one of both of them so it looked like she really, really missed him. And then she wondered if she did miss him or not. She missed things about him. But then she realized that she missed the things he showed her in the beginning, and how those things, like buying her gifts, and the attention, and the passion—which she'd realized was aggression— faded away fairly quickly. His representative had stopped showing up about three months in, and the following two years and seven months had been an emotional assault course, but she'd already announced the relationship on her socials so couldn't break up with him at that point in case she looked fickle to whoever had seen it. Dimple looked at the picture of both of them for a while before uploading the video, recalling the moment it had been taken. A few minutes before, he'd told her that she should stop eating chocolate because the fat was going to the wrong places.

"Who are you?" Janet's voice rang up from the kitchen and jolted Dimple out of her thoughts.

"Shit." She ran down the stairs and into the kitchen, where she saw her mum staring at Prynce, who was gently placing a lid on the rice pan, Danny, who was trying to figure out the microwave, and Lizzie, who was explaining it to him. Nikisha getting herself a drink from the fridge looked like it was about to be Janet's breaking point.

"Mum! I didn't think you'd be home till much later!" Dimple said, hugging her mum quickly.

"So you *are* here." Janet looked at her daughter, confusion lining her face. "And here I was thinking these strangers had broken into my kitchen to cook themselves dinner!"

"Oh," Dimple said. "They aren't strangers."

"Well, you could have given me some notice before you had so many friends round. But anyway, they're here now."

"We aren't her friends." Nikisha placed her drink down on the side as she turned to Janet, who narrowed her eyes as she focused on the four people in front of her.

"Mum, this is Nikisha."

Nikisha smiled.

"This is Danny."

Danny waved, walked over to Janet, and pulled her into a hug she definitely didn't want.

"Lizzie."

Lizzie nodded and crossed her arms.

"And Prynce! The youngest. Obviously."

Prynce beamed at Janet, his teeth lighting up the kitchen.

"How you doing?"

"I see." Coldness dripped from Janet's voice as realization set in. "They're your half brothers and sisters."

Dimple could see her mum's mind going very fast.

"I don't think we need to say 'half.'" Nikisha smiled. "Blood is blood."

Dimple's stomach turned as she pictured Kyron's blood on the kitchen floor. So much was happening in her head.

"When did . . . this happen?" Janet asked, motioning her hands around the kitchen.

"I saw Dimple in Croydon a few weeks ago, and we said how much of a shame it was that we were all adults and we didn't know each other. So here we are. Getting to know each other," Nikisha said, lying.

"Mmm," Janet said. "Well, continue making yourselves at home, won't you? Dimp, can I chat to you for a sec?"

Janet pulled Dimple out of the room the way she would when she was young and in trouble; a very small and specific pinch on the arm that nobody could quite see the severity of.

When she'd ushered her daughter into the very small utility cupboard and closed the door behind them, Janet looked at Dimple very sternly for a long time.

"They're gonna think something is weird now," Dimple said. "Why are we talking in the utility cupboard, Mum?"

"Because I don't want them to hear us!" Janet hissed.

"Yeah, no, I definitely got that. But what d'you need to say to me now that you couldn't say when they were gone? They haven't moved in."

"Why are Cyril's kids in my house, Dimple?" Janet said, louder than the first time.

"They're not 'Cyril's kids,' they're my siblings!"

"Half-siblings," Janet said, correcting her daughter. "Don't forget it. And why is it you haven't seen them for how many years and now here they are in my kitchen, eating my food?"

"Mum. What?" This was the first time Dimple had seen her mum like this. She didn't like who she was seeing either.

"Well, you have to ask yourself, don't you? Why haven't you had them in your life up until now? They've obviously seen you on the Internet and they think you're doing well, and that you've got money, and they want some!"

Dimple wanted to laugh at how far from the truth her mother's understanding was.

"No, Mum," Dimple said. "I got in touch with Nikisha a few days after me and Kyron broke up. I think I needed a big sister."

She knew how much this would hurt her mum. Which was and wasn't the desired effect.

"You sat in your room for all that time and didn't talk to me, but you got in touch with a stranger?" Janet couldn't believe the betrayal.

"A stranger?" Dimple said in disbelief. "Anyway, excuse me. I need to get back to them. Don't worry, we'll all eat and I'll have them out of your precious house soon."

Dimple squeezed past Janet and made her way back into the kitchen. Prynce was spooning rice out onto plates and Danny was struggling with the warmed-up container of curry chicken.

"I got a plate out for your mum," Prynce told Dimple. "She hungry?"

"No, she's going to have a bath," Dimple said. "She's had a long day."

"Actually, I think I'll eat with all of you first," Janet said as she entered the kitchen. "Let's sit down. We can sit around the table in the conservatory."

As decreed by Janet, they all sat around the large wooden table in the conservatory, uncomfortably. Janet sat at the head of the table, with her daughter to her left. Lizzie sat next to Dimple, and next to Lizzie and opposite Janet sat Danny. Prynce propped himself on the table by his elbows to the left of Danny, and Nikisha was next to him.

"So," Janet said. "What do all of you do? Let's go round the table."

She picked up her fork, speared a piece of chicken, and looked to her right.

"Nikisha?"

"I do this and that," Nikisha answered her. "But I've got two children who keep my hands pretty full."

"Ah, and how old are they?" Janet asked.

"Nicky is nine, and Amara is two." Nikisha smiled. "They're really special kids."

"What a gap!" Janet smiled back at Nikisha. "Same dad?"

"Oh yes." She nodded.

"I see." Janet's smile tightened.

"It's like history repeating itself, I guess." She smiled back at Janet. It was like passive-aggressive smiling tennis.

"And you, Prynce?"

"I don't have any kids," he answered.

"No." Janet looked at him quizzically. "Your job."

"Oh." Prynce laughed. "I do this and that, too, I guess. But mainly make money from doing delivery driving. Well, biking. Like, food and that."

"Right." Janet looked pointedly at her daughter. "By food do you mean drugs?"

"Ha, no." Prynce laughed again. "By food, I mean food that people eat."

"And you two have the same mum?" she asked. "Obviously I lost touch with your dad many years ago, but I did hear something like that."

"Yes," Nikisha said. "Obviously our mum was someone Cyril couldn't forget."

"Indeed." Janet pursed her lips. "And you, Daniel?"

"It's Danny," Danny said, correcting her. "Danny isn't short for Daniel or anything. It's Danny on my birth certificate, passport, driving license, everything."

"I see!" Janet said. "How unusual."

"Is it? But yeah, I'm a plumber," Danny told her.

"And you were in prison before that?" Janet asked.

"Mum!" Dimple sat up in her chair. "Why would you ask that?"
Danny nodded.

"I was, you know."

"I do know." Janet took a sip of her wine. "I heard of your case a few years back. You know I'm a barrister, don't you?"

Danny nodded once more.

"And I'd recognize that surname anywhere."

"But it was what it was," Danny said. "I was younger then. Reckless. But I don't regret it."

"You don't regret doing what you did?" Janet asked. "Surely you must."

"No, I mean, I regret what I did, yeah, but I don't think it makes me a bad person, if that makes sense. And I'm not embarrassed about my past. Like . . . I don't regret that I did something in my past. 'Cause I've grown from it. And we all make mistakes, don't we?"

"But that was a very big mistake, wasn't it?" Janet smiled again.

Danny didn't answer.

Janet pressed on. "And you, Lizzie?"

"Elizabeth to people I'm not close to, thanks," Lizzie said. "I'm training to be a doctor."

"Oh!" Janet exclaimed. "So at least one out of all of you has a proper job!"

"Mum!" Dimple yelped again. "I'm so sorry."

"No, I'm including you in that, Dimple." Janet took another sip of wine. "You know I don't see sitting in front of a camera three times a week and showcasing things that get sent in the post that clog up my hallway a proper job."

"Well, I'm not a doctor yet," Lizzie said. "And I don't see my job, or see myself, as more important than Prynce delivering food or Danny fixing a boiler that provides an entire block of flats with hot water."

"I see your mother raised you well!" Another sip of wine.

"She did," Lizzie said. "And being a single mother wasn't easy for her."

"Well, I know what that's like." Janet laughed, but the laugh was fooling nobody. "That Cyril Pennington. He was really something. How often do you all see him? I know Dimp hasn't seen him since she was—how old were you, Dimp? Weren't you around twenty?"

Dimple, who was fuming, didn't want to speak to her mum, let alone about her dad.

The rest of them said variations of "I haven't seen him in years" almost in unison.

"I see." Janet nodded slowly. It was a hard thing for her to realize that she'd had a child with a man who had effectively abandoned all of his children. "Well, at least Dimple has had me as both of her parents. And I am fiercely, fiercely protective of my girl. And if anything at all were to happen to her, if any harm were to come to her, I would do everything in my power to ruin the persons responsible in every single way a person could be ruined."

"Well," Nikisha said. "It's a good thing we all have that in common, isn't it?"

Nikisha and Janet stared at each other like two fierce neighborhood cats, both of which were ready to strike at any second.

"I think it's time for us to go." Lizzie broke the silence and stood up.

"But I haven't finished," Danny said, heartbroken at the idea of leaving a plate with even one grain of rice left on it.

"You have," Lizzie told him. "And we'll wash up before we go."

"No, you don't have to do that." Dimple jumped up and started gathering the plates. When they were all teetering in a dangerous pile, she walked her half-siblings out as Janet waved a goodbye that was way too petty for a woman of fifty-two.

"I am so sorry," Dimple groaned as her half-siblings filed out of the front door and stood, looking like they'd gone through the washing machine on a fast cycle, on the path in front of the house. "I think it was just a shock to her."

"It's okay, we get it." Danny crossed his arms.

"Er, speak for yourself, Danny," Lizzie said. "Not to be rude to your mum, and I never want to be rude about someone's parent, but she's an adult woman! What does she get out of basically accusing us of coming into your life to fuck you over, or steal from you, or, I don't even know, just be sus to you in *any* way?"

"I'm sorry," Dimple groaned again. "She's just really protective. She always has been. She was the sort of mum to get in fights with the children who bullied me at school. All the teachers were scared of her."

"She still has a lot of healing to do, clearly," Nikisha muttered as she walked away. "Let us know about the video."

"What video?" Dimple asked.

"The appeal video," Prynce said.

"Oh God, I forgot about that." Dimple rolled her eyes at herself. "I will."

"And not over text." Nikisha pointed at Dimple.

"We can use WhatsApp surely, though?" Prynce asked. "It's encrypted, isn't it?"

"Not over text," Nikisha repeated. "Or WhatsApp. I don't care what they say about that encryption business. We don't trust any of it."

"Oh, before I forget," Prynce said. "It's my birthday next week and I'm having a little *gathering*. Would be nice if you could all come."

Dimple watched them amble down the path and laughed to herself when she heard Danny say how hungry he was. She watched them drive away, waving as they turned out of her street, and slammed the front door as she went back inside.

"Whose door are you slamming like that?" Janet called from the conservatory.

"Mum, how could you do that?" Dimple asked as she stormed back in. "They're nice people and I'm happy I have them in my life! They aren't here because they've seen me on the Internet, which to you isn't even a real job anyway. They're here because what's wrong with being connected to each other?"

Janet laughed nastily.

"You're too young. No, you aren't even too young, you're too *naïve*. You don't know anything about people and their motivations, Dimp."

"No, Mum, you're just projecting your shit because you're pissed off with Cyril." Dimple picked up the stack of plates and was determined not to let them fall while she was trying to make an important point.

"I'm not pissed off with that man!" Janet spluttered. "He isn't worth my energy, never was!"

"Whatever, Mum." Dimple tottered into the kitchen and messaged Roman, asking him to come and get her.

Dimple scraped what was left on the plates into the bin. As she stacked the dishwasher, Janet stumbled into the living room, glass in hand, and threw herself onto the sofa.

Dimple took a glass out of the cupboard and held it under the water dispenser that was built into the expensive fridge. She felt a bit embarrassed by the luxury of it. She was looking at everything a bit differently these days.

"Here you go." She padded over to Janet, took the wineglass away, and replaced it with the glass of water.

"I'm fine. I don't need water."

"Just drink the water." Dimple sighed. "I'm going out."

"Where are you going?"

"I'm just going out," Dimple called over her shoulder as she ran up the stairs and into her room. She closed her laptop and threw a change of clothes into a bag. By the time she was done, Roman had messaged her to say he was outside.

Dimple thundered down the stairs and opened the front door. "Bye!"

"Dimp?" Janet called after her.

"What?"

"Nikisha said you bumped into each other in Croydon for the first time. But you said you got in touch with her after you broke up with Kyron. Which one is it?"

"Er." Dimple should have known her mum's eagle ears would have picked up on that. "Both. See you tomorrow."

Dimple grabbed her coat, ran out of the house, and got into Roman's car.

———————

"You seen this?" Jenna asked, rolling over onto Kyron. He felt his dick stir as her bare breast landed on his chest.

"Seen what?" Kyron asked, opening his eyes. He still wasn't feeling 100 percent. He was drowsy, still in pain, but hadn't charged his phone. Priorities always in place, he hadn't gone home yet either.

He'd come to stay with one of his hookups while he tried to piece together what had happened. Jenna was cool. Everything in her little studio flat was pink, but she was cool. He liked that she was one of those girly women who had fairy lights and candles. She liked giving him head, too, and didn't mind that he never reciprocated. What he didn't know was that she was getting it somewhere else but was clever enough to keep all of her *own* links separate. She liked all of the guys in her rotation, but had told them she was busy this week. Looking after Kyron was a full-time job. She'd cooked for him, cleaned the wounds on his head and face, and made sure he took the painkillers she'd bought him.

"This." Jenna handed her phone to Kyron and pressed play on a video while he held it a few centimeters above his face.

"Hey, everyone, happy Monday." Dimple's voice played out. "I hope you're all good. I'm so sorry I've been quiet, but I've been thinking about you all. And thank you so, so much to anyone who messaged me."

Kyron watched the video. When it had finished, he handed Jenna's phone back to her.

"Why's your ex done that?" Jenna asked.

"I'm guessing my mum put her up to it." Kyron shrugged.

"She's racking up views off your name you know," Jenna said, looking through the numbers that the video had racked up. "You see, I would never do that."

"Why you watching her videos for?"

"Someone sent it to me! Everyone has been sharing it, it's everywhere."

Kyron didn't say anything. He didn't even really hear what Jenna had said.

"Have you let her know you're okay yet?" Jenna asked.

"Who? Dimple or my mum?" Kyron said, snapping back to reality.

"Why would I ask you if you'd let your ex know you were okay?" Jenna asked Kyron, lifting herself and her bare breast away from him.

"Come back, man," Kyron said, pulling her back into him. "I'll go home in a couple of days. Just need to chat to my boy first, see what he knows."

———————

Kyron had had so much rest that he'd tossed and turned all night till he gave up on sleep altogether. He got to Roman's early in the morning. He knew Roman was probably going to be up before the sun was for work. As he turned onto the street, he saw Roman's door open, and watched Roman step out of the house. Kyron went to cross the street, but stopped abruptly when he saw Dimple step out after him.

Kyron pulled his hood up and hid behind a van, watching through the van windows as Roman and Dimple exchanged a few words and tender touches before getting into his car and driving away. What the fuck was going on, and when the fuck did this start? Kyron was so angry he thought he was going to smash the window of the van he was hiding behind.

———————

Roman had to be at the betting shop he worked at to open up, so had dropped Dimple home at six thirty in the morning, an hour or so before Janet would be awake. Dimple kicked her sneakers off and slinked up the stairs, but stopped when she heard snuffling coming from the living room. She turned and went back down and tiptoed toward the sound.

She saw her mum lying on the sofa, wineglass in hand, and sighed as quietly as she could before creeping over and removing it. Dimple was too frustrated to feel sorry for Janet. She didn't want this to be happening again. She thought her mum had left all of the drinking alone a couple of years back after some intensive therapy, and yet here they were. She weighed up the two options: She could wake up her mum and risk an argument right here and now while she was drunk, but ultimately get her mum into bed; or she could leave her and maybe have the argument another time. She'd spent enough nights pouring her mum into bed, so she padded out of the living room quietly, took herself upstairs, and had a shower.

When she'd wrapped the towel around herself, she picked up her phone and sat on the edge of the bath. Why so many notifications?

Dimple opened the YouTube app, her eyes widening as she saw how many people had watched her plea for help. She went on to Twitter. Same thing. Instagram, too. Hundreds of people had shared her video, and ten times as many people had followed her.

Dimple went back to YouTube and scrolled through comment after comment that had been left under her video. So many well-wishers, so many people telling her Kyron would be fine but that they'd keep an eye out.

"Poor Kyron! He'll be found soon in Jesus name."
"I swear I saw him yesterday in Ladbroke Grove."

One comment made her stomach turn.

"This girl isn't convincing at all. She probably killed him and buried the body."

Dimple didn't sleep a wink that night. The followers were great, but the adrenaline of so much exposure pulsed through her veins. The notifications had carried on coming thick and fast throughout the day, the digital attention increasing before her eyes. But that comment, that one comment, had stuck with her and was going round and round in her head.

"She probably killed him and buried the body."

"Can we go another way?" Dimple asked her Uber driver as the car went to turn left after Loughborough Junction station.

"This is the quickest route, miss." The driver shrugged, carrying on past the Tesco Express on the right and flicking down his indicator.

As the car turned onto Loughborough Park, Dimple started to feel sick. The night they tried to hide Kyron's body began to replay in her mind, frame for frame. Not that it had ever stopped running through her subconscious, but to revisit the scene of the actual almost-crime was overwhelming. She opened the window to get some air as they turned the corner where the building site sat, and panicked when she saw yellow tape strung up on the railings. Had Kyron actually gone to the police? And they were assessing the area as a crime scene? What if there was CCTV? Her heart started racing.

"Can you just stop here a sec?" Dimple asked the driver. "I'm not feeling very well."

The driver screeched to a halt and Dimple opened the door and leaned out of the car so she could look at the building site closely.

Something close to relief fluttered through her when she saw that the tape wasn't police tape, but was actually warning tape accompanied by a sign about dangerous chemicals being used. Dimple's heart rate slowed down.

"I'm okay now," Dimple said, closing the car door. "Just felt a bit funny."

"Are you sure, miss?" The driver turned around and looked at her, worried this girl was going to mess up the back of his car. "You're only going a couple of minutes—maybe you should get out and walk."

"No, no." Dimple knew that if she tried walking, she wouldn't make it without falling over. "I'm fine, I promise you."

"Dimple!" Kyron's mother, Lynette, collapsed into Dimple's arms at the door before Dimple could even get her shoes off.

Their dog, a bulldog named Larry, rolled onto Dimple's feet.

"Hi, Lynette. How are you doing?" Dimple asked, even though Lynette's face was telling her exactly how Lynette was doing.

Kyron's face was so similar to Lynette's that Dimple had often wondered if his dad had even been in the room at the moment of conception. The same smooth, carob-colored skin, the same dark brown eyes lined with thick, straight lashes, the same deep Cupid's bow that led into a wide, soft mouth that showed big white teeth when it smiled.

"Come in the kitchen, darlin', I've put some food on. Is it warm enough in here for you? I know how cold you get." Lynette turned and walked ahead, her sliders smacking the laminate flooring as she went.

Dimple didn't want to stay and eat, she wanted to get in and get out.

"I'm fine, Lynette, I ate not too long ago!"

"Don't be silly!" Lynette smiled with soft, kind eyes. "You've never come here and not eaten."

That's where they parted ways, Dimple thought as she walked into the warm, fragrant kitchen, and Larry trotted along behind her, panting loudly. Kyron had the same eyes as his mum, but his were always cold, always suspicious. Lynette's eyes were always searching for the good in people. It was these eyes that made Dimple feel so guilty that she wanted to rip her heart out and hand it to Lynette. She hated seeing anyone in such emotional agony, let alone this woman who had been one of the saving graces of being in such a roller coaster of a relationship for almost three years.

Dimple pulled out a chair from the kitchen table and sat down. Lynette had already laid out a table mat and a knife and fork for Dimple.

"So, any news?" she asked Lynette.

Lynette sparked the stove on and lifted the lid from the pot in front of her. Slowly, she took a wooden spoon that had been sitting in a cup of water on the side and stirred the contents of the steaming pot. Dimple held her breath the whole time she watched her. It went on for ages; it was like watching a sloth climb up and down a tree.

"Nothing," Lynette said finally. "Let me just warm this a little more for you."

Dimple started to worry that Lynette knew everything, and that there was poison in the food. She decided that she'd eat it anyway, and if there was poison in there she'd die and at least the living hell of life as it was would be over with.

She leaned down and stroked Larry, who was now snoozing heavily at her feet.

"The last time I saw him was a couple of weeks ago," Lynette said. "He was always in and out, as you know, but he'd been here for his dinner the night before I went off to Antigua with Ernest. The next day I texted him to say I'd landed, he replied saying I should send him pictures, but then the pictures stopped going through a couple of days later, but I didn't think anything of it. I called him to see if he could pop to my sister's and check on Larry but it went through to voice mail, and that was it, Dimp. I came back early because you know me, I panicked that something had happened to him when I hadn't been here, but when I got home there was no trace of an accident, or a break-in, or anything."

"And it's been how long now?" Dimple asked, even though she knew it had been exactly one week and four days since they'd tried to bury Kyron's body round the corner from his mum's house.

"Well, I don't know, Dimple. He messaged me on the Friday, I came back early on Wednesday night, so let's say two weeks or so since I heard from him." Lynette dished some food out for Dimple.

"Thanks, Lynette." Dimple stood and reached for the plate, feeling so guilty that she hoped it was actual poison.

"And I've called the boys, I've called the hospitals, but nothing. Nobody has seen my son."

"Oh dear," was all Dimple could manage.

"Here you go, darlin'." Lynette popped the lid off a glass bottle of ginger beer and placed it on an Antigua coaster in front of Dimple. "Your favorite—I'll always remember."

Dimple smiled a thank-you and loaded her fork with rice. She told herself she had to force it down or else she'd look guilty.

"But, darlin', how are you coping with it all?" Lynette asked, pleading with those kind, soft eyes again.

"Coping with what?" Dimple asked, mentally steadying her hand so it didn't shake the rice off the fork.

"Well, you and Kyron were together for a long time." Lynette finally sat down opposite Dimple. "I know you called it a day, but heartbreak still hurts, doesn't it? And I know how much he loved you. Even though he could be a bit of a handful."

Dimple's eyebrows went up at the idea that Kyron could be a *bit* of a handful. The man was an emotional terrorist.

"I'm missing him, obviously, Lynette," Dimple said. "I thought that when I hadn't heard from him it was because it was finally done this time. You know we spent so much time going back and forth, and baaack and forth."

Lynette nodded along to the slow, convincing rhythm of what Dimple was saying.

"And so I miss him, yeah, I really do. But us being over was for the best, you know? And now I'm just waiting for him to . . . appear again so I can give him a hug." Dimple let tears come to her eyes and she pushed the plate away. "I'm sorry, I don't think I can eat any more," she whispered.

"Oh, darlin'. Don't worry, I'll put this in a container so you can take it away." Lynette placed a coarse hand on Dimple's.

"What have the police said?"

"You know the police, Dimple." Lynette gazed over Dimple's shoulder at the picture of Kyron as a baby that sat above the radiator. "Their first thing was to say he'd just show up. Then after a week of me calling them every night, lunchtime, and evening, and going down to the station, they said it was probably gang related. Imagine that! They didn't even think it to themselves. They just said it to me. 'Was he in a gang?' they asked me. 'Well, boy like him, he's probably got himself involved in trouble with something like that.'"

Fat tears started to roll down Lynette's face.

"He wasn't even like that, Dimple," Lynette sniffed. "And even if he was, it doesn't make him not worth looking for, not worth finding."

All Dimple could do was jump up from her seat and pull Lynette into a hug, even if it did mean dislodging Larry. It made her feel like the worst person in the entire world, especially because Lynette felt so small in her arms.

Dimple eased away from Lynette and went over to the kitchen counter. She ripped a piece of kitchen roll from the holder and went to wipe Lynette's tears, but realized she was truly making a mockery of the situation if she was going to hide a man's body and then wipe the tears from his mum's face when she cried, especially as he was probably lying dead in a bush due to the injuries they could have sorted out if they'd just taken him to hospital.

She sat back down and handed the kitchen roll over. Lynette took it and blew her nose loudly.

"Thank you, darlin'," she whispered.

"You don't have to thank me," Dimple told her. "But I'm still keeping an eye out in case anyone has seen him. They'll know to come to me."

Before she left, Dimple asked to use the bathroom, to which Lynette didn't even reply and just waved her up the stairs because her and Kyron's house had basically been Dimple's second home for the last three years.

Dimple washed her hands and, before she went back down the stairs, crept into Kyron's room. The curtains were closed. The bed was unmade. The room seemed suspended in time. She knew Lynette wouldn't want to touch it until she saw her son again. It smelled like him. The smell of 1 Million by Paco Rabanne, the fragrance Kyron wouldn't leave the house without wearing, hung in the air faintly.

Dimple remembered the last time she was in there. It was a couple of weeks back when she'd told him she thought that things should
finally, definitively, be over between them. She'd cried before he'd
got angry, he'd done everything he could not to cry, they'd had sex,
she'd said she meant it and had left, then she'd gone to Roman's and
just lay next to him, which had felt nicer than having sex with him.

Dimple sat on the edge of Kyron's bed and wondered if she was
a bad person until Lynette walked into the room and interrupted her
thoughts.

"He'll come back, Dimp, don't you worry." Lynette smiled, sitting down on the bed next to Dimple. "I can feel it."

Dimple was ashamed when the hope that he didn't come back
popped into her head. Everything would be easier if he just . . . stayed
gone. And at that point, they heard a key in the door.

"Mum?" Kyron called out from the hallway. Dimple's blood ran
cold when she heard his voice.

Kyron closed the door behind him, shivering as the hot air from
inside hit him.

"Lord have mercy! Ky?" Lynette screamed, jumping up from the
bed, using Dimple's thigh as a springboard. "Is that you?" She wailed,
running out of his door and thundering down the stairs. "Where
have you *been*? Do you know what you've put me through?"

Lynette went to hit Kyron, thought better of that, so went to hug
him, but stopped when she saw the stitches at the back of his head in
the mirror by the front door.

"Ky?" Lynette stumbled backward in horror, saving herself from
falling to the ground by holding on to the banister at the bottom of
the steps. "What happened to you?"

"I'm fine, Mum, I'm good," Kyron told his mother. "It looks
worse than it is, trust me."

The inner lioness stirred in Lynette as she got ready to go and
rip the throat out of whoever had hurt her son.

"Who did this to you?" she roared.

Kyron had never heard this tone from Lynette. And believe, she'd shouted at him a lot. He watched his mum as she turned and ran back to the kitchen.

When she got back to the hallway, she was holding the biggest kitchen knife she had.

"Who. Did this. To you?" Lynette repeated, holding the knife up in the air.

"Mum, Mum, none of that, please," Kyron said, reaching for the knife.

"Kyron, I'm not joking!" Lynette roared again, moving the knife out of her son's reach.

"Mum, can you calm down, please?" Kyron said. "My head is banging and you're doing bare shouting."

The hallway was filled with the sound of Lynette breathing heavily, loudly, through her nostrils.

"What *happened* to you? Please tell me," she asked Kyron, moving around her son so she could take a close look at his injuries.

"Put the knife down, though," Kyron told her.

Lynette set the knife on the table by the front door and put her hands up to Kyron's stitches.

"Don't touch them, Mum." Kyron winced as he felt her fingers heading toward the wound.

"Who did this to my baby?" Lynette wailed. Tears had started to fall. Kyron was surprised it had taken this long for her to cry.

Dimple, who had been frozen at the top of the stairs, slowly descended the steps, eyes on the floor so she didn't fall. It was time to face the music. She was ready to accept a life in prison, after Lynette had beaten her up.

When Kyron saw Dimple coming down the stairs shakily, he wasn't *surprised* to see her in his house. Dimple was always one to go where the emotion was. He wondered if Roman was there, too, knowing that he'd have to firm his anger and deal with them both later.

It took Dimple a few seconds before she could look at Kyron.

When she did, her heart sank to her knees. He looked awful. His body looked weak. His usually rich skin was ashy, dull. The scratches on his face had scabbed over. His shape-up, sharp as a razor on any other day, had grown out.

"I don't think you're gonna believe me, Mum." Kyron shook his head, looking at Dimple.

Dimple gulped, ready to explain herself, throw herself to the ground crying, do whatever it took to be immediately forgiven.

"How you mean?" Lynette came back round to face her son, her cheeks soaking wet. "I saw you looking fine two weeks ago and now you've come back with . . . with . . . *this* on your head, your face is *ruined*, and you're telling me I won't believe you? Try me!"

"I dunno, Mum." Kyron shook his head slowly.

Dimple narrowed her eyes as she tried to understand what Kyron was doing.

"What do you mean?" Lynette stared at her son, searching for the answer in his eyes.

"I mean I don't know, Mum," Kyron repeated. "I don't remember who did this."

Kyron, like most men, lied. And actually, quite convincingly, most of the time. But he had one tell, one that Dimple had clocked over the years. When he lied, the story he was spinning went on and on. It would go to weird and wonderful places as Kyron tried to convince both the person (usually Dimple) and himself that he was telling the truth.

And so the simplicity of his response made Dimple realize: He really didn't remember.

"Nikisha!" Dimple shouted at the phone. "Where are you? It's Kyron!"

Nikisha sighed the biggest sigh Dimple had ever heard. She could almost feel Nikisha's breath on her ear through the phone.

"I'm seeing you in a bit, can't you wait? What did I say about the phone?"

"I know, but he's back!" Dimple shouted. "He turned up at his mum's when I was there and—"

"Did you speak to him?" Nikisha asked.

"No, his mum jumped on him and was crying and it all felt a bit like *EastEnders* so I said I'd leave them to it."

"Okay." Nikisha took a deep breath. "Carry on acting like everything is normal until he says anything."

"The thing is, Nik . . . I think he's *forgotten* everything. But you want me to gaslight him?" Dimple asked. "It's not in my nature."

"Well, you'd better make it your nature," Nikisha said. "It's just a bit of damage control. You need to make him think everything is fine. Lie. Convince him you still love him."

"I don't *not* love him. It might have been over, bu—"

"Dimple! Focus!"

"Okay, okay," Dimple said. "His mum invited me round to his welcome home party. I'll let you know how it goes."

"Welcome home party?" Nikisha was confused. "Didn't you say he just got back?"

"Yeah, but that's just how Lynette is," Dimple told her. "Any reason to throw her son a party."

"Dimple," Nikisha said.

"Mmm?"

"Find out *what* he knows. And don't tell the others until we're all together."

———————

The next evening, despite Kyron wanting the scars on his face to heal more than they already had before any people (girls) saw him, Dimple made her way, anxiety propelling her, to Kyron's speedily organized welcome home party. Despite his wishes, and his injuries, Lynette had always loved a party, especially one for Kyron, so when

Dimple arrived, she had to squeeze her way through all the family members who'd gone to the house to celebrate his return.

His cousin Trina opened the door and hugged Dimple hello and thanked her for making the video, before she was pulled away to help in the kitchen by her sister Makeda. Trina was probably Kyron's most loyal cousin; at his last birthday party she'd kicked Roman out for making a joke during Lynette's speech. So if she was hugging Dimple, she probably didn't know anything.

Dimple made her way into the house, wondering what her role should be here. How should she act? What should she say to people? She wasn't Kyron's girlfriend anymore, but should her role here be "trying to get him back"? Or should she just be his friend now? They'd never been friends, so this would be a weird time to start, but if she convinced him and everyone else that she wanted him back, she could go some way to finding out the last thing he remembered from that night.

She found Kyron standing in the kitchen, surrounded by people. Next to him was a slim, dark-skinned girl with big eyes framed by a set of lashes Dimple wished she had, a delicate nose, and full lips. The girl pushed her body close into Kyron's, but Dimple didn't feel jealous of this girl, who she readily accepted was much better-looking than her. She just didn't care about Kyron like that anymore. This girl could have him. But *he* needed to think she wanted him.

She finally caught Kyron's eye as she walked in and smiled widely at him, waving as she moved past his uncles who were playing dominoes loudly at the kitchen table. He looked back at her but didn't smile.

When Dimple finally got to him, he stepped away from the girl and toward her stiffly. He let her hug him. She pushed her warm, soft body against his to remind him of the good times, but he didn't hug her back.

"You good?" Dimple asked him. "Are we good?"

Kyron nodded slowly.

"I'm good."

"And I'm Jenna." The girl with the eyelashes smiled in a way that was not friendly.

"Nice to meet you." Dimple smiled back in a way that *was* friendly.

"Why is she here?" Jenna asked Kyron.

"Oh, don't start." Kyron closed his eyes in annoyance.

"How you mean, 'don't start'?" Jenna asked.

"Where's your friend?" Kyron asked Dimple, ignoring Jenna.

"Which friend?" Dimple asked, confused. He knew full well she didn't have friends like that.

"Here he is," Kyron said, gesturing toward the kitchen door as Roman walked in.

"What d'you mean?" Dimple asked before she saw the look on Kyron's face. He obviously knew.

Dimple, and everyone else in the kitchen, watched as Kyron pushed through his family, his fist raised, before he brought it crashing into Roman's jaw.

"What's going on?" Trina screamed, making her way between them.

"Him and her," Kyron growled, pushing Trina out of the way before he raised his fist again and swung a second time. This time, Roman dodged it and pushed Kyron away from him. He wasn't going to hit Kyron back because he knew he was in the wrong, but he was going to defend himself.

"Kyron!" Trina screamed again. "Have you lost your mind?"

"What's happening?" Lynette asked as she ran into the kitchen.

"How many years we known each other, bro?" Kyron shouted as he charged toward Roman, this time wrapping his arms around Roman's waist as he propelled them both backward into the wall.

Roman struggled as he tried to push Kyron off him.

"Boys!" Lynette shouted as she watched Kyron and Roman crash into the dining table, falling into everyone who was in their way.

"Get off me, man!" Roman twisted himself out of Kyron's grasp and shoved him away.

Dimple's hand flew to her mouth as Kyron stumbled backward and hit his head on the kitchen counter. Her stomach turned as she watched not-so-distant history repeat itself.

Kyron landed on the floor and Lynette ran over to him, screaming like a banshee. Dimple held her breath for what felt like a lifetime until she saw Kyron's eyes flicker, then open slowly.

"I'm all right, I'm all right," he said as a couple of his boys pulled him up. Instead of going for Roman again, who was braced for round two, Kyron stood still, as the events of that night finally trickled back into his memory.

He looked around the room for Dimple, but she was already gone.

"So you'll still fight for her?" Jenna asked Kyron. "Fuck you. We're done."

"We was never started," Kyron sneered.

The next morning, Dimple woke up and, with only one eye open, checked her phone. Among the new followers letting her know that Kyron had been found safe, one text stood out:

Kyron:

250 bags

That didn't last very long, Dimple thought, anxiety knotting her stomach. She knew there'd be repercussions, but she hadn't guessed they would be financial ones. She screenshotted his text and sent it over to Nikisha, who replied straightaway with an address and a time:

243A Sunset Drive
Thornton Heath
CR7 8FT
4 p.m.

––––––––––

"Is this 243?" Dimple's Uber driver asked her.

"Yeah, this will do, thanks," Dimple said quickly, jumping out. She eyed the door with no number suspiciously before the net curtains in the front window twitched and were pulled across to reveal Nikisha, who gave a quick wave.

Dimple opened the broken gate and walked up the path, arriving at the front door as it swung open.

"Come in, come in." Nikisha smiled, ushering Dimple in. "Shoes off."

Nikisha was wearing an oversized teal sweater and light blue jeans. Her feet were in a pair of fluffy gray slippers. Dimple tried to work out exactly how old her elder sister was from her outfit, but gave up as she kicked off her as-expensive-as-they-were-uncomfortable sneakers.

She followed her elder sister into what was meant to be a living room but was instead a storage room for furniture. Everything about that room was precarious and unfinished. Someone seemed to have wallpapered only half of the room, and the rest was a color that was only slightly more depressing than beige.

"Is this your place?" Dimple asked, looking for somewhere to sit.

"No." Nikisha shook her head. "I'm kind of staying here for a friend of mine who goes away for a few months at a time. Sometimes my housing situation is a bit here and there, so I house-sit for him. At the moment he's in Calgary. Ever been?"

"I haven't, actually," Dimple replied. "You?"

Dimple wondered if it was that Nikisha had nerves of steel, or that she was just good at hiding what she was feeling. The doorbell rang, putting a welcome stop to their awkward small talk.

"Who could that be?" Nikisha asked as she left the room.

Dimple perched on the side of an old cabinet as Lizzie walked into the room, her bright and tight floral dress filling the room with some much-begged-for color.

"Oh," Lizzie said, weirdly surprised to see Dimple in front of her. "Hi. How you doing?"

"Yeah." Dimple shrugged. "I think I'm all right. How about you?"

Nikisha popped her head into the room.

"I'm making some food. Are either of you hungry?"

"No," Dimple and Lizzie said in unison, their almost identical tone of voice not lost on Nikisha.

"Suit yourselves." Nikisha nodded, making her way to the kitchen.

Dimple tried to talk normally to Lizzie until she realized that recent events hadn't bonded them for all eternity and gave up altogether.

Danny arrived next, letting his sisters know that he couldn't stay for long because he had to collect Marley from nursery in the next hour.

"But what's this about?" he asked Nikisha. "Why have you brought us to some secret HQ?"

"When Prynce gets here Dimple will explain everything," Nikisha told him. "Find somewhere to sit if you can."

Danny sat on the floor between Dimple, who was still perched on the cabinet, and Lizzie, who'd managed to find a stool under the stairs.

"Don't you want to sit on something?" Dimple asked him.

"Nah, I've been on the floor all day, no point stopping now," he said. "And my overalls are dirty anyway. Don't want to mess up this . . . stuff."

He turned to look at Nikisha.

"Who's cooking?"

"I'm making a stir-fry," Nikisha answered. "You want some?"

Danny nodded and Nikisha left the room again.

"You two girls okay?" Danny asked his sisters, looking up at them.

"It's so funny. You could be nonidentical twins, you know. What are they called, Lizzie? It's like, maternal or fraternal or someth—"

"How do you think we'd be okay?" Lizzie yelped. "Have you slept? Because I haven't! And my girlfriend keeps asking why I'm suddenly addicted to watching the news!"

"Even if he was missing, I don't think that's how they'd do it, though," Danny said. "This isn't American TV, remember. No faces on milk cartons and that. Maybe on a T-shirt, though. But I don't know how often we have missing reports for people on the news."

"And we definitely don't if they're Black. Look what happened with Richard Okorogheye. The way they handled that was *disgusting*," Nikisha said as she stepped back into the room, a plate in each hand. She handed one down to Danny and sat on a large wooden desk opposite her half-siblings. "What is it the police said to his poor mum? *If you can't find your son, then how can you expect us to?*"

Nikisha put the steaming plate down next to her and took her phone out of her pocket as the doorbell rang.

"That must be Prynce now."

"I'll get it," Dimple said, getting up.

"No, it's fine, I'm closest to the door," Lizzie told her, jumping up and out of the room.

When she came back in and sat down on the stool, Prynce was behind her, wrapping up a phone call. Most of his locs were in a knot at the top of his head, with a few loose tendrils trailing down onto his navy-blue Nike sweater.

"All right, Kayla, I'll see you later. You too." He put his phone into his pocket. "Ah, it's everyone!" he exclaimed happily. "What's good, everyone?"

"Kayla? Is she number four or five?" Dimple asked him. "I've lost count."

"Dimple, you're saying that like these girls are disposable to me." Prynce shook his head, his locs dancing around his big smile. "I care about them *all*."

Dimple rolled her eyes.

"Anyway, what's going on? Why we all here?" Prynce smiled as he looked around the room.

Nikisha sat back at the table, Danny was concentrating on his stir-fry, Dimple looked like she hadn't ever slept a day in her life, Lizzie's jaw was visibly clenched tight. Prynce decided to perch next to Dimple on the cabinet as she looked the most stressed and he thought his presence would offer support by vibe osmosis.

"This is, like, a trap house," Prynce said, looking at the walls. "Is this why you've never let me come here? Do the kids come here? I hope not. Danger *everywhere*."

"You're probably all wondering why you're here," Nikisha said, ignoring Prynce as usual.

"*I'm* not wondering why we're here," Lizzie piped up. "I'm going to guess that it's something to do with—" She looked up at the ceiling. "Is anyone else here?"

Nikisha shook her head.

"Kyron knows," Dimple said flatly. "He remembers. Well, I'm guessing he remembers."

"Whaaat?" Lizzie jumped up so quickly that the stool fell backward. "What do you mean?"

"I went to his mum's and he just . . . turned up," Dimple said, her voice wavering. "And at first, when he saw me, I thought he was going to say something in front of her, but then when she asked what happened to him and where he'd been, he said he didn't remember."

"Okay, so when *did* he remember, then?" Danny asked, crossing his arms as he always did when he was trying to work something out.

"Well, *then* his mum had a welcome home party for him, 'cause Lynette *loves* a party, and then his boy Roman turned up, and I don't know how Kyron knew about me and Roman—"

"What about you and Roman?" Prynce asked.

"Well, we've been kind of in it for a while," Dimple said quickly.

"In what?" Prynce asked.

"What do you think?" Nikisha sighed, looking at Prynce.

"All right, all right." Danny uncrossed his arms and waved his hands to stop this line of conversation.

"I hope you don't mind me saying this, but you're not a very good storyteller, are you?" Prynce said. "You take too long to get to the point and somehow you still leave out all the good bits."

"As I was saying," Dimple said. "Kyron was all *where's your friend?* and I was, like, *who?* because I didn't know who he meant, and then Roman walked in and he was, like, *there he is*, and then there was a tussle, and *then*—actually, this is quite interesting—"

Lizzie cut in. "Is it?"

"Yes!" Dimple waved Lizzie's question away. "I would have said that Kyron is stronger than Roman, but it seemed to be kind of even. I think Roman was holding back, actually."

Dimple looked around and saw that none of her siblings wanted this kind of detail.

"Long story short, Kyron fell again, hit his head again—God, it was horrible to see a second time around—and when he got up, there was this look on his face that told me he remembers."

"When was all of this?" Lizzie demanded. "How long have you been sitting on this information?"

"This all happened in the last couple of days! I'm not hiding stuff from you!" Dimple said.

"Well you can't blame me for asking questions, can you?" Lizzie pursed her lips. "Given why we are where we are."

"Lizzie," Nikisha warned her half sister. "Dimple, continue."

"So I left sharpish, didn't say bye to anyone, and the next day he messaged me, and all it said was 'two hundred and fifty bags,'" Dimple told her siblings.

"Ah, so he's on a blackmail ting?" Prynce asked. "Makes sense, makes sense."

Lizzie glared at Prynce.

"What?" Prynce said. "He's well within his rights to ask for compensation—we was literally gonna bury him in the ground."

"How am I going to find two hundred and fifty thousand pounds, though?" Dimple bit her lip.

"Not trying to be rude or anything like that, but haven't you got money?" Prynce asked. "Isn't your mum rich?"

"I mean, we're comfortable, but I don't think she has a quarter of a mill to lend me, Prynce." Dimple rubbed her temples.

"It's not just your problem, Dimple," Nikisha said. "It's on all of us."

"Speak for yourself," Lizzie blurted out.

Everyone turned to look at her.

"Sorry, but it's true!" Lizzie said.

"Okay, well, how about this," Nikisha said. "When Dimple talks to Kyron and sees *what* he can remember, if he can't recall you or your involvement, how you helped to clean up his blood, and how you sat in the back of the van talking while he was probably playing dead, then you can opt out and leave us to it."

Lizzie rolled her eyes while Dimple dealt with the wound of what Lizzie had said. She knew Lizzie was right, though. This shouldn't have been on them, it was all on her.

"Here's how we play it for now," Nikisha said. "Dimple, you're going to go and talk to Kyron. See what he remembers. I personally haven't ever been blackmailed before, but I suspect the best thing to do is admit to nothing. In case he wants a recording of you saying what we did."

"But Dimple said he won't go to the police," Danny said. "So what does a recording matter?"

"He'll put it on social media," Dimple exclaimed. "He knows that'll ruin me, and I've only just come up!"

"Or all of us," Prynce said. "I dunno about you lot, but I don't want people searching my name on Twitter and they see that in the winter of this year I tried to bury a body."

"Why do you care about social media in *any* of this?" Lizzie asked in total disbelief.

"We need to think of an alibi in case he does decide to say what happened," Nikisha told her siblings. "We need to have somewhere we were that night. To protect ourselves, and to protect Dimple if the police, anyone, whoever, suspects anything."

"But we hadn't seen each other for years before that night. They're not going to think we all got together to hide a body, are they?" Prynce asked. "So we're really doing it to protect Dimple."

"Yes, Prynce," Nikisha said firmly. "Unless you're giving solutions, you're just talking for the sake of it."

"All right!" Prynce exclaimed. "Just making sure we cover all bases!"

"But Karen," Dimple whispered.

"Fucking Karen," Danny spat, even though it wasn't in his nature to swear.

"We don't know who she saw, remember?" Nikisha told them. "We'll cross that bridge if we come to it."

"Maybe we could ask Dad to be our alibi?" Dimple said, and all of her half-siblings burst into laughter that carried on for, in Dimple's opinion, too long.

Dimple felt her face go hot.

"I was just saying," she whispered.

"We could say we were all here, but it's better for us to be somewhere with a witness," Nikisha told her half-siblings.

"I—I don't think we should pull anyone else into this, d-do you?" Dimple stuttered.

"Well," Lizzie said, "the only person I was with was my girlfriend, and there is no way I'm getting her involved."

"None of my friends are going to go for that," Prynce said. "I jumped off *Vanguard* when I got your call though, Nikisha."

"What's Vanguard?" Lizzie asked Prynce, annoyed. "Why are you making words up at a time like this?"

"Relax, it's the new *CoD*."

"What is *CoD*?" Lizzie's temper was rising.

"*Call of Duty*, man!" Prynce said, holding his hands up. "Just chill, Lizzie?"

"What about one of your girls?" Danny asked his half brother in an attempt to defuse the situation. "You could say you were with them."

"I'm not tryna pull any of them into any of this." Prynce shook his head. "'Cause next thing you know, someone is saying if they can give me an alibi, I can give them a label, and I'm too young for all that."

"You know I had my son—*your* nephew—when I was two years older than you," Nikisha said to her youngest brother.

"And that's all cool. But I can't even look after myself, sis," Prynce told her. "You know that."

"I mean, followers or googling or not, we did try to bury his body rather than taking him to a hospital," Lizzie said. "I think he's gonna be pretty angry at her. Is it safe for Dimple to go alone?"

"She can just tell him she was scared," Prynce said. "It's not like that's a lie."

"Why don't we just try and get the money?" Danny said.

"From? Look," Nikisha said. "Dimple needs to talk to Kyron. And in the event of anything, anything at all, we need to get one story straight. Unified."

"Can't we just say he's lying?" Lizzie asked. "Isn't it our word against his?"

"It might be his word against ours, but people love a story, don't they?" Danny told them all. "Especially 'cause Dimple is trying to be famous. It might even help you, Dimple, actually?"

"First of all, I don't want to be famous, *second* of all, if I did, *that* is not the route I'd want to take to get me there." Dimple crossed her arms.

"You can't be famous with a couple hundred followers," Prynce informed his siblings.

"Actually, since I uploaded the Kyron video I've got seventeen thousand followers on Insta and *loads* of YouTube subscribers," Dimple said, correcting him.

"That's all right but it's not *that* many," Prynce said. "One of my friends does natural hair videos and she's in the hundreds of thousands. Maybe you could start doing that if we get through all this without anything coming out."

"Thanks for the suggestion." Dimple punched Prynce on the arm.

"Can't we all just say we were in our own houses?" Prynce asked, rubbing his arm.

"We could," Nikisha said. "But that means Dimple is out on her own. And you're forgetting about Karen, Prynce."

"I don't want you all to be dropped into anything because of me," Dimple said quietly. "It's my fault. I should have called the ambulance, or the police, or—"

"—called the who?" Nikisha said, cutting Dimple off. "Have any of you ever had a good experience with the police?"

The half-siblings all shook their heads.

"Obviously goes without saying for you, Danny, after your stretch," Nikisha said.

"Are you ever going to tell us why?" Lizzie asked.

"Nothing that bad, sis." Danny returned to his food. "Well, depends what you think is bad."

Lizzie narrowed her eyes.

"But," Dimple said. "Maybe I should have just called the police. I could have just explained that he fell."

"We don't need to go over this again." Nikisha held her hands up. "Let's stop dwelling on it. No wardens of the state are looking after people like us, so we did what we had to do. But the best thing is, he's fine."

"Yeah, fine enough to be asking for two hundred and fifty grand." Danny laughed. "Dimple, you couldn't find yourself a man who has any shame?"

"Sorry, just to divert us back to the point," Lizzie said. "Are you saying we need a plan, then, to figure out how we're going to get a quarter of a million pounds?"

"Let's have a break and regroup in half an hour," Nikisha said. "But keep thinking."

"Has this place got a garden?" Prynce asked Nikisha.

"If you can call it that," she said. "It's mostly weeds. Go out there at your peril. Through the kitchen—the key's in the door."

Prynce jumped up off the cabinet and pulled a vape out of his pocket.

"What's in there?" Dimple asked him.

"What d'you think?" Prynce smiled. "Want some?"

"Please." Dimple put her hands on Prynce's shoulders and steered him out of the living room.

"Wait, shoes!" Prynce said, bending down on the way and grabbing two pairs of sneakers. "I'm assuming these expensive ones are yours? How much they cost?"

"They were gifted." Dimple rolled her eyes at herself and pushed Prynce toward the garden.

"You're strong, you know!" Prynce laughed as he went hurtling down the hallway.

Surrounded by weeds that came up past their thighs, Dimple and Prynce stood close to each other, sharing the one solid block of concrete that had been placed arbitrarily in the garden.

"So you do actually want to be"—Prynce took a drag on his vape, a slim black thing that looked no different in size and shape than a tube of liquid eyeliner—"an influencer?"

Dimple nodded. "I was trying to be for so long."

"And how was that for you, then?"

Dimple shifted her weight from one foot to the other. "Well it wasn't what it is now," Dimple told him.

Prynce passed her the vape, then looked up at the sky. His dark skin seemed to absorb the final offering of sun the winter afternoon gave them and hold it in there, glistening.

"How you mean, 'it wasn't what it is now'? You must have more to say than that now you've got the numbers."

Dimple took a small pull.

"I thought I'd like it more. All those people talking to me, all the time."

"But why did you think you'd like it at all? Why did you even want to be that?" Prynce asked. " 'Cause it's not like it was an option at your school careers fair."

"Because I'm a people person," Dimple told him.

"Are you?" Prynce asked her. He wasn't so sure. "Don't you have to be an extrovert to be a people person? You aren't very outward facing. You see Dad? From what I remember, *he's* a people person."

There was a trace of admiration for their dad in Prynce's voice that surprised and annoyed Dimple. When had Prynce last seen him?

"It's not just about that. And the whole thing is harder than you realize, so."

"Okay, okay," Prynce said, narrowing his eyes to think about it. "But, like, it's not that hard to do, is it? Like, all you need to do is talk to a camera and get sent stuff."

Dimple took a deeper pull as Prynce stepped away from her and waded into the weeds. He bent down and grabbed a handful, pulling them from the earth.

"Yeah. I don't follow you or anything, 'cause I don't have social media, obviously. But look at when we helped you with that video— it's not like what you do is hard."

"Why don't you have social media? What's wrong with it?" Dimple asked Prynce. "You one of those people who think they're on a higher plane because they don't have Instagram?"

Prynce carried on through the garden, bending and pulling, bending and pulling. He started to build a pile of weeds by Dimple's legs.

"Nah. Not that. I just think it's easy to get sucked in to a fake life-style," he said. "I know *you* know that none of it's real, blah blah. But do your thing, init. Let other people validate you."

"Remind me what your job is?" Dimple asked, folding her arms.

"I'm not making a dig or anything, you know?" Prynce said. "I'm just asking questions. It's not that deep. You don't need to be spiteful."

"Okay, well, I'm asking you a question," Dimple mimicked Prynce's voice, so well that he jerked his head back, impressed.

Prynce bent over again. "I dunno what I want to do yet."

"I see."

"But, like, last thing I'll say on this . . ."

"Mmm?"

"Don't you feel a bit like you're feeding into people's insecuri-ties? Genuine question. And, like . . . aren't you insecure yourself? You know what I mean?"

It was Dimple's turn to jerk her head back, amazed that her brother could ask such pointed and rude questions as if he was asking her what the time was.

" 'Cause, like, I don't see how you couldn't be insecure. If I was, like, putting myself out there all day every day for people to watch me, I'd just be paranoid that people were always watching me. Where does it stop?"

"You're a Sagittarius, right?" Dimple asked her brother.

"What month is that?" Prynce cocked his head as he asked.

"December."

"Yeah." Prynce nodded. "I'm the ninth. But I don't know about any of that stuff. You'll have to tell me what a Sagittarius is like."

"Flighty," Dimple said. "You like your freedom. You probably think of yourself as an intellectual. And, most annoyingly, you're blunt. Text me your time of birth later and I'll tell you your big three."

"My big . . ." Prynce was lost. "Anything positive about us?"

"You're loyal." Dimple shrugged. "And quite fun. But probably because you're not dragged down with worries like the rest of us."

"Ha!" Prynce laughed. "Do you think it helps you to apply these—what can I call them?—'astrological tropes' to people because you're insecure in who *you* are? Like, projecting an identity onto people of what *they* are somehow gives *you* an identity?"

"It's more that I care about people so much that I want to know as much about them as possible without them having to tell me. And I'm not insecure," Dimple said to Prynce. "And if you'd watched any of my videos you'd know how much I try to empower myself, and women like me."

"Okay, relax," Prynce said, making his way back inside the house. "Empowerment," he muttered to himself as he slunk back through the kitchen. He still didn't believe what Dimple was saying. And he still didn't believe in star signs either.

CHAPTER
EIGHT

TWO FEAR-FILLED AND UNEASY days had passed since Kyron's message. Every time Dimple tried to call him, it went to voice mail, and when she'd messaged him none of her texts had gone through. He hadn't posted anything since his return. Not even any links to his shit music that nobody ever listened to. As Dimple got ready for Prynce's birthday party, she tried to call Lizzie to see if she wanted to head there together. When Lizzie sent her to voice mail after two rings, Dimple ignored the all-too-familiar feeling of rejection that nestled in her chest.

"Who was that?"

Lizzie watched her girlfriend Patrice's soft curves jiggle as she reached into the high kitchen cupboard for a sachet of Lemsip.

"Lizzie?" Patrice ran a manicured hand across her shaved head as she waited for the kettle to boil. "On the phone. Who was that?"

"Nobody." Lizzie shrugged, turning her phone over. "Probably a cold caller."

"Mmm." Patrice tore open the sachet and poured its contents into a mug on the kitchen counter.

"You sure you don't want to come?" Lizzie asked. "Though you probably shouldn't. You don't look too good."

"What, so you're ashamed of me?" Patrice laughed, her usually infectious chuckle turning into a coughing fit.

"Maybe I should stay home with you," Lizzie said, concerned.

"No, I'm fine! It's just a cold. I sound—and obviously look—worse than I feel. You should go and spend time with your siblings."

"*Half-siblings.*"

"You're still on that?" Patrice shook her head as she poured boiling water onto the yellow medical powder in the mug.

"You should wait till the water cools down," Lizzie said.

"Oh my God, don't change the subject," Patrice scoffed as she turned to look at Lizzie. "I think it's nice that you're connected to them! When we have babies they'll need aunties and uncles to babysit. If you think I'm staying at home 24/7 you've got *me* wrong."

"Our babies aren't going anywhere near those people," Lizzie said quickly. "No way."

Patrice shot Lizzie a disappointed look.

"What's your problem with them?"

"Where do I start?" Lizzie folded her arms and leaned on the kitchen counter. "Nikisha is a know-it-all."

"That must be hereditary, then." Patrice smiled, reaching into the cupboard for a jar of honey.

"Prynce doesn't take anything seriously. It's like being back at school and having to sit next to the class clown," Lizzie carried on, ignoring Patrice's comment. "And Danny is a bit stupid."

"You know, just because he's not a medical student, or a *creative*, or working in finance, doesn't mean he's stupid," Patrice said. "You're sounding kinda judgmental."

"No, no." Lizzie shook her head. "Okay, maybe he's not *stupid*. As in, he's smart, but I don't know how much common sense he has. Like his common sense has been replaced by blind optimism. If that makes sense."

"And what about Dimple? Surely you get on with her? You're the same age."

"She's the worst one," Lizzie said. "Always got a problem, always feeling sorry for herself, always the victim. You can't have a conversation with her without her bursting into tears."

Patrice stared at Lizzie for a while.

"What?" Lizzie asked.

"This isn't you," Patrice said. "This definitely isn't the Lizzie I fell for."

"Well, the Lizzie you fell for was technically an only child and didn't have to deal with a bunch of people she doesn't have anything in common with."

"And the Lizzie I fell for was a lot nicer than this," Patrice said, shuffling past Lizzie. "This energy of yours? I don't like it. I'm gonna take this Lemonsip to bed. I'll see you later. Have fun."

"It's called Lemsip," Lizzie said, correcting her.

"Bye!" Patrice slammed the bedroom door behind her.

———

"Happy birthday, Prynce!" Danny shouted very loudly as he, Dimple, and Lizzie entered the house. They'd arrived at Prynce's mum's doorstep at the same time, and Dimple was *elated* not to be walking in by herself.

"Do you know what an inside voice is?" Lizzie asked Danny.

Danny ignored this. He'd always had this special skill of managing to block out vibe killers.

Prynce looked up from pouring a second bottle of rum into a punch bowl on the rickety table and smiled at his half-siblings.

"You made it!" He walked over and pulled them into something resembling a group hug.

"Obviously!" Danny said. "I'm not missing my little brother's birthday!"

"You did miss the previous twenty-four of them," Lizzie reminded him, handing Prynce a bag containing a perfectly wrapped gift.

Dimple took the room in while they waited for the other guests to arrive. Prynce and his mum, Bernice, who was currently out of the house, as always, lived in a five-story house on the edge of Battersea, the rent for which was heavily subsidized. It hadn't been taken the best care of, and every corner that Dimple had seen was filled with clutter. Papers, dozens of tins of food, arbitrary pieces of Robert Dyas equipment that had been bought and never used: All had been pushed into every spare inch of the room to make space for more . . . things.

"Is it your mum who's the hoarder or is it you?" Dimple asked her half brother.

"Go up and look at my room," he told her. "Top floor, straight ahead."

Dimple, curious as she was to learn as much as she could about her brother, turned on her heel and moved towards the stairs.

"You coming?" she asked Lizzie and Danny.

Danny was already walking toward the food on the table, but Lizzie was up for exploring.

"Might as well." She shrugged. "After you."

They walked up the four flights of stairs, slightly out of breath when they got to the top.

"We're getting old," Dimple huffed. "When I turned twenty-five I could have done this, like, five times over."

"You sure?" Lizzie asked her.

"Yeah, you're probably right." Dimple conceded her lack of fitness as she opened the door to the most immaculate room she'd ever seen.

"Oh. Okay then," Lizzie said, walking across the thick gray rug and sitting on a bed that looked like it had been made by someone who'd spent a stint working in hotel cleaning. The sheets were tucked so tight she almost bounced up off them.

"How are you doing, though?" she asked Dimple. "Everything been okay? You heard from Kyron again?"

Dimple walked around the room to get a better sense of who Prynce was, and also to be nosy. She stroked the books on his shelf. Lots of philosophy, lots of nonfiction. Nothing that looked very fun to her, nothing that she wanted to borrow. Not that she was into books at all.

"No. I've been trying, but . . . it is what it is. Anyway. How are you?" When Dimple wasn't ready to talk about the several emotions she was feeling at any given time she deflected the question back onto who asked it.

"If I told you how I was, you wouldn't understand," Lizzie said.

"Well." Dimple blinked at her half sister. In this moment she felt strong enough to engage in an emotional standoff with a Leo. "You never know. I might understand more than you think."

"Okay." Lizzie took a deep breath. "Don't take this the wrong way, but my life was fine until you all came shouting and crying and arguing into it."

"How can I not take that the wrong way?" Dimple asked, rejection hitting her like a punch to the chest.

"You see, look at your face!" Lizzie rolled her eyes. "I knew you'd make this about you."

"Okay, well, sorry, I guess?" Dimple crossed her arms. "Please continue."

"I don't think that's unreasonable to say, Dimple," Lizzie scoffed. "Before you lot, I didn't feel like I was going to vomit every time I heard a siren. I was doing well in my exams. Now I can't concentrate for more than a minute without imagining what prison is going to be like. Plus, I'm pretty sure my girlfriend thinks I'm cheating on her because I keep disappearing on her! She hasn't let me touch her ever since I got home that morning because I can't say anything to convince her that I wasn't at some girl's house until five in the morning."

"What did you tell her?"

"I told her a friend had an emergency."

"So you haven't told her about us?" Dimple asked.

"I have, but not properly," Lizzie said. "I need to figure it out for myself first."

"You mean you need to figure us out for yourself first?" Dimple said, trying to clarify. "I don't think it's that hard."

"To you, maybe." Lizzie shrugged. "But I think you needed us more than we needed you."

"What?" Dimple felt like she was about to cry. She should have known she wasn't strong enough to engage in an emotional standoff with a Leo. "Because of the Kyron stuff?"

"Not just that." Lizzie shook her head. "I don't mean to be rude, but . . . your life outside of all of this . . . well, it wasn't real, was it?"

"Shall we go downstairs now?" Dimple asked, smiling to hide the sting of Lizzie's assessment.

"I think that's a good idea," Lizzie said, standing.

Dimple and Lizzie trudged down the stairs and faced a sea of people, including Nikisha, who had just burst into the house.

"Hello, little sisters." Nikisha smiled, hugging them when they met at the bottom of the steps. "Welcome to my childhood home."

"Was it this messy when you lived here?" Lizzie asked.

"Yep. Which is why I got the fuck out when I was sixteen. Prynce won't ever leave, though. He's managed to make the top floor his sanctuary. Nobody is allowed in there. That's how he survives the hoarding."

"We were just up there!" Dimple told her.

"Well, he must really trust you." Nikisha grinned, then looked around at Prynce's friends who were filling the hallway in an annoying way. "Do you lot want to move through to the kitchen?" she asked a group of boys who were looking at Dimple and Lizzie nervously. They hadn't conquered older girls yet.

"We're thirty. *Not* your age-mates," Lizzie told them as they shuffled off, dragging their box-fresh sneakers across the floor.

"Is my mum here?" Nikisha asked Dimple and Lizzie.

"Not that we've seen," Dimple said.

"She's not here, then," Nikisha said. "You would have heard her before you saw her. Even from upstairs. Anyway. Let's go eat!"

It had been a long time since Dimple had been around twenty-five-year-olds. She stared at them with caution. What did they like to do? What sort of things did they think about? Were they vastly different from her? Did they share any of the same interests? She almost wanted to interview a group of them to have these questions answered. She thought about the person she was at twenty-five. She didn't have a handle on her emotions now, but at least at thirty she knew why she was doing, thinking, and feeling the things she was.

Five years ago, she was sort of just existing recklessly. She could see that in Prynce, but only a bit. He already seemed a lot wiser than she'd been back then, or even was now. She caught a glimpse of him laughing with one of his friends and smiled. She didn't remember laughing much when she was twenty-five. It was all intense heartache and trying to figure out who she was. That was when the obsession with being an influencer had begun. That was when she'd decided that projecting an image of herself to "the world" would protect her from how harsh the world was.

Her chain of thought was broken when she locked eyes with Danny, who was talking to one of Prynce's female friends and looking panicked.

"You okay?" she mouthed at him.

He kept widening his eyes, which Dimple didn't understand until she saw that he clearly needed saving from the conversation.

Dimple walked over to him and said she needed his help with something, excusing both of them from his conversation and pulling him into the hallway.

"Thank you so much." Danny exhaled. "She came over and asked me if I was Prynce's big brother, I said yeah, and all I did was ask her how she knew him, Dimp. That's all I said. And guess what she said to me? She told me that she didn't know him as much as she wanted to get to know me!"

Dimple laughed at her half brother's shock.

"She's no older than Prynce, Dimp!" Danny folded his arms to protect himself. "I'm so much older than her!"

"Relax, relax." Dimple laughed again. "I'll protect you from her if she propositions you again."

"I didn't like that at all."

"Danny, haven't you got a child? With a woman? How can you be so stressed about talking to another one?"

"Yeah, but *that* woman is also thirty-three," Danny said. "I don't know where these young ones have got all this vim from!"

Dimple carried on laughing at Danny, but stopped when she heard a familiar but not-so-familiar voice at the front door.

"How is everybody?" Cyril Pennington asked everybody and nobody in particular as he came through the door, standing still so everybody at the party could observe his presence, even though nobody did.

Dimple hadn't expected him to look so old. The last time she saw him, he looked closer to the pictures of him she'd found in an old photo album under her mum's bed. He was still handsome, but now, he was smaller. He smiled, still flashing that gold tooth that replaced his front one, but his skin was sallower round the cheeks, and there were now lines around his eyes that deepened when he smiled. His dark skin didn't shine like it had that last day she'd seen him. Instead, it was dull, lacking the richness she'd been so envious of when she'd been younger.

Cyril moved his way through the young bodies that filled the hallway, smiling at the girls and holding a fist out to the boys. All largely ignored him, but he carried on smiling, his delusional optimism making him forget that he didn't have the charm he used to.

Why didn't he ever come to *her* birthdays? Dimple wondered. Was it that her mum had never invited him? Even so, he could have *tried* to come round. It didn't seem fair that he was here. Maybe he just liked Prynce and Nikisha more. Maybe he liked *their* mum more than he liked Janet. But if that was the case, why should she have been the one to suffer?

Cyril's smile dropped when he saw Dimple and Danny standing in front of him, and he very nearly frowned when Lizzie walked out of the kitchen and joined them, handing them each a can of Ting.

Lizzie turned to look at what her half-siblings were staring at, and saw Cyril standing there, looking even smaller than he had when he'd first walked in.

They all watched him decide whether he'd turn and run out of the door or face them all. He decided on the latter.

"Well," he said, walking over to them. "I didn't expect to see you three here."

He went to hug Lizzie, who pressed a hand against his chest and said a firm no.

He went to hug Dimple, who hugged him back because, in that moment, she felt sorry for him.

He went to shake Danny's hand, who reciprocated awkwardly because he didn't dislike his dad, he just didn't know him.

"You're all so big," Cyril remarked. "And look how *gorgeous* you are, Dimple. Shocking vibes! You must have children by now, surely—some man mussa breed you by this point? Wow. And who knew I could have produced such a serious weapon? But I know you didn't get it from me, that your mother's Indian genes coming through. How is Janet?"

"Yeah," Dimple said, reeling from the million terrible things her dad had said. "She's good, you know."

"Are you going to ask about my mum, Cyril?" Lizzie asked him.

"Well, I can tell Kemi raised you to be as serious as she is. And you've got her forehead." Cyril laughed. "And how is big Danny boy? Solid! Built like a *tank*."

"I'm good." Danny shrugged.

"You know, I heard about you in the prison," Cyril said.

"I did write to you," Danny told his dad. "And I sent you a visiting order."

"And I did mean to come, I really did," Cyril said, lying. "But you know things are busy, and I lost the paper you sent, and then when I went to write you back, things just took me over. But I was sending good vibes, son. I know you didn't mean to do what you did." Cyril looked past his children and into the kitchen. "Now, that rum punch is calling me. Check you lot in a little while. You're not going anywhere?" he asked, not waiting around for the answer.

"Did either of you expect that to be as disappointing as it was?" Lizzie asked Dimple, who didn't quite have the words, and Danny, who just looked sad.

They turned to watch Cyril walk through the kitchen and immediately over to the punch bowl. He picked up a plastic cup from the upturned stack next to the bowl, dipped it in, downed the contents, then dipped it in again as Prynce walked over to him.

"My bwoy!" Cyril exclaimed, pouring more drink in his cup and throwing his arms around Prynce, who embraced his dad back. "Happy birthday to you!"

Prynce stepped back, placed his hands together, and bowed a thank-you.

"Twenty-three today!" Cyril shouted. "Wow."

"Twenty-five." Nikisha corrected him as she walked in from the garden carrying a couple of plastic chairs. "Hi, Dad. Little help?"

Cyril took one of the chairs from her and put it down right next to him.

"Anyway, I'm just passing," he said as he eyed a young Black girl with shoulder-length braids walking past him. He nodded in approval as she placed a hand on Prynce's shoulder and squeezed it.

"Hey! You must be Kayla!" Dimple said enthusiastically, hoping she'd correctly remembered the name of the last girl she'd heard Prynce talking to.

From the look on Prynce's face, Dimple realized her mistake.

"Kayla?" the girl asked. "I'm Jana."

"Sorry, I thought I heard someone say your name was Kayla earlier! Ignore me!" Dimple forced a laugh.

"Okay." Jana looked at Dimple like she was mad as she left the room.

"Sorry, sorry, sorry!" Dimple groaned as Prynce laughed.

"That yours?" Cyril asked.

"Huh?" Prynce turned to their dad, confused.

"Your girl, your ting, your squeeze?" Cyril laughed.

"She's a good friend," Prynce said. "A very good friend."

"Friend?" Cyril snorted. "Come on, boy. You sure you're my son?"

Prynce narrowed his eyes at Cyril.

"Do you lot want anything?" Prynce asked Dimple, Danny, and Lizzie, who'd moved in from the hallway so they could watch their dad perform his warped idea of fatherhood.

"I'm quite hungry, actually," Dimple said.

"Me as well," Danny replied.

"Make yourself useful, then," Nikisha said to Dimple. "There's some patties in the freezer next to you, put them in the oven."

"I'll let you women run the kitchen," Cyril said, squeezing past his bemused children and disappearing off into the hallway.

"How long shall I put these on for?" Dimple asked, pulling the clear bag of savory yellow half disks out of the freezer.

"Put the oven on low, then check them after forty-five minutes," Nikisha replied. She fell into work mode quite quickly, and in work mode there was no space for pleases or thank-yous or even any niceties.

"How low is low?" asked Dimple, who was good at following instructions but only when they were clear. "And should I put them on foil, or on a tray, or—"

"Dimple!" Nikisha exclaimed. "Have you never used a kitchen before?"

Dimple felt embarrassment run through her. Her face went hot. It was true, Janet was the cook in the house and clearly, Dimple couldn't even be trusted to handle a bottle of vegetable oil without there being consequences.

"It's all right, I'll figure it out." Lizzie took the bag of patties from Dimple. She knew that Dimple was still raw from their conversation in Prynce's room. Not that she regretted anything she'd said. "You go and enjoy the party. If enjoy is the right word."

While Lizzie got to work on the food, Danny went to call his mum and check on Marley, Prynce went outside to smoke with his boys, and Nikisha started to move around the kitchen picking up party detritus, black bag in hand. Dimple went back up to Prynce's sanctuary of a bedroom for a breather. The music in the house was so *loud*, and watching her brother's friends dancing to it and film-ing each other instead of dancing together and talking to each other made her feel old, even though she only had five years on them. Maybe this subconscious aversion to influencer culture was why she hadn't ever properly blown as one. It wasn't that she *wasn't* grateful for the flurry of attention and activity that came from what happened to Kyron, but it wasn't that she *was* either.

On the second-floor landing outside the bathroom, she saw Cyril talking to Jana, the girl with the braids from the kitchen. One of Prynce's many, many friends.

". . . you know, a girl like you?—and I can tell just from looking at you, you're a sensible girl, good head on her shoulders—you need a older man. Not to be running round with little boys. You're mature, you see me?"

"Dad! Can you leave this poor girl alone?" Dimple stepped in and Jana immediately slipped away and down the stairs.

"Dimple! I was just chatting to the girl!" Cyril laughed, pulling his daughter under his arm. The fabric of his denim jacket muffled the sound of the music for a second, warping it in her ears.

Dimple wondered how he could act like he'd only just seen her yesterday when in reality it had been over a decade. She wondered if all those years of absence hurt him as much as they hurt her. She wondered if he'd do anything for her, the same way she'd do anything for him.

"Anyway," Cyril said. "I've been meaning to catch up with you."

Dimple had a horrible feeling about where this was going. She knew where it was going, though, so leaned closer to him so she could hear him properly over the various party sounds and get it over and done with.

"So I hear say you're doing quite well for yourself," Cyril said, his face so close to hers that the rum on his breath felt hot on her skin. "On the Internet."

"No." Dimple shook her head. "I wish."

"'Cause you see." Cyril pulled his daughter closer, ignoring what she'd said. "I've got myself in a couple sticky situations."

"What kind of sticky situations?" Dimple asked, even though she already knew.

"Ah, you know. Few investments here didn't go the way I planned, bit of money spent over there that I thought I'd get back somewhere else, you know how it is."

Dimple felt sad for herself, and sad for him. He was meant to be her parent; she was meant to be able to go to him to ask for money, but instead here he was telling her all the ways he'd failed, even in a financial sense, so much so that he felt there was no other way than to ask his child to bail him out.

"I'm not really sure I can help you, Dad," Dimple told him as she slipped out of his uncomfortably close grasp.

"How you mean?" Cyril asked her. "You can help your old dad out, surely?"

"Well, I don't think I earn money in the way you think I do," she explained. "Like, it might seem like I have money because I have nice things, an—"

"Dimple, your face is all over the Internet!" Cyril said, interrupting her. "You can't tell me that all these people who send you things to talk about aren't giving you money for it! I might not be a young, technological man, but I'm clued in on this stuff."

"Dad, it really isn't like that. On the Internet it might look like—in fact, it doesn't even *look* like I'm doing well. And I used to buy most of those things and say brands sent them to me. It's only now that—"

"You don't even know how much I need, Dimp." Cyril sat down on the stairs leading to Prynce's room. Dimple desperately wanted to be in there, and not out here having this conversation.

"How much do you need?" Dimple asked.

"Fifteen," Cyril told her.

"Fifteen pounds?"

"Ah, so my daughter's a joker like me!" Cyril laughed a little too hard.

"Fifteen hundred?"

Cyril shook his head.

"You're asking me for fifteen thousand pounds?" Dimple couldn't believe what she was hearing.

"You'll get it back at some point," Cyril told her. "I can't tell you when, but you'll get it back. I can work out some kinda . . . installment program where I give you what I can when I can. But I just need a lump sum to get my affairs in order. And then I can figure the rest out."

"Dad, I don't have that."

"Your mother must have been putting aside money for you?" Cyril asked her.

"I mean, yeah, but—"

"All right, let's say two thousan'."

"That's a drop." Dimple raised her eyebrows.

"Well, fifteen is—how can I say it?—desirable," Cyril said. "The two, well, the two is essential. Got a couple of people asking for it."

Dimple stared ahead, trying not to cry. Why didn't he love her for something other than what she could give him?

"Come on, help your old dad out." Cyril nudged Dimple. "I know you've got it."

Maybe if she did this thing for him, it could be the start of a relationship of trust, Dimple thought. And maybe this installment program he mentioned would be a reason for them to at least talk every so often.

She pulled her phone out of her pocket.

"What are your account details?" she asked him. "I'll do it now."

"You can do it from the phones?" Cyril exclaimed. "Backside! I thought I was going to have to drive you to the bank!"

Cyril pulled a small piece of paper from his pocket that held his bank details and handed it to her. As Dimple typed the numbers into the banking app on her phone, she felt deep, deep discomfort in her chest.

"You might as well make it three while you're here," Cyril said.

Dimple sighed, nodding slowly as she transferred three thousand pounds of the money her mum had been saving for her over the years that she'd promised she wouldn't touch unless it was for a good reason. This was coming directly out of the blackmail fund, and it burned her to lose it. Even if Cyril did hear his daughter sigh, he didn't care what it meant.

"Done," she said.

"You see!" Cyril smiled. "Nice to help your old man, isn't it?"

Dimple waited for him to say thank you.

"I think my phone is ringing," Dimple said, lying, when she realized his gratitude wasn't coming. She got up and squeezed past Cyril. She didn't want him to see her cry. "I'm going to have to take this, sorry."

She ran up the stairs into Prynce's room and held her phone to her ear.

"Hello?" she said loudly. "No, sorry, I'm at a party! Can you hear me? I'll just close the . . ."

Dimple closed the door and experienced the closest thing to quiet she'd had in hours. She walked across the gray rug again, flopped onto Prynce's bed, and burst into tears. If she'd known seeing her dad would go from bad to really much worse she wouldn't have bothered coming today. But then she looked up and saw a picture of childhood Prynce dressed up as some sort of superhero on the windowsill and she smiled through her tears. He was worth it. This weird new family setup was worth it. Feeling like she belonged somewhere was worth it, even though Nikisha was bossy, Danny wasn't always on the same page as everyone else, Lizzie was still mean, and Prynce spoke before he could think about what his words could do.

Dimple lay back on Prynce's bed and scrolled through her phone. She couldn't believe she had so many followers now. And so many invites, not that she was in the right frame of mind to go anywhere. Invites to events, to be part of campaigns, to model for all of these brands that she'd never heard of but would be happy to endorse if it meant free shit. Dimple wondered if it was time to get a manager.

"You okay?" Prynce asked, walking in. "Sorry, I know there's a lot of people here. Haven't been able to spend a lot of time with you lot."

"Oh no, it's fine!" Dimple told him, sitting up. "Are you having a good time? Sorry I snuck up here, and sorry for making myself so at home."

"Nah, don't apologize. You can even go to sleep if you want!" Prynce smiled. "It's nice seeing all my peoples, but it's nice knowing you lot are here as well."

"Not Dad, though, fucking hell." Dimple exhaled. "You know I caught him telling that girl, your 'friend'—which we'll discuss in a sec—that she needed an older man?"

Prynce laughed.

"I've heard him say worse, trust me."

"How close are you to him?" Dimple asked.

"Not close at all, trust me," Prynce told her. "Why's your face like that?"

"Well, I just feel a bit sad because when Dad came in and saw Danny, they did this weird handshake, which was all formal and cold, and then when he saw you, you had a big hug."

"Lizzie didn't hug him, did she?" Prynce asked.

"No, of course not, but it's different, isn't it. She actively doesn't like him. But Danny wants Dad to like him. When I looked at Danny's face he looked like a lost puppy."

"Ah, shit."

"Yeah. And I don't know if the right thing for you to do is, like, say something? Because it's not like it's your fault that he hugged you, it's just . . . well, I dunno. I'm sure Danny's fine. He always seems weirdly cheerful, though. And I don't know if that's how he actually is or how he thinks he needs to be."

"I know what you mean," Prynce agreed. "If Dad comes up, I'll chat to him about it. But I don't wanna say it in a forced way, if you know what I mean."

"I do. Now that we've all sort of found each other I don't want Dad to start making problems between us. And I don't want to moan, but he asked me—"

Dimple stopped speaking as Danny and Lizzie walked into the room. Danny was holding a plate in one hand and a patty in the other. The patty was going in his mouth, obviously.

"There you are." Lizzie was holding a plate with two patties on it, which she handed to Dimple before taking a seat next to her and Prynce on the bed.

Danny sat on the floor in front of them all.

"You love the floor, don't you?" Lizzie said to him.

"Well, I'm not gonna sit next to you all so we can talk in a line, am I?" he asked her, taking another bite.

"Anyway, as I was saying before you two came in." Dimple took a bite into the flaky pastry before she continued. "Dad cornered me and asked me for fifteen grand. Fifteen grand, can you imagine?"

Danny shook his head.

"He did what?" Lizzie asked.

"I know! He started moaning about his money problems and said he needed some money to sort his shit out," Dimple explained, looking down at the floor as shame rose up her body from the ground. "He said he'd be able to pay me back in installments. Can you believe that?"

"He did what?" Lizzie repeated.

"Did you not hear her?" Danny asked.

"No, I did, but I just can't . . . Wait, so you're telling me this man—who hasn't spoken to you for how many years?—sees you at a party. And when I say a party, let's remember that it's a party for his youngest son who we only met however many years ago when Cyril told us not to grow up and fuck each other. And when he happens to see you—at a party, and not because he actually reached out to you to spend time with you—he asks you for money?" Lizzie finally drew a breath. "Did he even ask how you are?"

"I don't . . . think so, actually." Dimple tried to remember. "But, like, don't work yourself up over it. It's not like I'm going to give him any."

"Yeah, but it's the principle." Lizzie jumped up. "Where is he?"

"Don't get yourself worked up, Lizzie," Danny said. "He's not worth it."

"I don't care about worth it or not!" Lizzie shouted. "What the fuck has this man done in any of our lives to be asking for anything? Let alone fifteen fucking K?"

Dimple knew it wasn't worth telling anyone that she'd given him any money at all. Not just because they'd all line up to fight him and that would probably ruin Prynce's birthday, but because, more than anything, she was embarrassed that all it took was a few words from him for her to cave. It burned more that she felt embarrassed that she wasn't as strong as the rest of them.

"What's going on in here?" Nikisha asked, stepping into Prynce's room. "Who's doing all this shouting?"

"Why didn't we know Cyril was going to be here?" Lizzie asked Nikisha. "I'm gonna go and find him."

"He's gone. But would it have made a difference if you'd known?" Nikisha closed the door behind her and took a seat at Prynce's tidy desk. "Would you not have come to celebrate our brother's birthday?"

Lizzie pursed her lips.

"I just would have liked to have geared myself up for it. I didn't expect to see him today, and all he did was treat us like strangers and ask Dimple for money."

"That, younger sister, is Cyril for you," Nikisha said. "Get used to it."

"How do you two not mind?" Lizzie asked Nikisha and Prynce.

"What do you mean?" Nikisha asked her.

"How have you been used to that as your dad in your life?"

Nikisha laughed.

"You know he's not in our lives, right? Never has been."

"Really?" Danny asked. "It seems like you guys are quite close to him."

"Nope." Nikisha shook her head. "This is the first time we've seen him in a long time. Not as long as the rest of you, but a long, long time. He only came by because he knew our mum wasn't going to be here. Last time he came around he left and had to go to the hospital to get stitches."

"My mum told me he was off raising you, Nikisha," Lizzie said. "And then you, Prynce."

Prynce shook his head.

"Ha!" Nikisha shouted. "Raising? That man has never raised anything."

"And Nikisha basically raised me, so," Prynce added. "He really, really hasn't been about."

"So," Dimple started. "This guy really just nutted five times and never looked back."

"You know I heard there might even be a sixth," Nikisha said.

"On the way?" Lizzie spluttered.

"No." Nikisha shook her head. "Older than me. But I'll let you know when I know for sure, 'cause . . ." She exhaled loudly.

"Dimple, what's happening with Kyron?" Danny asked, checking that Prynce's bedroom door was closed. "Has he messaged you again?"

"No, I'd have said if he had. And I can't get through to him," Dimple told him.

"It's time for you to . . . spend some time with him," Nikisha said slowly.

"Right, I'm leaving the room for this conversation." Danny stood up and exited swiftly.

"You're pimping me out," Dimple spluttered as Danny closed the door behind him.

"It's not pimping when he's your ex," Nikisha said.

"Are you sure about that?" Prynce asked. "I think pimping is still pimping when the framework of pimping is in place, despite who is who."

"Shut up, Prynce," Nikisha said.

"How can you tell me to shut up on my birthday?" Prynce looked hurt.

"He has a point, though," Dimple said. "Also I feel like we shouldn't use the term 'pimping.'"

"Isn't there another way?" Lizzie asked. "What if it doesn't work? What if Dimple tries to seduce him or whatever, but he's not into it? He's not responded to her messages, has he?"

"You have to make sure he's into it," Nikisha said to Dimple.

"Sounds like a warning," Lizzie said, looking concerned by Nikisha's command.

"You know what?" Prynce said.

"What?" Dimple asked.

"I can't believe Dad left without saying goodbye," he said finally.

"Seriously?" Lizzie asked him. "That's literally the most on-brand thing he could do."

Prynce nodded.

"Yeah, good point."

CHAPTER
NINE

DIMPLE SAT ON HER bed and took a deep breath as she called Kyron's phone. With every ring, her stomach was getting tighter and tighter. She'd been calling him for days, and every time, the fear and unease was the same. After what felt like an eternity, it went to voice mail. She messaged him.

Dimple:
I miss you x

A second after she put her phone on her bedside table, she got a text.

Kyron:
You home?

She stared at the message before she replied.

Dimple:
Yeah I am. You coming? Xx

Another text came through.

Kyron:

Yh, later. Make sure no one else is there

Dimple's mum wasn't home until later.

Dimple:

I'm alone xxx

Dimple showered. She shaved her legs, even though it broke her waxing routine. She did her makeup. She took her underwear off and put on the smallest dress she could find, the one Kyron said she wasn't allowed to wear out, but could wear for him. Then she sat on the sofa and anticipated a very difficult conversation.

"Hey," Dimple said as casually as possible as she opened the front door. "You okay?"

Kyron snorted as he moved past her.

"I been better."

The scabs on his face had healed so they were scars, and he'd made it to the barber's. His trim was short enough to show the almost-healed gash on the back of his head. Dimple closed the front door behind him and followed him as he walked slowly into the living room.

"Is there anything you wanna say to me?" Dimple asked him. She figured it was better to find out what he knew before she said anything she shouldn't.

Kyron ignored this as he sat down on the sofa. He was trying to act cool, calm, collected, but he was on high alert. He didn't trust this girl anymore. With every day that had passed, he'd pieced together more and more of what he could remember from that night. It was only little bits, and he'd heard more than he'd seen. He remembered hearing voices that weren't Dimple's, but had no idea who those voices belonged to. Being back here didn't sit right in his belly. Like his body could tell something bad had happened to him in this spot.

"Do you want a drink?" she asked. "Or some food?"

"Some food?" Kyron asked, confused. "You're just gonna act like everything is normal?"

"I know we've broken up, but I still care about you," Dimple said, sitting next to Kyron and putting a hand on his thigh.

"Care about me?" Kyron laughed. "Bro, you had me wrapped in a tarpaulin in the back of a van."

"I can order us something to eat?"

"What kind of game is this?" Kyron laughed.

Dimple looked at Kyron and blinked. He hadn't taken his phone out. She wondered if it was recording them in his pocket.

"I want things to go back to how they were, Ky," Dimple said, moving closer to him, making sure that her dress rode up her bare thigh.

Kyron snorted again, but his eyes darted to Dimple's naked skin. He hated how predictable he was.

"Don't you?" Dimple asked, leaning into Kyron and kissing his neck lightly.

"This isn't gonna work on me," Kyron said.

"No?" Dimple whispered into Kyron's ear before biting his lobe gently. Her hand wandered over to his zipper. She could feel that he was hard. The plan, if it was a plan, was working.

Kyron pulled Dimple onto his lap. She kissed him, reaching her hand to the back of his head to stroke it.

He let out a yelp of pain and jerked his head back. Dimple's eyes widened. How could she forget where he'd hit his head? She wanted to ask if it was okay, if he was still in pain, but she couldn't, so instead she quickly pulled the dress down so her breasts popped out.

Kyron's eyes focused on them and he held one in each hand before he buried his face in them. He kissed the soft skin between her breasts before he started sucking and biting her nipples.

"That's it." Dimple sighed, trying to hide a yawn. This was so easy, she thought. "Shall we go to my room?"

Dimple stood up over Kyron, wriggled out of her dress, and dropped it onto the floor.

"Yeah," Kyron said, standing up and pulling his T-shirt off.

"Why don't you take the rest off?" Dimple wanted him to leave his phone downstairs.

"All in good time," Kyron said.

When they got up to her room, Dimple got on all fours, the way Kyron liked her to.

"Nah." Kyron shook his head. "Lie on your back."

Dimple did as she was told as Kyron made his way over to the bed and lay on top of her, jamming his fingers inside of her. Dimple winced. They'd been having sex for such a long time that while he should know what she liked, he always followed the same formula that worked for *him* without ever checking that it did anything for her.

It would start with kissing, then he'd flip her over and ease his fingers inside while never going anywhere near the clitoris, then when he felt like she was adequately wet, he'd push himself inside of her, and forty-five seconds later, he'd be finished. He'd never check if she came. She used to wonder if it was because he was too embarrassed to ask in case her answer was no, but after a while she realized that he actually assumed that when he came, she did.

Dimple wondered if this new position meant that something new and potentially exciting was coming. She also wondered if the bump on the head was the reason for this change.

Kyron withdrew his fingers from her, then sat back and stared at her.

"Actually," Kyron said, disrupting Dimple's train of thought, "I want you to play with yourself."

"Oh, okay." Dimple didn't really understand this new assignment. "Like how?"

"Do what feels good," Kyron told her. "But I want you to close your eyes while you do it."

Dimple felt self-conscious, but she knew that she needed to do what he said. She moved her hand down and closed her eyes like he'd asked.

Dimple started to rub her index and middle finger across her clitoris slowly. She felt too uncomfortable to get any pleasure from this act, and could feel more with her fingers than she could from her clit.

"Keep going," Kyron commanded.

Dimple continued, her discomfort growing. She slowed down when she heard Kyron fiddling with something.

"And don't open your eyes," he said.

Obviously, Dimple opened her eyes. As she did, she saw Kyron hide his phone behind his back.

"What are you doing?" Dimple asked him, sitting up.

"Nothing," Kyron said quickly, and a little too firmly. "I'm taking my jeans off. I needed to empty my pockets."

"Ah, okay," Dimple said. She wasn't convinced but she needed to speed this up. "I just want you inside me."

Kyron stood up, putting his phone into his pocket as he did. He unzipped his jeans and pulled them, and his boxers, down enough so that only his erection was out.

"You not taking them off?" Dimple asked him.

Kyron shook his head.

"Turn around."

Dimple got on all fours.

"Nah, nah, lie on your front." Kyron positioned Dimple how he wanted her, and mounted her so his knees rested on the backs of her thighs. He eased himself into her from behind, and forty-five seconds later, he pulled out, turned her around, and deposited a splash of warm white liquid on her stomach.

When Dimple came back from the bathroom, Kyron wasn't in the bedroom.

"Ky?" she called, listening for him. She heard a noise from downstairs so pulled on a big T-shirt and ran down.

Kyron was in the living room, putting his sweater on.

"You're going already?" Dimple asked him. Did her plan work? And so easily?

Kyron didn't say anything.

"We good, though?" Dimple asked him.

"Good?" Kyron looked at her and smirked. "What I said still stands."

Dimple decided that, on balance, it made sense to play dumb.

"What did you say?"

"Two fifty," Kyron said.

Dimple looked at him, blinking. She wanted to laugh at herself. Why did she think sex would stop blackmail?

"And, 'cause you're smarter than you look," Kyron said, "I've got this as insurance."

Kyron pulled his phone out of his pocket and showed her a picture of herself, legs apart, fingers on her clitoris. Face and everything. She wondered if the picture would be any nicer to look at if she'd been pulling a better face.

"Kyron," she said. "I told you we could never do that. I trusted you, how—"

"Trusted me?" Kyron laughed, leaving the room and heading toward the front door. "Don't talk to me about *trust*."

"What are you going to do with that?" Panic coated Dimple's voice.

"I told you, it's insurance," Kyron said. "You know what I want. I've kept what happened to myself till now, even after I found out you been fucking my boy. But you've got a month to give it to me. Or I tell everyone what you did, and this picture goes out."

Dimple wanted to be sick. She also didn't know which was worse. People knowing she was on her way to being a seasoned criminal, or everyone seeing her looking unattractive while she played with herself.

"One month," Kyron said, opening the front door.

"Okay." Dimple nodded as she watched Kyron laugh down the front path.

———————

"I was trying to do what I needed to do!" Dimple told her half-siblings as they sat around her living room the next evening.

"And did it work?" Lizzie asked, knowing the answer.

"It didn't, no," Dimple replied.

"'It didn't, no,'" Lizzie mimicked Dimple. "And it's somehow even worse. Why did you let him take a picture of you?"

"Hey, hey!" Dimple shouted. "He obviously did it in secret! And I feel bad enough without you victim-blaming me!"

"Just so we're all clear, I didn't tell you to do that," Lizzie said.

"No, I know, but Nikisha did!" Dimple said.

"You should have put the pussy on him the minute he walked through the door," Nikisha said, shaking her head.

"Are you . . . *allowed* to say that to me?" Dimple asked, shocked. She wasn't a prude, but she didn't think she'd be doing pussy talk with her big sister.

Nikisha laughed.

"I'm your big sister, I can say what I want. Besides, we're all big people, I've got a pussy, you've got a pussy, we have sex—"

"Okay, okay," Danny said, cutting Nikisha off. "Please, come on. I don't wanna hear all that stuff."

"Get used to it," Nikisha told him.

"Okay, all that aside, what you're saying is, we need to find that money else you're gonna be exposed in one of two ways?" Prynce said. "Or maybe both. I don't trust that guy."

"We aren't going to find the money." Dimple started to cry. "I might as well just accept it. At least this way it's only me who's affected."

"Can I ask one thing?" Prynce raised his hand.

"It better be something useful," Nikisha said to her little brother.

"Is it *that* bad if the picture comes out?"

All four siblings turned to glare at Prynce.

"I'm just saying! Maybe Dimple can spin it, turn it into a positive? You said your whole thing was about empowering women, why not do it like this?"

"I am *not* empowering women like this!" Dimple shrieked.

"It was just a suggestion," Prynce said. "Do you even have that many followers anyway? Who's even gonna see it and know who you are?"

"At my last count, just over fifty thousand on Instagram," Dimple told him. She never, ever thought saying that would have filled her with dread.

"Wow, that's great!" Danny smiled at Dimple.

"Under any other circumstances, yes." Dimple sat forward and let her head loll into her lap.

"You can't tell there was blood all over this floor," Prynce remarked. "We did a really good job."

"My life is over," Dimple groaned, ignoring Prynce.

"Don't think like that!" Danny rubbed Dimple's back. "I've got, like, a few grand in savings!"

"Unless it's two fifty, there's no point bringing it up," Lizzie scoffed.

"Well, what are you offering?" Prynce asked her.

"I don't think I need to offer anything," Lizzie said. "Besides, Patrice would notice any money going missing."

"So you just want our sister's . . . personal parts on the Internet?" Prynce asked Lizzie.

"There are revenge porn laws," Lizzie said.

"It doesn't sound like he cares about any of that," Danny said.

"Don't cry, Dimple. Something will work itself out," Nikisha said. "It always does."

When Dimple woke up the next afternoon, after a night of tossing and turning, she had five missed calls from Nikisha. Fear paralyzed her for a few seconds. She felt sick at the thought of checking social media. Oh, how the mighty had fallen, and so *soon*. All of those sponsorship deals taken away before she could get the chance to review one little mascara. All she could do was lie on her back and imagine herself exposed for all the world to see, or in prison. As soon as she caught herself thinking about how much her skin-care routine would suffer if she was locked up, she snapped out of it.

She called back, but Nikisha didn't answer, so Dimple sobbed as she scrolled the news, waiting to see pictures of herself and her half-siblings on the screen, ATTEMPTED MURDERERS emblazoned across their faces in red.

She jumped from news outlet to news outlet, the tears coming thick and fast as she searched for the warrants for her arrest, when Nikisha finally called back and put her out of her misery.

"He's said something, hasn't he?" Dimple wailed. "Everyone knows!"

"It's Grandma," Nikisha said flatly, no trace of familiarity with the woman she referred to in her voice.

"Whose Grandma?" Dimple asked. "What?"

"Our grandma," Nikisha told her. "Dad's mum. Delores."

"Oh." Dimple sat up, stopped crying immediately, and wiped the tears from her face. "What about her? I don't know her."

"She's really ill," Nikisha said. "We're all going there later on. Just in case."

"In case she dies?" Dimple asked. "That's not very optimistic."

"Optimism isn't my thing," Nikisha said. "I'll pick you up in an hour."

"Do I need to bring anything?" Dimple asked.

"Like what?" Nikisha laughed.

"Well, what kind of thing should I wear?"

"I dunno! It's not an occasion, Dimple. In an hour."

Dimple pulled herself from her bed and got dressed. She felt relieved, of course, but beyond that, she couldn't really place this new emotion that was coming through. She didn't have any memories, none at all, of her dad's mum. But that didn't mean she didn't care, for lack of a better word. Death was fucking horrible; but how much was she allowed to care when she didn't know someone? Even if it was because of that person that she was here? She looked out of the window. Gray, unclear, like her thoughts. She pulled on a long black dress and a pair of tights, and put on some very minimal makeup in case she had to cry on demand. Sometime later, Nikisha pulled up outside. Prynce and Lizzie were already in the car.

Prynce was on the phone, smiling into it, lust-drunk.

"Hello, little sister," Nikisha said. "How are you?"

"Not good," she said, climbing into the back next to Lizzie.

"When *are* you good?" Lizzie asked, pulling her scarf tighter around her neck. "Turn the heating up, please."

"How are you all?" Dimple asked everyone, ignoring Lizzie's question.

"I'm good, you know!" Prynce answered. "Just been doing this and that, but I feel like there's good energy in the air, you know?"

"Oh! You're off the phone!" Dimple said. "Who was it this time?"

"My friend Jordan."

"Boy or girl?" Dimple asked.

"*Woman*," Prynce said.

"You might want to calm that good energy down when we turn up at our dying grandmother's house," Nikisha told him.

"Or you could spread it around," Dimple said. "I could take some of that good energy."

"You see the problem with you, Dimple?" Prynce asked, turning to look at her.

Dimple leaned her head against the car window.

"No, but I'm sure you'll tell me."

"You're just always a bit sad," Prynce said.

"It's because I'm a Cancer," Dimple replied.

"You're doing that thing again," Prynce said, facing the front.

"Doing what?"

"Astro Twitter."

Dimple laughed a bit. Prynce turned back to Dimple.

"The other day I told one of my friends what you told me."

"What did I tell you?"

"My big three or whatever? I said that I was a Sagittarius, Scorpio moon, Leo rising."

"What did she say?"

"She said that any man who knows his big three is a slut."

Dimple laughed at that.

"It's all nonsense, you know," Lizzie said.

"No, it's not," Dimple shot back.

"Of course it is! How can the stars in the sky decide what your whole personality is going to be?"

"Look," Dimple said. She'd gotten into this before and knew the best possible route of shutting down people who didn't believe in the zodiac. "Are you religious?"

"Nope." Lizzie shook her head. "My mum is, but it's not for me. Even though I tell her it is."

"Okay, but if you were, it's a system of faith, a system of belief, isn't it?"

Lizzie paused to think about it, then nodded in agreement.

"I guess."

"And would you ever tell your mum, who believes in this system, that it was 'all nonsense'? And don't say yes just to win the argument, because I know you wouldn't."

Lizzie thought about it for a second. She didn't disagree, so she had no retort.

"She's got you there," Prynce said from the front.

"All right, so what are Cancers apart from sad, then?" Lizzie asked.

"It really is mainly sad," Dimple said. "Crying. Moody. But quite loyal. Loving, depending on who deserves it. And we go into our shells, as the crab would suggest."

"And what about those pincers?" Prynce asked.

"Yeah." Dimple nodded. "They come out when we're ready."

They drove in silence for a second.

"Does anyone know what time Dad was born?" Dimple asked. "I want to do his birth chart."

"You tell him about birth charts and see how fast he calls you a witch." Nikisha laughed.

When they arrived at the house of Cyril's mother, Delores Ricketts (née Pennington), a huge former council house in Brixton, the gold Jeep was already parked outside. Nikisha parked behind it just as Danny turned up in his work van and beeped a hello.

"Look at that." As they walked past it, Prynce pointed at a set of deep and jagged scratches in the gold Jeep.

"Which woman do you think did that?" Lizzie said. She'd already had enough.

"Maybe it was an accident," Dimple replied.

"Your naïveté isn't an act, is it?" Lizzie asked her.

"Huh?" Dimple asked back.

"Don't worry." Lizzie shook her head.

They all waved at Danny as they stopped outside the battered gate and waited for him.

"How's it all going, people?" he asked when he got to them, hugging each in turn. "What's this woman's name again?"

"Danny! This woman is our grandmother, Delores," Nikisha said as they approached the front door. "And Dad loves her, so he's going to be distraught. Act accordingly."

"Why are we even he—" Lizzie couldn't get her sentence out before the door swung open and Cyril stood in front of them, not looking distraught at all.

"My children!" Cyril smiled proudly, his gold tooth winking at them.

They all sort of mumbled varied hellos while they waited for their dad to invite them in.

"What you waiting for?" Cyril laughed. "Come in, nuh?"

The house felt cold. The wallpaper was peeling and the carpet wasn't saying much either. They filed up the scuffed stairs behind their dad. Dimple noted that the house had a smell she'd smelled before. Like Clorox and dried lavender.

"Have any of you been here before?" Prynce asked from the back of the line.

"I . . . think so, actually," Dimple answered, wondering why these walls felt familiar to her. Maybe she *had* known her dad's mum. "Have you?"

"Yeah." Prynce shrugged. "Me and Nikisha used to come here sometimes. When we were young-young, though."

When they approached the first floor, the heart of the house back in the day, Dimple finally remembered that she'd been brought here, only once, when she was young. Maybe ten, maybe eleven. But the actual memories of the day were fuzzy, and they weren't quite coming to her.

Danny shook his head.

"I've never been here."

"Me neither," Lizzie said, careful not to touch anything, not even the banister. "How long do we have to be here?"

"Stop it," Nikisha said, trying to take the situation seriously by trying not to laugh. "But not long."

"She's in here," Cyril said as they arrived at a closed door. The paint was chipping off the wood, and the handle had fallen off.

He pushed the door open slowly and Dimple winced at the volume of the creak.

Cyril stepped into the room and beckoned for his children to follow him in.

Nikisha stepped in first, then Danny, then Lizzie, and finally Prynce. Dimple stayed in the hallway, looking from the broken banisters to the pictures on the walls. They were mainly of family members she'd never be able to recognize. She stepped closer to a picture of her dad as a child. He looked about ten, and he was in Jamaica, standing in front of a small shack. He looked genuinely happy. And not like now, not like the pseudo-happiness he projected to fool everyone into thinking everything was good; he actually looked happy. He was beaming. He had all his teeth, and all of them were white. He was holding a thick stalk of sugar cane that had been bitten in one hand, and a pair of smart shoes in the other, presumably Clarks, which were completely at odds with his grubby T-shirt and shorts.

"That's where I grew up." Cyril's voice made Dimple jump.

"Oh! You scared me!" Dimple's hand went to her chest. "I know. It's Jamaica. Clarendon, right?"

"Clarendon." Cyril nodded. "But, I mean, that's the house I grew up in."

"That?" Dimple pointed at the shack behind him. "But that looks like a shed."

"It was enough," Cyril told her. "We didn't need any more than that."

"Your family still live there?"

"Where else would they live?"

"Wait—where did you shower?" Dimple asked. "Did you have water facilities?"

Cyril laughed.

"A bucket was the shower."

Dimple considered this for a second.

"How come you never took me—or any of us—there?"

"Because, my dear, I know you English kids need—wha' you jus' call dem? Water facilities."

"Well, we'd make do," Dimple told him.

"One day," Cyril told her. "The house is bigger now."

Dimple knew she'd have to make her own way there if she ever wanted to go.

In the moment of silence they shared while they looked at the shack on the wall, anxiety started to build in Dimple's chest. Should she mention the money she'd given him? Was *he* going to mention it? Was he going to ask for more? She broke the silence the only way she knew how.

"Dad, do you know what time you were born?"

"I don't even really know which date mi born," Cyril told her.

"What do you mean? Isn't it the fifth of August?"

"They walked to the town to register me on the fifth," Cyril said. "I could have been born any day before dat."

"Right."

A passionate, rattling cough from Delores's bedroom signaled that Dimple should go in and join everyone else. She walked into the room. It smelled musty, stuffy. The curtains were closed, but a dim lamp in the corner lit it enough for Dimple to see that the room was clean. Apart from the bed, a bedside table next to it covered in pill bottles, a chair in one corner and a sink in the other, the room was bare. Her half-siblings were standing in a cluster at the foot of the bed.

Dimple shuffled up behind Prynce.

"Dimple?" Delores croaked. "Is you?"

"Er, yeah." Dimple nodded, not moving.

"Come mek mi see yuh."

Dimple stepped around Prynce and Lizzie and moved toward the bed. She looked down at the small figure that was almost lost in the sheets that were pulled up to her chin. Her eyes were nearly closed, and her skin was sallow. The biggest thing about her was the baby-blue bonnet on top of her head.

"The las' time mi see yuh, yuh was big as a house," Delores said.

Dimple didn't know what to say to that. What was there to say? *Yes? Thank you? I've slimmed down since then, maybe, and hopefully to your preference? What kind of house do you speak of? Semidetached or a small cottage?*

"But now you look more like dis one, wi' di African mooma." Delores pointed her dry, cracked lips toward Lizzie.

"I don't know who dis one favor," Delores said. "Prob'ly him white side. But him nose is Black."

Danny laughed awkwardly.

"How are you feeling, Delores?" Nikisha asked, needlessly loudly. "You're looking very small! And frail!"

"Why yuh shouting?" Delores asked. "And who you callin' Delores? Me is yuh grandmother, yuh mus' address me as such."

None of them said anything. They didn't know this woman to have recognized her on the street, let alone call her Grandmother.

"Anyway, we were just passing to say hello," Nikisha said on behalf of the siblings.

"To say goodbye, you mean," Delores grunted. "Yuh never pass by before. An' yuh come only to see mi deat' bed."

"That's not true!" Dimple protested quietly.

"Yeah it is," Prynce whispered to her.

"We just didn't know we were welcome here, that's all!" Dimple said. "And I speak for all of us when I say that if we knew we could come here, we would have been here a long time ago."

"Don't speak for all of us, please." Lizzie closed her eyes and shook her head.

"I'm trying to be *nice*," Dimple shot back to her sister.

"Speak only for yourself at all times," Lizzie said, folding her arms.

"How are your mothers?" Delores asked, her voice cracking halfway through the question. "I always told Cyril to bring them, mek me meet them *all*."

Danny piped up first. "Mine is good, thanks," he said. "She's cleaning at the school round the corner from where we live. And helping me look after my son, Marley, when I've got him."

"Mmm." Delores nodded. "So you look after your pickney?"

"Yeah." Danny shrugged, not wanting to look at Cyril in that moment. "Of course."

Cyril didn't want to look at Danny either. He pretended to be checking something on his phone.

"So you don't take after your daddy in that regard." Delores laughed, coughing and spluttering so much that the Pennington children jumped back.

"Death is not contagious." Delores sighed, recovering from the laugh as she wiped spittle from her mouth.

"And your mother?" She pointed a trembling finger at Nikisha and then Prynce, the effort of which tired her out just as much as the coughing fit.

"She's good!" Prynce replied politely. He didn't want her to curse him on her way out. "She's doing her own thing. We never know what it is, but we know she's busy, so. That's good."

"Your mother and Cyril were alike in that way. Both loved to be on road. Neither of them could stay still enough to look after anybody. Couldn't even look after themselves. It's a shame."

"Well, me and Prynce were both fine," Nikisha told Delores. "More than fine."

"So you say." Delores nodded. "But I see something different in both of you. A loneliness."

"I'm not lonely." Nikisha shook her head. "Are you, Prynce?"

"Well, that depends, you know. I think in a way, everyone is lonely. But then I think, I was born alone, I'll die al—"

Nikisha held a hand up to stop Prynce from continuing.

"And your mother." Delores looked at Lizzie. "I don't remember meeting her."

"You wouldn't have," Lizzie said.

"And why is that?" Delores smiled. "She think she's better than the rest of the baby mothers? Like you think you're better than your brothers and sisters?"

"No I don't." Lizzie stepped forward. "I . . . don't. Not at all!"

"We should make a move," Nikisha said to Delores. "And let you rest. You aren't making sense, Grandma."

"Oh, I'm making more sense than I've ever made." Delores nodded slowly. "I know you all more than you know yourselves. You're from me."

"You're *from* me?" Prynce mouthed, furrowing his deep brow.

"I haven't forgotten about Janet," Delores said to Dimple. "I think she's the only woman Cyril ever cared about. And he didn't even care about her that much, else he wouldn't have had this one here."

Delores looked over at Lizzie again.

"Okay, Mum, that's enough." Cyril finally stepped in. "She doesn't mean it."

"Your dad was just afraid of love," Delores told her grandchildren. "And it was my fault."

"It's time to go." Cyril, panicked that his (worst-kept) secret was out, gestured that his children leave the room.

"We're going already?" Prynce asked.

"Yes," Nikisha said, leaving the room.

"That was a short visit," Prynce said.

"It wasn't short enough," Danny said, exhausted.

"Goodbye," Delores called out after them.

"Bye," they said in unison as they trudged out of the room.

———————

The next day, Nikisha called Dimple.

"She died last night in her sleep."

"Oh my God," Dimple said. "Do you think—"

"No, Dimple, I do not think our visit is what finished her off."

"But are you sure?" Dimple asked. "Because I feel like we could have been a bit nicer."

"To a woman like that?" Nikisha laughed. "There's no point

being nice to women like that. Did Prynce tell you we used to go there?"

"Mmm," Dimple said, trying to figure out if she should feel more sad. Or even any sadness at all. She didn't feel any, after spending that small bit of time with Delores. Instead, she was thinking about whether or not she should eat now, then do yoga, or do yoga when she got off the phone to her sister and make brunch.

"We went there a few times. Dad would tell our mum he was taking us for the weekend and he'd drop us off there on Friday evening, say he'd come and take us out for dinner, then we wouldn't see him till Sunday night when he dropped us back home. And trust me, she was horrible to us. She wouldn't acknowledge us, she wouldn't even feed us properly. It wasn't neglect or anything, the portions were just so *small*. And she'd *always* tell us to say our prayers before we ate, before we went to bed, before we did *anything*. I used to have to sneak food for me and Prynce from the kitchen. And believe me, I'd be saying my prayers that she didn't notice. The beatings she doled out were horrible."

"Do you think we'll have to go to the funeral?" Dimple asked, rolling out her yoga mat, wondering if her followers would like to see her doing this session.

"Oh, definitely," Nikisha said. "Nine night first, though."

"Why are we like this?" Dimple sighed, kneeling on the mat. "So many practices and we don't even know her. I don't want to dedicate a week and a half to this woman."

"It's okay," Nikisha said. "It's only going to be one night. But the funeral you'll have to come to."

"Hopefully it'll be in Jamaica," Dimple said. "Nice to get some sun."

"No, it'll be at her church in Clapham."

"Was she a pastor?"

"Dimple," Nikisha said. "Please. You're like Prynce. Sometimes you just *say* stuff. I'll speak to you later."

"Well, she might have been," Dimple said to herself as she put the phone down. "I can't know everything."

Her phone buzzed with a message from Nikisha.

Nikisha:

And call Dad. Tell him you're sorry his mum's dead.

Dimple looked for her dad's number. She couldn't remember the last time she'd called him. She typed "Dad" into the contacts search bar.

Dad

DAD

Dad 2

Dad Jamaica

Dad Jamaica Line 2

Dad New

Dad New new

Dad recent

Dad THIS ONE

She scrolled the list. She tried Dad THIS ONE. It didn't connect. She rolled her eyes, tried Dad recent. It started to ring. She felt nervous, and didn't know why.

"Hello?" he answered eventually. He sounded like he usually did.

"Hi, Dad," she said gently.

"Who's dis?" Cyril asked.

"Your daughter," Dimple said. "Are you okay?"

"Which one?"

"Ha-ha," she said flatly.

"Lizzie?" Cyril asked.

"It's Dimple, Dad!"

"Sorry, mi neva know," Cyril said. "You all sound similar."

"Don't apologize," Dimple said, grateful for the apology even though it was, as it always was, disingenuous. She couldn't believe he couldn't tell his children's voices apart. "How are you doing, Dad?"

"I'm all right, how are you?" Cyril replied. "The sun is out."

"Oh." Anxiety washed over Dimple. He didn't know. He didn't know his mum had died, and she was going to have to break the news to him. She was going to ruin his day, his life, by telling him his mother had died.

"Dad," she said. "I've just spoken to Nikisha. She told me about your mum."

Dimple thought this way maybe she could share some of the blame with Nikisha.

"Okay," Cyril said, his tone largely unchanged.

"I'm sorry, but she's dead." Dimple used the voice she always used to deliver the saddest news. Similar to the one she used when she was announcing that she and Kyron had broken up, but a little bit less dramatic.

Cyril didn't say anything for a while.

"Dad?"

"Sorry, sorry, I was just looking for something."

"What? Looking for what?"

Cyril sighed.

"I know about mi mother, Dimple."

"You know?" Dimple yelped. "Why don't you sound sad, then?"

"Wha' yuh waan mi fi do?" Cyril asked her in a tone she'd never heard before. He sounded close to angry. "Lay down an' die wid her?"

"No," Dimple said quietly, tears filling her eyes.

"But listen, every cloud has a silver lining. When I sell that house, all my debts, dem gaan."

Dimple held her breath and waited for him to say he'd pay her back. The Kyron blackmail fund was no closer to being reached even though she'd just been paid an insubstantial but better-than-exposure amount to post some products from a natural skin-care range. These were the perks of fifty-two thousand followers.

"So! My mother never died for nothing. I'll let you know when the funeral is."

When Dimple got off the phone, she cried on his behalf. Or maybe she cried for herself. She'd always longed to have a dad in her life, but now that she did, it was shit.

"Nikisha?" Dimple answered the phone. "Thank God you called. I need to talk about my feelings."

"I've been roped into helping Dad sort out the funeral, so I'm bringing Nicky and Amara for the night. Is your mum home?"

"No, she's at a detox retreat till Thursday," Dimple said. "Don't worry, we're not going to have an event like last time."

"You think I'm scared of your mum?" Nikisha laughed.

"I know you aren't," Dimple said. "It's me who's scared of the both of you together. I thought I was going to have an anxiety attack sitting round a table with the two of you. All of that passive aggression almost killed me. Never again. But . . . is Dad okay?"

"I don't know," Nikisha told Dimple. "I don't ask about things like that."

"But he's lost his mum, Nikisha."

"I'm not concerned with people's feelings the way you are, Dimple," Nikisha said. "I get things done."

A few hours later, Dimple heard her niece and nephew before she saw them. When she opened the door, a small boy, Nicky, ran into her thighs and hugged them tight. Amara walked in absentmindedly after her brother, not paying any attention to who or what was inside.

Nikisha smiled a wide hello as she got to the door.

"Amara, TAKE OFF YOUR SHOES!" she shouted into the house, and Amara toddled back toward the door and kicked her shoes off. She turned and ran back into the house, screaming for no reason other than being two years old.

"Er, hello!" Dimple looked down at her nephew, who was still hugging her thighs. "Do you like crisps?"

"Say hello to your aunty," Nikisha said to her son.

Nicky looked up into Dimple's eyes and blinked.

"Hello, Aunty!" He smiled, his new adult front teeth slightly too big for his mouth.

"Let go of her now," Nikisha said. "And go and take your sister's coat off."

Nicky released Dimple's thighs from his grasp before he ran into the house to look for his sister.

"I think I'm a bit awkward around kids," Dimple told Nikisha. "I haven't really hung out with them before."

"What do you mean, you're awkward around kids? They're kids, they don't care about you or your personality." Nikisha put a big overnight bag down on the kitchen counter. "In here is everything you'll need for the night. Changes of clothes, toothbrushes and toothpaste, all of that. Amara has a special soap for her eczema, but don't worry about anything too much because Nicky knows how everything goes. If you get stuck, he'll let you know, trust me."

"And what time are you collecting them tomorrow?" The panic in Dimple's voice was not hidden well, and Nikisha obviously laughed at her.

"Early afternoon," Nikisha said. "I just have some stuff to sort and these two, they don't help."

"Are you leaving right now?"

"Would you like to talk about your feelings now, or when I come back for these two?" Nikisha asked flatly.

"Now, please," Dimple said.

"Okay, tell me what's happened. I've only got— Amara, that does NOT go in your mouth! OUT! NOW!"

Nikisha ran over to her daughter and held her hand out as Amara spat one of Janet's small ornamental beads into it. Nikisha shook Amara's spit off it and placed it back on the side table.

"It's okay, I'll give it a rinse later." Dimple grimaced.

"Sorry, carry on."

"You were the one saying something."

"What was I saying?" Nikisha asked.

"You said, 'I've only got.'"

"Yep. I've only got a few minutes, so be quick."

"I don't think I can talk about my feelings under time pressure," Dimple groaned.

"Well, you're going to have to."

"Okay, fine. I just, I feel like I feel guilty all the time. Like I've got myself in a pit of guilt that I can't get out of. The Kyron thing being the main thing," Dimple whispered. "Which I think I'm going to have PTSD about for a long time."

"Right, okay," Nikisha replied efficiently.

"And then obviously there's the stuff with Roman that I feel guilty about, and I just keep thinking, am I a bad person?"

"You aren't a bad person— Nicky, PLEASE can you keep an eye on your sister?"

Nicky looked up from the book he was reading for a brief second, looked at Amara, then carried on reading.

"Sorry, go on," Nikisha said.

"It was you! You were saying I wasn't a bad person."

"Right," Nikisha said. "You aren't a bad person, you did what you had to do. Women are just made to feel bad for making the choices that they need to make. Do you think men feel bad about having two women? Look at Dad."

"I mean, the Kyron thing is pretty bad. I should probably feel bad about it."

Nikisha nodded.

"Stand in your choices, little sister. That's all the advice I can offer you."

Dimple looked over at her nephew and remembered the picture of Kyron as a child.

"I don't know if I can."

"What else can you do, Dimple?"

Dimple truly did not know.

"Do you?" she asked her half sister.

"Do I what?"

"Stand in your choices."

"My choices are right here in front of you," Nikisha said, nodding at Nicky and Amara. "I stand in, and with, them every single day."

———————

When Nikisha had said goodbye to her children, Dimple closed the door behind her and went back into the living room. She looked at the two small people in front of her and wondered how they'd all get through the next few hours.

It took a few minutes, but as soon as Amara realized that her mum had gone, her lip trembled. The lip tremble turned into a small wail.

"She won't stop now," Nicky said from behind his book, a warning that made way for an almost continual wail from Amara that only stopped every few seconds when she needed to breathe.

Dimple called Lizzie.

"Hey, Lizzie. Are you free? . . . No, sadly for me the screaming isn't the TV. It's Nicky and Amara. Well, mainly Amara. She absolutely loves screaming . . . Would you mind coming to help me? I'm sorry to ask."

She wasn't sorry to ask at all. Dimple ended the call when Lizzie agreed to come and help her.

"What do I need to do here?" Dimple asked her nephew. "To stop the screaming."

"I dunno." Nicky shrugged, putting his book down. "But I'm thirsty."

Dimple went to the fridge and pulled out a carton of apple juice. She chucked it over to Nicky and instead of him catching it, it hit him square in the chest.

Even Amara stopped wailing at the hollow thud of the impact.

"Why did you do that?" Nicky asked, rubbing his chest. "I don't even like apple juice."

"Sorry!" Dimple ran over to her nephew. "I thought you'd catch it."

"But you didn't tell me you were going to throw it."

Today was the day Dimple would realize how literal children were.

Amara picked herself up and waddled over to her brother. She hoisted herself up onto the sofa with some difficulty and started to pat Nicky on the chest where the juice had hit him.

"Should I have done that?" Dimple asked Nicky. "I didn't know if it hurt you. Do you want a hug or something? But you might not like hugs, I don't know! I didn't like hugs when I was young. Sorry, I'm oversharing. I don't think I'm *that* good with kids."

"I'm okay, Aunty," Nicky said.

After Dimple went into the hallway to take some deep breaths, she returned to the living room to find Amara sleeping next to her brother, who was reading.

"She fell asleep quickly," Dimple remarked, and Nicky ignored her.

An hour later, Nicky had eaten and was still reading peacefully, and amazingly, Amara still wasn't awake. Dimple was about to text Lizzie to tell her not to bother coming when the doorbell rang.

"I was about to say you didn't need to come," Dimple said as she opened the front door.

"Oh. Well, I'm here now." Lizzie kicked off her loafers. "But I don't hear any screaming."

"Yeah, it was weird, she sort of instantly fell asleep." Dimple led Lizzie into the living room. "Nicky, you remember your aunty Lizzie, don't you?"

Nicky looked up from his book and blinked at both of his aunts.

"He won't," Lizzie said. "The last time I saw him he was tiny."

"Hello, Aunty Lizzie," Nicky said dutifully.

Lizzie smiled at him.

"You're polite."

"Thank you," Nicky replied.

"Don't be too polite, though." Interesting advice from Lizzie to her nephew. "You don't want people to think they can walk all over you."

"Lizzie, he's nine," Dimple reminded her as she wandered across the room to the kitchen area. "You want a drink?"

"No, thanks, I brought my water." Lizzie pulled a pink bottle out of her bag, followed Dimple, and put it on the counter. "After your mum last time I didn't want to take anything from this house in case she charged me for it."

"I'm sorry about her, really," Dimple said. "She's not here for a while. But mainly, she wouldn't do that. I don't know what got into her."

"She feels a way." Lizzie shrugged. "If I came home and all the kids of the man I thought was going to be my husband were in my house, I might be a bit . . . spiky."

"But it's not your fault that our dad didn't turn out to be the man of her dreams."

"It's whatever. You okay, though?"

"Are you okay down here with your sister, Nicky?" Dimple called across the room. "Me and Aunty Lizzie are going to go upstairs for a chat. Just call us if you need anything."

Nicky ignored her again.

"He's not always polite," Dimple told Lizzie as she led the way up the stairs. "This is the second time he's ignored me."

"Stop being so sensitive." Lizzie rolled her eyes. "He's nine, like you said."

They walked to Dimple's room.

"You spoken to Dad?" Dimple asked Lizzie. "Silly question, of course you have."

"No," Lizzie said. "I'll say I'm sorry at the funeral."

"Seriously?" Dimple was taken aback. "His mum died, Lizzie."

"I know," Lizzie said as they got to Dimple's room. "But when anything has happened in my life, he hasn't called me. I'm not going to pretend we have a relationship when we don't."

"I see," Dimple said, making herself comfortable on the bed. Lizzie pulled out the chair from Dimple's dressing table and sat down.

"What's happening with Kyron?" Lizzie asked.

"Nothing," Dimple told Lizzie. "As far as he knows, I'm trying to find the money."

"Right. And can I ask you another question?" Lizzie asked in a tone that unsettled Dimple.

"Yeah, anything," Dimple said nervously.

"I don't want you to take this the wrong way," Lizzie said. "But . . . I just keep thinking about that night."

"Okay . . ."

"Why *didn't* you call the police?" Lizzie asked. "I know we've said the whole 'people don't trust the police thing,' but still."

Dimple, who always thought the worst, and spent all her time worrying about the worst, had anticipated this question.

"Are you asking if I pushed him?"

"If you did, I don't judge you," Lizzie said, sitting down. "I obviously don't know the full story and I don't know about your relationship, but . . . I kind of feel like I have to ask. I hope you understand that."

Dimple blinked a bit before she took a deep breath. Then she got up and closed the door in case Nicky heard anything. She didn't know a lot about children, but she knew that often they heard more than anyone thought they did, and the last thing she wanted was for Nicky to go to school and start talking about a man called Kyron being put in the back of a van.

"I would never, and have never, hurt anyone intentionally," Dimple said. "Physically," she added. "The relationship was bad, but there was no way I would have done that, whether I knew he was going to hit his head like that or not. He came at me, tried to strangle me, I scratched his face—which is why I didn't call the police first—and then when he came at me again, he slipped over. I know I've already said this to you, and the reason my story hasn't changed is because it's true."

"Right," Lizzie said. She liked dealing in facts.

"I thought that if the police turned up at my house and saw him on the floor with scratches on his face, they'd think I attacked him. Even though, yeah, I'm small, and I had bruises on my neck that I had to cover with makeup for the next two weeks, I still didn't think that they'd believe me." Dimple spoke so quietly that Lizzie had to strain her ears to hear her. "They never believe us."

Lizzie moved her chair closer to Dimple.

"Did he do that often? Like, hurting you?"

"No, not physically. And that's why I scratched him, like, out of shock, you know?"

"But why did he do that?"

"I don't know. Well, I know why he was angry, but I don't know why he put his hands on me." Dimple lay back on the bed. "Well, actually, I think it was two things. We'd broken up for the millionth time, but this was the first time I uploaded a video saying it was over, and he didn't like that. And he was obsessed with the idea that there was someone else."

"But there was," Lizzie said flatly.

"What?"

"There was," Lizzie repeated.

"Mmm." Dimple nodded.

"Can you see where I'm going here?" Lizzie leaned forward.

"It was complicated. And it's done now." Dimple shrugged, feeling very judged. "Roman won't answer my calls, so."

"So his paranoia didn't come from nowhere, then?"

"What are you saying, Lizzie?"

"Nothing!" Lizzie held her hands up. "I'm just trying to get all the facts, that's all."

"For what?"

"I don't want you to take this the wrong way, but I know that you're very all about you, and that's, whatever, that's just the way you are."

A punch to the gut for Dimple.

"But you know we're all affected by what happened that night, right?"

"I know," Dimple said. "You've already told me you're struggling and stuff, and I'm sorry. Does your girlfriend still think you were cheating?"

"I'm not talking about me; have you checked on Danny? He might seem cheerful all the time but I think he's trying to keep it together because he's our big brother. And I'm pretty sure Prynce is smoking a lot more since it happened."

"You didn't know them before, so you don't know those things are true." Dimple wasn't someone to get very angry, but she felt stirrings of something close to that inside her. Her Cancer crab pincers usually never came out, but Lizzie was drawing them out. Why was she saying all this stuff?

"Okay, fine, maybe it's easier for you to believe that I'm projecting my own stuff onto them, but have you *asked* them?" Lizzie asked. "And I know that Nikisha seems like she has everything together, but I truly doubt that she does. She's just doing that big-sister thing of holding everyone down, but she's as fragile as anyone. She's just older than us and is used to being a parent."

"I do care about other people's feelings, you know," Dimple told Lizzie.

"But in conjunction to yours, it seems like," Lizzie shot back.

"Have you got a problem with me, Lizzie?"

"I don't!" Lizzie exclaimed. "I just think you could *think* about other people. You're suddenly in this world where everyone looks at you, so now you think even the people around you, even us, are your audience. And we aren't!"

"I—I know you aren't!" Dimple sat up and looked Lizzie in the eyes that were almost identical to hers. "You keep forgetting that I didn't call you that night, I called *Nikisha*! You all decided to come."

"And you keep forgetting that we didn't know what we were stepping into, it seems!"

"So you're saying that if you knew, you wouldn't have come?"

"Obviously not!" Lizzie furrowed her brow as she stared hard at Dimple.

That hurt Dimple, even though Lizzie's response was reasonable.

"I would have come for you if I'd known you needed me." Dimple was on the verge of tears. She didn't understand how they'd gotten here. "Do you not like me very much, Lizzie?"

Lizzie scoffed.

"Don't be so sensitive!"

"Answer the question!"

"I don't know you, Dimple," Lizzie said. "All I know is that we have this thing in common."

"As in blood, or the Kyron thing?"

"The latter," Lizzie said. "The blood thing, too, but it's not like we can say we know each other like sisters."

"Not because I haven't tried, Lizzie."

"When you say tried, what do you mean? Calling me up in the middle of the day to come and help you with Nikisha's kids doesn't make a sibling bond," Lizzie snorted.

"Yeah, but I—" Dimple stopped her sentence because she had

realized that, actually, Lizzie was right. "Well, I'm sorry. I thought I'd done more."

"Okay. Well, you haven't."

"But . . ."

"But what?"

"But you can also try with me, you know. It's not been easy."

"Who said anything about easy?" Lizzie asked. "None of this has been easy, especially when you get pulled into something criminal you didn't ask to be pulled into."

Dimple blinked for ages.

"I don't know what it's like to have to be someone's sister!" she told Lizzie.

"And neither do I, Dimple," Lizzie said as she stood. "But I guess we might as well work it out together. Have you got any coloring pencils? I bet you do. I bet you were part of that mindful coloring book movement."

———

The next afternoon, after several ordeals—including Amara breaking everything she went near, and Nicky sleepwalking into the hallway and almost falling down the stairs—Nikisha came to collect her children.

"Was everything okay?"

"Yeah!" Dimple said, lying. "Did you have a nice evening?"

"It was fine." Nikisha nodded. "I'm glad aunty duties went so well. Now I know I have a babysitter on call."

Dimple withered inside. She smiled on the outside and said, "Yes!"

"Did you get my message about the nine night?" Nikisha said.

"Yeah, but do we *really* have to go to that?" Dimple asked.

"What kind of question is that?"

"I'm just asking!" Dimple said. "I dunno, it just feels weird not ever seeing someone your whole life, then suddenly feeling really involved."

"You know what your problem is?" Nikisha asked.

"No, but I'm sure you'll tell me."

"You feel too much," Nikisha said.

"Tell me about it," Dimple said, wondering if this was her whole identity given that both of her sisters had said this within twenty-four hours of the other.

CHAPTER
TEN

DIMPLE TURNED TO HER mum as she parked in the closest spot she could find near Delores's house.

"You know, you didn't have to come."

"I know I didn't," Janet said, turning the wheel smoothly as she parallel parked. "But despite everything, when you were born, Dimple, your grandmother was the first person to visit me. And for that alone, I'm going to pay my respects."

"Was she?" Dimple asked.

"Yep." Janet nodded as she turned the engine off, her keys clattering in the hand she was trying to stop from shaking. "I told your dad I was in labor, but for some reason that was never made clear to me, he couldn't make it. So he sent her in his place. After me, and the midwife, she was the first person to hold you."

Janet was still telling Dimple this new information about Delores as they walked up to the house, but her focus changed when they got to the front door.

"God, they really let this house go." Janet shook her head as she sneered at the weeds that had overtaken the front garden. "Your grandmother used to be so house-proud."

The front door opened and a short and stocky woman wearing

jeans and a black blouse appeared. She blinked at Janet and Dimple with eyes she shared with her big brother, Cyril.

"Lavinia." Janet smiled. "I'm sorry for your loss."

"Janet!" Lavinia stepped back in shock. "I didn't expect to see you here."

"And yet." Janet walked into the house. It looked almost exactly as it had when she'd stepped foot in it decades back. Just older. Like she was. "Here I am."

"Is that you, Dimple?" Lavinia asked, taking Dimple in. "You look the *same*! Still a big girl! You take after your mother in that regard."

"Yep." Dimple covered her soft stomach with her hand. "So everyone keeps saying."

"How are you all doing?" Janet, who had long gotten used to these comments from Cyril's family, asked Lavinia as she followed her through the house.

"Well, you know," Lavinia said. "It was hardly a shock, and we're glad she's not in pain anymore."

"She lived a long life," Janet said sympathetically as she entered the front room behind Lavinia. "A very long life."

"You two help yourselves to food and drink. I'm just going to see if I can find Marvette," Lavinia said, squeezing Janet's plump arm gently before walking away.

"Who's Marvette?" Dimple asked her mum as she watched Lavinia move through the room.

"Your aunt," Janet told her. "Your dad's youngest sister. She's a bit of a funny one. Didn't have any children. Used to keep herself to herself. I was quite scared of her, actually."

"Why?" Dimple asked. "It's not like you to be scared of anyone."

"She used to look at me in a weird way," Janet replied. "Like she was looking *through* me."

The room was full of people Dimple guessed were extended family members and friends of her grandma. They stood around talking energetically and eating with abandon as though somebody hadn't died. Sitting on the sofa in front of them was Danny, his son Marley on his lap, and an older white woman who was a third of Danny's size squeezed in next to him.

"Mum, I'm gonna go and say hello to Danny."

"So you're leaving me as soon as we get here?" Janet asked her, scared that Marvette would appear and look through her the way she did in the nineties.

"No! I was just—I'll stay with you," Dimple told her mum. "Do you want something to eat?"

Janet shook her head.

"No, I won't stay long."

"Little sis!" Danny clocked Dimple and stood up, lifting Marley and balancing him on his hip as he moved toward her and Janet.

"This is Marley!" he said, jostling his son gently. "Marley, say hello to your aunty Dimple. And this is Janet, Aunty Dimple's mummy. Say hello!"

Marley looked at Dimple and Janet, then buried his face in his dad's shoulder.

"He's shy." Danny laughed. "I don't think he likes being around so many people."

"How are you, Danny?" Janet asked coldly.

"Yeah, I'm good, you know." Danny smiled. "Work, and this one keeping me busy."

"I see your mum came here, too. Tracy is her name?" Janet knew full well that the woman who had come before her was Tracy Smith.

"Yeah!" Danny nodded. "I know she was close to Delores back in the day, so."

Janet looked over to the sofa. An older man and woman she recognized as Cyril's sister Tessilda and her husband, whose name she didn't remember back when she met him and definitely wouldn't remember now, had taken Danny's place. They were laughing with Tracy. It stung Janet. Cyril would *always* speak so favorably about

Tracy. She always used to hear about how "nice" Tracy was. All these years later it hurt to see that play out in front of her. She could be nice, too. Just in a different, more concealed way.

Dimple didn't want her mum to drink alcohol, especially not after the detox retreat she'd had to hear so much about, so she squeezed through to the dining table and filled two little plastic cups with ginger beer for them. When she made her way back, Dimple stood close to Marley as Danny held him and tried to engage him in some way, but Marley was still having none of it.

Dimple was about to give up on peekaboo with her nephew when she saw Nikisha and Prynce walk into the room. Behind them was a slim woman in a tight white dress who looked almost exactly like the two children she'd given birth to. Bernice was an undeniably attractive woman, and Janet, who had clocked her seconds after Dimple did, had always known this. Her girlfriends had, often with spiteful delight, clued her in when they'd seen Cyril out and about with his women, and for some reason, she saw Bernice as her main competition. Maybe because Cyril had gone back to her. Janet eyed Bernice's trim frame and wished she'd worn something that was more flattering.

"Is this the rest of the Pennington clan?" Bernice asked loudly as she pushed through Nikisha and Prynce and sashayed toward Dimple and Danny. She ignored Janet. She was well aware of who Janet was and, ironically, had always seen Janet as her main competition.

"This is Bernice," Nikisha said when she and Prynce had caught up to their mum.

"Nice to meet you." Dimple smiled.

"Aren't you pretty?" Bernice screeched, cupping Dimple's face with a rough hand. "And nice and big! And look at all this hair!"

Bernice buried her hands in Dimple's curls before she turned her attention to Danny, who already looked a bit worried about how she'd size him up.

"And who is this big man before me?" Bernice shouted, standing back and looking Danny up and down. "Such a big man could never be Cyril's son."

"Ha-ha," Danny said instead of laughing. He wasn't one for attention, and that was never going to change. "My mum's brothers are tall, so."

"Must be!" Bernice laughed loudly before finally turning her attention to Janet.

"And your name is?" she asked, knowing full well what Janet's name was.

"I'm Janet." Janet extended a hand to her historic competitor.

"I know *you*! Baby mother number three!" Bernice screeched again, batting Janet's hand away and pulling her into a big, overbearing hug. "Well, I am *Bernice*, baby mother number one. The original. And I see the white baby mum over there."

When Bernice let go of her, Janet pursed her lips before taking a big sip of her drink. She wished the ginger beer that she gulped down could have converted into the strongest rum in existence right there in her hand.

"I know the other one isn't turning up," Bernice screeched, then let out a cackle. "Too stush. She never liked the rest of us."

Watching Bernice in action, Dimple could see why Nikisha was the way she was. There was something about being forged in chaos that made somebody so focused and organized. It was both a trauma response and a survival technique.

"Your daddy here yet?" Bernice asked, looking around the room. "I bet he's not. That man runs on his own time, I swear."

"I haven't seen him and I've been here awhile," Danny said, shifting Marley onto his other hip.

"Where are Nicky and Amara?" Dimple asked Nikisha.

"With their dad. I couldn't be bothered to bring them here."

"Do you think Lizzie will come?" Danny asked Nikisha.

"Nah. I spoke to her earlier. She said she'll come to the funeral to pay her respects, but that's her limit."

"You talking about the Nigerian one?" Bernice asked, inserting herself into the conversation verbally and physically, pushing Janet out of the way as she stood close to Dimple. "Whew, I remember when I first bucked baby mother number four! Me and her went *at it*! I didn't think either of us was gonna make it out alive, you know. The police had to come and break it up."

Janet wasn't going to compete with this *braggadocious* woman. She made her way over to the drinks table, leaving Dimple with this new family she obviously wanted to spend more time with.

"Let's go and say hi to Tracy," Nikisha said to Prynce, nodding toward the corner of the room that Tracy stood in.

"Have you met her before?" Dimple asked them.

"Yep," Prynce said, walking over to Danny's mum.

"That was abrupt," Dimple said to herself as she watched Nikisha follow their brother across the room. She watched Tracy pull Prynce into her and give him a huge kiss on the cheek that he immediately rubbed off, which made Tracy laugh. Dimple was going to go over there, but her mum was looking at the drinks table a little too passionately, so she went to intervene there instead.

Around an hour later, Cyril finally arrived. He'd been held up at the betting shop. When he walked into the front room, he thought his eyes were deceiving him when he saw Bernice in one corner of the room, Tracy in the other, Janet by the drinks table, and the children they shared in the middle. He held his breath as he looked for Kemi. The only reason the nine night hadn't turned into a bloodbath was because she wasn't here. She was dignified, yes, but there was something about Bernice that sent that out the window.

Cyril wondered whom to say hello to first. The kids could wait; he'd seen them more recently. He decided to approach them in order of who'd given him children. He moved through the room, thanking friends of his mother who expressed their condolences, but with his focus still on his women. When he reached Bernice, who was talking to his sister Lavinia, he smiled his most charming smile at her and pulled her into a tight embrace. Lavinia sucked her teeth and walked away.

"What happened, you fell in the bottle of aftershave before you left the house?" Bernice asked Cyril when he was close enough for her to smell him. "How you doing, *Fireshot*?"

Bernice clapped the father of her children on the back roughly as she hugged him.

"It's been a long time. You're looking well. Tired, but well." Bernice could never resist a dig.

"Not as well as you." Cyril looked her up and down, remembering the last time they'd been intimate. He'd always be drawn to Bernice's fire, even though it always burned him.

"Don't start with all that." Bernice laughed, throwing her head back. "I'm here to pay my respects. And I don't want to make the other two jealous."

"I'll catch up with you properly later," Cyril said as he crossed the room, making his way over to Tracy.

Tracy's eyes lit up when she laid eyes on Cyril. The thing about Tracy was, she'd never expected anything of Cyril. She knew the type of man he was when she'd first met him, and had never asked for anything more than that. She knew what the score was, and she knew that he knew that she knew, too. They'd never, ever had one conversation about what they as a pair would "be." A man like Cyril would never stay *still*, and that was fine. He'd given her Danny, and that was good enough.

"How are you, my love?" Tracy moved toward Cyril and kissed him on the cheek. "I'm sorry about your mum."

Cyril put a hand on Tracy's slight shoulder and squeezed it gently.

"Thank you, darlin'," he said, noticing how much older she looked. Gray streaks ran through her once-blond hair, and the crow's-feet around her kind eyes had deepened. She was still beautiful to him, though.

"I see you never stopped feeding Danny up," Cyril remarked.

"Oh, he's my big boy." Tracy smiled widely. "And isn't Marley *gorgeous?*"

Cyril hadn't met Marley yet, and brushed off the creeping embarrassment he felt about that, and everything else where Danny was concerned.

"Come and say hello to your grandson!" Tracy pulled Cyril over to Danny and Marley.

Danny was nervous. Not as nervous as Cyril was.

"Hi, Dad." Danny smiled. "This is Marley. Marley, this is . . . your grandad!"

"Call me Cyril," Cyril said to Marley, holding out a fist. "Gimme a spud, likkle man."

Marley stared at his grandad, blinking his long lashes at him slowly while taking his face in. He reached his arms out to Cyril, who stepped back.

"I don't hug and dem tings dere!" Cyril laughed nervously. "You teaching this boy to be soft, Danny?"

That hit Danny harder than any punch he'd ever felt.

"Come on, Marley, let's get you something to eat," he whispered to Marley, hugging his son tighter than he ever had.

"Cyril." Tracy shook her head at the father of her son, disappointed. Not that she expected any more from him.

"How's your mum?" Cyril asked her, changing the subject. "She still in the same place?"

"Nah." Tracy shook her head. "We moved her into a home a couple of years ago. She wasn't all there and it didn't feel right, us leaving her in the flat alone."

"Let me go and say hello to a friend I've just seen," Cyril said. Whether or not he'd heard what Tracy had just said, he'd never have been able to give an emotionally appropriate response.

Tracy nodded as she watched Cyril walk away. She knew that he'd be making his way over to Janet, and very happily let him go. Tracy had long stopped trying to hold Cyril's attention.

Janet was pouring herself another ginger beer when she felt Cyril behind her. She didn't need to look to know it was he who had placed his hands on her shoulders and squeezed them firmly. All these years later, she remembered how it felt when Cyril touched her.

She turned around, cup in hand, and felt some feeling she couldn't name stir in her as she looked into his eyes.

"Janet," Cyril said. "As beautiful as ever."

And to him, Janet really did remain one of the most beautiful women he'd ever seen. In truth, of all the women he'd been with, Cyril had always seen Janet as the one who got away. And not because of how she looked, or anything like that. Janet was the only woman who had ever been so totally forgiving of the way he was. He knew she wanted more from him, and he'd always promise it, but whenever he disappeared for days and weeks on end, she always understood, and stopped him before he could make excuses. She was so enamored with this man, who looked so cool, who played her songs, and who made her laugh, that she was happy for any little bit of time she got with him, even when him not being near her made her cry. And because Janet never gave him any trouble, Cyril *tried* to be as consistent as someone like Cyril could be with her.

In the time they'd spent together, he'd opened his eyes to all sides of her, and he was fond of every side that she'd shown him. He liked how driven she was, how determined she was. And he liked that she allowed him to be there for her when she was sad, too. This strong woman needing him made him feel like he had a purpose.

Cyril had taken Janet to meet his mum. This was a big thing to him. Delores already knew Bernice through working with her mum, and had met Tracy by accident when Cyril had taken her food shopping and they'd bumped into her and Danny in Tesco. But he was *proud* of the relationship-like thing he had going on with Janet. But when Janet had swiftly started to make strides in her career, being around her made Cyril feel inadequate. It made him feel small. He knew he wasn't going anywhere in his job. Why did he need to? He liked what he did, and he didn't want to put in a drop more effort than was necessary.

And so, annoyingly, once Janet had met Delores, Cyril scared himself into thinking that the relationship was a bit too real, which is where his misstep with Kemi came in. And when Kemi had told Cyril that she, too, was pregnant, a little voice in his head told him that the lives of both of those children and the women who carried them would be better if he wasn't involved.

He also knew he hadn't learned from the mistakes he'd made with Nikisha and Danny. Kemi had, very gracefully, kicked him to the curb when she saw him for who he was, and, wounded by his own decisions, he made himself scarce in Janet's life, too. He didn't explain anything to her, he just disappeared. And even though Janet had always been patient with him, she knew, deep in her stomach, that this time he wasn't coming back. And her like of drinking turned into her love of drinking, and that turned into a need of drinking.

"How are you, Cyril?" Janet asked, now pouring herself a stiff drink that she felt she deserved. Cyril Pennington was the only man who'd ever broken her heart. There had been men before him, and there had certainly been men after, but it was the scars of Cyril that still ran deep.

"I'm all right, Jan," Cyril told her. "Bearing up. But it's good to see you."

"I wanted to come and pay my respects," Janet said. "Your mum was certainly a character, and we didn't always see eye to eye, but I'll never forget that she was there for me."

"Like I never was, you mean?" Cyril asked her. He was always getting to himself before you could get to him.

"You said it, not me." Janet took a sip from her cup, her body relaxing when the rum hit her stomach.

"Dimple takes after you." Cyril smiled. "She's a pretty girl."

"Mmm." Janet nodded, looking over at Dimple, who was deep in conversation with Nikisha, Danny, and Prynce. "And she's a good girl, too. I'm very proud of her."

"So you're saying she doesn't take after me at all?" Cyril forced a laugh.

"I couldn't have dealt with that," Janet said. "She's like me."

"What, so you're saying I was so bad that you couldn't have my mini-me running around?"

"I don't know what you want me to tell you, Cyril." Janet sighed. "You know—"

"Cyril!" Bernice shouted as she walked over. "How come you're talking to number three more than you're talking to number one?"

Cyril winced as Bernice's voice cut through the room, as big and as sharp as a machete.

"She your favorite?" Bernice asked. "You better mind I don't get jealous."

"Now, now, Bernice." Cyril turned to her. "Stop all that talk."

"Well, I have to ask, don't I?" Bernice clapped a hand down on Cyril's shoulder. "Because you did breed me twice, but you can only talk to me for ten seconds before you come running over here!"

Janet drained the cup of rum. She didn't know why she had come here. She should have known this would happen.

Cyril tried to defuse the situation.

"I like you all the same."

"Let's see, shall we?" Bernice smiled wickedly before beckoning Tracy over.

"How you doin', darlin'?" Tracy asked Bernice. "Everything all right?"

Tracy wasn't scared of Bernice. She knew Bernice's bark was worse than her bite. And Tracy definitely wasn't scared of Janet. She felt sorry for her if anything. She could see how she felt about Cyril written all over her face, and guessed Cyril had had the same effect on this poor woman for a long time.

"I'm asking Cyril here who his favorite is." Bernice laughed.

"I'm sure Cyril doesn't have a favorite," Tracy tutted. She turned her attention to Janet, who now looked like she wanted to be anywhere but here. "You all right, darlin'? It's Janet, isn't it? I'm Danny's mum, Tracy. I didn't get to say hello earlier."

"Good to meet you," Janet said, pouring herself another drink. She wanted to turn into Captain Morgan himself at this point.

"I'm only playing!" Bernice screeched. "Cyril's favorite person is himself."

"All right, Bernice, all right," Cyril said firmly, taking hold of her wrist gently.

"Oh, you're telling me off now?" Bernice snatched her wrist away from Cyril.

"What's going on over there?" Dimple pointed toward the drinks table.

"Ah shit," Prynce said when he saw the look on his mum's face.

"We aren't getting involved," Nikisha said. "They're big people. Leave them to it."

"You know your problem, Cyril?" Bernice asked, her question silencing the room. "You're too greedy."

Cyril's sisters, who had come through from the kitchen, looked at each other and nodded in agreement.

"Your mother, God bless her soul, knew it, too. You were greedy for attention, greedy for women, and greedy for money. I bet you were late today because you were in the betting shop!"

"So yuh came here to embarrass me?" Cyril laughed, trying to hide his shame. "Let's all have a drink and cool off, man."

"You want me to drink with your other women? You must be taking me for *eediat*." Bernice threw her head back and laughed again. "A white woman and this fat bitch? Your standards slipped after me. No wonder you came back."

Janet's cheeks flushed with embarrassment. She'd argued against some of the most powerful barristers in the country, and had won, but was left speechless when she was standing in front of Bernice.

"I think that's enough," Tracy said, stepping forward.

"Who are *you* talking to?" Bernice asked, putting a hand on her hip and narrowing her eyes at Tracy.

"I'm talking to you, darlin'," Tracy said, all five feet of her squaring up to Bernice. "Did you come here to pay your respects or have an argument with a man who isn't worth your energy?"

Bernice sucked her teeth.

"You're right. *None* of you are worth my time."

Cyril looked over the heads of the mothers of his children, pretending someone across the room needed him.

"All right, one second!" he called across the room to this fictional person. "Ladies, it was nice seeing you."

Dimple hadn't heard what was said but looked over at her mum, who was swaying slightly, holding on to the table for support. She went over and gently held her mum by the arm.

"Have you been drinking, Mum?" Dimple asked.

"Well, you can't blame me, can you?" Janet hiccupped gently as she closed one eye and tried to figure out which of the Dimples in front of her was her daughter and which was the result of double vision.

"I'm going to put you in a cab," Dimple said.

"Are you coming home with me?" Janet asked, slurring her words. "Or you're staying here with your new family, I bet."

"No, Mum, I'm staying at a friend's," Dimple said, not wanting to stay here, but not wanting to go home. She went through the list of where she could go. She didn't want to see any more of her siblings, not this evening.

———————

When Dimple arrived at Roman's door, she rang the bell and smoothed her hair down nervously. Would he even want to see her after the embarrassing fight that couldn't even really be called a fight at Kyron's? She realized it would have been a good idea to think this through before turning up. She made a mental note to discuss with Nikisha next time they spoke why she was so subconsciously drawn to him, alongside the rest of her general feelings.

"It's you," Roman said, sighing when he opened the door and saw an emotionally worse for wear Dimple on his doorstep. He was happy to see her, but he wouldn't show it yet. "Didn't think I'd see you again now Kyron is back."

"Well, now that he knows about us, I don't think he ever wants to see me again, so."

"So you're only here because he knows about us?"

"Roman? What? *Please*."

"You coming in or you going to stand in the cold?" Roman stepped aside to let her enter.

Dimple walked in, happy to be there. She'd missed Roman's flat. It was comforting in its own way. She could smell that he'd been cooking oven food.

"One of these days you're gonna eat a salad and it'll change your life," Dimple told him.

"You want some oven chips?" he asked her.

Dimple shook her head.

"You've been losing weight, you know," Roman said, looking her up and down. "You didn't tell me you was on another diet."

"No, nothing like that."

"Ah, so now you've blown up on social or whatever you're changing up your image." Roman laughed. "So predictable."

"Not at all. And I wouldn't say I've blown up. A few more people just know my name, that's all." Dimple shook her head, dismissing what Roman had said. With each day that passed with her getting the online attention she'd craved, the more uncomfortable it made her. Especially with that fucking picture Kyron had. "I just haven't been feeling good."

"You're not pregnant, are you?" Roman asked, suddenly thrown into total panic. "Is it mine?"

"No." Dimple rolled her eyes. "I'm good. Just leave it. I don't want to talk about food. Or diets. Or socials. I'm just in a weird place."

"All right, well, sit down, relax." Roman left the room. Dimple heard him clattering around in the kitchen as she curled up on the sofa and turned the TV on. She couldn't focus on what was on the screen. She gave up and just stared at the ceiling.

He came back into the room and sat next to her.

"Lift up," she said.

Roman lifted his thigh and she tucked her feet underneath it. It was nice to feel tethered to someone.

"So what's been going on?" he asked her. "I ain't seen you for a while. You sure you and Kyron aren't back into it? Or is this a setup? You know me and him haven't spoken since that party?"

Dimple laughed and shook her head.

"You're the one who hasn't been answering the phone!"

"Yeah, 'cause everything just felt a bit long." Roman shrugged.

"But now you're here."

"Uh-huh." Dimple nodded. " 'Cause I missed you."

"Stand up," Roman said.

"Stand up? Why?"

"Stand up," Roman repeated, using the remote to turn off the television. The sound of silence swallowed the room.

"And I asked why," Dimple said again. This is how it always started.

"Stand up and see," Roman said, stretching out his thick arms and putting his hands behind his head. He stared at her.

Dimple stood up and looked down at him.

"Don't think you're anything special," she said, playing with him. "You're just a habit I haven't been able to break."

"You think I don't know?" he asked.

Still looking her dead in the eye, Roman reached up the side of her little skirt and slid his hand across her smooth thigh, feeling for her underwear.

"Fuck," he said.

"No underwear," Dimple whispered, closing her eyes as he moved his hand across her thigh to between her legs. It was all quite boring and quite easy for her, this sex stuff. She liked it, sure, but it wasn't her driving force.

"And you're nice and wet for me." Roman smiled, easing his thumb into her. "Always nice and wet for me."

"Don't get excited," Dimple said, more coarsely than she'd intended. "It's just biology or whatever."

"All right, you're entering the violation zone," Roman warned her.

Dimple smiled, still standing, and threw her head back as he moved his thumb to her clitoris. He made small circles, enjoying her physical response to his motion. They'd been fucking long enough for him to know exactly what she liked. He waited for her to bite her lip. That's when he'd insert his middle finger.

As soon as Roman could feel that Dimple was ready for him, he told her to take her clothes off.

"How do you want it this time?" he asked, pulling his tracksuit bottoms and boxers down and kicking them off. He held his erection in his hand.

"How do *you*?" Dimple asked, cocking her head to the side. It was easier to be told what to do when her head was swimming.

Roman smiled.

"I want you to sit on it."

"Okay. Condom," Dimple said. "Just so you *know* I'm not gonna get pregnant."

"Move on from that," Roman said as he jumped up from the sofa and disappeared into his bedroom. When he came back in, condom in hand, he sat down and rolled it on. She stood in front of him and let him take her in for a while. She liked the glaze that made his eyes shine while he stared at her from head to toe.

She lowered herself down, placing her legs on either side of him, taking his erection in her left hand and forcing him to look her in the eye while guiding him into her with the right. When she placed all her weight on him and felt him fill her up, he let out a deep, long groan. The second she began to move up and down on him, he was immediately consumed by her. It happened every time. As if this would be his last time with her, Roman ran his hands across every inch of her skin that he could find, ran his fingers through her hair; when he wasn't sucking her lips and letting her bite his, he was kissing her arms, her shoulders, her chin, her neck; he was taking her breasts into his mouth and licking her nipples.

Dimple was always surprised by how good he made her feel, how tender he was with her.

Dimple could never understand the way Roman took over her whole body when they were like this. It shocked her how quickly she'd orgasm when she was having sex with him. It was almost instant, this sensation that suddenly filled her, this urgency of pleasure that made her want to be able to suspend time and hold this feeling forever. But then she came, and it stopped.

Later, after the chips had burned and they'd spent an hour trying to air out the kitchen and get the fire alarm to stop shrieking, Dimple and Roman had gone up to his room to sleep. Roman had passed out, and Dimple had been lying silently next to him for two hours. Now that she'd had sex, she didn't want to be here either. Her grandma had died and her mum was drunk at home; this was the last place she should be. But where did she *want* to be? Who did she want to be? Who was she?

Eventually, sometime around five in the morning, she drifted off. When she woke up, she looked at her phone. It was just past 10 a.m. Roman was still asleep.

"Do you ever feel guilty?" she asked him, waking him up.

"Huh?" Roman answered gruffly.

"I said do you ever feel guilty?"

Roman cleared his throat before answering her.

"About what? Me and you?"

"Mmm, you don't really need to feel guilty about that anymore." Dimple shrugged. "More . . . in general."

"Not really," Roman said. "I think guilt is a wasted emotion."

"Tell me more?"

"Dimple, you woke me up to talk about *guilt*?"

Dimple blinked at Roman, waiting for him to answer the question.

"If I'm gonna do something, I'm gonna do it," Roman finally said. "So by the time I've done it, I've made an active choice to do it. No point feeling bad about something I chose to do, is there?"

"But what if you felt like you didn't have a choice?" Dimple asked him. "What if you did what you had to do because you were scared?"

"All right, you're talking in riddles now," Roman said, jumping out of the bed. He was always weirdly active in the mornings. "Unless you're gonna explain what you mean." Roman opened the blinds. Outside was bright, even though it was cold. "You should head out. 'Cause I've got some things to do."

Dimple laughed as she lay back down, pulling the duvet over her head. The freezing air whipped her as Roman pulled the duvet off.

"No, I'm serious," he said.

"You who never has anything to do but watch conspiracy theories on YouTube?" Dimple waited for Roman to tell her he was joking, but that never came.

"Oh, for fuck's sake." Dimple rolled her eyes as she climbed out of the bed. "This is why I stay away from Capricorns. You can be so cold!"

Ten minutes later, she was out of his house, chilly as she waited for the Uber to come. She couldn't believe he wouldn't even let her wait in the hallway. She began to see red until she had to realize he was probably protecting himself in his own way.

"Who's going to protect me, though?" she asked herself as the Uber arrived, knowing full well the only thing she needed protecting from most of the time was herself.

"Driver, would you mind turning the heating up?" she said, clipping her seat belt. "Or even on, please."

Dimple tried to think warm thoughts as the driver nodded, and the warm air blew weakly over her.

She called Nikisha. No answer. She tried Prynce. Nothing. She didn't feel like she had enough in common with Danny to call him, and after the last conversation she had with Lizzie, she was going nowhere near her.

She went to put her phone into her pocket when it started to buzz. Lynette.

"Act normal," Dimple said before answering the phone. "Hey, Lynette! How are you doing?" she asked, fake cheer coating her voice.

"Hello, darlin'! I was just calling to say that we're going to have a little get-together for Kyron's birthday. Just some family and his friends. And I know that things aren't the same between the two of you, but you have to be there."

Lynette obviously didn't know about her and Roman. She couldn't. She wasn't surprised that Kyron hadn't told her about it. Even though they lived under the same roof, his mum barely knew what her son was doing day to day, let alone what was going on in his personal life.

"I don't know if that's a good idea, Lynette," Dimple said, trying to find a way out of it that would appease her. "But it would be nice to see you soon. Maybe I can pop round when Kyron isn't there? I think he still needs some sp—"

"—I'll text you the details. Lots of love, sweetheart."

Lynette clicked off the call as Dimple's Uber pulled up to her house.

When Dimple got in, she undressed and bundled the dirty clothes she'd just removed into a heap. She walked into the bathroom, dumped them in the wash basket and turned the shower on. She stepped in, and while the hot water licked her skin, she thought about all of her various life crises for a while.

When she got out, she wrapped a towel around her body and looked at herself in the mirror. She surveyed a new cluster of spots on her forehead and thought about how ugly she was. She thought about how beautiful Lizzie was. She thought about their physical similarities, then, for the first time, about their differences. Lizzie's skin was better. Lizzie's eyes were clearer, they shone more brightly. Her smile was wider, her teeth were whiter, despite the fact that Dimple had spent so much money on Invisalign and whitening treatments. Lizzie's body was tighter, more toned. Lizzie held herself with such poise, such confidence. Dimple thought about how Lizzie was like the better, sharper version of her. Lizzie actually had her life together. She was in a functioning relationship, had an actual career ahead of her, was more focused.

But why? Dimple asked herself as she sat on the edge of the bath. Neither of them had a present dad. Both of them, from what Dimple could tell of Lizzie, had stifling mums. Maybe it was that Dimple was just too soft. Too soft and too scared to actually do anything that was out of her comfort zone. It was easy, in its own way, to pursue a career that didn't really have any stakes where she was concerned. Because she could just . . . turn the phone off and her mum would tell her everything was going to be okay. Lizzie couldn't turn her real life off. Quite the opposite. It seemed to be full, with so much to be happy about and so much to achieve and look forward to. Dimple didn't even have a proper relationship with either of the men she'd been having sex with. Kyron was cut from the same cloth as her dad. Both of them wanted parts of her on their terms only. And when it came to the pleasure and the safety she felt with Roman . . . it didn't sit comfortably inside her. It scared her.

Dimple dried herself off and padded into her room. She sat at her dressing table and reached for her most expensive serum, slathering it all over her face and dabbing extra on the new spots.

She pulled a T-shirt on and climbed into bed. When she woke up again, it was early evening. She sighed as she picked up her phone and started to scroll it mindlessly. Dimple crept past her mum's bedroom and down the stairs. She warmed up some leftover shrimp fried rice and ate it on the sofa in near darkness as she scrolled through all her social media accounts, looking at all the messages from people telling her either how great she was or how and where she could improve herself. She was used to these lonely, sleepless nights where her only company was digital, but they didn't get easier now that she had more followers. And these followers would definitely turn on her if she didn't pull Kyron's money together, and fast.

CHAPTER
ELEVEN

THEIR GRANDMOTHER'S FUNERAL WAS on a Wednesday, which felt to Dimple like a weird day for a funeral until Nikisha told her that that had been the cheapest day of the week to hold it. She stepped past faces she didn't know into the church and shivered. Not as a response to spirituality, but because it was much colder in there than it was outside.

She pulled her black scarf tighter around her neck and shoulders and squinted as she looked across the pews for her half-siblings.

All she could see were the backs of heads she knew she wouldn't recognize if they turned to look at her, and unknown children running round. The sound of a tambourine falling to the floor alerted her to the church band setting up in the corner.

"STOP running!" a stern woman's voice called across the church, and all of the children stayed still long enough for Dimple to recognize Nicky.

She walked over to him and bent down to his level. He looked up at her.

"Do you recognize me?" she asked him.

Nicky looked at her like she'd asked him the stupidest question in the world.

"You're my aunty Dimple," he said. "Why are you asking me that?"

"I dunno what kids can and can't remember, Nicky," Dimple told him. "Shall we have a hug?"

"No, thanks." Nicky shook his head. "My mum went back there."

He pointed to a group of adults emerging from a door by a statue of a peeling Black Jesus that was nailed to the lectern at the front of the church. Always one to stand out, Nikisha came striding toward her, a vision in black velvet. She smiled widely, waved at Dimple, and mouthed "wait there."

When she made it over to her, Nikisha explained that she'd been talking to their cousins about who was making what speech.

"Is that sort of thing not meant to be decided by now?" Dimple asked. "And who are these cousins you were speaking to?"

"Pretty much everyone in here between my age and Prynce's is our cousin," Nikisha told her, pulling Dimple out of the emotional spiral she could see she was just waiting to go on. "Apart from the men in the band. I went and spoke to them earlier and none of them are Penningtons."

"How many children did Delores have?" Dimple asked.

"Tune in," Nikisha told her. "You're about to find out."

A few minutes later, the service began. Dimple and the rest of her half-siblings squeezed themselves into the hard pew. Amara was on Danny's lap, and Nicky was sitting at Nikisha's feet playing a game on his phone.

"Where's Marley?" Dimple asked Danny.

"Oh, he's just parking up now," Danny told her.

"Okay, sarcasm. I'm just *asking*."

"Don't be so sensitive!" Danny laughed. "His mum thought he was a bit too young for all of this. In her words: 'He might be small but he picks up on energies, Danny.'"

The pastor, a top-heavy, dark-skinned Jamaican woman with shoulder-length dreadlocks that brushed her purple gown, started the proceedings by announcing: "The body is on its way. It's in traffic."

"Is she serious?" Dimple whispered to Nikisha.

"Deadly," Nikisha replied, nodding.

Lizzie leaned over Danny and whispered to Dimple, "Is Cyril even here yet?"

Dimple turned to look around to check. They were in the third row, so she was in prime position to see who was and wasn't in the church.

"I can't see him," Dimple said.

"Let's enjoy some praise and worship before Delores reach," the pastor suggested to the band, which immediately started to play its own unique version of "Nearer, My God, to Thee." They weren't all in the same key, but it was still a very good and boisterous effort.

Dimple noticed the bassist, who looked about the same age as her and Lizzie. He was taking his job very seriously. He was also very good-looking.

"Who's he?" Dimple nudged Nikisha.

"Who knows?" Nikisha shrugged. "Go and ask him."

"I'm shy!" Dimple hissed.

Nikisha couldn't be bothered to whisper anymore.

"Well, you'll need to figure out how to find some confidence if you want to know who he is."

"Shhh!" an older woman behind them hushed them. "Disrespectful!"

Nikisha turned round slowly.

"Do not shush me like I'm a child. Shush yourself. This is our grandmother's funeral," she said to the woman, who was so surprised at being spoken back to that she was stunned into silence.

Prynce, bored of making small talk with an older man at the edge of the pew next to him, asked to sit between Lizzie and Dimple. When he got there, he leaned over Dimple and tapped Nikisha on the leg.

"We're not going to the reception, are we?"

"Of course we are," Nikisha told him. "And you'd better pass the message down the line in case anyone thinks we can just do half the day."

"All right. But can we miss the burial?" Prynce asked. "It's too cold for all of that. And is Dad not here?"

"Call him if you want to know where he is." Nikisha looked at Prynce pointedly. "I'm not his keeper."

"I'm just saying, doesn't make sense that we're here if he's not."

The funeral procession arrived, and six pallbearers walked through the church doors, the coffin balancing precariously due to their various heights. Dimple scanned them all. Cyril was not one of them.

Once the coffin had been laid on the stand at the front of the church, just to the side of the pastor, the service could properly begin. First, a reading from the First Letter of Paul to the Thessalonians. Then a song. Nobody in the church seemed concerned with getting the tune or lyrics right. A slightly shaky poem from Tania, Delores's youngest grandchild. Another song. A reading from Psalm 23, which was, thankfully, slightly shorter than the First Letter of Paul. Danny had nodded off. Amara had started crying, so Nicky had taken her to the back of the church to play with some of the other kids. Momentum and general engagement in the funeral started to dip a bit after the first hour, but everyone woke up when three of Delores's grandchildren, the daughters of her third son, who had two different mothers, argued very openly about who of them should read their tribute first.

Somewhere between the argument and a terrible song written and performed by Delores's sister's son and his guitar—a song about an ex-girlfriend that had absolutely nothing to do with Delores—Cyril arrived. He shuffled through the door wearing a light gray suit and a faded Arriva baseball cap, strode to the front of the church, and sat down next to a crying woman Dimple understood was his youngest sister, Marvette. With no apology for lateness passing his lips, he looked around the church, greeting people across the room, smiling and waving as though they were all at an everyday family function.

Finally, it was time for the eulogy. Everyone in their row was very confused to see Nikisha pulling a folder from her bag.

"What are you doing?" Dimple whispered over to her.

"The eulogy," Nikisha told her, standing up.

"Yes, I assumed that was the case, but why?" Lizzie leaned over and asked. "We don't know these people."

"Nobody else wanted to do it." Nikisha slipped away from the pew and walked slowly and dramatically over to the lectern.

"Good afternoon, everybody," Nikisha began confidently. "I am Nikisha Theresa Pennington, the first grandchild of Delores. Thank you all for coming to celebrate her life today." Nikisha got comfortable at the lectern, as though she was about to deliver a motivational speech at a youth club, and not a speech about her grandmother's life and death.

"Delores Ricketts, née Pennington, was the first daughter born to Clarence Pennington and Rita Pennington, née Denton. She grew up in Red Ground, Coffee Piece, a small area that sits in the parish of Clarendon in Jamaica. Delores lived in a tiny home with her parents and her younger sister, Desrence."

Nikisha spoke clearly and calmly. Dimple wondered if she'd ever be able to speak to this many people in the same way. She knew the answer was no, but it was worth thinking about it.

"As a young woman, Delores was said to be bright, resourceful, and attentive." Nikisha smiled. "She would chop and sell sugarcane from a stall by the house she grew up in, and then, as she got older, would sell it at the markets, and around the parish, pushing bags of cane around on a cart she found broken on the side of the road and fixed by herself. Even though she didn't go to school, she would learn from the elders of the parish that she'd sell cane to, building her own education of Jamaica, and of the wider world as she went along."

"Why was Grandma the Oliver Twist of Jamaica?" Dimple whispered to Lizzie.

"Shhh!" Lizzie hissed back, even though this was the first thing Dimple had said that she'd found funny and she wanted to laugh.

Nikisha continued. "When she was fifteen, she met a young man named Zelbert who was selling guinep at the market on a plot next to hers."

"First the names Delores and Desrence, and now Zelbert?" Dimple whispered to Prynce as Nikisha paused to take a sip of water. Nikisha took her time with it. She'd always been a comfortable public speaker, long before she was the debate team captain at secondary school.

"They spent very little time together before he was sadly killed in a traffic accident," Nikisha continued.

"Bet you feel bad now," Prynce whispered back to Dimple.

"A few months later, Delores gave birth to Cyril, who took the family surname. Despite being a single parent, and her own parents ostracizing her, Delores carried on selling cane on weekends, and had learned enough by this point to get a part-time job as the receptionist to Israel Ricketts, the local dentist. Two years later, when Israel relocated to London, he took Delores with him. The plane left Kingston, Jamaica, on the fourteenth of February 1972. That was the last time Delores would ever see home, though I understand it was her regular wish to return there. She was said to have been shocked almost to death by the cold weather when she arrived in England. Perhaps that's why."

A few people laughed at this. Probably in solidarity, as they were cold, too, and the heating in the church hadn't been fixed yet.

"Instead, she stayed, and she built a life with Israel, who she married in the annexed registry office next to a church in Wandsworth in 1975. She and Israel had five children. Tessilda came not long after she and Israel married, then came Lavinia, Wally, Marvette, and Cornelius. At the age of thirty, when they'd amassed enough money,

Delores sent for her first son, Cyril, now fifteen, who joined them in the family home on Somerleyton Road, Brixton.

"Delores was a homemaker until 1973, when Israel bought a house and turned it into his own dental practice, where of course, she was reinstated as his receptionist. Together they ran that office for thirty years, until Israel sadly passed away from a heart attack in 2002. More tragedy was to come when their son Wally passed away two years after that in a traffic accident, and three years following that, Cornelius slipped while working on the tracks and was hit by a passing train.

"Delores, through her grief, kept the dental practice running until it was time for her to retire. She died happily at home, surrounded by family. She is survived by her sister, Desrence, her eldest son, Cyril, and her girl children Tessilda, Lavinia, and Marvette, as well as her thirteen grandchildren and eight great-grandchildren. Delores will be missed by her family and many friends. May she rest in peace."

Finally, it was over. Dimple, who was sobbing, obviously, closed the funeral program and looked down at the picture of her father's mother through blurring eyes. Delores was probably about the same age Dimple was when it was taken, smiling in her smart dress in front of the dental practice she and her husband ran. Dimple noticed that they had the same eyes, something she wouldn't bother pointing out to Lizzie, who had them, too.

Delores Ricketts's reception was in a church hall at the end of a one-way street in a quiet part of Wandsworth Dimple had never been to before. She and her siblings filed in, aware of the eyes that were on them now that people knew who they were. Lots of "Oh, so you lot are Cyril's kids?"; "How many mothers you got between you?"; and "You're lucky you never got his nose." All of them but Danny, who did get his nose, laughed at the comments politely.

When they got inside, they sat at one of the round tables that had been covered by a cheap white plastic tablecloth. They went for the one in the back corner of the hall, closest to the exit. In the middle of the table sat a large bottle of mineral water, a carton of Just Juice (orange), a stack of small plastic cups, and a handful of Ferrero Rocher.

"That's a nice touch," Danny said, reaching for one. He unwrapped it and threw it into his mouth.

"How did you know all that stuff about Delores?" Lizzie asked Nikisha. "For the eulogy."

"I asked," Nikisha told her.

"Asked who?"

"Her children, her siblings who are still alive," Nikisha said.

"Why?" Dimple asked. "And how?"

"None of you will ever have to do what I do," Nikisha said. "But as the eldest, I have a lot of responsibilities. I have to know things. Who is who, what is what. It's because I kept track of you all that we were able to come together."

Lizzie snorted.

"Yeah, thanks for that."

"It was so sad, wasn't it?" Dimple asked her brothers and sisters.

"Which part?" Prynce asked.

"The whole eulogy," Dimple said. "So this woman, our grandmother—"

"*Your* grandmother," Lizzie interjected.

"Whatever," Dimple said: "She got pregnant when she was fifteen by a man who died months later, her parents X'ed her out, she had to raise a baby while she was still a baby, then she ends up leaving that baby behind and moving to England where it's cold and miserable, and pushing out five kids for some man who was her employer. The whole time she has this son she's abandoned in Jamaica, and when she finally got Dad over here, I doubt that was a smooth integration. And then she just works and works and works, her husband dies, then two of her kids die—one of them the same way our dad's dad died, I hope you guys noticed that—and then after all that heartache and heartbreak, she dies."

"Well, when you put it like that . . ." Danny sighed, reaching for another Rocher.

"And I know you said she died happy, Nikisha, but that was a lie. She was miserable and we all know it," Dimple added.

"Artistic license." Nikisha shrugged. "I could hardly say some of the last people she saw were her five grandkids who didn't really know her, and her waste of a son."

"Would we call him a waste of a son?" Dimple asked.

Her siblings stared at her, daring her to challenge Nikisha's statement.

Dimple looked around the church hall, with its cream walls and high ceilings, old beams propping up the crumbling roof. From the door at the other end of the hall emerged the church band, including the handsome bassist.

In the corner nearby were a group of five men, including their dad, trying their hardest to set up the sound system, the components of which clearly weren't wanting to work together. The music that was already coming out of it fuzzed gently, almost inaudibly, cutting in and out until the right jack finally found its way into the amp.

"Look, it's like us the night we all had to sort out *the thing*." Dimple smiled, pointing at the men. "All trying to work together."

"That's not funny." Lizzie shook her head.

"It is quite funny," Prynce said, laughing.

"Hello, hello, why you lot sitting down?" Their aunt Marvette shuffled over to them, serving spoon in hand. "You need to help in the kitchen."

"Do we, though?" Lizzie asked her.

"Yes! Follow me!" Marvette barked, marching toward a side door next to a set of open shutters that the kitchen sat behind.

"It'll give us something to do," Dimple suggested, standing and pulling her black dress down over her bum. It was too short for a funeral. She knew it, and everyone else knew it, too.

"Is this how Jamaicans do things?" Lizzie asked, also standing.

"Try as you might, you can't avoid it," Nikisha said. "It lives within you."

They stood at the door of the kitchen. Marvette was in there, immediately losing her mind. She was unloading a box that was full of cartons of Capri Sun and multipacks of chips, stacking it all on a large metal surface next to foil trays from the caterer covered in white cardboard that hadn't been unsealed yet.

"You. The little one." She pointed at Prynce. "Take these out there and put them on the table for the kids."

"I'm not little," Prynce said under his breath, stacking three cartons of Capri Sun in his arms to prove it. "Why are people always saying that?"

"And you two," Marvette said, pointing at Dimple and Lizzie. "The age-mates. Put on aprons and start opening up the food."

Lizzie and Dimple looked at each other.

"Now, please!" Marvette insisted.

"Who's she talking to?" Lizzie asked Dimple.

"Let's just get it moving," Dimple said, reaching for two aprons on the counter.

"You, the big one, go and get the oven working. Your dad tells me you're a plumber. You can make yourself useful."

"Yes, ma'am." Danny smiled, getting to work on the industrial oven, immediately having to google how to ignite it. He was elated that his dad had both remembered what he did for a living and had passed that information on to at least one other person in the family.

"The soup." Marvette pointed to Nikisha. "*You* need to start serving the soup for the elders. Take the ladle and spoon it into the foam cups that are over there. And make sure everyone gets a chicken foot in their cup. I don't want any of them telling people that Miss Delores's family are cheap."

Nikisha walked over to the cups and started lining them up on the side.

"No!" Marvette squawked. "Put them on the tray and serve it in there, save yourself time!"

"It's going to be a long afternoon," Dimple said to Lizzie. She went to lean on her but thought better of it.

Once Danny got the oven working, Dimple and Lizzie emptied the foil trays of food, pouring curried goat, brown stew chicken, white rice, and rice and peas into gigantic pots on the stove to warm it all. While it was heating, they peeled the lids off the rest of the trays and laid out fried chicken, jerk chicken, peppered steak, escovitch fish, dumplings, macaroni and cheese, and roti, ready to serve it. Vegetarians had clearly been an afterthought, and vegans hadn't been catered to.

Marvette's job seemed to be to stand in the corner and keep the kitchen running, telling each of them what they were doing wrong, and how she could have done it better.

"Where are your kids?" Lizzie asked her. "Maybe they'll do a better job than us."

Marvette ignored her.

"Get the hard dough bread out of that bag and cut it and butter it," she told her. "People are ready to eat."

Working in that kitchen felt like working in customer services. Nobody was happy with the portion sizes. Things weren't hot enough. Things were too hot. The jerk chicken wasn't spicy enough. The fried chicken had too much crumb. The macaroni and cheese was too rich. Dimple and Lizzie heard it all, and Nikisha had had to step in more than once to stop Lizzie from climbing through the partition and fighting someone.

People kept trying to come into the kitchen to help themselves until Danny and Prynce very happily installed themselves by the door to act as culinary bouncers.

Dimple, who had hoped that the task would have brought her and Lizzie closer, hadn't been able to say one word to her sister beyond "Can you pass that over, please?"

When everyone seemed to be, in some small way, satisfied with their food, and was sitting down talking quietly among themselves, Cyril's five children could take a break. They each grabbed a plate and spooned whatever was left in the pots and from the foil trays onto it.

"If I didn't have those couple of Rochers earlier I would have dropped down," Danny said, spearing as much macaroni and cheese onto his fork as he could.

"Can we go now?" Lizzie asked. "I don't even know why we came here in the first place."

"Lizzie, we get it!" Dimple snapped. "None of us wanted or needed to be here, but we're here. We've shown our faces, we've paid our respects, we've done manual labor, now we can go. There's no point being so spiky and negative all the time. Sometimes we have to do things we don't want to do."

Prynce exhaled.

"Yeah, but you would say that, you're desperate to be a daddy's girl," Lizzie shot back with alarming speed.

"What?" Dimple spluttered. "No, I'm not."

"Yes, you are," Lizzie said.

"How?" Dimple scoffed. "What do I do to try and be a 'daddy's girl'?"

"You don't even need to do anything," Lizzie told her. "You're just one of those girls. Obsessed with what men think of them because they never got enough attention from their dad."

"Lizzie," Nikisha said sternly. "Don't do this."

"I'm not being rude, I'm just saying it how it is. We've all seen her videos—it doesn't take a genius to work out that men make her world go round," Lizzie said matter-of-factly. "Which I actually don't really get, because Dad gives you more attention than the rest of us."

"Okay, that's enough, Lizzie," Danny said gently.

"No, he— And what's wrong with my vid— And why would you— Why are you saying this?" Dimple could barely get her words out. "Why are you always so mean to me? I haven't ever done anything to you!"

"Mean?" Lizzie laughed. "I'm not being mean, you're just always on the verge of tears. If I ask you the time in the wrong tone your chin starts trembling."

"Eh!" A familiar voice demanded their attention from the opening in the wall. "Any food left?"

"You see!" Lizzie smiled nastily at Dimple. "Daddy's come to save you!"

"Lizzie, let me talk to you for a sec," Nikisha said, putting her hands on Lizzie's shoulders and steering her out of the kitchen.

Cyril staggered onto the ledge and his head lolled forward slightly. He reached into the kitchen and started to pick up and throw down anything he could reach. Plates, spoons, foam cups, anything.

"Come on, come on, pick up the service!" he laughed.

Dimple looked at her brothers for some sort of help.

"He needs something to soak it all up," Danny said. "Prynce, you get him some water, and the two of you can sit him down outside for some air. I'll bring some . . . bread out. Let me see if I can find any more."

"Ifff I die . . ." Cyril slurred from his precarious perch on the wall by the church hall. "No, when I die. When I go. When mi gaan. When I close mi two eyes fi good—"

Dimple and Prynce waited patiently for the rest of the sentence. Dimple held on to him to stop him from swaying all the way back and over the wall, while Prynce offered a cup of water to him; he knocked it out of his son's hand and onto the floor.

"What have I done in my liiife?" Cyril wailed quietly, his head falling back. "Who do I have? What do I have?"

"You've done loads, Dad!" Dimple tried to soothe him as she pulled him further forward. Even though the events of his life didn't seem to amount to much on the surface, she didn't feel like she was really lying. He had technically done a lot of things across the years, even if they weren't significant.

"Not one of mi children like me," Cyril mumbled. "What will they say at my funeral?"

"I think we should get him home," Dimple said. "He needs to sleep it off."

"No!" Cyril shouted, pushing himself off the wall. He swayed unsteadily on his feet. "Leave me, nuh!"

"Here, Dad, eat this." Danny approached the three of them with a slice of buttered hard dough bread wrapped in a piece of kitchen roll. Cyril walked past Danny, snatching it. He shoved the bread into his mouth and sort of did the action of wiping his mouth with the kitchen roll, which would have been effective if he hadn't just been wiping crumbs across his face. He threw the kitchen roll onto the floor and staggered back into the hall, straight past Nikisha and Lizzie, who were walking out.

"What should we do for him?" Dimple asked Nikisha when they made their way over to the wall. Lizzie was looking down at the floor, muttering to herself angrily.

"Nothing at all," Nikisha said.

"But what if he needs us?" Dimple felt bad; they couldn't just leave him there like that.

"He's a grown man," Nikisha told Dimple. "He's managed to get himself home from every other event he's drunk too much at without us before now."

"Yeah, but his mum hadn't died, Nikisha," Dimple said, trying to reason with her sister. "I know what you're saying, and I know he seemed fine, but when I called him he wouldn't even say he was upset. I don't think he knows how to process it."

"You're too nice, man!" Prynce laughed. "He should be the one making sure we're getting home okay!"

"Ah, he'll be fine, Dimple," Danny said. "Nikisha's right. He's eaten something, he'll sober up in a bit, one of his mates in there will take him home."

"Only once they've figured out the sound system," Prynce said.

"You two want a lift home?" Nikisha asked Prynce and Lizzie. "Danny, you might as well take Dimple."

"I'm good, you know," Prynce said. "I'm gonna go to Jana's."

"Oh! The one we met at your birthday?" Dimple asked.

Prynce nodded.

"This is the first time I've heard you talk about the same girl twice. This feels huge."

"Well, of all my friends, I guess she's the main . . . friend."

"Is that why we got to meet her?" Dimple asked. "Well, lucky her and lucky us."

The second they got into Danny's van, Dimple's skin started to feel sensitive. Every time her skin connected with the fabric of her dress, when the backs of her bare legs touched the van seat, when Danny put the heating on and the air blew onto her thighs, it hurt. Everything felt sharp, unusual.

"Why you wriggling?" Danny asked. "You cold? The heating will kick in soon."

"No, it's fine, I'm not cold," Dimple told him. "Just a bit . . . I dunno. Today was a lot."

"Is what it is, isn't it?" Danny shrugged, braking as they pulled up to a red light. "Did the funeral spin you out a bit? I know it's weird. 'Cause we didn't know her. I was thinking the other day whether or not I'd be more sad if I knew her properly. But I think I'm sadder now 'cause I never got to know her."

"For what it's worth, I don't think it would be easy either way," Dimple told her brother. "I think we just need to be glad, in a way, that we got to say goodbye."

"Yeah. You're right." Danny nodded, setting off again the millisecond the traffic light started flashing amber.

"Danny?"

"Mmm?"

"Are you okay about the Kyron stuff?" Dimple asked him.

"Not really," Danny admitted. "Are you all right about it?"

"Do you want to talk about it?" Dimple asked.

"Pfff." Danny let the air out of his mouth through gritted teeth. "I don't really talk about things too tuff."

"I've noticed. You're just 'cheery, cheery, everything will be fine' all the time. And that's fine if that's the real you! But it's not if that's how you think you have to be."

"Mmm." Danny nodded again. "It's both, I think."

Dimple gave him the space to keep talking. She saw getting feelings out of men like Danny as similar to getting close to a cat you wanted to stroke. If you got too close they'd run off, but if you left them to it enough by pretending you weren't desperate to be near them, they'd approach, even if it was with caution. And then they'd never stay long.

" 'Cause you know my first thing is always Marley," Danny began. "And then it's my mum, obviously. And if anything happens to me, Marley isn't going to grow up knowing me. 'Cause even though I'm not, like, certain his mum will do a good job taking care of him, I know my mum will. But still. What happens if I'm not there? I want to be his best friend, you know? I want him to know that I'm always there and that I love him. I want him to always be able to chat with me. I need to be, for him, what Dad wasn't for me. Well. For all of us."

Dimple wanted to hug Danny and ask him if there was some way he could adopt her.

"I hope you know that if it had been up to me, you lot wouldn't have all been pulled into this," she tried to explain. "I feel guilty about it all the time. Like, aaall the time."

"Ah, I know, Dimp." Danny smiled. "And I don't regret it. If it happened tomorrow, and I knew what we'd be doing, I'd still have come. 'Cause you lot are my third thing, now, after Marley and my mum. These past few weeks have been hectic, but I didn't know how much I needed you all."

"Same." Dimple tried to hold back tears. She knew Danny should still have the floor, emotionally. "Apart from Lizzie."

"Ah, I wouldn't worry about her too much," Danny said. "Seems like her bark is worse than her bite. That's what my mum says about that Bernice woman. I think it's the same."

"And just so you know, I'm going to figure out the money thing," Dimple assured her brother, and herself, even though she had absolutely no plan in mind just yet.

Danny pulled up outside Dimple's house. There was nobody else on the street, just the cold wind blowing through the trees.

"See you soon," Dimple said, reaching across and half hugging him over the gearshift. "Hopefully for a nicer occasion. Maybe I can come and hang out with Marley."

"I think he'd like that!" Danny said. "Chat with you soon. And don't worry about stuff so much. It just is what it is. We're doing the best we can."

"If you're sure." Dimple wondered if Nikisha had told Danny her fears. She hopped out of the van and ran to her front door. She pulled her keys out of her bag as she turned to wave Danny off.

Just as Danny pulled away from the pavement, Janet yanked the front door open.

"Hi, Mum." Dimple kicked her shoes off, the only ones she had that were suitable for a funeral, then her jacket, and headed into the kitchen. "How was your day?"

Dimple washed her hands, warming them under the hot water.

She filled the kettle and flicked it on. She didn't need to look at her mum to know she'd been drinking.

"So you were with your criminal brother today," Janet sneered. "And the rest of them criminals."

"Who are you talking about?" Panic shot through Dimple. Had Janet overheard something? What could she have heard? Dimple had been so careful.

"Your dad is the biggest criminal of them all. And the apple doesn't fall far from the tree."

Janet hiccupped.

"My dad isn't a criminal, Mum," Dimple told Janet, in a way relieved that her drunken ramblings weren't based in any truth.

"Emotionally, a criminal," Janet said.

"Mum, you were doing so good at not drinking." Dimple groaned. Janet was a completely different person when she was drunk. And not a nice one. "What's going on with you?"

It should have been obvious to Dimple that seeing Cyril at the nine night had knocked Janet back a few steps in her road to permanent sobriety.

"What's going on with me?" Janet asked, her voice trembling. "What's going on with me is that my baby is going to leave me. My baby, who loved me, who didn't need anyone else, is going to leave me now Cyril and his kids have decided they want her in their stupid lives."

"Where am I going, Mum?" Dimple asked her. "You've made this all up."

"No, I haven't," Janet grumbled. "I can see it happening. You're going to leave me the way your dad did. It wasn't enough for him to leave me, now he's come back to take you as well."

"He couldn't take me anywhere, Mum."

It was too much to deal with another drunk parent. Dimple walked out of the kitchen and pulled her thickest parka on.

"You just got in!" Janet objected. "You can't go anywhere!"

"I just . . . I'll see you later. I don't want to deal with this." Dimple left her key on the cabinet in the hallway and stormed out the door.

She regretted leaving the house as soon as the winter air hit her face, but powered on. She pulled her hood up, tightening it round her face.

She wanted to go somewhere, but once again didn't know where. She never knew where. She felt so disjointed inside herself. She didn't feel like she belonged to a place, didn't feel like her company belonged to a person. But she also knew that it was maximum 41 degrees Fahrenheit, and that she had to go somewhere.

Roman's was out, even though she missed him. He was being weird the last time she saw him and wanted to give it some time before she delved back into all of that. He still hadn't messaged her, but she couldn't really blame him for that. She didn't want to bother Nikisha again either, not after today.

Dimple checked the time on her phone. The whole day had been an exhausting blur that had begun at 9 a.m., but she was still surprised to see that it was only nine at night. It felt like it was five in the morning.

She called Lizzie, whom she didn't expect to answer.

"Hello?" Lizzie actually did answer.

"Hey, it's Dimple."

"I know."

"So I came out to the shop when I got back and forgot my keys," Dimple lied. "And my mum isn't answering her phone. Are you still up?"

"Er, yeah. We're still up. It's just gone nine," Lizzie said, more playing up the annoyance in her voice than hiding it.

Dimple heard a woman's voice in the background asking who was on the phone.

"It's Dimple. She needs to come round."

Dimple strained her ears to hear the rest of the conversation, but the dead silence on the other end of the line told her that Lizzie had muted the call. She waited for Lizzie to come back on the phone and say no.

"Do you need me to get you an Uber?" Lizzie finally said when her voice reappeared.

"No, it's fine, I can get one." Dimple almost collapsed with relief. "What's your address?"

A few minutes later, Dimple pulled up outside a new building in Elephant and Castle. She was confused by its exterior; it was all glass and angles and pointy architecture, so she had to check that it was the same building as the one Lizzie had sent. The names matched, so she ran out of her Uber and toward the wide glass doorway.

Underneath the text with the address was a follow-up that read:

My girlfriend doesn't know anything.
Be careful what you say.

"Twenty-three," she said to herself as she pressed the chrome numbers on the wall. She waited for a second, staring at the interface as nothing happened. Then she read the instructions. She pressed twenty-three again, then the little bell icon.

"It's open," a voice crackled through the intercom almost immediately. "Third floor."

Dimple pushed the door open and strolled across the clean granite flooring toward the lift, the doors of which were already open. She stepped in, and instead of looking at herself in the mirror again under the needlessly bright light—God knows she'd done that enough today—she turned to face the lift doors as they closed.

"Why am I here?" She panicked suddenly. Was this the person who was going to provide her with even an ounce of comfort? But it was too late; she'd already arrived at the third floor.

She stepped out and turned left, walking down the carpeted hallway, uniform white doors on either side of her. The owners of the flats had tried to mark their personalities by choosing doormats that ranged from IKEA basic to as jazzy as possible. Dimple glanced at an expensive-looking doormat with the words "Lose the Shoes" woven into it and wondered why anyone would bother spending so much money on something people were going to wipe their feet on.

She got to the end of the hallway and realized that twenty-three was in the other direction. When she finally found Lizzie's flat, Lizzie's already headscarf-wrapped head was poking out the front door. Dimple smiled at Lizzie, who didn't smile back.

"She found it yet?" Dimple heard a voice call from inside the flat.

"Yep," Lizzie called behind her. She stepped aside for Dimple. "Come in."

Dimple stepped into the flat, her eyes not quite settling on any one thing. Everything was too exciting to look at. There was already so much going on, decorwise, and she was only in the hallway. Directly ahead of her was a bedroom, bright prints on the bed, the walls—even the curtains possessed more color than anything in Dimple's bedroom.

"Thanks. I know it's kind of late," Dimple said as she followed Lizzie through into the open-plan living room. She looked at Lizzie's slim frame, her tight onesie acting as a second skin.

"Hi!" a loud, bright voice called across the room. "Do you want a hot drink?"

The loud, bright voice belonged to a woman who was wearing tracksuit bottoms and a tight vest. Dimple tried not to look at her visible nipple piercings poking through the fabric. They made her wonder whether or not Patrice and Lizzie had had sex since the night of the incident, and she felt so weird about thinking about that that she looked down at the floor.

"Okay. I'll introduce myself, shall I?" the girl asked, stepping toward Dimple while looking pointedly at Lizzie. "I'm Patrice, Lizzie's partner."

"Hi, I'm Dimple." Dimple smiled, holding her hand out.

Patrice laughed. "We don't shake hands in this house, we hug. Unless you're against that."

"No, not at all!" Dimple was relieved that Patrice didn't hate her as much as Lizzie did. She felt a bit sad when she realized she hadn't hugged anyone properly in a very, very long time.

She stepped toward Patrice and felt an unfamiliar comfort like no other when Patrice pulled her into a close, warm embrace.

"It's nice to finally meet you," Patrice said, releasing Dimple. Dimple wondered how soon was too soon until she could ask for another hug.

"And you too."

"Now," Patrice said. "Before I make you a hot drink, which I will, because you feel as cold as you look, do you want some trousers?"

Dimple looked down and realized that her parka had unzipped itself from the bottom up and her already too-short dress had ridden up.

"Yes, please." She nodded. "Yes."

"Don't just stand there, Lizzie, go and get your sister some tracksuit bottoms!"

Lizzie rolled her eyes.

"You want to give me your coat?"

"Oh. Yes, please." Dimple pulled her parka off and handed it to Lizzie, who took it in a way that felt a bit too close to snatching and left the room.

"Tea good for you?" Patrice asked.

"Yes, please." Dimple nodded again, wondering why she felt so shy that she couldn't generate any new words.

"Any milk preference?" Patrice flicked the kettle on and went over to the fridge. "I dunno why I'm asking you, we only have oat. Anything else makes me feel sick."

"Oat is perfect, thanks."

"Sit down, sit down!" Patrice ushered Dimple over to a circular table in the middle of the room and pulled out a chair for her. "Make yourself at home."

Dimple allowed herself to exhale deeply. She looked around the living room as the kettle tried its hardest to compete with the noise of what Dimple recognized as NTS Radio playing through a set of speakers on a shelf. Every bit of space on the white walls was covered by memories: pictures of things, of people Dimple assumed were friends of Lizzie and Patrice, snapshots of the couple on various holidays; there were stickers, little cartoons, ticket stubs from cinema visits, gallery trips, concerts. A large fiddle-leaf fig sat in the corner of the room, its leaves hanging across a television that Dimple guessed didn't get used much.

"Your flat is so nice," Dimple said, finally able to say some words without being prompted. She wondered if she'd done a good job of hiding her jealousy.

"Thanks," Lizzie said flatly as she came back into the room, handing Dimple a pair of tracksuit bottoms that Dimple could see were going to be too tight for her.

"Thanks. How long have you lived here?" Dimple asked as she pulled the tracksuit bottoms on, letting out a small, almost inaudible noise as she sat back down and they almost cut her in half.

"Almost two years, you know." Patrice smiled. "I realized the other day that it would be two years in March since I forced this one to pool all our savings and tie herself to me. Legally speaking."

Lizzie pulled herself up onto the counter, nodded, and crossed one slender leg over the other.

"Oh! You own it?" Dimple asked, jealous again. Lizzie really did have her life together.

"Shared ownership!" Patrice clarified. "We own a percentage. Can you imagine being able to fully own a flat in London?"

"Mmm," Dimple agreed, knowing she would never. A long time ago, she'd made peace with living with her mum until maybe she married some rich guy who installed her in his house.

Patrice finished making Dimple's tea and sauntered over to the table. She placed it on a coaster in front of Dimple and sat opposite her.

"Pretty, aren't you?" Patrice asked her. "Look at all that hair!"

"Thanks." Dimple smiled. It was easier to take compliments and pretend she appreciated and understood them than to bat them off.

"Lizzie, come here," Patrice said. "Come and sit next to her, I want to look at you side by side."

"No!" Lizzie protested.

"Can you just do it, please?" Patrice asked, though she wasn't really asking.

"Seriously?" Lizzie groaned.

"Seriously!" Patrice smiled.

Lizzie uncrossed her legs and slipped down from the counter. She walked over to Dimple and took the seat next to her.

"Pretty much the same eyes." Patrice nodded, looking at both half sisters. "Mad. Almost the same nose, almost the same mouth. Who do you look more like, Dimple? Your mum or your dad?"

"My dad, I'm always told. I look like the female version of him. With hair." Dimple almost felt guilty saying this in front of Lizzie. "But I think Lizzie is the beautiful one out of the two of us."

"Huh?" Lizzie turned to look at her.

Dimple turned to Lizzie.

"Well then, your dad must be really beautiful, 'cause you two are *baddies*."

"Don't you remember what Dad said to us at Prynce's birthday?" Lizzie asked, furrowing her brow.

Dimple shook her head.

"I can remind you: 'Look how beautiful you are, Dimple. Shocking vibes! Who knew I could have produced such a serious weapon?'" Lizzie said flatly.

"Oh for God's sake, you're still stuck on that?" Patrice huffed. "Some man you don't even chat to says one thing and you remember it for a hundred years? I wish you could remember when our anniversary was with as much clarity as you remember some of the dumb shit your dad has said."

Lizzie rolled her eyes.

"Yeah, but there's a difference between pretty and beautiful, isn't there?" Dimple said.

"What?" Lizzie asked.

"Like, yeah, I'm pretty and I'm cute or whatever, but you've got the kind of face that people actually think about after they've seen it. You're so striking. I don't have that kind of face."

"So shall I ask why you're here?" Lizzie asked abruptly, ending that line of conversation. "Man problems, I assume? You wanted to go to one of your links but nobody was answering?"

"No, actually." Dimple shook her head. "I just had to go for a walk to clear my head and forgot my keys, like I said."

"Didn't you say you'd gone out to get some shopping?" Lizzie asked.

"Your sister wanted to see you, Lizzie!" Patrice smiled. "And it's not the middle of the night, it's 10 p.m. We're thirty, not eighty. You can stay up a bit late just this once. You stayed up very late a few weeks ago, didn't you? You didn't even come home until five in the morning."

"All right, chill with the passive aggression." Lizzie held her hands up.

"You hungry, Dimple?" Patrice asked Dimple.

Before she could answer, Patrice went to the fridge and pulled out a container of what looked like pasta in some sort of sauce.

"That's my lunch for tomorrow." Lizzie frowned. "She didn't ask to eat anything. She's good."

Patrice looked at Lizzie.

"Let me talk to you in the bedroom for a sec?" Again, it wasn't really a request. And it was the second time Lizzie had been pulled aside that day. Dimple was very aware of that.

Lizzie got up and walked out of the room.

"Seriously, make yourself at home," Patrice said. "And eat! Forks are in there."

She pointed at a drawer by the sink.

"What is it?" Dimple asked.

"Kale, butter bean, and tomato pasta," Patrice told her.

"Fancy. I've never had kale before," Dimple said.

"We don't have a microwave, but just have a look around, you'll find the pots."

Patrice followed Lizzie out of the room. Dimple heard the bedroom door close behind her.

Dimple stood and went closer to the pictures on the walls. Her eyes were drawn to a photo of a slim, handsome woman she guessed was Lizzie's mum, baby Lizzie on her lap. Dimple smiled at how similar she and Lizzie looked as babies. Both round, with big cheeks and big smiles.

She went to look for a pot to warm up the pasta, being as silent as she possibly could. After she put the pot on the stove to warm it before she put the pasta in, she crept toward the doorway and strained her ears.

". . . but you're making it awkward, and why?" she heard Patrice say. "She's your sister!"

"My half sister!" Dimple heard Lizzie shoot back.

"You're saying the half ting *again*? You see, that's your problem. You're so pedantic! She's your blood, why are you doing fractions?" Dimple heard Patrice ask.

"Because she comes stepping into my life and I'm meant to drop everything to look after her?"

"Lizzie, can you hear what you're saying? If I can see how fragile that girl is, why can't you? She's obviously lonely, why else would she turn up here when I know for a fact you've been giving her a hard time since the five of you came back into each other's lives? Do you *truly* believe that she forgot her keys? Give her a break, please. What is it you said Nikisha told you today? That Dimple needs to be handled with care, right? So why are you trying to break her? What's she done to you?"

Dimple stepped away from the doorway and tipped the pasta from the container into the pot, stepping back too slowly as the tomato sauce splashed on her. She took a sip of her tea as Lizzie and Patrice came back into the living room.

"You found the pots, good!" Patrice smiled encouragingly. "You've got food on you."

"It's *kale*ing me softly." Dimple tried to make a joke. She knew it was a bad one. Why was she making jokes? Was she nervous? She must have been. Sometimes her emotions caught her unawares until they made her do or say something strange.

"Do you want to stay here tonight, Dimple?" Lizzie asked, a little bit through gritted teeth.

Dimple really did want to stay there. She wanted to be around two people who liked, loved, each other. She didn't want to be bouncing about from house to Uber to house to her bed.

"Only if you don't mind," Dimple said quietly. "I'll wake up first thing and go home before my mum goes out to work."

"Don't worry about rushing out." Patrice smiled. "I'm working from home tomorrow! We can get to know each other."

Whatever else Patrice had said in that bedroom had softened Lizzie a bit, so she wasn't as snippy. While Dimple was eating, Patrice took some time to get to know her by asking a million questions in a row and giving Dimple approximately three seconds between each to squeeze her answers in. Lizzie even laughed at a couple of things Dimple said. When it was time to go to sleep, as Patrice did her twenty-step skin-care routine and swapped tips with Dimple, Lizzie pulled out the sofa bed and covered it with pillows and a duvet for Dimple.

"How are you with noise?" Lizzie asked as Dimple came back into the room, a thick mixture of turmeric and honey on her forehead that Patrice had administered masterfully.

"Fine, I think. Why?" Dimple asked.

"The trains."

"The trains?"

Lizzie walked over to the window and pulled up the blinds. It was only when Dimple saw the train rattle past the track close to the window that she registered the noise it was making.

"Oh, fine," Dimple said. "I didn't even clock."

Lizzie went to pull the blinds back down, but Dimple stopped her.

"You can leave them up. I want to see them go past, if that's okay."

"Suit yourself, 'cause it gets bright in here." Lizzie shrugged. "Sleep well, then."

"You too."

Lizzie waited for Dimple to climb into her bed for the night before she turned the light off.

"Lizzie?" Dimple called out quietly, just before Lizzie could close the door.

"Yup?"

"Thank you." Dimple paused. "I really am grateful. Not just to stay here. But for you. Sorry if I haven't shown that. But I just—maybe I think because I've got a lot of emotions inside I assume they're coming out even when they obviously aren't."

"Trust me, they come out enough." Lizzie closed her eyes and nodded. "But you're welcome. I'm grateful for you too."

Dimple rearranged herself under the duvet and inhaled deeply. It smelled sweet, clean.

"If you want to stick around tomorrow, I'll be home at about seven," Lizzie added quickly before she closed the door with a soft click, leaving Dimple in what would have been darkness, had it not been for the white lights blinking above the train track outside.

The fridge began to hum gently as Dimple shuffled down even lower in her bed for the night, pulling the soft, sweet and clean duvet around her.

She lay there for a while, wondering what it took to find a love like Lizzie had found. She wondered if maybe she was too wrapped up in herself to actually be open to love. Then she wondered if her dad was to blame, that he was the reason she just settled for attention, rather than something that actually made her feel good. But then Dimple realized that Lizzie was in exactly the same boat as her, dadwise. And then she started to wonder if the key difference was that Lizzie liked women, and before she could explore that thought any further, a train went past and distracted her racing mind.

As it rolled past the window, slowing slightly, Dimple's eyes grew heavy as she tried to focus on the few people in the carriages. She was asleep by the time the train had made its way past the building.

———

The next morning, it took Dimple a few seconds to realize where she was. She was panicked at first, but calmed down when she looked across the room and saw a picture of a laughing Lizzie and Patrice next to the fiddle-leaf fig.

She rolled up from the sofa and went into the bathroom. As she relieved herself and rubbed her eyes at the same time, she smiled as she heard Patrice singing her own makeshift remix of "Lovin' You" by Minnie Riperton from the bedroom. Her singing voice was high, sweet, strong.

By the time Dimple had finished and splashed some water on her face, Patrice and her voice had moved into the living room.

"Good morning, good morning!" Patrice trilled. "How did you sleep?"

"I think that's the best sleep I've had in a long time," Dimple croaked. "Sorry. My voice isn't as good in the morning as yours is. I don't think any of me is very good in the morning."

"Same as Lizzie," Patrice told her. "She doesn't even say anything to me before she leaves the house most days. The trains bother you?"

"No, not at all. I quite like it," Dimple said, going over to the sofa bed and folding the duvet. "I watched them until I fell asleep."

"Oh, you're a trainspotter like Lizzie?"

"What do you mean?"

"I feel like the main reason she wanted to live here is so she could watch those trains go by. You and her have that in common as well."

"It's not about the trains," Dimple said. "I like thinking about who's in them."

"Who's in the trains? You mean people going about their business?"

"Whenever I see trains, I like to think about how many different lives are inside the carriage. Every person in that carriage is someone different, going somewhere different. I think the same thing about high-rises." Dimple paused. "Behind every light is a life. And there are so many lives different from mine. Helps to remind me not to always be so in my head about myself."

"Me and you don't see the world the same way." Patrice laughed. "When we first came to view this place, I was put off by the train tracks 'cause they're so close. It's like the platform is on the balcony—I didn't understand it. And imagine, Lizzie didn't care about wanting privacy, but I was convinced that every person who went past would be logging everything we were up to," Patrice explained. "Honestly, I was so annoyed about it and so angry that we'd committed to what was potentially a lifetime of noise and people looking in my yard that I refused to even hug your sister for a fortnight. I cited 'deep stress and disruption,' and then I just got used to it. Anyway. Breakfast?"

Dimple had fallen asleep again on the sofa while Patrice was in the bedroom doing some work. She'd insisted that she'd either go out or go home and give Patrice back her living room, but Patrice had promised that she worked best from bed. Dimple woke up when she heard the front door close, and when she heard Patrice shush Lizzie.

"Why are you shushing me?" Dimple heard Lizzie whisper from the hallway. "Is our flat a library?"

"Your sister is sleeping," Patrice whispered back.

"Oh. Is she okay?" Their whispers were as loud as their talking volume. Dimple could hear everything, if not more clearly.

"Yeah, I mean, nothing has happened today, and you're the doctor out of the two of us, but I think sis is obviously going through it." Dimple heard Patrice step into the hallway and kiss Lizzie hello.

"Anyway, now you're home I need to go and get some potatoes."

"Why didn't you ask me to get them on my way back?"

"It's fine, you spend some time with your sister." *Whisper whisper*. "I'm going to pass by my mum's anyway—I need to collect a package I accidentally got sent to her house."

Dimple heard Patrice pull her coat and shoes on and leave the flat. She sat up.

"Hello?" she called out.

"Hey!" Lizzie called back. "Just washing my hands, one sec!"

A moment later, she walked into the living room and smiled when she saw Dimple sitting cross-legged on the sofa.

"Good nap?"

"Sorry, I dunno why I'm so tired," Dimple apologized.

"Could be anything. Winter. Stress. Lack of sleep. Turning up at people's houses in the night."

Dimple apologized again: "I'm sorry. I left my keys at home on purpose. I just wanted to see you, I guess. And I didn't like how we always bicker, you know?"

"It's okay, it's okay," Lizzie said. "I was thinking when I was on my way home, why don't you stay here for a few days? It probably isn't doing you much good, being in that house."

"How do you mean?" Dimple asked.

"Mmm, something pretty traumatizing happened there," Lizzie told Dimple. "You're better than me. I definitely wouldn't be able to stay at that house. I'd just be replaying what happened over and over again."

"Yeah, I've been doing a lot of that." Dimple nodded, her eyes glazing over. "I don't think I made the connection, though. I just feel really bad, all the time, when I'm there. And you've met my mum, so you know what I'm dealing with at home. But I don't want to, like, impose."

"You aren't imposing. I wouldn't have offered if I didn't want you here," Lizzie said. "If you don't want to go home you can borrow some of our clothes. And you can buy some knickers. Honestly, I think Patrice would kill me if I let you leave. I dunno what it is about you, but she loves you off. She was texting me about you all day. And she doesn't usually like anyone new. How she was being, I don't ever see her like that unless she's known them for years."

Dimple wondered where Lizzie's change of heart was coming from. Whatever its origins, Dimple appreciated it.

"Well, that's nice." Dimple sat back on the sofa and pulled a blanket over her feet. "I don't feel very loved at the moment."

"Your emotions really run you, init?" Lizzie asked.

Dimple started to laugh, but her laugh turned into soft crying, and soft crying turned into sobs.

"All right, it's all right." Lizzie swooped over to Dimple and put an arm around her. "I'm here."

"Th-thank you." Dimple wept, burying her face in her sister's shoulder, which wasn't really built for comfort, but was nice to lean on all the same.

"I just . . . I am really lonely." Dimple carried on with the crying. "Like, all the time."

"But you have friends, don't you?" Lizzie asked.

Dimple had to take a few deep breaths before she could talk in proper sentences.

"I don't, really," Dimple finally said. "I had two best friends at school, Samaria and Kiira. And we used to be together all the time. But then when Samaria went off to university we lost touch, 'cause when she came back she'd want to hang out with all of her new friends. And Kiira moved to Japan to teach when we were, like, twenty-five. And trying to talk to each other and fill each other in over video chat isn't the same, is it?"

"And you didn't pick up one new friend from then till now?" Lizzie asked.

"I guess not." Dimple shrugged. "I didn't have a *job* job, so I couldn't meet anyone that way. And I spend a lot of time at home, so I guess my mum became my main friend."

"Yeah, but you talk to people on the Internet all the time—aren't any of them your friends? Surely you can just message one of them and ask if they want to go for a coffee, or go bowling, or, like, go to the park and take pictures of each other, something? You could say it's a photo opportunity and then *BAM*, you've tricked them into being your friend."

"I dunno," Dimple said. "I'm quite shy. And I feel like I'm not going to live up to the person I am online, so it's just easier to keep those things separate, even if it means . . . not hanging out with anyone."

"I say this with love, but the person you are online isn't that great."

"Thanks." Dimple laughed, sniffing.

"No, I mean, like, the person you are on the Internet isn't as good as the person you are in real life. All those emotions are a lot, but they're very real. And the real version of you is better than anything else."

"I guess I didn't think of it like that. I've always seen my emotions as a burden."

"You gotta like yourself a lot more than you do now, Dimple," Lizzie told her.

———————

It was almost midnight before Dimple looked at her phone. She'd turned all her social media notifications off because it was all depressing her too much. It was mainly people commenting that the last couple of videos she'd posted were pointless and boring. They were already turning.

Lizzie and Patrice had just gone to bed, and Dimple got under her duvet before she started to scroll through the notifications that had been allowed to come through. Dozens of missed calls and voice mails from her mum that she swiped away, and then she squinted at a message she'd received from Kyron.

She opened it.

Kyron:
Time's ticking.

CHAPTER
TWELVE

DIMPLE HAD SEEN *I Know What You Did Last Summer*, and the sequel, which actually she preferred, so she knew she didn't have the emotional fortitude to keep any of this up.

She sank lower down into the duvet and sobbed.

"Everything okay?" Lizzie padded into the living room softly. "I could hear you crying."

"Did Patrice hear?" Dimple sniffed as she sat up.

"No, she's already asleep." Lizzie shook her head. "And nothing, nothing can wake that woman up."

"Kyron messaged me," Dimple said.

"What does he want now?" Lizzie sighed. "It can't be more money, surely."

"He said time's ticking," Dimple told Lizzie. "Shall I call Nikisha?"

"Unless you've found the money, I think you should leave Nikisha alone for the night."

"Please don't be annoyed with me," Dimple said, more panicked than anything that this would make Lizzie hate her again.

"I'm not annoyed with you," Lizzie said, putting a hand on

Dimple's shoulder. "Well, I am. But you're my sister. So the annoyance is nothing new."

Dimple went back home. The day after Kyron had sent her the countdown message, she started feeling aware of every single one of her movements in Lizzie's flat. Every time she got up to wee in the night, every time she took a plate out of the cupboard, every time she had to ask to be let back in after a trip to the shop. She started to be so hypersensitive to her own movements that she was even annoying herself, and Lizzie didn't do much to make her feel at home.

It made sense to go back home and just try to avoid her mum as much as she could. The first day was fine. It was nice being around her things again, even though she'd only stayed at Lizzie's for two nights. Her attachment issues extended to her possessions, too. She could record the first video she had in a long time, explaining away her absence because her grandma had passed away.

In the video she spoke about how it was so important to connect to her family history, and to think about the women she came from, the place she came from. She spoke about how learning about the past of this strong woman had woken something up in her, a new determination, a new drive. She added that she'd like to go to Jamaica to trace her family history, if any travel companies wanted to sponsor her.

Prynce is going to have a field day with this one, she thought as she uploaded it.

When she'd finished, she picked up the phone and called her dad to ask him something. He didn't answer, but called back two days later when she was hanging her washing out.

"W'happen?" he asked her, sounding a little bit too cheerful when she answered immediately.

"Hey, Dad, how are you feeling?"

"All is bless."

"Are you sure? Because I worry a bit that you're not really processing things prop—"

"I said all is bless, Dimple," Cyril repeated. "Is funny yuh call because I did mean to ask yuh someting."

"I had a question for you as well," Dimple told him. It felt so novel, just casually being on the phone to her dad. She was sad that death had brought them together, but still.

"What is it? You go first."

"You know in the eulogy? For your mum? I was thinking about it, and I realized that she was a single parent, and her mum and dad, your grandparents, had disowned her for having you so young."

"That's right," Cyril said.

"But, Dad, who looked after you?" Dimple asked. "When she came to England?"

Cyril didn't say anything.

"Hello?" Dimple moved around in case she'd lost reception.

"Rita and Clarence." Cyril finally broke his silence. "An' let me tell yuh a joke."

"Okay?" Dimple didn't know what kind of joke to expect.

"I grew up in that little house you saw. You remember the one in the picture?"

"Yeah. The little shack."

"The little shack." Cyril laughed. "I lived there with Desrence, and my grandmother, Rita, and my grandfather, Clarence, until I was fifteen. And when I was fifteen, Desrence told me someone from England was sending for me. And I had an older cousin, Ivanjoe, who lived down the road, he was already scheduled to bc flying to England a few weeks later. So I got on the plane with him, and he took me to this address he had on a piece of paper he kept in his pocket. You know, even when we were on the plane I didn't ask who had sent for me. So imagine, imagine my face when I got to this big house in England and the door opened and I see a woman looking me up and down, telling me she's my mother!"

"Wait," Dimple said. "What?"

Cyril chuckled quietly.

"I don't understand," Dimple told her dad. "So you thought Desrence was your big sister? And that your grandparents were your mum and dad?"

"Well, nobody ever tell me different, and when my mother left I wasn't old enough to remember her. So that's how it went."

"Well, that must have messed you up quite a lot, no?"

"Messed me up?" Cyril laughed again. "My dear, it is what it is."

"Okay." It was Dimple's turn to be silent. She was used to feeling sorry for him, but this felt different. It was a different strata of sad, a new level of understanding when it came to where this man had come from. It was no wonder he had attachment issues.

"Now, I have a question for you," Cyril said.

"Yeah, sure, what is it?" Dimple asked, knowing what it was going to be.

"Yuh see, the funeral," Cyril said. "Well, it really cost me. And that money you gave me the other day, it finish. Becah me neva expect to haffi pay fi a funeral, let alone mi mother's, yuh zimmi? And so if yuh could gimme likkle more, just to tide me over until the will is all sorted and I can sell mi mother house."

Dimple felt so sorry for him that she asked him how much he needed and promised to transfer it as soon as they got off the phone.

"You're a good daughter, Dimple," Cyril said before he ended the call. That didn't feel good to hear.

Her mum got home just as Dimple was hanging the last sock on the drying rack.

"Are you ready to talk about it?" Janet asked, washing her hands at the sink.

"To talk about what?"

"To talk about the fact that you left the house days ago and didn't come back? And since you did, you've been in your room avoiding me for the last few days," Janet said.

"I don't think there's anything to talk about."

"And I won't allow it, not under my roof." Janet crossed her arms and leaned on the kitchen counter.

"There's nothing much to talk about, Mum." Dimple shrugged. "I didn't have family before, and I have family now. I like spending time with them, and I shouldn't have to feel guilty about it, and I shouldn't have to hide it from you."

"You have family now?" Janet spluttered. "So what did you have before? What am I? That's a very cruel thing to say, Dimple."

"But here's the thing, Mum. It's not cruel. And you know what I mean, but you've made it about yourself! I've been lonely, Mum. And you're my mother and I love you, and that shouldn't be a question, but now these four people are in my life, and I love them as well, because they're my blood. It's not about me leaving you behind, it's about me getting to know them."

"And what about your dad?" Janet asked, completely disregarding Dimple's heartfelt speech. She'd seen enough of her daughter's videos to know she was well skilled at saying exactly what made people feel good.

"What about him?"

"Have you been spending time with him?"

"Only at the funeral. Why?"

"Has he been asking you for money?"

"What?"

"*Has* he been asking you for money?" Janet repeated.

"No!" Dimple said, lying. "Why would you ask that?"

"Because that's what he does, Dimple," Janet said. "That's what he did to me, for a long, long time. Before and even after you were born, he'd pop in and out of my life. He'd come back with the excuses, which I believed because I loved him too much to think he'd lie to me. Then he'd stay around for a week, maybe two. He'd look after me, he'd tell me how he'd changed, and then he'd ask for a bit of money to tide him over. I'd give it to him, then he'd go again."

"Well, he hasn't asked me for any money," Dimple said. "But I'm sure he's different now, Mum. I know you cast people into eternal damnation, but they can change, you know?"

"Yeah, and why do you think it is that I 'cast people into eternal damnation'? Because of your dad! I'm just trying to protect you from him! From all of them! Look at that brother of yours! Has Danny told you why he went to prison yet?"

"No." Dimple shook her head. "And I don't need to know, unless he wants to tell me."

"Well." Janet pursed her lips. "Let's see if he's your family once you know."

Dimple threw her head back.

"You didn't want to talk about things at all, did you? You wanted to do what you usually do: be bitter, be mean, be manipulative, act like you're the only person I've got and try and turn me against everyone. But it won't work. And I'm going to walk away from this now."

"You never used to be like this, Dimple!" Janet shot back. "The other day we were best friends!"

"Because you never encouraged me to *have* any friends, Mum." Dimple walked out of the room and left Janet there with that specific brand of guilt.

Dimple fired up the search engine and typed in "Danny Smith-Pennington prison." Nothing came up. She tried "Danny Smith-Pennington court." No results. She closed her laptop. She didn't need to know what he did. But then she heard Janet saying, "Let's see if he's your family once you know," in her head, and she let her mind run a little bit, and because she knew that some crimes were definitely unforgivable, she opened the laptop again and tried "Danny Smith-Pennington sentenced."

That did it. Next to the top result was a blurry picture of a much younger Danny. He looked like he was in his midtwenties. The picture was alongside an article from the *South London Press* that read

"Men Sentenced for Kidnap of Friend." Danny was scowling into the camera. His hair was longer, unkempt, no shape-up.

Dimple clicked through and skimmed the article as quickly as she could, her eyes darting across the screen. As she tried to take in what he did, she lingered on the picture of him. Even though he was scowling, he looked more sad than angry. Underneath was a picture of another man. Mixed-race, too, but with skin darker than Danny's. He had green eyes, and thick, deep brows that framed them.

Dimple finished reading the article and closed her laptop. She texted Danny and asked if they could speak.

An hour later, she was sitting at Tracy's kitchen table. Marley was toddling around the kitchen babbling to himself, not at all interested in Dimple and her nervous energy.

"Hi, Marley!" Dimple said in a voice she thought a child would respond to as she cupped the chipped mug of tea in her hands. "It's Aunty Dimple! Do you remember me?"

She went to take a sip but her stomach was acting up and the idea of swallowing it made her feel a bit sick. She let it dribble back into the mug, checking that Marley didn't see. Even though he was only one and a half, Dimple didn't want to feel judged by a toddler.

"You all right, darlin'? Tracy asked from behind a mound of washing in her arms as she walked into the dimly lit kitchen. "Danny'll be home in a sec."

"Yes, thanks," Dimple replied, wiping her mouth with the back of her hand as discreetly as possible.

"How's your mum doing after the nine night?" Tracy asked. "That Bernice. I can't believe what she said to her. Your mum has a beautiful figure, and so do you."

"Er, I think she's fine."

Dimple didn't want to know what Bernice had said because she didn't want to carry the weight of feeling sorry for her mum. Instead, she watched Tracy shove the washing into the drum of the machine and stand back, observing it.

"We got a new one of these," Tracy said, picking up a box of washing powder. "And I'll tell you what. It has just got too many buttons. What am I doing? A spin cycle, or sending the dirty clothes to the moon?"

Dimple smiled as Tracy pulled out the drawer and poured the powder into it while Marley waddled over and clung on to her legs.

"Nanny's coming, darlin'," she said to her grandson as she slammed the drawer shut and pressed some buttons. The machine beeped a response before it whirred to life. "That should do it. If it gets too loud we can go in the other room."

"I like your kitchen," Dimple said, looking around it. It was one of your standard subsidized housing kitchens. The appliances that it had come with were all a little battered, but humming away to let you know they were still working. The dark gray covering of the countertop was peeling at the edges, and the cupboards, light brown and made of laminate wood, had the handles removed on the bottom rows, presumably so Marley didn't hurt himself on them. The handles on the top set of cupboards were sharp at the edges.

Danny, plumber in residence, had obviously installed a new sink and taps that were slightly out of place, just a little bit too fancy for that kitchen. But the aesthetic worked because it had to.

"Do you?" Tracy laughed. "I don't! But it's where we live."

"It's nice." Dimple nodded. "It's homey."

Tracy picked Marley up and walked over to the cupboard. She pulled out a baby biscuit and put it in Marley's little fat hands, then made her way over to the table at which Dimple sat.

She pulled out a chair and eased herself down while Marley got to work on his snack. Dimple noted that Tracy had dyed her hair a brighter shade of blond since the nine night.

"You look more like your dad than the rest of them. Even the boys! But I suppose that was always going to be the case with Danny." Tracy smiled. "And there are traces of Cyril in Prynce. When he laughs, I think. And sometimes there's a little look he does—I can't quite describe it—where I can see your dad in him. Though saying that, Cyril was never that small at twenty-five."

"I didn't know you'd met the rest of them."

"Oh yeah!" Tracy exclaimed before she took a sip of her tea. "I met Nikisha first, obviously. Cyril is so silly, he used to drop her off here when she was a little baby and tell me she was his niece. Danny wasn't born yet, and here I was, maybe a little naïve, thinking that this nice man who drove the buses and used to help me carry the shopping was already good with kids. By the time I was pregnant with Danny, I'd spent enough time with Nikisha to know she was his daughter. But I didn't care. She was such a lovely little girl."

"Really? It didn't matter to you that he lied?"

"I didn't care at all! When I had her I'd just take her out with Danny, treat her like my own. And I saw all the looks people gave me, walking around with a little Black girl, but it didn't matter. Anyway, that all stopped when she was about five, when Bernice caught wind of it. She's a one, as you know by now. Anyway, Cyril had been saying he'd been the one looking after her, but she caught him in the betting shop one Saturday and asked where her daughter was. Can you believe it?"

Dimple wasn't surprised by this at all.

"You I met when you were around three." Tracy nodded. "And only once! Cyril turned up at mine, and I hadn't seen him for months, maybe even a year, but he turned up on the doorstep with you! And you were all big hair and deep dimples and this sad little face, and he asked if I could look after you for the night."

"And did you?" Dimple asked.

"Of course!" Tracy laughed. "I love babies! You don't remember it, do you?"

Dimple shook her head.

"You cried a lot," Tracy said. "But not big wailing or anything, you were just sort of whimpering and sniffling to yourself. I ended up just sitting you on my lap until you cried yourself to sleep. Such an emotional little thing."

"Weren't you annoyed that he just kept turning up with these kids for you to look after? Or not even annoyed—like, upset, or something? I mean, I get that you probably clocked that he wasn't a great boyfriend, but, like, wasn't it weird that he wouldn't explain who we were?"

"No." Tracy smiled. "Not at all. I knew the score with your dad, darlin'. I had his number the day I met him! He was never going to settle down. He's not settled in himself, is he? I used to joke that being a bus driver was the perfect job for him. But it's not his fault. All the stuff with his mum, and his dad, it's no wonder he can't stay still. Constantly looking for something."

Dimple opened her mouth to ask more about this.

"Anyway, then I met Elizabeth," Tracy said. She loved a chat. "Well, I wouldn't say I met her, but I saw her. Only once, as well. I saw her and her mum—remind me of her name?"

"Kemi?"

"That's it, Kemi. I saw her and her mum, Kemi, on the high street. Elizabeth must have been about ten, but I knew she was Cyril's daughter the second I saw her. And when I asked him about her, he knew there was no point in lying." Tracy laughed. "In fact, I didn't even ask! I said, 'Oh, Cyril, I saw your other daughter the other day, the one with the gorgeous Nigerian mum,' and he just nodded. And actually, I first met Prynce when he was about fourteen. I reckon Cyril got a telling off when Bernice found out he'd been bringing Nikisha here so he stayed away with Prynce. Which was a shame. But I know they'd met each other, the boys, by this point. I think when he took you all to the park that day. Anyway, Danny was away, and Prynce needed somewhere to stay for a few months. Think Cyril and Bernice were a bit worried about the people he was hanging out with, so he was here for a while, keeping his head down. It was Nikisha's idea, if you can believe it. She'd come and visit him every weekend, sit down with him and do his homework. Between me and you, that girl raised herself, and then Prynce, too."

"Yeah, I got the sense of that. But, Danny was away where?" Dimple asked.

"He was inside, my darlin'. But you knew this, didn't you?"

"Oh, of course." Dimple nodded. "Sorry."

"Why are you sorry?" Tracy asked her. "Nothing to be sorry about. I'm not sorry. My son is who he is. The way you all are the way you are, the way your dad is who he is. And I don't know you all, but I'll still care about you and look after you all if it comes to it. Whatever type of person you are, whatever you do, good or bad."

"But why?" Dimple asked. "You don't need to do that."

"I'm a mum, darlin'." Tracy smiled. "That doesn't stop at having one kid. Speaking of which, I think this one needs a little rest."

Tracy stood, an almost floppy Marley in her arms, at the same time they heard Danny's keys rattle in the front door.

"That's good timing," Tracy remarked as Danny walked into the kitchen.

"Hello, everybody!" He smiled at his mum and sister before swooping over to Marley and giving him a kiss on the head. "Oh, he's about to go down, is he?"

"Yeah, darlin', he's been up all day if you can believe it."

"He eaten properly today?"

"Well, he's eaten more than he did yesterday, which is good," Tracy told her son. "I wouldn't worry too much, Dan. It was probably just a little virus he picked up at nursery, like I said."

"You're right." Danny nodded. "Okay, well, if you don't mind putting him to bed, I'll go out in a bit and pick us up something for dinner?"

"Sounds good to me. And, Dimple, if you want to stay the night, I can make up the sofa for you," Tracy said as she started to leave the kitchen with her grandson.

"Oh, I'm good, thanks." Dimple smiled. "But thank you! That's very kind of you."

"Suit yourself, darlin'. And don't be a stranger!" Tracy called back from the hallway. "You've slept here before, you can sleep here again, anytime you like."

"Why is your mum so nice?" Dimple asked Danny as he washed his hands at the kitchen sink. "What's the catch?"

Danny let out a small laugh.

"Yeah, she's not like that all the time, don't be fooled."

"I mean, you've met my mum, so."

"Yeah, true." Danny laughed again. "Nah, my mum is good, don't get me wrong. She's a kind woman. But trust me, she can get angry, and she can dig me out. But as she's got older, I think she just got less angry and a bit more . . . accepting of things."

Danny sat down opposite and seemed to collapse further in the little wooden chair.

"Hard day at work?" Dimple asked her brother.

Danny nodded. "It's always a hard day at work. But it's all right! I'm home now. Getting back and seeing Marley before he goes to bed always reminds me why I work so hard."

Dimple smiled at this. "I like how much you love Marley," she said. "Not that parents don't love their kids. But you light up when you talk about him. It's a beautiful thing."

"I mean, yeah." Danny smiled. "He's easy to love. He's a beautiful boy with a beautiful soul. It's funny, actually. When I look at him, I always wonder how Dad could have walked away from any of us. Well, that's not funny at all, but you know what I mean. You'll experience it yourself when— Sorry, *if* you ever have kids. All I want to do is be around Marley."

"Maybe because Cyril was never around us?" Dimple wondered aloud.

"Maybe." Danny nodded again. "Or maybe because he's a part of me. I can't imagine not wanting to protect him."

They sat in silence for a while. "Danny," Dimple said, even though she didn't really want to spoil the moment.

"You want to know, right?" Danny collected himself, ready to get serious. "When I got your text, I guessed as much."

Dimple nodded.

"Sorry."

"Nah, don't be sorry." Danny smiled. "I'm just glad you gave me the chance to explain—well, there's nothing to explain, really. 'Explaining' makes it sound like I didn't do what I did. But I did it, so I guess I mean I'm glad you're giving me the chance to talk about it."

"Well, you're my brother, so." Dimple shrugged. "Can't just cast you off."

"Basically." Danny wriggled out of his work jacket. "Let me get into it now, no point in building it up. I had this friend when I was younger. I met him in primary school. Year *one*. That's how far back we went. He lived on the other side of the estate, so we used to roll together morning till night. Do you want another cup of tea? I'm gonna have one."

"Oh. No, no, thank you." Dimple pulled her discarded mug of tea toward her and put her hand over the rim.

Danny stood up and filled the kettle by the fancy sink. As he did, he put all of his weight on his left leg. His other leg was stretched out, the toe of his foot touching the floor lightly.

"I do that." Dimple pointed. "Have you seen me do that?"

"Do what?" Danny asked as he put the kettle back on its base.

"I stand like that," Dimple said. "Like a ballerina. When I'm washing up."

"Ha!" Danny laughed. "Finally we got something nice from Dad. Not that it's of any use."

The kettle started to fizz and bubble as Danny pulled a mug from the cupboard and fished for a teabag in the glass jar on the kitchen counter.

"Anyway, as I was saying," he continued. "My friend Jerome. He was my chargie, you know? Proper rider. He'd follow me anywhere and I did the same for him. You know when your parents say, 'Oh, if that person jumped off a cliff, would you follow them?' If Jerome had somersaulted off a cliff, I would have done ten somersaults after him."

"I've never had a friend like that," Dimple said. "But it's nice that you did. Or do. Are you still friends now?"

Danny shook his head slowly.

"Nah, nah. One day, when we were both twenty-two, so, like, young, and *dumb*, Jerome got into it with some guy from Sunnyhill estate, a few minutes down the road. Over some girl. Some girl that Jerome had only seen a couple of times! Anyway, this guy, I'm not gonna say his name 'cause it doesn't really matter, I think he must have been jealous, 'cause now he was properly loved up with this same girl Jerome had seen a couple times. So he came round here, shouting about how Jerome thought he was the king, and how the girl said he was shit in bed— Sorry."

"No worries. I am thirty years old."

"Yeah, but still. Anyway, saying how Jerome couldn't beat, and how he was a bowcat, and all of this childish stuff. Jerome had a temper, but that day he was calm. Like, weirdly calm, even though bare people were there and could hear this guy saying all this stuff, and they were all laughing and that. 'Cause everyone on the block knew Jerome, and even though they knew him, they didn't know him like *that*. He was quite a private person up until that point. I kept asking him if he wanted to do anything, but he just kept saying, 'Nah, it's okay, it's okay.' So I didn't think anything of it. Well, I thought it was a bit weird, but I was, like, whatever. If he doesn't mind his business being out there, then okay. I mean, I was glad it wasn't me, but anyway."

As Danny finished making his tea and sat in front of her, Dimple smiled at how much her brother had inherited Tracy's love of telling a story in as much depth and detail as possible.

"I didn't hear anything from Jerome for a couple days, but I wasn't that worried, 'cause even though we was always together, sometimes we wasn't, and that was cool."

Dimple nodded.

"But one night, like at about two in the morning, my phone rang, and it was his number, so I answered, like, 'You all right, bro?' and he was, like, 'Yeah, I need a favor,' and I was obviously, like, 'Anything, my guy.' So he tells me he's going to come and collect me 'cause I needed to do something for him. I'd fallen asleep in my clothes so I just jumped up and was, like, 'Yeah, cool, come for me whenever,' and he calls me up like twenty mins later and he says he's downstairs in a van. I dunno where he got a van from, but I got in it, 'cause why wouldn't I?"

Danny took a well-deserved breath before he got up and opened another cupboard. He pulled out a packet of Jammie Dodgers.

"Biscuit?"

"No, thank you." Dimple shook her head as Danny sat back down and ripped the packet open.

"So we're in this van, and he starts driving. And after a while—and, like, when I say a while, I mean an hour—I'm, like, 'Where we goin', man?' and he says nothing. And 'cause he's my guy and I trust him, I just fall asleep. 'Cause I'm not really a person who can just fall asleep around anyone, is the thing. So that shows you how I thought, 'Yeah, my boy has got me.' A few hours later, I wake up, and we're in, like, deep country. Jerome is pulling up outside some little house and I'm thinking, 'Is this guy taking me for a minibreak or something?' He hops out the van, I follow him, and he goes into this little house. He's not saying anything, so I ask him why we're there and whose house it is, but he just keeps saying nothing. It's still dark, 'cause it's early, early morning, and this little house doesn't have lights that work or anything, so I'm just feeling my way around and falling over bits of wood on the floor and shit. And he had a flashlight, yeah. Jerome had a flashlight."

"Actually, Danny, can I have some water, please?" Dimple asked, her mouth dry. Where this story might go was making her nervous.

"Course." Danny jumped up and went over to the sink. He picked up a glass off the drying rack and turned the tap on.

"I installed a filter in here." He pointed to the cupboard under the sink as he let water fill the glass. 'Cause of my job, I can't drink tap water after the pipes I've seen."

"Thanks." Dimple took the full glass of water from him and gulped down a big sip.

"So where was I?" Danny sat back down and threw a whole biscuit into his mouth.

"Jerome had a flashlight."

"That's it," Danny said as he chewed. "Jerome had a flashlight. And I'm following him through this mad cottage, like one of them haunted houses you get at the carnival, and we get to this room in the back. And Jerome turns the flashlight off and I hear him shuffling around when he gets in the room. And I hear this flicking, 'cause he's got a lighter. So he's lighting these candles, and I see that he's got a mask on, like a bally, face all covered apart from eyes and mouth, and I say, 'Bro, what's going on?' and he says, 'Say nothing,' and I'm, like, 'Okay.' So I look around the room, and I see my man in the corner! The one who came to the estate saying Jerome was a bowcat and all that."

"What's he doing in the corner?"

"He's all tied up, and his face is bloody, eye swollen, and he's got a sock in his mouth, and he doesn't even look scared or anything, he just looks pissed. If anything, I was the one who was scared," Danny told Dimple. "So Jerome says to me that he's got some things to do, and I need to watch this guy for him, and obviously I wouldn't have chosen to do that, but he's my boy, so obviously I do it. I asked him for how long, and he says just a couple of hours, and he'll be back by the morning and he'll bring me breakfast and that."

Danny ate another biscuit.

"So, morning comes and goes. And all I have is my phone, but I don't have reception, so I can't call him and see where he is. And I'm hungry but I can't even use the map to find a shop. And even if I knew where the shop was, I didn't wanna walk through fields and that to get to it, 'cause Jerome had the vehicle init."

"And are you and this guy saying anything to each other?" Dimple asked. "Or are you just sitting opposite each other in silence?"

"I'm not even in the same room as him, mate, I felt so bad," Danny said. "And he smelled really bad, 'cause I dunno how long Jerome had had him there for, but he'd pissed himself, and I didn't want to be in the room with that."

"And how long were you there for?"

"So, the whole day passes," Danny said. "And I can't lie, I'm vex 'cause I'm in the middle of nowhere with this guy, there's no food, no water or electric, I had to take a shit outside and wipe my arse with leaves, my phone has died by this point, and I'm really hungry. I walk around outside a bit, and the only person I see is some guy and his dog, and the man is eyeing me like he's all suspicious 'cause obviously he probably hasn't seen many people my shade bowling round, but I just wave and say something like I'm on a nice walk. But he doesn't say anything so I just don't think about him again. Anyway, night comes, so I go in that room and light the candles again 'cause even I'm a bit scared of the dark and I'm thinking this guy must be even more scared than me 'cause he's probably scared for his life as well by this point."

Danny threw another biscuit into his mouth and chewed it slowly before washing it down with a gulp of tea.

"Right, so. I go back to the room next to the one the guy is in, and all there is for me to do is look out the window at the moon. So I'm doing that for a while, and I can start to smell, like, a bonfire?

And I hadn't ever really fucked with bonfires before, but I remember one bonfire night my school did once, and the smell was the same. But after a bit, it smells like it's really close and I'm, like, that's not right. And I look at the door of the room I'm in and I see smoke coming up from under it, so I jump up and open it, and I see that the room next door, the one the guy is in, is on fire."

"Jesus Christ," Dimple whispered.

"But he's all right! One of the candles on the other side of the room has fallen and the flame is going up the wall over there, so the fire hasn't got to him yet. But I run over and I untie him, and as soon as he's untied, he's up and he's off. I turn to go after him, but, like, this bit of wood that's on fire falls down on me from the ceiling."

Danny held his arm up and showed Dimple the burn mark she'd seen that ran across his forearm. "I saw you look at the burn that night."

Dimple touched it gently while Danny continued. Like Danny, the scar was softer than it looked.

"And so I'm screaming and for a second I'm thinking, like, should I try and put this fire out, and how do I do it? But then I'm, like, wait, why do I care about this house? So I run out, and obviously I can't see any trace of the guy. And there's no point in me trying to run through these fields of wheat or whatever looking for him, so while this cottage burns, I just wait outside it. Nowhere else for me to go, not in the dark, and not on foot. The fire engine comes to put the fire out, but when I hear it coming I hide in some bushes nearby 'cause I think it's police. But when the fire's out and they've gone, I go back to where it was and just sit next to all the burned wood and that on the floor, waiting for my boy to come back. A couple hours later, it's morning now, I'm freezing cold, I could have died in a fire, and Jerome finally drives back when all the drama is over, and he asks, 'What happened?' Just like that. He sees me looking like I've gone through the wars, I'm standing in front of ash, and he asks me 'What happened?' And imagine, this guy didn't even bring food for me."

Dimple blinked back at Danny. His obsession with food was going to get him killed one day.

"So I jump in the van with him and explain what happened, and he drives us round looking for this guy, but we don't find him. Bit like that night, actually. Driving around looking for Kyron really messed my head up."

"I'm sorry—" Dimple said.

"It's not your fault." Danny smiled. "Anyway, by this point I'm, like, 'Look, take me back to the ends, please, I need to eat, I need to shower, I need to sleep.' And I think I'm probably in shock to be honest, because that fire was mad. It was so scary, Dimple. And I couldn't really breathe and it was bare hot. So we drive back, and Jerome tells me not to worry about anything. He says the guy won't make it back, and if he does, he won't say anything. So I'm, like, 'I dunno about that,' and he's, like, 'The less we say about it for now the better,' and he's my boy innit, so I think he's coming up with some kind of master plan or some alibi or something. But I'm so tired that I just fall asleep instead of telling him we need to get our stories straight, and when I wake up we're back on the block, I'm in the van by myself 'cause I'm assuming he's hopped out when we got back. I go in the flat, Mum isn't here 'cause she's at work, so I have a shower to wash the fire smell off me, and I eat something finally, and I go to sleep. I must have slept for so long cause I heard Mum come in and ask if I wanted dinner, but I was too tired to say yes. When I woke up again, it was morning and the police were knocking the door down. And when I say they were knocking down the door, I mean, like, knocked off the door you walked through *off* its hinges. When Mum got home she didn't know what had happened, but she had no door and the flat was wrecked. Her neighbor told her that I'd been taken away, 'cause the whole estate had seen what had happened, basically. More than anything I felt bad for my mum. I was worried that everyone on the estate had seen that happen and they'd think she was a bad parent or whatever."

"Wait, so, the guy made it back and went to the police?" Dimple asked Danny.

"Not even, you know. Basically, he'd got out of the burning cottage, and he'd run and run until he saw the same man walking his dog that had seen me the day before. And the man with the dog had called the police because he was obviously, like, 'Why are all these Black boys running round my little village,' or whatever. So the police had picked up the guy I was meant to be watching 'cause he was trying to make it back to London on foot, and eventually the police got it out of him that he'd been kidnapped and all of that. And the police must have assumed that whoever had kidnapped him had had a weapon, which is why they fucked up the flat like that. They probably would have done it anyway, though. They don't usually need an excuse to treat us like animals."

"So you and Jerome went to prison?" Dimple said. "I'm hoping he went for longer."

"Well, the guy didn't see Jerome's face, 'cause Jerome always kept his mask on. He was the smarter one out of the two of us, and he didn't even bring me a mask! But yeah, he obviously knew it was him, but he's not gonna snitch. And the man with the dog saw my face outside the cottage and called me out in the lineup. And I wasn't gonna snitch either, so. Yeah."

"So you went to prison for six years," Dimple said flatly, "because you wouldn't actually say what happened?"

"It was meant to be twelve, but the sentence usually gets halved."

"And what happened to Jerome?" Dimple asked. "You're not friends with him now, are you?"

"Never heard from him again, Dimple. The last time I saw him was before I fell asleep in the van with him. Nobody knows where he went after that." Danny laughed sadly, shaking his head. "Imagine. After all of that. But, you know, it is what it is."

"What do you mean, 'It is what it is'?" Dimple scoffed. "You didn't technically do anything wrong."

"That's not how things in this life work, Dimple." Danny shrugged. "Bad things happen to good people, and the other way around. And the thing is, I didn't have to help Jerome. I coulda said no. Coulda let that guy go free. But I didn't. I did somersaults off the cliff instead."

CHAPTER

THIRTEEN

DIMPLE SAT UP AND blinked awake, her eyes finally focusing on the graying stone ceiling above her. The fluorescent bars of bright white light hurt her eyes, so she closed them again as she rolled onto her side. The scratchy fabric of her gray tracksuit irritated her skin. She cleared her throat and reached over to the small cupboard on the side for her plastic cup, draining it of the last dregs of water that were inside.

"You're up, then."

Her eyes followed the voice, and her gaze landed on Lizzie, who was lying on the bed opposite.

A loud bell made them both jump.

"Did you sleep okay?" Dimple asked her sister.

"Of course I didn't fucking sleep okay," Lizzie said. "How the fuck would I sleep okay?"

The bell kept chiming.

"It's time for breakfast," Lizzie said. "You better get up."

"I'm sorry," Dimple groaned. "I'm sorry, Lizzie."

"Sorry isn't going to cut it," Nikisha said from the corner of the room, between the door and the small sink that sat in the corner.

"The same," Prynce spat, suddenly appearing at the end of the bed. "My life is ruined because of you."

The bell went again.

"We have *children*, Dimple," Danny said, sitting on the bed next to Lizzie. "Marley, Nicky, Amara. What are they gonna do?"

"I know, and I'm sorry," Dimple choked. She tried to keep apologizing, but the words were getting caught in the dryness of her throat. She coughed and reached for her cup again even though she knew it was empty.

"We're stuck in here for life and it's all your fault!" Lizzie screamed, her voice filling the entire cell. "It's all your fault."

Dimple coughed and coughed, her hands reaching up to her throat and her mouth as she tried to apologize again.

"You need to get up," Nikisha said, walking over to her.

"What?" Dimple rasped. "I can't."

"You need to get up," Prynce repeated.

"Dimple, get up." Lizzie jumped up from the bed and put her hands on Dimple's shoulders, shaking her.

"Dimple!" Danny shouted.

Dimple opened her eyes for real and saw Janet standing above her, her hands on her shoulders. The bell of her alarm chimed on repeat next to her head.

"Jesus," Dimple gasped. Her heart was pounding hard. She sat up, brushed her mum's hands from her shoulders, and turned her phone alarm off.

"You were having a bad dream," Janet said, sitting on the end of the bed. Dimple wondered if it was wine she could smell on her mum, or if she was still in some sort of dream state.

"Was I?" Dimple asked, reaching for the glass of water on her bedside table.

"I walked past your room and I could hear your alarm, so I left you, and then when I came back past the alarm was still going and I could hear you saying sorry over and over again."

Dimple tried to steady herself.

"What time is it?" she asked her mum

"It's just after ten," Janet told her. "But don't get up just yet, rest a bit. And tell me what's wrong, Dimple."

"Nothing is wrong." Dimple swung her shaky legs out of the bed and stood up. "I need to get ready. Do you mind?"

"What do you need to do today?" Janet asked a little bitterly. "Seeing one of Cyril's children?"

"I'm seeing all of them, actually," Dimple shot back. "Our dad has asked to see us."

The "hmmm" that passed through Janet's throat was loud.

"Why are you even home?" Dimple asked her mum.

"I've got an appointment at eleven so I'm going into work after," Janet said. "Anything else you'd like to know?"

"No." Dimple shook her head. She flopped back onto the pillow before she had to get ready for the day.

———————

A couple of hours later, just around the corner from her late grandmother's house, Dimple saw a familiar face crossing the road and coming toward her.

"Hi, Marvette, how are you?" Dimple asked her aunt.

"I am fine, Dimple, and yourself?" Marvette answered curtly.

Dimple made the little bit of small talk with her aunt that she could, ranging from how the weather was to the traffic that was building up next to them.

"You seen your useless daddy?" Marvette pursed her lips and put her shopping down by her feet.

"I'm just on my way to Grandma's to see him now," Dimple told her. "But he's having a bit of a hard time—I hope he's okay."

"I'm the one having the hard time, let me tell you that." Marvette was ready to misplace some anger. "That funeral almost bankrupted me. I had to beg and borrow and steal, asking people on my knees to help me out. And your daddy didn't put one penny toward it, but even now I'm hearing he's telling people our mother didn't have a good enough send-off? Disgusting. Tell him from me that his days are numbered."

Dimple could tell Marvette meant that.

"I'm really sorry, I thought he— Well, he told me he—"

"And I hate to say it." Marvette cut Dimple off, not caring at all about anything to do with her brother. "But the house selling so quickly is a godsend. We couldn't even spend any time in there to properly say goodbye, but we had to do what we had to do."

Tears sprang to Marvette's eyes, surprising Dimple.

"Take care of yourself, Dimple." Marvette sniffed and picked up her shopping bags. "I hope you'll be sensible with the money. Unlike your waste-of-space father."

As she watched Marvette shuffle away, a lot was going through Dimple's head. Was she surprised that her dad had lied about the money? Not so much. It was very much a "not shocked but disappointed" situation. Her main worry was that she'd been weaving so many lies recently that she was turning into her dad, and she was concentrating so much on this transformation that she didn't have time to wonder what her aunt had meant about being sensible with money.

———————

"I have a favor to ask you all," Cyril said to his five children. They blinked back at him from the beaten sofa in their late grandmother's house.

"What is it?" Nikisha asked.

"Well." Cyril laughed. "It's funny, actually."

They all knew it wouldn't be funny.

"So you see this house?" Cyril asked, gesturing to the four walls around them.

"Mmm?" Nikisha responded impatiently.

"Yuh cyaan believe how much it's worth."

"Okay?" Lizzie said. "What's that got to do with us?"

"So," Cyril said. "My mother, she was a funny woman."

"Was she?" Danny asked. "Funny weird or funny like she was a joker?"

"Both." Cyril laughed a laugh that made his children uneasy.

"Where is this going?" Nikisha asked.

"Nikisha!" Dimple exclaimed. "He's getting there!"

"So soft," Nikisha muttered under her breath.

"Well," Cyril said again. "It doesn't look like much, but this house is worth a million. *A million*."

He always meandered in and out of patois, but when he talked money he always spoke like an Englishman.

"I'd believe it." Danny shrugged. "It's a five-bedroom house in the middle of Brixton."

"Even though it's ex-council?" Lizzie asked.

Danny nodded.

"Yeah."

"Well, there's that, *and* the money from the old dental practice. And after that teefin' government take away the inheritance tax, that's a *lot* of money," Cyril said. "My mother, funny as she is, she lef' a quarter of it all to Tessilda and her kids, a quarter to Lavinia and her family, a quarter to Marvette. And the rest, she left to . . . all of you."

"All of who?" Prynce asked in disbelief.

"The five of you," Cyril replied. "She always did tell me I should have been better to you all. So I think this must be her way of punishing me or teaching me a lesson. Whatever yuh waan call it."

"Whoa," Dimple said.

"But she didn't even like us," Lizzie said, confused.

"You don't have to like someone to love them," Cyril said. "But see, my sisters, they've already found a buyer. One posh white couple who have had their eye on the house for a while. And the people who rented the practice will buy it. So look, I worked it out," Cyril said, pulling a tatty piece of paper out of his pocket and unfolding it slowly. "And so, after it all sells, Tessilda, Lavinia, and Marvette will each get about two hundred and thirty thousand."

"And so will we, as per your calculations," Nikisha told Cyril.

"Well, so, about that," Cyril said before clearing his throat. "You know I'm not in the best position, financially."

"Okay." Nikisha shrugged. She wasn't going to pretend she cared.

"If that money gets split five ways, you all get forty-six thousand, or thereabouts."

"Or thereabouts?" Lizzie snorted. "There's no point pretending you haven't worked this out to the penny."

"And so I was thinking that the best way to do it is that you each take a nice sum of five thousand from that. You can each get yourselves something nice, maybe go on a holiday, or something. And you can give me the rest. That seems like the fairest way to sort it."

"Sorry?" Nikisha spluttered. "Fairest to who?"

"To me!" Cyril said. "She was my mother. And I've learned my lesson. Trust me."

"What lesson?" Lizzie asked him.

"Well, the lesson that . . . that I . . . that . . ." Cyril laughed nervously. "What can I say? I'm still learning."

"No, Dad," Nikisha said. "No. Anything that woman left to us, we're keeping it."

"But—but—" Cyril couldn't find the words.

"Did you think we'd say yes?" Nikisha asked him.

"You know your dad needs it," Cyril said to Nikisha.

"You think we don't know about the money you've been taking from Dimple?" Nikisha stood.

"I didn't tell you that!" Dimple exclaimed.

"You didn't have to." Nikisha shook her head. "When you told us he'd asked, we knew you would."

Dimple felt her face flush with embarrassment.

"You see, Dad, you might act like you're too cool to care about what goes on, but we know you're smart." Nikisha turned her attention back to Cyril. "I know you didn't ask Dimple for the money because it looks like she's the one who's got it, it's because you know she's the most naïve of all of us."

Cyril didn't know how to respond to that. It wasn't like Nikisha was wrong. He couldn't argue with her, or laugh it off like he usually did.

"We're keeping the money, Dad," Nikisha told Cyril. "Let's call it accrued child support. With interest."

Cyril looked betrayed.

"Look at you lot. No honor among thieves," he tutted, shaking his head.

"*Thieves?* Call us what you want, Cyril. We don't owe you anything, and we wouldn't take what we don't deserve." Nikisha walked to the door. "Come on, you lot. We're leaving."

Cyril's children filed out of the house and gathered on the street outside.

"As much as I hate this, we'll give the money to Dimple to pay off Kyron," Nikisha told her siblings. "Any objections?"

"No, no, no." Dimple shook her head. "No, you can't do that, no."

"It's not up to you," Nikisha said firmly. "Danny?"

"Yep." Danny nodded.

"Lizzie?" Nikisha looked at Lizzie.

Dimple knew Lizzie would say no.

"Fine by me," Lizzie said. "I just want this gone."

"Prynce?" Nikisha asked her youngest brother.

"Course!" Prynce smiled. "What are the chances of getting the money like that? Mad."

"There we go." Nikisha looked at Dimple. "Tell him when the house sells, he'll get it. You can make up the rest, right?"

Dimple didn't know what to say.

"Stop opening and closing your mouth like a fish and say thank you," Nikisha told her.

"Thank you, thank you!" Dimple spluttered. "I just— I don't deserve this!"

"We aren't doing this for you," Nikisha reminded her. "We all need this to go away. You just need to make sure he doesn't think there's more where this came from."

"I'll make sure he knows," Dimple said.

"Please don't try and do the thing where you have sex with him again," Lizzie said.

"None of that chat, please," Danny told her.

"It'll be sorted," Dimple said. Her siblings didn't believe her.

They were right not to. On her way home, Dimple went to Kyron's house and explained that he'd get his money as soon as the house sale went through. He seemed satisfied with that, but said he was still going to keep the picture of her.

"You haven't even said sorry that my grandma died," Dimple said to Kyron.

"You didn't know her," Kyron said, laughing.

"It's the principle," Dimple said.

"So what, you're a girl of principles now?" Kyron asked.

"Please delete that picture, Kyron," Dimple said.

He shook his head.

"Nope."

"When are you going to delete it?"

"When I get my money," Kyron said. "Aren't you grateful you're getting an extension?"

"Grateful?" Dimple yelped. "You've got something that could ruin my life!"

"It's not gonna *ruin* your life." Kyron smiled at her, narrowing his eyes. "It'll fuck it up, maybe. Ruin is a bit strong."

"How can you talk like this?" Dimple asked him. "We used to love each other, Ky."

"U-used to love?" Kyron stuttered. "Love? How much did you love me when I was in the back of that van? You're a forgetful girl, Dimple."

———————

A week had passed since she'd seen her brothers and sisters, but to Dimple, it had felt like longer. She was . . . lonely, again. Her Internet popularity had pretty much faded. The last video she'd posted got as many views as her old ones had, before the Kyron video. And she was just as melancholy as she was before (and during) her time in the ring light.

Nikisha had her hands full with Nicky and Amara because their dad started seeing someone (he hadn't told Nikisha, she could just tell), so he'd dropped them off with her so he could "go away for a few days with a friend." Danny had decided he was going to try to give things a proper go with Marley's mum, so was mainly uncontactable because, ironically, as a Gemini, he wasn't good at focusing on two things at once. Lizzie was "really actually focusing on revising, Dimple," and because Dimple took that as rejection, she told herself there was no point trying to hold on to the few days Lizzie had been nice to her. And Prynce was just young and unfocused, so it wasn't like she could make a solid plan with him.

Without any looming threat of incarceration or similar, there was no reason for her and her siblings to spend time together. One afternoon, though, when she was indulging in some deep and moody feelings, Kyron messaged her to remind her that she owed him. In true Dimple style, she'd been ignoring all of that in the hope that he'd forget, or that the amnesia he'd had after the knock to his head would come back.

She ignored his message, putting her phone back on her bedside table, but as soon as the screen touched the surface, another message from Kyron came through:

Kyron:

There's still time for you to get that Internet fame you've always wanted.

She called Nikisha, who answered while she was trying to stop Amara from indulging in her new favorite pastime, which was opening the front door and running out into the street.

"Hello?" Nikisha said breathlessly. "Everything okay? One sec. AMARA! Can you not— Nicky, go and grab— No, grab her. Sorry, Dimple, what were you saying?"

"We aren't giving him the money," Dimple said firmly. "He's a prick. He doesn't deserve it."

By the end of the day, after three more phone calls made by Dimple that were similarly dramatic, all of the siblings were standing around in their late grandmother's house. It was empty now that her remaining children had taken what they wanted from it and Nikisha had a key because she knew someone who was going to clean the whole place on the cheap. After most of Delores's possessions that were worth anything had been distributed in the will among the rest of her grandchildren, it was for her children to sort out the house.

Cyril had been first in, obviously, and had taken all of the electrical appliances. He'd sold those at the Cash Converters on Streatham High Road, getting himself a whopping four hundred pounds for about two thousand pounds' worth of his mother's stuff.

Tessilda, Delores's eldest daughter, hadn't really wanted anything but her mother's wedding ring. She had one son and three daughters, and, ignoring the fact that he was clearly gay, and lived with his boyfriend, wanted her son to give it to a wife one day.

Lavinia only wanted the big armchair that sat in the corner of Delores's bedroom. When she was a young girl, she used to go into her mum's room and sit in that chair, listening to her talk about what it was like when she first came over to England. She didn't care if her mum told the same story ten times over. Something about that story made her feel like she was connected to Jamaica.

Marvette, the one who'd had to go in there and sort everything out and make sure it was cleaned, hadn't wanted anything. She just wanted to know that the right thing had been done by her mum.

"So, do you have a plan that you didn't want to message over, or you just wanted to get us all in one place because you didn't have things to do today?" Lizzie asked, leaning on the wall in the empty living room.

"I don't really have a proper plan." Dimple shook her head. "But I was weighing it up, and I just don't think it's right that he gets an amount of money that could change all of our lives. It's not like he earned it."

"In a way he kind of did, no?" Prynce asked. "I'm not sticking up for the guy, but, like, what we did was kinda messed up."

"I hear what you're saying." Dimple dismissed her little brother's very valid point. "But, like, there's so much we could do with that money! Nikisha, you've got two kids to raise. Danny, you could, I dunno, buy a van that has more room in it. Lizzie, you could buy Patrice a big wedding ring, and Prynce? Well, I dunno. But it's so much money!"

"Yes, but what are you going to say to Kyron?" Lizzie stared at Dimple, desperate for an explanation.

"Nothing," Dimple said. "He can say what he wants, he can post the picture, I don't care anymore. It'll be another Internet *thing* that'll come and go."

"Is this you wanting another burst of attention?" Lizzie asked.

"Yeah, I'm not so sure about that, mate," Danny said. "Maybe you don't mind a picture like that of yourself floating about the Internet, but I do."

"What do you mean?" Dimple held a hand up to silence Danny as she moved over to Lizzie.

"Well, all of the attention you got from Kyron going missing died down pretty quickly." Lizzie shrugged. "I'm just wondering if this is part of a new plan to get Internet famous or something. But I think you're forgetting that it's not just a picture he has, and if he wants to tell people that we all tried to bury him, he can definitely do that."

"You think this is about attention?" Dimple asked Lizzie, narrowing her eyes. She didn't like confrontation at all, but Lizzie was always running her mouth unchallenged, and Dimple was tired of it. It took a long time for her buttons to be fully pushed, but when they were? They were. "Kyron doesn't even KNOW about you lot. He hasn't said anything about any of you!"

"Well, we don't know that for sure, do we? Are you telling me it's *not* about attention?" Lizzie asked. "You're the queen of pretending you don't want attention while doing a really good job of getting it."

Dimple blinked at Lizzie while the rest of the siblings turned to look at her. Where had this come from? Maybe Lizzie was stressed by her upcoming exams, but still.

"What?" Lizzie held her hands up in defense. "I'm just saying what we're all thinking."

"Don't speak on my behalf, please, Lizzie," Danny said in a tone nobody had heard before.

"It's not about speaking on your behalf, is it, Danny? It's about me not saying anything to upset Dimple because you love her so much," Lizzie snorted. "Is it because she 'looks the most like Cyril' and you're so desperate to be close to him?"

"Watch your mouth," Danny said.

"Well, it's not like you're gonna do anything to me, is it?" Lizzie asked. "Or are you gonna kidnap me?"

"Lizzie," Nikisha said firmly.

"Oh yeah." Lizzie nodded slowly, narrowing her eyes as she lasered in on Danny. "I've seen the articles."

"No, Lizzie," Danny said, hurt by Lizzie's dig. "I'm not gonna kidnap you. And I wish you'd asked me about it, instead of going looking. But what you forget, 'cause you're so lippy, is that people have feelings. And just 'cause I don't talk about mine doesn't mean they aren't there. I've gone through a lot and I'm trying to deal with all of it all the time. But you wouldn't know that 'cause you don't care enough to see it."

"Yes, I do!" Lizzie said.

"Do you?" Prynce asked, jumping in to defend his big brother. "Because all you do is dig us out and act like you're better than us."

"Why am I under attack now?" Lizzie yelped. "We've had to come to this house to sort out Dimple's shit yet *again*, and everyone is turning on me?"

"Nobody is turning on you, Lizzie!" Prynce laughed, trying to keep things as light as they could feel at that moment. He didn't want to say anything, but felt like he'd given Lizzie enough grace these last few weeks. "You turn on yourself and all of us before we even have a chance to. But even *you* have to admit that you give us all a hard time, come on!"

"I don't think anything is funny, Prynce." Lizzie narrowed her eyes at him. "But I guess everything is funny for you when you take absolutely nothing in your life seriously!"

Prynce laughed, unintentionally proving her point.

"Come on, man, I'm only twenty-five. I don't have to take things seriously!"

"Let me ask a quick question: Do *you* feel a way when everyone says Dimple looks the most like Cyril?" Lizzie continued. "Is that why you've worked so hard to be just as useless as him? Is that how you've decided you're going to carry on his legacy? That, and all the girls in your phone?"

"Be careful with your words, Lizzie," Nikisha said.

"Yeah, well, you would jump in to protect your baby brother," Lizzie spat. "With your special little bond because you're 'full' siblings."

"You're all my full siblings," Nikisha told her calmly. "I don't subscribe to the idea of halves and wholes. But full siblings or half-siblings, I wouldn't carry on talking like that if I were you."

"I'm not scared of you, Nikisha!" Lizzie scoffed. "You think 'cause you're the eldest you've got any power over us? What is it that you do, apart from tell people what to do?"

"Lizzie, you need to calm down," Danny said.

"No, I don't!" Lizzie shouted, her voice bouncing through the empty house. "From the very beginning, all Nikisha has done is give orders. Cast your minds back to the night she called us, out of no-where, and dragged us into this. What did Nikisha do that night? Nikisha didn't lift one finger! I was the one cleaning—"

"Yeah, so was I," Prynce said, interrupting.

Lizzie continued. "Danny was the hired help 'cause he had a van. The boys had to lay down the body while me and Dimple—who I haven't even got to yet—had to wrap it up, all while you're standing over us keeping your hands clean! But maybe that was your plan all along? And even when Dimple fainted, you were sitting on the sofa! It was up to me to look after her!"

"Carry on if you need to. Get it out of your system." Nikisha stared at Lizzie while she finished.

"I don't think that's a good idea," Danny said.

"It is," Nikisha said calmly.

"Why is it a good idea?" Dimple asked Nikisha. "Why do you think it's okay for her to be horrible to us all?"

"She needs to speak her truth," Nikisha told Dimple.

"Were you speaking your truth when you said I was fat?" Dimple asked.

Nikisha laughed.

"What?"

"When we were young," Dimple recalled. "That day Dad came to collect us all, in the gold Jeep, when he took us to the park. You said that I should sit in the front because I was the biggest one and I was taking up the most space in the back!"

"That wasn't nice of me," Nikisha said. "I was young, too, remember. And I think I'd just got used to it being me and Prynce. I was being territorial. And I'm sorry."

"Well, that stayed with me for years, Nikisha," Dimple said. "Imagine how scared I was about being dragged from my house and shoved in a car with all these people who were supposedly related to me and then you, my oldest sister, who I'm already scared of but still in awe of, calls me fat for no reason? I was still figuring my body out."

"Dimple! How can you hold on to a memory from a hundred years ago and expect an apology?" Lizzie turned to Dimple, pointing a finger in her face. "You're the reason we're here! I got pulled from *my* house to help you!"

"It's not me who called you all!" Dimple held her hands up. "I didn't want to pull you into anything! I called Nikisha and she called you all! If it was up to me—"

"That's the thing about you, Dimple!" Lizzie was gearing up for a strong finish. "I have never, ever in my life met anyone who was so obsessed with being a victim as you are. Everyone else is to blame for every single thing that goes wrong in your life, as well as every single little emotion you feel. It's everyone's problem and we all get drafted in to deal with it. If you'd simply called the police when Kyron had smashed his head open, we'd all just be living our lives! But instead, the last couple of months have been about worrying whether or not the police are going to be knocking at our doors! And at the same time, making sure you're okay. Making sure you don't feel too bad. Making sure you don't feel like you're to blame for anything. Making sure you aren't too upset."

Dimple's throat started to prickle. She knew the tears were coming but she wasn't going to let them out yet.

"You know what, Lizzie? You need to shut the fuck up." The

words sprang out of Dimple's mouth, surprising her. "You would have had a problem with me anyway. I wouldn't be able to do anything right in your eyes, despite what happened. Years ago, I messaged you asking if you wanted to meet up. You ignored me. I messaged you again, because I really meant it. I really wanted to be your sister. I wanted to know if we were going through the same things. I wanted to know if you were feeling the same things I was feeling. I wanted to know if it was hard for you growing up feeling like you'd been left behind by someone who just couldn't be bothered to be a parent. But you ignored me again. And ever since we've been in this, which I am *sorry* for, you've had something against me that runs much deeper than you getting the call that night. And I don't know what it is, but I don't care anymore."

It was Dimple's turn to point in Lizzie's face.

"You, Lizzie, are not a good person. You are spiteful, and you are judgmental. And I really thought things would be good between us after I came to stay with you. We had this big conversation where you actually softened, and it was amazing. 'Cause out of everyone, of all five of us, *you're* the person I wanted to be around when I felt bad. And I think it's because on some level I wanted forgiveness, you know? I think I wanted you to forgive me for the fact that we're the same age because Dad got our mums pregnant a week apart, and because I was born first, that somehow feels like it's my fault. But I've seen the way you always looked at me. I could see on your face how much of a nuisance you thought I was. You even stopped trying to hide it after a while! But I don't need anything from you, and I know that now. I don't need forgiveness, because I didn't do anything wrong. And it's okay that I don't like you. How can I, when you don't like yourself?"

Dimple stopped shouting, her chest rising and falling as she tried to regulate her breath.

"You know what?" Dimple started to cry. "I don't give a fuck about the money, about Kyron, about my pussy on the Internet, or about *any* of you. Well, no, that's not true, you know I do, in general. But right now, I don't!"

They all watched as Dimple stormed out of their late grandma's room, and listened as she thundered down the stairs and slammed out of the house.

"I didn't know she had that in her." Prynce nodded, watching her from the window as she crossed the street and ran down the road.

CHAPTER
FOURTEEN

DIMPLE WASN'T USED TO the concept of forgiveness, or moving on from pain. That's probably why she didn't have any friends. She dwelled on things that hurt her so much that they ate up little parts of her that she couldn't get back. That didn't always work both ways, though. Sometimes she thought she should be forgiven because she just felt so deeply that she couldn't help what she'd said and done, and sometimes she felt so bad about what she'd said and done that she didn't think she deserved to be forgiven. So it was a shock to her system when, instead of begging for her forgiveness, or making her apologize for anything she'd said, her siblings just . . . carried on as normal the next day. There was no space for dramatics, no room for tears or harbored anger. It was like they'd all just gotten everything out of their systems, and the focus was back on getting Kyron to delete any and all pictures he'd taken of Dimple in a compromising position and keeping the money.

Dimple had a loose plan, aided by having seen Lynette when she was getting her hair done, and being invited once again to Kyron's birthday party, even though she'd tried to ignore the digital flyers for it that Lynette kept forwarding her on WhatsApp.

"What you doing today?" Janet asked as she walked into Dimple's bedroom without knocking, as usual. "I thought maybe we could go out for breakfast?"

"No, I can't. It's Kyron's birthday thing," Dimple told her mum as she stood up and opened her wardrobe. She searched through it anxiously. What should she wear? She couldn't go sexy, but she couldn't go leisure wear. Hard decisions.

"Things are back on with Kyron again?" Janet asked, exhausted. "Dimple, *please*. I cannot keep up. And I don't think you should either."

"They aren't! Lynette invited me, and you know what she's like."

"Do you want me to come with you?"

"No!" Dimple replied gruffly, and a little too quickly. "Not at all, thank you."

"All right, all right." Janet threw up her hands as she stood. "I get it. You don't need me, Dimple. I'm receiving that loud and clear."

"It's not that, Mum," Dimple said. "I'll always need you. I just don't need you today."

"Oh." Janet nodded. Emotional permanence was not one of her strengths. She always needed a reminder that Dimple wasn't going anywhere. "Okay, then."

"I love you, Mum," Dimple said. "You're still my best friend. And Cyril won't ever come close to that. You were the one who was there."

"Damn right I was," Janet told her daughter. "When you come home, let's talk about me doing the . . . detox thing for a bit longer."

"I think that's a good idea." Dimple smiled.

Janet walked out of the room and hummed to herself as she went down the stairs. Dimple went back to the wardrobe when the buzz of her phone alerted her to someone calling. From where she was standing, she could see that it was Nikisha.

"Hello?" Dimple answered.

"You all set for today?" Nikisha asked.

"Yep." Dimple replayed the conversation she'd had with Nikisha about how to conduct herself at Kyron's birthday.

"Text me the address, and call me if you need me."

Dimple was going to get an Uber, but she was feeling claustrophobic enough so decided to walk. It was still cold outside as winter blazed on, but the sun was shining at the very least. As she'd approached Lynette and Kyron's house, she saw multicolored birthday balloons tied to the door and laughed to herself. Lynette would never stop treating Kyron like he was her baby boy. That's why he was so entitled. He was just a big fucking kid who had always gotten his own way. She took a deep breath as she approached the door, and pressed the bell with an unsteady finger.

The door opened while Dimple was looking down at her sneakers, wondering if she should have gone for something smarter. When she looked up, she locked eyes with Roman.

"You're here?" he asked, stepping aside so Dimple could enter the house. "Lynette said you was coming, but I didn't think you would."

"Your car isn't here, I didn't think you—"

"You know how me and Kyron are. We fight it out, then don't chat for a bit, then one of us asks if the other wants to play *Halo*, and then things are just cool until it happens again."

Dimple looked past him and saw that the house was once again full of people. Kyron wasn't even as nice as she was, but he still had so many friends. How was that fair?

"Well, maybe I should start playing video games—maybe that way you can be nice to me? What kind of headset should I get?" Dimple couldn't believe what she was hearing. Did she mean so little to both of them that them falling out over her could be solved with an Xbox?

"You mean more to me than he does," Roman told Dimple. "It's just all a bit technical, with you and him being together for so long. And you know that."

"Do I?" Dimple smiled at Roman, wishing it took more than a few words for her to soften. She wished she was more like Lizzie in that respect.

"You know you do." Roman smiled down at her.

"Well then, you can still be nice to me!" Dimple said.

"I am nice to you." Roman frowned at her.

"I know you believe that." Dimple sighed. "But one of these days we're going to have a conversation about what that actually looks like."

"Look who it is," Kyron said, coming down the stairs. "I hope I'm not interrupting you two."

"Nah, it's not like that," Roman said, backing away from Dimple.

"Nah, it is like that." Kyron looked at them both. "And I would appreciate it if whatever you were doing wasn't done in my face. Lemme chat to her a sec."

"Do your ting, man," Roman said, taking a second to look into Dimple's eyes before he went into the living room.

Dimple didn't know which way this was going to go. She also couldn't believe that clearly Roman had been forgiven while she was still a jezebel in Kyron's eyes.

"Happy birthday." Dimple smiled. "I was gonna bring you a present, but I thought maybe that was a bit weird."

"That money is going to be a good enough present for me," Kyron told her, smiling with glee. "And then you and your codefendants will be fine."

Dimple's stomach dropped.

"Which codefendants?"

"I know you didn't move me by yourself," Kyron told her. "I just don't know who helped you."

"Anything I did, I did by myself. You know I don't have any

friends." Dimple shrugged, trying to hide her nerves. "I'm going to say hello to your mum."

Dimple walked down the hallway toward the kitchen, where she could see and hear signs of life. She saw Lynette, who was, as usual, at the stove, and before she made her way over, she messaged Nikisha, I don't think I can do this, and put her phone away.

As she made her way through the kitchen, exchanging hellos with Kyron's friends and family who felt like complete strangers to her now, she tried to ignore Kyron. She could feel his eyes boring into her.

She wanted to make herself useful, because obviously she felt weird being there, and performing normalcy was exhausting, so she took over from Lynette and carried on frying the dumplings, not minding the stray splashes of hot oil that jumped out of the pan and stung her arms.

She flipped them with a fork, spearing the golden-brown ones that were ready, dropping them onto a plate covered with a kitchen towel. Larry the bulldog was sitting by her feet, keeping her company. Dimple wondered if he'd still love her if he knew what was going on.

This arduous task kept her mind suitably occupied until she heard a familiar voice by the kitchen doorway.

"I am so happy that your son was found safe and well." Nikisha was smiling widely, her hand already on Lynette's shoulder. "I remember when Dimple told me he'd gone missing! As a mother myself, I wondered how you, also a mother, felt."

Dimple dropped the fork and scooted over to them.

"Hi, Nik! What are you doing here?" she asked, her voice climbing an octave with every word.

"Well, little sister, I knew that today, especially after everything that's gone on with you and Kyron, was going to be really hard for you." Nikisha turned to Lynette. "You know, Dimple has been crying on the phone to me every night. It's been so hurtful, even to me, to see her like that. She loved him so much."

"Oh, Dimp." Lynette squeezed Dimple's shoulder. "Poor you."

"That first heartbreak is always the worst," Nikisha said. Dimple thought her sister was pushing it.

"Well, look, if you're Dimple's sister, then you're family, too. Make yourself at home, eat, relax."

"Do you know what, Lynette?" Nikisha said. "I'm actually having a childcare emergency, so I need Dimple to look after my babies while I go and tend to something. I'm going to have to take her, if that's okay?"

"I understand completely." Lynette nodded. "But you both come back anytime! And take some food when you go!"

Lynette was pulled away by a woman who was trying to alert her to the unattended frying pan catching fire.

"Did you have to go that hard?" Dimple asked Nikisha as they moved into the hallway.

"You're welcome," Nikisha said.

"Sorry, thank you, thank you." Dimple hugged her sister, who didn't move.

"Do you not like physical contact?"

"It's only now you've noticed?" Nikisha laughed as she stepped with shocking purpose into the living room.

"Wow," Dimple said, following her in. "Yeah. Where are you going?"

"I'm gonna chat to this Kyron yout." Nikisha looked around the room.

"I don't think that's a good idea," Dimple said. "I just want to get out of here. We can figure everything out another time."

"I didn't ask what you thought, little sister," Nikisha said, clocking him across the room.

"Honestly, I—" Dimple said, but Nikisha was already moving toward him.

"There he is," she said, walking slowly over to an unassuming Kyron, who was talking to Roman in the corner by the sofa.

Dimple didn't know what was going to come of the conversation, and she couldn't just stand and watch it, so she turned back into the hallway, where she sat on the stairs and panicked.

Kyron looked up when Nikisha, who was smiling, arrived next to him and put a hand on his forearm.

"Hi, I'm Nikisha. We haven't met properly. Let me talk to you a sec?"

Kyron turned away from Roman, who recognized Nikisha from the car parked outside his house a few weeks ago.

"Cool, cool." Kyron smiled, not realizing who she was. He just thought a really good-looking woman who was slightly older than him wanted to chat, and he heard that older women had more experience, so to him it was win-win.

"Come on, then!" Nikisha was still smiling. "Let's go into the hallway."

Kyron followed Nikisha, starting to put two and two together when he saw Dimple sitting on the stairs.

"I'm going to keep this quick," Nikisha said to Kyron, stepping toward him so she was close enough to hear his heartbeat.

"Right, so," Nikisha said. "Dimple, my little sister, who you know very, very well, has told me, and our sister, and our brothers, that you've taken a few pictures of her. And that you're planning on using these pictures—of someone who is vulnerable, not in a good mental place, someone who invited you round to get you back because she loved and trusted you, and missed you—against her? And you're, what, planning on holding it over her until when?"

Kyron didn't know how to answer. In truth, he hadn't really thought about it. His only plan was to keep it in his arsenal to get her to do what he wanted.

"I'm not going to get into what I know and what I don't about what may have happened to you. But I *do* know you don't care about the police, and you don't care about the law in that way. And yeah, Dimple could go to the police and say you have this picture of her.

And you and I both know that the police would ignore her until you actually did something with it," Nikisha said. "But lemme tell you something. You having that picture in your phone means something much worse for you."

Nikisha leaned closer to him.

"What happened to you was an accident. The only reason you're still here is because it was an accident. But you see me? I will make something happen that will seem like an accident, and it will be anything but."

Kyron could tell that Nikisha was serious.

"Did you see that little video Dimple put out asking people to look for you?" Nikisha asked Kyron.

"Yeah." He shrugged.

"It was convincing, wasn't it?" Nikisha smiled. "And unless you want her to have to record another video telling everyone something terrible happened to you and that she's sorry that you're gone, I suggest you delete that picture, right now, in front of me, and you never speak to my sister again."

"Why, who do you know?" Kyron stepped to Nikisha, feeling threatened.

"Who do I *know*?" Nikisha asked him, smiling. "That's my baby sister, Kyron. And I will do anything I need to for her. Do you understand me?"

"All right, man." Kyron shrugged. "I don't even have it, I deleted it a while ago."

"I'm not stupid, give me the phone." Nikisha held her hand out.

"It's gone, man, I told you," Kyron whined. It was amazing for Dimple to see this man, who she'd only ever seen as commanding and demanding, behaving like a teenage boy.

"You've got some pictures as well, haven't you, Dimple?" Nikisha asked.

"Pictures of what?" Kyron snorted.

"When you put your hands around my little sister's neck and al-most killed her, Kyron," Nikisha told him. "Your fingers left very nasty bruises."

Kyron looked uneasy.

"And, you can cry on demand, can't you Dimple?" Nikisha asked her sister.

"Yep." Dimple nodded.

Kyron's eyes darkened. He'd lost. He handed his phone to Nikisha, who deleted the X-rated picture of Dimple. She went into the deleted images folder, as well as the cloud, and got rid of the pic-ture permanently before handing the phone back and patting Kyron on the chest.

"Look how easy that was." Nikisha smiled. "And, this should probably go without saying, but just before we go"—she looked Kyron dead in the eye—"if you contact her again, if you go near her, if you send one message to her, I will ruin your entire life and not lose one night of sleep worrying about it."

"How you mean, ruin my life, man?" Kyron growled.

"In every way possible that a man's life can be ruined," Nikisha replied. "And you see my threats? They aren't empty. And as insur-ance, I've been chatting with your little friend Jenna."

"Huh?"

"It was easy to find her on socials. You might not have tagged her, but she used to comment on all of your pics till you upset her. And I don't want to stoop to your level, but she's got some pretty embar-rassing videos of you I don't think you'd want anyone to see that she's sent over to *me* when I told her you were still in love with my sister."

Nikisha held eye contact with Kyron, not blinking, until he was forced to look away.

"Whatever, man." Kyron looked at the floor.

"Let's go, Dimple!" Nikisha said cheerfully, heading toward the door. "Bye, Lynette!"

"Bye, darlin'!" Lynette called back. "Remember what I said! Come back soon!"

"We will!" Nikisha trilled.

"Thank you so much, Nikisha." Dimple smiled, relief washing over her as she climbed into the passenger seat of Nikisha's car. "Listen, that was pretty terrifying. You even scared me."

"Dimple," Nikisha said very seriously as she started the engine. "I need you to stop being a liability. To yourself and to the people around you. It's time to grow up now."

Dimple's stomach flipped. The adrenaline from Kyron's take-down and the shock of her own telling-off were a horrible cocktail.

"Okay," Dimple said quietly. "I'm sorry."

"You're always sorry, Dimple." Nikisha sighed as she drove them away. "I'm not angry, and I'm not saying you need to toughen up, but you need to know who you are, and take accountability for who that person is. That's when you'll stop apologizing for everything."

"I think I need to talk to Dad."

"About what?" Nikisha asked her, not taking her eyes off the road.

"I dunno." Dimple shrugged. "Maybe it'll give me, give *us*, a sense of who we are?"

"I know who I am, Dimple," Nikisha said. "But if you need to talk to him to understand him, then you should do that."

"I think we need answers from him, you know? 'Cause the one thing we have in common, apart from being his kid, is that he . . . left us, you know? And we're all in our feelings about it, even if we don't know it. And that isn't going to go away until we actually talk to him about it. I don't think. And you might say you don't need it. But I think we all do."

"Well." Nikisha sighed. "Talk to the rest of them and see."

The next day they were standing, in a line, on Cyril Pennington's doorstep. The stone walls around the door had crumbled, the steps were cracked, the handrail had rusted, and the paint on the window frames had faded, but it was the entrance to the same studio flat he'd always lived in.

The gold Jeep, though, was parked outside, sparkling clean, looking like it did all those years ago when he'd taken them to the park. The jagged lines that had been scratched into his car were nowhere to be seen. Dimple guessed that some of the money she'd given him was why.

"Ready?" Nikisha asked.

"He knows we're coming, right?" Danny asked her.

"Not exactly, but that doesn't matter," Nikisha told him.

"He doesn't know?" Lizzie shouted. "We can't ambush him!"

"Er, yes, we can," Nikisha said. "We're his children."

"I dunno, you know," Prynce said. "But we're here now."

Nikisha pressed the doorbell for flat A twice, hearing the two sharp rings fill the hallway of the building.

"Is he even in?" Dimple asked just as the door swung open and Cyril Pennington stood in front of them all. He was wearing a navy-blue fleece and a pair of stonewashed jeans. He hadn't had a haircut for a while, so his gray hair was scruffy, fuzzy, patchy in places.

He looked like he'd seen five ghosts.

"What you all doing here?" he spluttered.

"Well, we're obviously here to see you," Nikisha told him. "Shall we come in?"

"I wasn't expecting visitors," he said as Nikisha moved past him and the rest of his children followed.

The flat wasn't dirty, but it was messy. While everything was clean, nothing had a place. Nothing but the sound system and the records, obviously. They all looked around, wondering where to sit.

"I can't offer you anyting to eat or drink, I'm afraid." Cyril laughed nervously. He felt more vulnerable than he ever had in his *life*. He was standing in front of his five children and he couldn't even offer them anything that wasn't tap water.

He went over to the kitchen sink, balancing on one leg, the other leg pointed delicately, as he ran himself a glass of water.

"Everyting all right wid you all?" He turned around and smiled at them. "You all look well. You been treating yourselves wid that money from the house?"

"Dad." Nikisha held a hand up to stop the small talk. "They'd like some answers."

Cyril looked at his children.

"What kinda questions you have for me?"

"What was the real reason you didn't visit me when I was in prison?" Danny asked.

Cyril looked down at the floor and smiled as he shook his head.

"I did think to come, and I did get your, wha' dem call?"

"Visiting orders," Danny said. "Yeah, you said the other day."

"Yes. But I thought to myself, what good would that do?"

"It don't really need to do any good, though, does it? Would have been nice to see my dad when I was locked up. It was hard, Dad," Danny said.

Dimple was pleased that Danny was expressing some feelings.

Danny stared hard at his dad, waiting for a proper answer.

"I don't know wha' yuh want me fi tell yuh." Cyril shrugged. "Is all in the past, Danny."

"Right." Danny accepted that he wasn't going to get the answer he'd been waiting for longer than he'd like to admit to. "Fine. Understood."

Lizzie took a deep breath.

"Why didn't you try harder with me? Or Dimple?" she asked. "We're the same age, Cyril. It would have been nice to know that we were each separately important, and not just the product of two nights of passion you had with two different women seven days apart!"

"Me never plan that one." Cyril sighed. "Things just happen, Lizzie."

"No, I know that things just happen, but after things just happen, you can talk about them, did you know that? You know you could have spoken to us at any point and told us we mattered to you."

"But who told you that you didn't matter to me?" Cyril asked her. "Not me."

"You didn't have to say it, it's how I felt, Cyril!" Lizzie took her line of questioning up a notch. "Why didn't you wear condoms, Cyril? Then you wouldn't have five people who have been longing for you to be in their lives standing in your house and demanding answers from you!"

"And who are you to demand anyting from me?" Cyril asked her. "Yuh never know how hard *I* have it!"

"Dad, I can't lie, you can't really use that one against us," Prynce said, cutting in. "I know I don't know much, and I'm the youngest— not tryna disrespect you, 'cause you're my elder—but even you can see that if you don't tell us about what you've gone through, we won't know. You can't just think we're gonna puzzle everything together and understand it, man."

"You're right about one ting." Cyril nodded, smiling, that gold tooth flashing again. "I am your elder. I don't have to answer to *any* of yuh. The same way I never answered to your mothers."

"No, you don't have to, but you could, Dad!" Dimple told him. "Why are you being defensive? We haven't come here to ask you for anything you aren't able to give us! It's not like I'm the one asking you for money, Dad."

"So you're throwing that in my face?" Cyril laughed to himself, trying to engineer himself as the victim.

"Dad! You're my parent! You've never given me anything! Not a *hug*, or a piece of advice, let alone money!" Dimple said. "And the only time you ever talk to me, it's literally *about* money, and only that!

I don't think you've ever even asked me how I am! And you weren't even there when I was making a penny!"

"So what, me cyaan ask for help?" Cyril snorted as he shook his head. "What's the point in having all these kids if none of you can help me?"

"When have you ever helped us, though?" Dimple asked. Everyone knew she was about to cry, so it was no surprise when fat tears fell down her face instantly. "When Nikisha had kids and Danny was in prison and Lizzie's been working hard to train as a doctor and Prynce has been growing up in a society that tells him he doesn't have any value—where have you been to help with babysitting, or go to a prison for even one afternoon to visit your son, or ask Lizzie how her exams were, or to tell Prynce that he's going to grow into an amazing and kind and inquisitive person worthy of being alive, whatever he does?"

"Okay." Nikisha put a hand out to signify that she was about to speak, sensing that not much good was going to come of the conversation. "What we all need to know from you is: Are you ready to have a relationship with us? And that doesn't mean speaking to us every day, or coming round at short notice to babysit, and even be a grandad, or anything like that. We just want to know if you're prepared to be there, as our dad."

Cyril looked around at his five children.

"No." Cyril shook his head. "I'm sorry."

"And why?" Nikisha asked him, crossing her arms.

"Because . . . I don't have it in me," Cyril told them. And that was the first time an honest word had come out of Cyril's mouth.

———————

Nikisha, Danny, Dimple, Lizzie, and Prynce trotted down the crumbling stone steps. When they got to the bottom—balancing between not knowing what to say, wanting to say everything, and saying nothing at all—all they could do was blink at each other. For a couple of minutes, they were silent, taking in what had happened.

"Shall we go to the park?" Dimple said.

"Yeah." Danny nodded. "Why not?"

"Danny, I'll jump in with you, need to talk to you about something," Prynce said.

"If it's girls, bro, I dunno, I'm not the best person to ask," Danny told him.

"You're my brother, so you are," Prynce said.

"Which car you going in, Dimple?" Lizzie asked.

"Er, probably Nikisha's?" Dimple looked at Nikisha, who nodded. "Why?"

"I'll come with you." Lizzie linked arms with Dimple and steered her toward Nikisha's car.

"Wait, lemme grab you a sec, Dimple," Prynce said.

"You okay?" Dimple asked him, breaking away from Lizzie.

"Yeah." Prynce nodded. "I just wanted to say something to you quick."

"Okay?" Dimple had no idea what it could be.

"I've been thinking about this a lot. You remember, a while ago, I said you weren't much of a people person?"

"Yeah," Dimple said. "It didn't do wonders for my confidence, but it's whatever. I know you more now. I know you didn't mean it like that."

"Yeah, I kinda did mean it like that," Prynce said. "But I've been thinking about it a lot, and . . . I don't think you're a people person in the way you think you should be, or the way *I* said you should be."

Dimple furrowed her brow.

Prynce continued. "I think that you're a people person in the way that you get people. You see people. And, like, *properly* see people. You see us, you see who we all are, in our own way. And you don't judge us for it. You don't ask people to be who they aren't. And I don't think many people are like that, so, yeah. I rate it."

"Thanks, Prynce," Dimple said, her eyes filling with tears once again.

"You know I'm not good with the tears, man," Prynce said, burying his sister in a hug.

They got to the park. Clapham Common, for old time's sake. They each got an ice cream—apart from Lizzie, obviously a vegan, and Danny, who was accepting of his lactose intolerance, who got ice lollies—and stood in a circle like they had when Nikisha was nineteen, Danny was seventeen, Dimple and Lizzie were almost fourteen, and Prynce was nine and a half.

"It's a weird feeling, isn't it?" Dimple said.

"What is?" Prynce asked her.

"Being dumped by your dad." Dimple shrugged.

Danny laughed.

"Just because he rejected us, time and time again, doesn't mean we were ever, or are ever, going to reject each other," Nikisha told her siblings. "And don't forget it."

"I love you all," Dimple said earnestly.

"We know." Nikisha smiled.

"Can you say it back, then?" Dimple asked her big sister.

"I love you all, obviously," Nikisha said firmly. "And I'm always going to be here for you, no matter how much it fucks up my life."

"But because it's your duty? As the eldest?" Dimple said, imitating Nikisha.

"No," Nikisha said. "Because I wouldn't have it any other way."

"I love all you lot, till the end!" Prynce smiled. "Thought I'd join the love-in."

Dimple looked at Lizzie expectantly.

"What, we're going round in a circle? I love you too, obviously, why wouldn't I?" Lizzie rolled her eyes, annoyed. "All of you, even though you get on my nerves."

"All right, I'll take that from you, Lizzie." Danny nodded. "And same."

"We get on your nerves?" Dimple asked her big brother.

"No." Danny shook his head. "The love thing."

"Say it properly or it doesn't count," Dimple said to him.

"I don't really say that, you know," Danny said. "But I do."

"Do what?" Dimple knew she was pushing it.

Danny forced this new and unfamiliar phrase from his mouth. "Love you all."

"And you know Cyril loves us in his own way," Nikisha told her brothers and sisters.

"Yeah." Dimple nodded. "And it matters and it doesn't, I guess. But just 'cause he's half the reason we got here, doesn't mean he's our reason we're here now. And I'm still sorry for the reason we all got . . . literally here, together."

"Nah. I'm glad I got the call that day." Danny smiled. "What a difference a day makes."

"What a difference a *dad* makes," Prynce said.

"That night," Lizzie said, correcting Danny and ignoring Prynce's wordplay entirely. "And *I'm* not glad about that, and I'm gonna have to use the money from Delores to pay for therapy fees, but I'm glad we made it back together."

"Do you think we'd be better people if he'd been in our lives properly?" Prynce asked his siblings.

"Nah." Dimple shook her head. "I think we'd have been worse. But we're all right as we are. We're good people."

EPILOGUE

"NICE TO BE BACK." Danny said, adjusting his tie as he looked up at the peeling Black Jesus at the front of the church. Where Black Jesus had previously been nailed to the lectern by his hands (obviously) and his feet, his lower half had crumbled away, leaving him even more committed to his heavenly Father from the waist down.

"I wouldn't say it was *nice* to be back," Dimple said, bouncing the sleeping baby up and down in her arms.

"Well, it's just a turn of phrase, isn't it?" Danny shrugged. "Are you trying to wake her up?"

"No." Dimple shook her head.

"Stop bouncing her up and down, then," Nikisha said as she made room for Nicky, who was fourteen now, and Amara, who was seven.

"You shouldn't tell a new mother what to do," Prynce said, poking his head through his sisters from the pew behind.

"How would you know? There's space for you along here." Nikisha made room for Prynce. "Amara, you and Nicky go on the other side with Marley and Aunty Tracy."

"Fine," Amara said. "But give me your phone."

"I don't think you finished asking the question." Nikisha stared down at her daughter.

"Please," Amara added. She went to sigh, but thought better of it. Nikisha handed Amara the phone.

"There you go."

Amara took the phone before her mum could change her mind and moved across the aisle with Nicky as Prynce took their place.

"Where's your girlfriend?" Dimple asked.

"Which one?" Prynce asked, completely unironically. "Baby's looking healthy!"

"Can you not refer to her as *baby*, Prynce? You know her name is Evie."

"Sorry— Evie's looking healthy," Prynce said, correcting himself. "I think because you've given her the same name as an old woman my young brain has blocked it out."

Dimple rolled her eyes and nuzzled her face by Evie's tiny ear, whispering that she should ignore her rude uncle.

"Has anyone spoken to Lizzie?" Danny asked, leaning forward and looking down the aisle.

"She's been a bit quiet these past few days, but Patrice said they're coming, so I guess we'll see them . . ." Dimple trailed off as she looked around the church. It had been five years since they'd been here, and apart from everything looking a bit more worn than it had before, it was all kind of the same. The people, too. Time had passed, but their looks hadn't.

"Oh look, there they are!" Danny waved at Lizzie and Patrice as they entered the church wearing matching black dresses.

"Why have you dressed like twins?" Prynce asked them when they'd made their way through the people who hadn't found their seats yet.

"Hi, Prynce, nice to see you too," Patrice said, hugging him. "Basically, we both bought the same dress and didn't consult each other about it. And by the time we were both ready, neither of us had the time to change."

"I could have found the time—" Lizzie said.

"So we could be late for today? Of all days?" Patrice asked her. "I don't think so."

Dimple stared at Lizzie until Lizzie finally looked up and made eye contact with her.

"You okay?" Dimple mouthed.

Lizzie nodded before looking down at baby Evie and smiling.

"She's getting so big," she mouthed back.

"Lizzie, why don't you squeeze in there with your brothers and sisters and I'll go keep an eye on Nicky and Amara?" Patrice said.

"Sure," Lizzie said, squeezing Patrice's hand before sidling in next to Prynce.

"You look well," Prynce said. "It's been a while."

"It's been about a week, Prynce." Lizzie rolled her eyes. "I needed to sleep for five days after that nine night. It wasn't easier than the first one we did."

"Yeah, I guess." Prynce shrugged. "Things have been busy." Is your mum coming today?" he asked. "The mystery lady."

"I think the question is: Is *yours*?" Dimple asked, joining the conversation and handing the still-sleeping baby to a very eager Danny so she could stretch her arms for a bit.

"You think Bernice would miss it?" Nikisha asked, pulling an iPad out of her bag.

"You're not taking that up there, are you?" Dimple asked.

"Why wouldn't I?"

"I dunno, it just seems a bit . . . modern," Dimple said.

"What's wrong with that?" Prynce laughed.

"I don't think it's a good look for you to be laughing, Prynce," Lizzie said.

"Laughing is how I hide my pain. Don't you know that by now?" Prynce asked Lizzie.

"Oh! So you've been going to that therapist I suggested?" Dimple smiled at Prynce.

"Is Roman coming?" Nikisha asked Dimple. "I hope you're not doing all the parenting and letting him live a stress-free life. The biggest mistake I made was not letting their dad look after Nicky and Amara from birth."

"He's meeting us at the hall. He's gone to collect the drinks," Dimple told Nikisha as rain started to hit the stained glass windows. "And no, Roman's not like that at all. He's more hands-on than I am, actually. He's the one who does all the nighttime feeds. And most of the day ones, actually."

"Good." Nikisha nodded.

"He's like the opposite of Dad." Dimple shrugged. "In lots of ways. And it took me a long time to accept that. And to be open to that."

"Dimple," Nikisha put a hand on her sister's shoulder. "Let's get into your emotions around Roman and Dad later."

Before Prynce saw his mum, he heard her enter the church. Bernice was sobbing loudly and wiping her tears on a handkerchief modeled on the Jamaican flag that she produced from the sleeve of her tight black bodysuit.

"You go and deal with her," Nikisha told him. "And do *not* let her come up here."

Prynce slipped away and moved through people who had filled the church but were talking among each other so energetically that they still hadn't managed to find a seat.

"Your mum is coming, right?" Danny asked Dimple.

"She's here." Dimple pointed to Janet, who was sitting politely in the back, reading diligently through the order of service she'd been given at the church doors.

"Oh, I didn't say hello," Danny said apprehensively.

"You can say hello later," Dimple told him. She's going through something back there and I think she needs to be left alone for a bit."

"She been drinking?" Danny asked.

"No, no," Dimple shook her head. "She's doing good recently. Taking things one day at a time, but yeah. Doing good."

"I'm with you." Danny smiled and crossed his arms as he looked at Janet, who was fixed on that order of service. He guessed it was easier for her to focus on something she could hold in front of her than to think too much about why they were all there.

"What a day, eh," Danny said as thunder rumbled on, a quiet growl that moved above the church. "What a day."

"Shouldn't this have started?" Lizzie asked Nikisha.

"Coffin isn't here yet," Danny told them. "They're gonna text me when it arrives."

"Everything going okay with work this week?" Nikisha asked Lizzie. "You know, I've tried to call but you seem to have misplaced your phone."

"Well, I'm a doctor now." Lizzie smiled and crossed her arms, which Danny noted happily. It was still never lost on him when his siblings showed the same mannerisms that he did. "I've got doctor's business to be doing, not sitting on the phone to you while you shout at Amara. And I don't appreciate it when you all text me with your medical worries."

"Who is *that*?" Dimple gasped as a striking woman entered, gliding glamorously through the church doors. The rest of her siblings turned around to look, and were all suitably curious. It seemed as though the rain that had started falling outside hadn't dared to touch her; her black dress bedazzled with black sequins, her long braids, and her makeup were all flawless.

"Oh. That's my mum," Lizzie said casually.

"Your *mum*?" Danny asked. "Forgive me for what I'm about to say, but—"

"Don't say it." Lizzie held a hand up to stop Danny from continuing.

"Respectfully, I can see why Cyril went after her," said Prynce as he slid back into his seat. " 'Cause even me, at twenty-nine—"

"Prynce," Lizzie said.

"It's a compliment!" Prynce told Lizzie as he and everyone else in the church watched Kemi, head held high, slink into a seat a few rows behind them.

"Coffin's here!" Danny said cheerfully, looking at a text on his phone. "Ready, Prynce?"

"Nah." Prynce shook his head. "But let's do this."

It is hard for six people of equal heights to carry a coffin on one shoulder, and, like the last time, it is much harder when six people ranging from five foot six to six foot three are tasked with the job. Luckily, the coffin didn't fall on the floor, although it threatened to do so more than once. It certainly made the opening to the proceedings as memorable and thrilling as goings-on at that particular church always seemed to be.

The service seemed to go by both quickly and as though time would stretch forever. The pastor had obviously recycled the same order of service that had been used for Delores. Maybe that had been Cyril's request, or maybe the pastor was just lazy. Nikisha did not cry, Danny shed one tear, Dimple sobbed so much that Danny had to hold the baby for the whole service, Lizzie visibly held her sadness in, and though he was silent, Prynce let his tears fall freely down his face.

"And now, with the eulogy, Cyril's eldest daughter, Nikisha." The pastor stepped aside from the lectern as Nikisha, modern iPad in hand, made her way up to the front of the church.

"Hello, everybody, and thank you for coming," Nikisha said. "This is my second time delivering a eulogy in this church. The first time for my grandmother, Delores Ricketts, and this time for her son, and my father—*our* father—Cyril Pennington. I didn't think I'd be here so soon, but there we go."

Nikisha took a sip of water and willed her voice not to shake.

"Cyril Pennington was born to Delores Pennington and Zelbert, surname unknown, in Red Ground, Coffee Piece, in the parish of Clarendon in Jamaica. Delores moved to London in 1972, when

Cyril was two years old. He was raised by his grandparents, Clarence and Rita Pennington, and his aunt, Desrence, living happily in the same house he was born in, until the age of fifteen, when his mother sent for him. It was only then that Cyril learned that Desrence was not in fact his big sister, but his aunt. When he came to England, Cyril moved into the house Delores shared with her husband, Israel, and their children, Cyril's half sisters: Tessilda, Lavinia, and Marvette, on Somerleyton Road, Brixton."

Nikisha looked over at Lavinia and Marvette. Lavinia nodded as she listened intently, as though listening to a radio show, and Marvette looked sad. Not devastated, but sad. Their eldest sister, Tessilda, had moved to New York with her husband a couple of years ago and hadn't bothered to come back for Cyril's funeral. Their children were there, though, attending as guests rather than family members.

"I've spent a lot of time asking around to piece together the bits of our dad's career, and this is what I've got: He worked as a soundman for a few clubs back in the day before trying his hand as a presenter for a local radio station. He drove buses on the side, and this turned into a full-time job as time went on. And the more he drove, the less time he had for music professionally, but it was still a huge part of his personal life. His colleagues Deborah and Tony told me that before every shift, Cyril would make his way to the depot with his boom box and play his song of the day for anyone who was in there. He'd smile whatever their reaction and tell them the same thing: That one day he was going to be a world-renowned DJ. Dad, you might not have got to be a world-renowned DJ, but me, my brothers, and my sisters remember the songs that DJ Fireshot used to play when you'd drive us around in that gold Jeep." The congregation laughed. The gold Jeep was clearly infamous, as was DJ Fireshot's musical career that had never really gone where it needed to go.

"I don't have a lot to say about Cyril—sorry—our dad personally. I've been tasked with delivering his eulogy because I'm the eldest, but

I probably know the least about him out of me and my four brothers and sisters. If I'm honest, I definitely had the least time for him." Nikisha stopped for a moment and looked over at them all. "He was a man who largely kept his feelings and his dealings to himself. But having spoken to the people who knew him, what I came to learn about our dad is that Cyril Pennington was, above all, a people person. A cheerful man. A social man. He liked to laugh, and to make people laugh. An extrovert, he led with happiness and confidence. He was truly a man who didn't dwell on the bad. Life to him was about finding happiness in the smallest things. As a father, and I'll be real here . . ." Nikisha paused.

Dimple's heart stopped beating, Prynce looked concerned, Lizzie looked over at Patrice, and Danny wondered if he was going to have to go up there.

". . . as a father, I believe that he had good intentions."

All the siblings breathed an audible sigh of relief that carried through the church.

"And I believe that he cared, in his own way, for me, my sisters, Dimple and Lizzie, for my brothers, Danny and Prynce, and for his grandchildren, Nicky, Marley, Amara, and Evie, who luckily he got to meet briefly before he passed. And the belief that he cared for us all has to be enough. So goodbye, Dad. Thank you for the times we did have with you. You will be missed. And I want to say thank you to our mothers, Bernice, Tracy, Kemi, and Janet. They raised us for you too."

When they left the church, the rain had stopped. Their mums had made their way to the wake, and Janet had taken baby Evie. She presented it as taking Evie off Dimple's hands, but the truth was that she had been obsessed with her granddaughter since she was born, even though she'd never been Roman's biggest fan.

"P, can you take the rest of the kids with you, please?" Lizzie asked Patrice, who was already deep in conversation with her niece and nephews. "We're going to make our own way there."

"I couldn't believe it when Marvette dropped these off." Nikisha held up the keys to the gold Jeep.

"I couldn't believe the Jeep actually worked," Danny remarked, crossing his arms.

"Why?" Lizzie asked him. "You think he was going to let that Jeep die before he did?"

"It's a bit too soon for jokes like that," Dimple sniffed.

"All right, crybaby," Prynce said, putting an arm around Dimple. "Let's get in."

Nikisha opened the door on the driver's side, climbed in, and stroked the steering wheel. She'd only driven the gold Jeep a couple of times since it had been given to them, but the act felt so familiar to her. Danny climbed into the passenger seat next to her, opened the glove box, and started rummaging around.

"Prynce, you get in the middle." Lizzie opened the back door. "You're the smallest."

Prynce threw his head back in anger before doing as he was told.

"Let's not start all of that again." Dimple squeezed in next to Prynce and raised her eyebrows at Nikisha through the rearview mirror.

"I don't know how many times I need to tell you lot that I'm catching up to Danny," Prynce said. "Why can't you see it?"

"We can't see what isn't there," Lizzie told him as she clipped herself in next to him. "You in, Dimple?"

"I'm in." Dimple nodded.

"Found it!" Danny exclaimed. "I knew it would be in here some- where."

"What is it?" Prynce asked, poking his head between Nikisha and Danny.

"Can you sit back and put your seat belt on?" Nikisha shouted at Prynce, sliding the key into the ignition and turning it, allowing some small emotion to hit her as the Jeep rumbled to life.

"Professor Nuts!" Danny held up the CD he'd retrieved from the glove box. "Remember this?"

"How could we forget?" Lizzie crossed her legs and let a small smile pass her lips.

"DJ Fireshot's favorite song," Nikisha added, checking the mirrors, looking at her siblings squashed into the back seat rather than paying attention to what was behind the Jeep. When Dimple's swollen eyes met Nikisha's through the rearview mirror, she winked at Dimple to let her know that it was all . . . okay.

Danny took the CD from its case carefully and slid it into the drive, crossing his arms while he willed it to work.

When the song began and boomed through the speakers—the soundtrack to that very strange day all those years ago when they'd been taken to that park—Cyril Pennington's five children knew that their dad, as absent as he was, could only have been himself. And that that was, in the way that it had to be, enough.

"Run that back!" Prynce shouted over the music. "For Cyril."

Danny smiled as he started the song again, his fingers pressing the tiny buttons on the archaic CD drive.

"For Cyril!" Nikisha, Danny, Lizzie, and Dimple repeated, as the gold Jeep pulled away from the curb and sped down the street, demanding attention from everybody it passed in the way that it always had. The way that Cyril always had.

ACKNOWLEDGMENTS

I have many people to thank, not just for the support while I wrote this, a novel I didn't think I'd be able to finish, but for being there. The first person I'd like to thank is myself, because YOU are the person I'm in constant conversation/argument with, and getting this novel out was dependent on us being on the same page in many senses. So thank you, Candice, for cooperating with Candice.

Thank you to my editors, Katie Espiner and Alison Callahan, for your patience, your guidance, your wit, and your ability to steer me toward the unlocking of thoughts I wouldn't have gotten to on my own. Separately and together you are so instrumental to me being able to write a novel that feels entirely complete, this time around and the last.

Thank you to my supreme agents, Jo Unwin and Deborah Schneider, for keeping things going on both sides of the pond, and a special shout-out to Nisha Bailey for everything you do, and with such kindness.

Cait Davies, Leanne Oliver, Maura Wilding, I can't believe I get to work with the best in the fucking business. Thank you so much for everything you've done and have been doing since *Queenie* touched road in 2019.

Thank you Zoe Yang for keeping me on the editorial straight and narrow, and thank you AGAIN Sophie Wilson for coming in with your keen eye for detail and for mistakes. Before you got to *People Person*, it wasn't what it is now.

Hadil Mohamed, I can't believe what you've done here. You've managed to take these characters out of my head and give life and vision to them in a way that's even more real than I imagined. Your talent is inspiring and unending. Thank you. Mylène Mozas, you're a marvel! Thank you for creating a cover that I loved the second I saw it. Thank you also for bearing with my endless neuroses around aforementioned cover.

To the family members I chat to: Nan, Mum, Selena, Claude, Esther and Sweetie, Kai, Aunty Heidi: Thank you for bearing with me since 1989 and beyond even though I don't always pick up the phone. And Sharmaine Lovegrove, my adopted big sister! I can't believe the unlimited love and care and advice you give to me. I absolutely don't deserve it.

And my *friends*. As you, and I'm sure everybody, know, I have a lot of emotions that I can't really ever contain on my own, and it's thanks to all of you that I'm not crying every minute of every day. But let me be specific with my thanks:

Hattie Collins: If I didn't speak to you about every single thing I was doing every single day, then how would I get through any of it? Pain is the essence, the game is a lesson, and I'm grateful that I have you to navigate it all with.

Danielle Scott-Haughton: Pimping? Oh boy.

Selcan Tezgel: For the Turkish rice, and everything else. You are more special than you know.

Aimée Felone: The FBI man knows why I love you and if I say it here everyone will know too much.

Hayley Camis: My astrological and general soul mate. I love you even when that Scorpio tail stings me.

Emma Dennis-Edwards: My number one travel companion. Thanks for the unrelenting chaos that is being your friend, and for the late-night parked car conversations.

Lemara Lindsay-Prince: MY chargie! For the food, the kindness, everything, everything. My fellow Caribbean-uncle-sitting-in-a-chair-watching-the-world-go-by.

Yasmin Joseph: "BaAaBe!" If I tried to list all of the inside jokes we've managed to collect in the last year I'd be typing for weeks, so instead I'm going to thank you for being such an incredible force in my life.

Platinum Pussy Energy: My hoame gurlz. You really keep me going you know: Bolu Babalola, the wittiest and the wisest. Bridget Minamore, for the frantic but somehow levelheaded assessments. Daniellé Scott-Haughton, for the heartfelt reasoning. Emma Dennis-Edwards, for the unending intel (whether it's true or not) and again, honestly, for the chaos.

Dave Evans: For your pragmatism, for all the food you've brought me, and for your surprise notes on this novel. You continue to go above and beyond for me and I am grateful in so many ways.

Danielle Vitalis: Why are you so good? Tell me.

Ryan Bowes: If you ever play anyone the crying voice notes I used to send you at four in the morning I will have to kill you, but that I could even send them to you shows how much I love and trust you.

Isabel Mulinde: My sister, always. Forever.

Zezi Ifore: For being my cat in slider.

Tobi Oredein and Bola Awoniyi: I feel very grateful to have watched my favorite couple turn into my favorite family unit. It's an inspiring and beautiful thing to have witnessed.

Cicely Hadman: For helping me make sense of my emotions for over a decade.

Anya Courtman: For half a life of friendship. My fox till the end.

Daniel Kaluuya: For the wisdom. For being so near even though you're always so far.

Mannie Mensah: For being *the* most stylish and *the* most incredible woman, always there, always golden.

Morwenna Finn: For many things, but mainly for always watering my plants. Thanks, babe.

Hannah Howard: I don't know anyone else who can get to the root of my problems as quickly and as insightfully as you do.

Selina Thompson: 0121 stand up!

Michael Cragg: Once again for the £200 that I probably still owe you but you've been too polite to ask for.

Florie Mwanza: The day we get married will be the day that I am finally happy.

Edem Wornoo: How lucky am I to have found a little brother at this point in my life.

Jesse Armstrong: For always being so kind, and for always wanting to listen.

Caleb Nelson: Genuinely: For that thirty-on-one fight we witnessed in Ruskin Park. Kim and the outfit change really saved summer 2020 for me.

Julian Obubo: For always listening to my erratic voice notes about whatever thing we're into that week or for whatever thing has upset me that week.

Obioma Ugoala: For your open mind and your open heart.

Lettice Franklin: For seeing it all and loving me anyway.

Eishar Brar: For the zodiac assessments and many more things.

Polly Norton: For always inspiring me in so many ways.

Zainab and Indira: For lentils, lengas, and for feeding me food and feeding me books. Zainab, you are an endless fount of knowledge; Indira, you are an endless fount of Cancerian kindness.

Black Girls Book Club: For everything you've done for me, and have done for us. The Black literary space is nothing without you.

Zadie Smith: For every email you send me that is even wiser or even more random than the last. I love it.

Nikesh Shukla: For the care.

To Sophie Francois and Michelle Nyangereka: Thank you for helping me sort out my body and my mind, respectively.

To all the mothers of others who unknowingly mothered me when I needed it: Aunty Alice, Janet Edwards, Sharon Young, Marilyn Lindsay-Waugh, and Purllett Hogan.

To my extended families: the Courtmans, the Permauls, the Lovegroves, the Woodhams, the Forresters, the Forrester-Browns; thank you always for your open arms.

To my New York contingent: Gregory Greene, Ashley Clark, Aminatou Sow, Somalia Seaton, Mateo Askaripour, Renée Chung, Joshua Thew; thank you for being my home away from home.

To everyone I've thanked here, the love I have for you is endless. I don't want to imagine the version of myself I'd be if it weren't for each and every one of you.

If I've forgotten anyone I'm sorry, but I was typing these out at 4 a.m.

And, as always, #BlackLivesMatter

ABOUT THE AUTHOR

Candice Carty-Williams was born in south London in 1989, the result of an affair between a Jamaican cab driver and a dyslexic Jamaican Indian receptionist. She is a culture writer, and author of Book of the Year Award–winning *Queenie*, as well as the young adult novella *Empress & Aniya*. In 2016, Candice created and launched the Guardian and 4th Estate Short Story Prize for underrepresented writers, the first inclusive initiative of its kind in book publishing. Candice is the ex-Guardian Review books columnist, has written for *Guardian* (obviously), *i-D*, *Vogue*, *The Face*, every iteration of the *Sunday Times*, *BEAT* magazine, *Black Ballad*, and many more publications. Her *Sunday Times* bestselling debut *Queenie* received wide acclaim, and was described as vital, disarmingly honest, and boldly political. *People Person* is her highly anticipated second novel.